The Viking Portable Library

POETS OF THE
ENGLISH LANGUAGE

Edited by

W. H. AUDEN

and

NORMAN HOLMES PEARSON

VOLUME I: LANGLAND TO SPENSER

VOLUME II: MARLOWE TO MARVELL

VOLUME III: MILTON TO GOLDSMITH

VOLUME IV: BLAKE TO POE

VOLUME V: TENNYSON TO YEATS

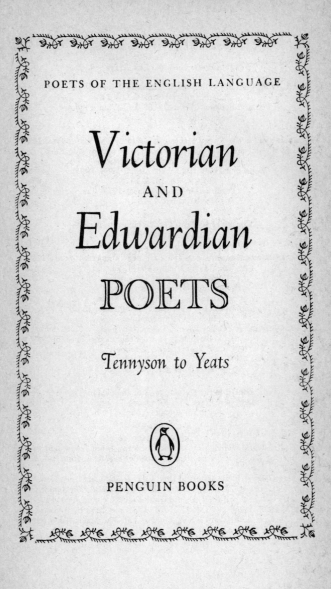

POETS OF THE ENGLISH LANGUAGE

Victorian
AND
Edwardian
POETS

Tennyson to Yeats

PENGUIN BOOKS

Penguin Books Ltd, Harmondsworth,
Middlesex, England
Penguin Books, 625 Madison Avenue,
New York, New York 10022, U.S.A.
Penguin Books Australia Ltd, Ringwood,
Victoria, Australia
Penguin Books Canada Limited, 2801 John Street,
Markham, Ontario, Canada L3R 1B4
Penguin Books (N.Z.) Ltd, 182–190 Wairau Road,
Auckland 10, New Zealand

First published in the United States of America by The Viking Press 1950
First published in Great Britain by Eyre & Spottiswoode 1952
Paperbound edition published 1958
Reprinted 1960, 1962, 1963, 1965, 1966, 1968,
1971, 1972, 1973, 1975
Published in Penguin Books 1977
Reprinted 1978

LIBRARY OF CONGRESS CATALOGING IN PUBLICATION DATA
Auden, Wystan Hugh, 1907–1973   ed.
Poets of the English language.
(The Viking portable library [49–53])
CONTENTS.—V. 5. Tennyson to Yeats.
Biographical notes. New York, Viking Press, 1950.
Includes bibliographies.
1. English poetry (Collections)   2. American poetry (Collections)
3. English poetry—Bio-bibl.   4. American poetry—Bio-bibl.
I.   Pearson, Norman Holmes.
[PR1175.A76   1977]   821.'008   50–9508
ISBN 0 14 015.053 6

Printed in the United States of America by
Kingsport Press, Inc., Kingsport, Tennessee
Set in Linotype Caledonia

ACKNOWLEDGMENTS

Grateful acknowledgment is made to those listed below and on the
following page for permission to include selections from the books
named.

Mrs. George Bambridge and Doubleday & Company, Inc., New York:
Life's Handicap, The Seven Seas, Puck of Pook's Hill, The Jungle Book,
and *Rewards and Fairies,* by Rudyard Kipling, copyright 1891, 1893,
1894, 1905, 1906, 1910, 1918, 1921, 1931 and 1933 by Rudyard Kip-
ling; also to A. P. Watt & Son, London, and The Macmillan Company
of Canada, Toronto.

ACKNOWLEDGMENTS (*continued*)

Harper & Brothers, New York: *Bolts of Melody, New Poems of Emily Dickinson*, edited by Mabel Loomis Todd and Millicent Todd Bingham, copyright 1945 by Millicent Todd Bingham.

Little, Brown & Company, Boston: *Poems* by Emily Dickinson, copyright 1914 by Martha Dickinson Bianchi.

Charles Scribner's Sons, New York: *Songs & Poems* by John Jay Chapman, copyright 1918, 1919 by Charles Scribner's Sons, 1947 by John Jay Chapman; *The Town Down the River* by Edwin Arlington Robinson, copyright 1910 by Charles Scribner's Sons, 1938 by Ruth Nivison; and *The Children of the Night* by the same author; Scribner's and Constable and Company, Ltd, London: *Selected Poems of George Meredith*, copyright 1897 by George Meredith, 1925 by William M. Meredith.

The Clarendon Press, Oxford: *The Poetical Works of Robert Bridges*.

Columbia University Press, New York: *The Complete Poems of Emily Jane Brontë*, edited by C. W. Hatfield.

Gerald Duckworth & Co., Ltd., London: *The Dawn in Britain* by C. M. Doughty.

Harvard University Press, Cambridge: *Melville's Billy Budd*, edited by Frederic Barron Freeman.

Henry Holt and Company, Inc., New York: *A Shropshire Lad* by A. E. Housman; also The Society of Authors, representatives of the author's estate, and Jonathan Cape, Ltd., London, publishers of A. E. Housman's *Collected Poems*.

The Macmillan Company, New York: *Collected Poems* by Thomas Hardy, copyright 1925 by The Macmillan Company; also Macmillan & Co., Ltd., London, and the Trustees of the Hardy Estate.

The Macmillan Company, New York: *Captain Craig* by Edwin Arlington Robinson, copyright 1902 by Edwin Arlington Robinson; *Poems, The Green Helmet & Other Poems*, and *Responsibilities* by William Butler Yeats, copyright 1906, 1912, and 1916 by The Macmillan Company; also Mrs. Yeats, A. P. Watt & Son, London, and the Macmillan Company of Canada Limited, Toronto.

Sir Francis Meynell and Burns, Oates & Washbourne, Ltd., London: *Complete Poetical Works of Francis Thompson*.

Oxford University Press, London, and the poet's family: *Poems* by Gerard Manley Hopkins.

Contents

CONTENTS

CONTENTS

CONTENTS

CONTENTS

CONTENTS

CONTENTS

CONTENTS

CONTENTS

Introduction

The limiting conditions for inclusion in this volume are two: the poet must have been born before 1870 and his poem must have been published before August 1914. These two dates have not been chosen at random. The first is doubly significant: it is the year of the Franco-Prussian War, when Europe, the City of *L'esprit français,* is challenged from within by the *Blut und Eisen* spirit of the Barracks;[1] and it is the year in which the dogma of Papal Infallibility is proclaimed, when the oldest and most powerful Christian Communion declares in the most spectacular way possible that in matters of Faith the Liberal conception of truth as conditional and arrived at by experiment and discussion has no place. As the year when the First World War broke out, 1914 marks the final break-up of Europe. The experiences of mass mechanical warfare and organized propaganda were proof that, whatever the nature of man might be, it was not what the European intellectuals as a group had said it was.

For America these dates are not exact but they are sufficiently close to its decisive years to be serviceable. In the Civil War of 1861-65 the United States had a foretaste of total war with modern weapons, and 1917 ended

---

[1] In view of the subsequent history of Germany, it is important to remember that it was France, not Prussia, which declared war in 1870. The initial betrayal of Europe was the *coup d'état* of 1851, and Napoleon III, with his combination of force and appeal to the masses, was, as De Tocqueville realized, a novel and sinister phenomenon, the first dictator of the modern type.

its isolation from the Old World. Henceforth, whatever kind of civilization was to emerge would be a joint creation.

The nineteenth century is the European century. In so far that neither England nor America is part of Europe, the poetry with which this volume is concerned can be called provincial. To say this is not in any way to detract from its value. In literature, indeed, one is inclined to feel that the really new, the revolutionary, works appear not in Europe proper but on the peripheries—the Russian novels and the plays of the Norwegian Ibsen—or outside her altogether, in America.

Whatever one may feel about Poe's own work, it is impossible not to see that he is the father of one kind of "modern" poetry. However little to one's taste both the manner and the content of Whitman's poetry may be, the revolution in sensibility which he effected is indubitable, and one is reluctantly compelled to agree with D. H. Lawrence:

Whitman, the one man breaking a way ahead. Whitman, the one pioneer. And only Whitman. No English pioneers, no French. No European pioneer-poets. In Europe the would-be pioneers are mere innovators. . . . Whitman like a strange, modern, American Moses. Fearfully mistaken. And yet the great leader.

Studies in Classic American Literature

In style and craftsmanship the poetry of the nineteenth and the twentieth centuries has extended, developed, and refined the discoveries of the early Romantics. To a degree hitherto unknown, each poet sets out, like Milton, to create a personal style; he invents a particular genre of poem suited to his cast of temperament—the Tennyson idyl, the Browning dramatic monologue, the

Patmore ode; for each poem he tries to find the form uniquely suited to its subject and vice versa. No previous period can show such a wealth of variety in stanzas, newly contrived or revived from the past, such metrical invention, from classical meters to sprung rhythm to dithyrambic free verse. The advantages of this variety and individual freedom are obvious, its disadvantages perhaps less so: a personal form and manner sometimes become more of a prison than would a traditional style shared in common, precisely because they are the poet's own; what was once his face can, if he himself change, turn into a mask without his realizing it.

If, then, we look for any point of division, any sign of a decisive change, in the period between, say, Wordsworth and the present day, we shall not find, as we find between Pope and the Romantics, any startling break in style. The dividing line between "Victorian" (to use an English term internationally) poetry and "modern" poetry lies between the poets for whom the ideas and hopes of liberal Christian humanism are still valid, and those for whom they are not. Thus Browning, Hugo, Longfellow are Victorian; Hopkins, Baudelaire, and Whitman are modern.

THE LIBERAL BARD

The poets I have called for convenience Victorian inherit the beliefs of Romanticism and the French Revolution and become their official spokesmen; they are listened to by the general public in a way that their predecessors were not, for the revolution has succeeded and is therefore now respectable.[2] There are, of course, differences between the various countries: in Catholic

[2] In America, with its relative provincialism and its proliferating sects, the sermon of the Liberal Bard was concerned

countries like France, liberalism is more directly political and anti-clerical, more explicitly concerned with *Liberté, Egalité, Fraternité;* in Protestant countries, the liberalism is more concerned with religion. The poets preach a religion in which the values and even the cult are to remain Christian but the Christian dogmas are to be regarded as myth, that is, poetic truth. If this is the case, then the poets are, of course, the real priests of society, the oracles on all social problems and values.

Their trouble was that they could never quite believe it; they were all haunted men, with a room in the house which was kept locked and from which they had to distract the attention of visitors. It is significant that the poem of theirs which opens that room most dramatically professes to be a nonsense poem, "The Hunting of the Snark." The snark, that is, the meaning of existence, turns out to be a Boojum—existence is meaningless. They were all of them uneasily aware of the possibility that the liberal creed might only hold for talented and successful people like themselves, for men who might speculate upon the meaning of existence in general but never had to put the personal question "Why do I exist?" because they were enjoying themselves in the exercise of their talents and the glory such exercise brought them. However many adoring disciples might sit at their feet, outside the cozy circle there was a shadow who was by no means friendly, to whom their genius for inspiring speech was a joke, and who spoke himself in a very different vein.

---

less with religious doubts than with the importance of culture. One should never underestimate the value of Longfellow's attempt to secure democratic respect for smoothness, correctness, and craftsmanship in poetry and through translation to make European literature available to the youth of the Republic.

I am a sick man. . . . I am a spiteful man. I am an unattractive man. I believe my liver is diseased. However, I know nothing at all about my disease, and do not know for certain what ails me. I don't consult a doctor for it, and never have, though I have a respect for medicine and doctors. Besides, I am extremely superstitious, sufficiently so to respect medicine, anyway (I am well-educated enough not to be superstitious, but I am superstitious). No, I refuse to consult a doctor out of spite. That you probably will not understand. Well, I understand it, though. Of course, I can't explain who it is precisely that I am mortifying in this case by my spite: I am perfectly well aware that I can't "get even" with the doctors by not consulting them; I know better than anyone that by all this I am only injuring myself and no one else. But still, if I don't consult a doctor it is out of spite. My liver is bad, well—let it get worse!

> Dostoevski, *Notes from Underground*

So speaks the victim of the French Revolution and liberalism. Emancipated from the traditional beliefs of a closed society, he can no longer believe simply because his forefathers did and he cannot imagine not believing —he has found no source or principle of direction to replace them. He is not a genius, he is not socially gifted, his work is not important or interesting, so that self-love and the thirst for glory cannot motivate his life; his self-consciousness can only turn in destructively on himself, his freedom waste itself in freakish, arbitrary, spiteful little acts. "I swear, gentlemen," he says, "that to be too conscious is an illness—a real out-and-out illness."

Liberalism is at a loss to know how to handle him, for the only thing liberalism knows to offer is more freedom, and it is precisely freedom in the sense of lack of necessity that is his trouble. When a man knows what he wants, liberalism can help him—when a peasant exploited by his landlord desires a farm of his own, for example, liberalism can fight for land reform. But ask this man what he wants and his only answer is a fantastic daydream.

> Then the band would play a march, an amnesty would be declared, the Pope would agree to retire from Rome to Brazil: then there would be a ball for the whole of Italy at the Villa Borghese on the shores of the Lake of Como (the Lake of Como being for that purpose transferred to the neighborhood of Rome); there would come a scene in the bushes, and so on, and so on. . . .
>
> Dostoevski, *Notes from Underground*

He is a dangerous customer because he is desperate and can only imagine destructive change. Moreover, the real object of his resentment is not any exploiting class or concrete injustice but the man of talent who enjoys and profits from the consciousness that makes him suffer. He is anti-humanist, anti-liberal, in terms of democracy, above all anti-intellectual. The thought of a tyrant who will provide him with a myth of terror, of the prospect of a total war as a cult, are not unwelcome to him.

The confidence of the liberal humanist was not seriously shaken by the natural sciences, which were based on the presupposition that, whatever his origin, whatever the relation of his mind to matter, man was capable of a disinterested search for an objective truth which was universally valid. The dangerous assault came later from the half-sciences, like sociology, anthropology, and psychology, which are concerned with man as an interested actor. Their exhibition of the mind's capacity for self-deception, of the unconscious effect upon its thinking of social status and sex, their demonstration that the customs and beliefs of other peoples could not be dismissed as merely savage, irrational, and quaint but must be accepted as rival civilizations complete in themselves, cast doubts on the finality of any truth.

Again, in practical politics, the pure liberal doctrine of laissez-faire was proving unworkable. The Companies Act of 1862 in England and the legal advantages conferred by the American courts on corporations were symptoms of a modification of the liberal gospel; the gradual appearance of the social welfare state, first in Bismarck's Prussia, was another.

THE MODERN POET

The break with liberal humanism exhibits itself in various ways. In France the poets rejected the political ideals of the French Revolution; *"l'esprit belge,"* Baudelaire called it. And they rejected the notion of the poet as bard, of poetry as a popular religion. Poetry was, for them, to be a religion for poets only. The others must find their salvation with the priest or the philosopher. The poets are no longer interested in the others. In the Protestant countries, aestheticism did not come on so quickly or go to quite the same lengths. The notion of the bard persisted, but the myth was no longer liberal Christianity.

Wagner was the first, as Yeats has been the latest, to create a whole cosmology out of pre-Christian myth, to come out openly for the pagan conception of the recurrent cycle as against the Christian and liberal humanist conception of historical development as an irreversible process. Though the characters in *The Ring* wear primitive trappings, they are really, as Nietzsche pointed out, contemporaries, "always five steps from the hospital," with modern problems, "problems of the big city." Other poets turned to Stoicism or Platonism; a few were converted to orthodox dogmatic Christianity.

THE WHITMAN MYTH

Whitman's polemic exaltation of the human body is directed not against the Puritan ascetic, but against the emancipated liberal intellectual. To the former the body with its passions is a formidable enemy who threatens the salvation of his soul; his error lies in his taking the body too seriously. To the latter, on the other hand, the body is a mere thing, of no importance in itself whatever except as the instrument which feeds his mind with experiences; while working he forgets to feed and rest it, when in search of "copy" and inspiration he drives it into debauchery.

As against the intellectual's dogma that what all men have in common is a consciousness of possibilities and consequently a capacity to make history by realizing them, Whitman asserts that all men, whatever their talents, education, or race, are equal in the flesh; each has a body which needs the same things and suffers in the same way and does not partake in history but goes through the same cycle in every generation.

The good of the body is health, which cannot be thought of in liberal terms, for words like freedom or possibility do not apply to it. To sustain physical health so much food, shelter, light, and so on, neither more nor less, are *necessary*.

In their re-emphasis on the sacredness of the flesh, Whitman, Nietzsche, and other protestants were not alone; the cult of the Sacred Heart and the dogma of the Immaculate Conception were expressions of a similar insight on the part of the Catholic Church.

EPILOGUE

In 1914 a revolution was set in motion which has involved the whole world and is still going on. If every revolution can be represented graphically by a symbolic figure—the Papal Revolution by a twin Warrior-Priest, the Lutheran by a God-fearing paterfamilias, the English by a country gentleman, the American by a pioneer, the French by an intellectual—then the contemporary symbol is a naked anonymous baby. It is for the baby's right to health, not for the freedom of any person or class to act or think—for a baby is not yet a person and cannot choose or think—that the revolution is being fought everywhere in one way or another. A baby has to be controlled, it has to be indoctrinated, it cannot be told more of the truth than it can profitably understand, so the present revolution is authoritarian and believes in censorship and propaganda. Since its values are really derived from medicine, from a concept of health, it is hostile to any nonconformity, any deviation from the norm. It is precisely, therefore, the exceptional man, the man of talent, the man who works alone, the man whom the French Revolution liberated and admired, who has become the object of greatest suspicion.

The difference between the poets in this volume and the contemporary poet is in their relation to the state and society. The former were either admired or left alone; the latter are suspect, and the campaign to control them by bribes or threats is likely to intensify.

What will happen is anybody's guess. Perhaps history is forcing the intellectual, whether scientist or artist, into a new conception of himself as neither the respectable bard nor the anarchic aesthete, but as a member of the Loyal Opposition, defending, not for his own sake only but for all, the inalienable rights of the individual person against encroachment by an overzealous government, with which, nevertheless, even though the latter deny it, he has a bond, their common love for the Just City.

A Calendar of British and American Poetry

GENERAL BACKGROUND	DATE	DIRECT HISTORY
Gauss, *Disquisitiones Arithmeticae:* higher mathematics developed as an independent science	1801	
Pestalozzi, *Wie Gertrud ihre Kinder lehrt:* doctrine of direct experiences for the child in education		
	1802–03	Scott, ed., *Minstrelsy of the Scottish Border*
Louisiana Purchase	1803	
Code Napoléon	1804	Blake, *Milton;* "Jerusalem"
Lewis and Clark Expedition	1804–06	
Beethoven, *Fidelio,* first performance, rewritten in present form and presented 1814	1805	Scott, *The Lay of the Last Minstrel*
		Southey, *Madoc*
		Wordsworth, *The Prelude,* written; this version first published 1926
	1806	Byron, *Fugitive Pieces*
		Scott, *Ballads and Lyrical Pieces*
Hegel, *Phänomenologie des Geistes*	1807	Moore, *A Selection of Irish Melodies*
Charles and Mary Lamb, *Tales from Shakespeare*		Wordsworth, *Poems in Two Volumes:* including "Intimations of Immortality"
Mme de Staël, *Corinne*		
Fichte, *Reden an die deutsche Nation*	1807–08	
Goethe, *Faust,* Part I	1808	Bryant, *The Embargo*
		Scott, *Marmion*
Lamarck, *Philosophie zoölogique*	1809	Byron, *English Bards and Scotch Reviewers*
		Campbell, *Gertrude of Wyoming, A Pennsylvanian Tale*
Schlegel, *Vorlesungen über dramatische Kunst und Literatur:* a key book of European Romanticism	1809–11	
Porter, *The Scottish Chiefs*	1810	Crabbe, *The Borough*
Mme de Staël, *De l'Allemagne*		Scott, *The Lady of the Lake*
Goya, *Los Desastres de la guerra*	1810–13	

A CALENDAR

A CALENDAR

GENERAL BACKGROUND	DATE	DIRECT HISTORY
Lamartine, *Méditations poétiques*	1820	Merci"; "Lamia"; "Isabella"; "Hyperion," etc. Shelley, *Prometheus Unbound* Wordsworth, *The River Duddon*
Lamb, *Essays of Elia*, periodical appearance	1820–23	
Cooper, *The Spy* James Mill, *Elements of Political Economy:* first English textbook on economics Saint-Simon, *Le Système industriel* Scott, *Kenilworth*	1821	Beddoes, *The Improvisatore* Bryant, *Poems,* expanded 1832 Clare, *The Village Minstrel* James Gates Percival, *Poems* Shelley, *Adonais; Epipsychidion* Southey, *A Vision of Judgement*
Hazlitt, *Table Talk*	1821–22	
De Quincey, *Confessions of an English Opium Eater* Scott, *Peveril of the Peak*	1822	Byron, *The Vision of Judgement* Beddoes, *The Bride's Tragedy* Darley, *The Errors of Ecstasie* Rogers, *Italy,* Part I
Samuel Brown's gas engine: internal combustion Cooper, *The Pioneers; The Pilot* The Monroe Doctrine	1823	
Carlyle, *William Meister's Apprenticeship:* a translation from Goethe Scott, *Redgauntlet*	1824	
Landor, *Imaginary Conversations of Literary Men and Statesmen*	1824–28	
Mitford, *Our Village*	1824–32	
Coleridge, *Aids to Reflection* Hazlitt, *The Spirit of the Age*	1825	E. C. Pinkney, *Poems*
Manzoni, *I Promessi sposi*	1825–27	
Grimm, *Irische Elfenmärchen*	1826	Hood, *Whims and Oddities,* first series
Graham's Magazine, published in Philadelphia	1826–64	
Cooper, *The Prairie* Heine, *Buch der Lieder* Niepce's first camera image	1827	Clare, *The Shepherd's Calendar* Keble, *The Christian Year* Poe, *Tamerlane and Other Poems* Mrs. Sigourney, *Poems* Simms, *Lyrical and Other Poems* Alfred and Charles Tennyson, *Poems by Two Brothers*

A CALENDAR

A CALENDAR

GENERAL BACKGROUND	DATE	DIRECT HISTORY
Carlyle, *French Revolution* Dickens, *Pickwick Papers* Emerson, *The American Scholar* Hawthorne, *Twice-Told Tales*	1837	
Carlyle, *Sartor Resartus* Hugo, *Ruy Blas*	1838	Tupper, *Proverbial Philosophy*
Stendhal, *La Chartreuse de Parme*	1839	Bailey, *Festus* Longfellow, *Voices of the Night* Very, *Essays and Poems*
Faraday, *Experimental Researches in Electricity*	1839–55	
Carlyle, *Chartism* Dana, *Two Years before the Mast* Poe, *Tales of the Grotesque and Arabesque*	1840	Browning, *Sordello*
	1840–47	Barham, *The Ingoldsby Legends*
Carlyle, *On Heroes, Hero-Worship, and the Heroic in History* Emerson, *Essays*, first series Newman, *Tracts for the Times, No. 90; Remarks on Certain Passages in the Thirty-Nine Articles*	1841	
	1842	Browning, *Dramatic Lyrics* Macaulay, *Lays of Ancient Rome* Tennyson, *Poems*
Borrow, *The Bible in Spain* O. W. Holmes, *The Contagiousness of Puerperal Fever* Kierkegaard, *Either/Or* John Stuart Mill, *A System of Logic* Poe, *The Murders in the Rue Morgue* Surtees, *Handley Cross*	1843	W. E. Channing, *Poems* Hood, "Song of the Shirt" Longfellow, *The Spanish Student*
Ruskin, *Modern Painters*	1843–60	
Disraeli, *Coningsby* Musée de Cluny opened: medieval arts and crafts	1844	Barnes, *Poems of Rural Life in the Dorset Dialect* E. B. Browning, *Poems* Cranch, *Poems* Emerson, "The Poet," in *Essays: Second Series* Lowell, *Poems* Patmore, *Poems*
Engels, *Die Lage der arbeitenden Klasse in England*	1845	Longfellow, ed., *The Poets and Poetry of Europe: his-*

A CALENDAR

A CALENDAR

A CALENDAR

GENERAL BACKGROUND	DATE	DIRECT HISTORY
Holmes, *The Autocrat of the Breakfast Table*	1858	Morris, *Defence of Guenevere*
Charles Darwin, *On the Origin of Species*	1859	Fitzgerald, *Rubáiyát of Omar Khayyám*
Meredith, *The Ordeal of Richard Feverel*		
John Stuart Mill, *On Liberty*		
First popular Rogers group of domestic sculpture: "The Slave Auction"		
George Sand, *Elle et lui*		
Boole, *A Treatise on Differential Equations*	1859–65	
	1859–85	Tennyson, *Idylls of the King*
Collins, *The Woman in White*	1860	Stedman, *Poems, Lyrical and Idyllic*
Pattison, Baden Powell, and others, *Essays and Reviews*: introducing higher criticism of the Bible into England		Swinburne, *The Queen Mother and Rosamond*
		Timrod, *Poems*
		Tuckerman, *Poems*
Beginning of American Civil War	1861	Palgrave, ed., *The Golden Treasury*
Holmes, *Elsie Venner*		D. G. Rossetti, *The Early Italian Poets: translations*
Max Müller, *Science of Language*	1861–64	
Homestead Act: opening of Western lands in U.S. to settlement	1862	Clough, *Poems*
		Meredith, *Modern Love*
Herbert Spencer, *A System of Synthetic Philosophy*		
Turgenev, *Fathers and Sons*		
New York exhibition of Düsseldorf paintings	1863	
Hawthorne, *Our Old Home*		
Huxley, *Man's Place in Nature*		
Lincoln, "Gettysburg Address"		
Paris, Salon des réfusés: beginning of 1863 Impressionism		
Renan, *Vie de Jésus*		
Taine, *Histoire de la littérature anglaise*		
	1863–74	Longfellow, *Tales of a Wayside Inn*
Newman, *Apologia pro Vita Sua*	1864	Christina Rossetti, *Goblin Market and Other Poems*
Rodin's sculpture of "Man with the Broken Nose" rejected by the Salon; accepted 1876		Praed, *Poems*
Matthew Arnold, *Essays in Criticism*, first series	1865	Lowell, *Commemoration Ode*
		Read, *A Summer Story, Sheri-*

A CALENDAR

GENERAL BACKGROUND	DATE	DIRECT HISTORY
Confederacy surrenders; Lincoln assassinated; 13th Amendment ratified, abolishing slavery Dodgson (Lewis Carroll), *Alice's Adventures in Wonderland* Lecky, *History of the Rise and Influence of Rationalism in Europe* Mendel, *Versuche über Pflanzenhybriden* Ruskin, *Sesame and Lilies* Wagner, *Tristan und Isolde*	1865	dan's Ride and Other Poems* Swinburne, *Atalanta in Calydon* Whitman, *Drum-Taps*
	1865–67	Longfellow's translation of *The Divine Comedy*
Dostoevski, *Crime and Punishment* Field's first successful transatlantic cable *Le Parnasse contemporain* Ruskin, *The Crown of Wild Olive; The Ethics of the Dust* Shaw, *Josh Billings: His Sayings*	1866	Melville, *Battle-Pieces* Newman, *Dream of Gerontius* Swinburne, *Poems and Ballads, I* Whittier, *Snow-Bound*
Clemens (Mark Twain), *The Jumping Frog of Calaveras County* DeForest, *Miss Ravenel's Conversion from Secession to Loyalty* Ibsen, *Peer Gynt* Nobel invents dynamite Marx, *Das Kapital, Kritik der Politischen Oekonomie*	1867	Matthew Arnold, *New Poems* Emerson, *May-Day and Other Pieces* Harte, *The Lost Galleon and Other Tales*
	1867–94	
L. M. Alcott, *Little Women* Collins, *The Moonstone*	1868	Sill, *The Hermitage and Other Poems*
	1868–69	Browning, *The Ring and the Book*
	1868–70	Morris, *The Earthly Paradise*
Matthew Arnold, *Culture and Anarchy* Clemens (Mark Twain), *The Innocents Abroad* Flaubert, *L'Education sentimentale* Galton, *Hereditary Genius, Its Laws and Consequences* Suez Canal opened Transcontinental Union Pacific railroad completed	1869	Gilbert, *The "Bab" Ballads* Morris, translation of *Grettis Saga* Whittier, *Among the Hills*

A CALENDAR

A CALENDAR

A CALENDAR

GENERAL BACKGROUND	DATE	DIRECT HISTORY
Henry James, *The Portrait of a Lady*	1881	
Stevenson, *Virginibus Puerisque*		
Howells, *A Modern Instance*	1882	Bronson Alcott, *Sonnets and Canzonets*
Standard Oil trust formed		
Whitman, *Specimen Days and Collect*		
F. H. Bradley, *The Principles of Logic*	1883	Bridges, *Prometheus, the Fire-giver*
Brooklyn Bridge opened		Riley, *The Old Swimmen'-Hole*
Clemens (Mark Twain), *Life on the Mississippi*		Swinburne, *A Century of Roundels*
Fabian Society founded		
Howe, *The Story of a Country Town*		
Stevenson, *Treasure Island*		
Lester Ward, *Dynamic Sociology*		
Bismarck's laws providing sickness, accident, and old-age insurance	1883–89	
Nietzsche, *Also sprach Zarathustra*	1883–91	
Clemens (Mark Twain), *Huckleberry Finn*	1884	Dixon, *Odes and Eclogues*
Lang, *Custom and Myth*		Guiney, *Songs at the Start*
		Symonds, *Wine, Women, and Song: translation of medieval Latin students' songs*
Hertz's discovery of radio waves and photoelectricity	1885	Stevenson, *A Child's Garden of Verses*
Hudson, *The Purple Land*		Tennyson, *Tiresias and Other Poems*
Laforgue, *Les Complaintes*		
Pater, *Marius the Epicurean*		
Whistler, *The Ten o'Clock Lecture*		
Burton's translation of the *Arabian Nights*	1885–88	
Daimler invents internal combustion engine using gasoline	1886	Kipling, *Departmental Ditties*
		Tennyson, *Locksley Hall Sixty Years After*
Hardy, *The Mayor of Casterbridge*		F. Vielé-Griffin, *Cueille d'avril*
Henry James, *The Princess Casamassima*		
Laforgue, *L'Imitation de Notre-Dame la Lune*		
Royce, *California . . . A Study of American Character*		
Dewey, *Psychology*	1887	Meredith, *Ballads and Poems of Tragic Life*
Edison's kinetoscope patented:		

A CALENDAR

A CALENDAR

GENERAL BACKGROUND	DATE	DIRECT HISTORY
Mahan, *The Influence of Sea Power on History, 1660–1783*	1890	
Richard Strauss, *Tod und Verklärung*		
Wainwright Building, St. Louis, designed by Louis Sullivan: First skyscraper using steel skeleton		
Whistler, *The Gentle Art of Making Enemies*		
Melville, *Billy Budd*, written; first published 1924	c.1890	
Bierce, *Tales of Soldiers and Civilians*	1891	Dickinson, *Poems*, second series
Dewey, *Outlines of a Critical Theory of Ethics*		Melville, *Timoleon*
Garland, *Main-Travelled Roads*		Stuart Merrill, *Les Fastes*
Gauguin leaves for Tahiti		
Gissing, *New Grub Street*		
Hardy, *Tess of the d'Urbervilles*		
Howells, *Criticism and Fiction*		
Leo XIII, *Rerum Novarum:* rights of labor		
Shaw, *The Quintessence of Ibsenism*		
Wilde, *The Picture of Dorian Gray*		
Hauptmann, *Die Weber*	1892	Kipling, *Barrack-Room Ballads*
H. A. Lorentz announces electron theory		Tennyson, *The Death of Œnone*
Page, *The Old South*		Yeats, *The Countess Kathleen*
Nordau, *Entartung:* degeneration of European culture	1892–93	
F. H. Bradley, *Appearance and Reality*	1893	Meynell, *Poems*
Bridges, *Milton's Prosody*		Francis Thompson, *Poems*
Final Honour School in English established at Oxford		
Wilde, *Lady Windermere's Fan; Salome*		
World's Columbian Exposition, Chicago		
Yeats, *Celtic Twilight*		
Debussy, "Prelude à l'après-midi d'un faune"	1894	Carman and Hovey, *Songs from Vagabondia*
Hearn, *Glimpses of Unfamiliar Japan*		Santayana, *Sonnets and Other Verses*
Kipling, *The Jungle Book*		
Moore, *Esther Waters*		

A CALENDAR

GENERAL BACKGROUND	DATE	DIRECT HISTORY
Turner, "The Significance of the Frontier in American History"	1894	
Yeats, *The Land of Heart's Desire*		
The Yellow Book: fin-de-siècle English magazine	1894–97	
Brooks Adams, *Law of Civilization and Decay*	1895	Crane, *The Black Riders and Other Lines*
Conrad, *Almayer's Folly*		Lionel Johnson, *Poems*
Crane, *The Red Badge of Courage*		
Diesel engine invented		
Freud, *Studien über Hysterie*		
Maitland and Pollock, *The History of English Law before the Time of Edward I*		
Marconi invents wireless telegraphy		
Pinero, *The Second Mrs. Tanqueray*		
Wells, *The Time Machine*		
Röntgen, *Ueber eine neue Art von Strahlen:* discovery of X rays	1895–96	
Fenollosa, *The Masters of Ukioye*	1896	Dickinson, *Poems,* third series
Frederic, *The Damnation of Theron Ware*		Dowson, *Poems*
Hardy, *Jude the Obscure*		Housman, *A Shropshire Lad*
Jewett, *The Country of the Pointed Firs*		
Puccini, *La Bohème*		
William James, *The Will to Believe*	1897	Robinson, *The Children of the Night*
Meredith, *An Essay on Comedy*		
Tyler, *The Literary History of the American Revolution*		
Hearn, *Exotics and Retrospectives*	1898	Hardy, *Wessex Poems*
Shaw, *Plays Pleasant and Unpleasant; The Perfect Wagnerite*		Wilde, *The Ballad of Reading Gaol*
		Yeats, *The Wind among the Reeds*
Dewey, *The School and Society*	1899	Markham, *The Man with the Hoe and Other Poems*
Norris, *McTeague*		
Arthur Symons, *The Symbolist Movement in Literature*		
Veblen, *The Theory of the Leisure Class*		

A CALENDAR

GENERAL BACKGROUND	DATE	DIRECT HISTORY
Clemens (Mark Twain), *The Man That Corrupted Hadleyburg* Dreiser, *Sister Carrie* Freud, *Die Traumdeutung* Santayana, *Interpretations of Poetry and Religion*	1900	Quiller-Couch, ed., *The Oxford Book of English Verse* Stedman, ed., *An American Anthology, 1789–1900*
Royce, *The World and the Individual*	1900–01	
Kipling, *Kim* Thomas Mann, *Buddenbrooks* Quantum theory originated by Planck Shaw, *Three Plays for Puritans*	1901	Hardy, *Poems of the Past and the Present* Moody, *Poems*
Debussy, *Pelléas et Mélisande* Henry James, *The Wings of the Dove* William James, *The Varieties of Religious Experience*	1902	De la Mare, *Songs of Childhood* Masefield, *Salt-Water Ballads* Robinson, *Captain Craig* Stickney, *Dramatic Verses*
Butler, *The Way of All Flesh* Dewey, *Studies in Logical Theory* Ford Motor Company founded Gissing, *The Private Papers of Henry Ryecroft* London, *The Call of the Wild* Shaw, *Man and Superman* Wright brothers' first successful airplane flight	1903	
	1903–08	Hardy, *The Dynasts*
Camera Work, a quarterly, edited and published by Stieglitz	1903–17	
Henry Adams, *Mont-Saint-Michel and Chartres* Barrie, *Peter Pan*, produced Beerbohm, *The Poets' Corner* A. C. Bradley, *Shakespearean Tragedy* Chekhov, *The Cherry Orchard* Ellis, *A Study of British Genius* G. Stanley Hall, *Adolescence* Henry James, *The Golden Bowl* Hudson, *Green Mansions* Steffens, *The Shame of the Cities* Synge, *Riders to the Sea* Veblen, *The Theory of Business Enterprise*	1904	George Cabot Lodge, *Cain, A Drama* Moody, *The Fire Bringer*
More, *Shelburne Essays*	1904–21	

A CALENDAR

GENERAL BACKGROUND	DATE	DIRECT HISTORY
Einstein enunciates theory of relativity	1905	
Freud, *Drei Abhandlungen zur Sexualtheorie*		
Huneker, *Iconoclasts*		
Paris, Salon d'Automne: "Les Fauves," post-Impressionism		
Russian Revolution of 1905		
Edith Wharton, *The House of Mirth*		
Santayana, *The Life of Reason*	1905–06	
H. W. and F. G. Fowler, *The King's English*	1906	Doughty, *The Dawn in Britain*
Galsworthy, *The Man of Property*		
Jung, *Diagnostiche Assoziationsstudien*		
W. S. Porter (O. Henry), *The Four Million*		
Sinclair, *The Jungle*		
	1906–10	Saintsbury, *History of English Prosody*
Henry Adams, *The Education of Henry Adams*	1907	Colum, *Wild Earth*
Beerbohm, *A Book of Caricatures*		Joyce, *Chamber Music*
Bergson, *L'Evolution créatrice*		
Cabell, *Gallantry*		
Gorki, *Mother*		
Gosse, *Father and Son*		
Synge, *The Playboy of the Western World*		
Sumner, *Folkways*		
Rilke, *Neue Gedichte*	1907–08	
Bennett, *The Old Wives' Tale*	1908	John Jay Chapman, *The Maid's Forgiveness, a Play*
The "Eight" founded (New York): the "Ashcan School" of artists		Doughty, *Adam Cast Forth*
		George Cabot Lodge, *Herakles*
E. M. Forster, *A Room with a View*		Pound, *A Lume Spento*
Anatole France, *L'Ile des pingouins*		
Georges Sorel, *Reflexions sur la violence*		
Frank Lloyd Wright, *In the Cause of Architecture, I*		
Van Wyck Brooks, *The Wine of the Puritans: A Study of Present-Day America*	1909	Pound, *Personae*
		Sterling, *A Wine of Wizardry*
Peary's discovery of the North Pole		
Schönberg, *Klavierstücke* (Three Pieces for Piano-		

GENERAL BACKGROUND	DATE	DIRECT HISTORY
forte): beginning of atonal style	1909	
Stein, *Three Lives*		
Strauss, *Elektra*, an opera		
Wells, *Tono Bungay; Ann Veronica*		
Norman Angell, *The Great Illusion: A Study of the Relation of Military Power in Nations to Their Economic and Social Advantage*	1910	Lomax, *Cowboy Songs and Other Frontier Ballads* Robinson, *The Town Down the River*
Babbitt, *The New Laokoön: An Essay on the Confusion of the Arts*		
Croce, *Problemi di estetica*		
Mme Curie, *Traité de radio-activité*		
Huneker, *Promenades of an Impressionist*		
Pound, *The Spirit of Romance*		
Russell and Whitehead, *Principia Mathematica*	1910–13	
Amundsen's discovery of the South Pole	1911	Rupert Brooke, *Poems* Chesterton, *The Ballad of the White Horse*
Irving Berlin, "Alexander's Ragtime Band"; W. C. Handy, "Memphis Blues"		Masefield, *The Everlasting Mercy*
Fenollosa, *Epochs of Chinese and Japanese Art*		Pound, *Canzoni*
Jung, *Wandlungen und Symbole der Libido*	1912	De la Mare, *The Listeners and Other Poems* Jeffers, *Flagons and Apples* Lindsay, *Rhymes to Be Traded for Bread* Harold Monro, ed., *Georgian Poetry*, first series *Poetry: A Magazine of Verse* established Elinor Wylie, *Incidental Numbers*
Brooks Adams, *The Theory of Social Revolution*	1913	William Rose Benét, *Merchants from Cathay* John Gould Fletcher, *The Dominant City*
Apollinaire, *Les Peintres cubistes*		
Armory Show, New York: Introduction to America of modern Continental art		Frost, *A Boy's Will* D. H. Lawrence, *Love Poems and Others*
Bohr's application of the quantum theory to the structure of the atom		Lindsay, *General William Booth Enters into Heaven and Other Poems*

A CALENDAR

GENERAL BACKGROUND	DATE	DIRECT HISTORY
Randolph Bourne, *Youth and Life*	1913	Watson, *The Muse in Exile*
Cather, *O Pioneers!*		William Carlos Williams, *The Tempers*
Freud, *Totem und Tabu*		
D. H. Lawrence, *Sons and Lovers*		
Thomas Mann, *Der Tod in Venedig*		
Proust, *Du Côté de chez Swann*		
Stravinsky, *Le Sacre du printemps:* ballet		
Joyce, *Dubliners*	1914	Aiken, *Earth Triumphant*
The New Republic and *The Little Review* established		Frost, *North of Boston*
O'Neill, *Thirst and Other One-Act Plays*		*Des Imagistes, An Anthology,* including poems by Aldington, H.D., Flint, Williams, Joyce, Pound, etc.
Panama Canal opened		Amy Lowell, *Sword Blades and Poppy Seed*
Stein, *Tender Buttons*		Yeats, *Responsibilities*
World War I begins		

Alfred, Lord Tennyson

(1809–1892)

The Kraken

Below the thunders of the upper deep;
Far, far beneath in the abysmal sea,
His ancient, dreamless, uninvaded sleep
The Kraken sleepeth: faintest sunlights flee
About his shadowy sides: above him swell
Huge sponges of millennial growth and height;
And far away into the sickly light,
From many a wondrous grot and secret cell
Unnumber'd and enormous polypi
Winnow with giant arms the slumbering green.
There hath he lain for ages and will lie
Battening upon huge seaworms in his sleep,
Until the latter fire shall heat the deep;
Then once by man and angels to be seen,
In roaring he shall rise and on the surface die.

Mariana

> Mariana in the moated grange.
> —*Measure for Measure.*

With blackest moss the flower-plots
    Were thickly crusted, one and all:
The rusted nails fell from the knots

1

That held the pear to the gable-wall.
The broken sheds look'd sad and strange:
    Unlifted was the clinking latch;
    Weeded and worn the ancient thatch
Upon the lonely moated grange.
        She only said, "My life is dreary,
            He cometh not," she said;
        She said, "I am aweary, aweary,
            I would that I were dead!"

Her tears fell with the dews at even;
    Her tears fell ere the dews were dried;
She could not look on the sweet heaven,
    Either at morn or eventide.
After the flitting of the bats,
    When thickest dark did trance the sky,
    She drew her casement-curtain by,
And glanced athwart the glooming flats.
        She only said, "The night is dreary,
            He cometh not," she said;
        She said, "I am aweary, aweary,
            I would that I were dead!"

Upon the middle of the night,
    Waking she heard the night-fowl crow:
The cock sung out an hour ere light:
    From the dark fen the oxen's low
Came to her: without hope of change,
    In sleep she seem'd to walk forlorn,
    Till cold winds woke the gray-eyed morn
About the lonely moated grange.
        She only said, "The day is dreary,
            He cometh not," she said;
        She said, "I am aweary, aweary,
            I would that I were dead!"

About a stone-cast from the wall
  A sluice with blacken'd waters slept,
And o'er it many, round and small,
  The cluster'd marish-mosses crept.
Hard by a poplar shook alway,
  All silver-green with gnarled bark:
For leagues no other tree did mark
The level waste, the rounding gray.
      She only said, "My life is dreary,
        He cometh not," she said;
      She said, "I am aweary, aweary,
        I would that I were dead!"

And ever when the moon was low,
  And the shrill winds were up and away,
In the white curtain, to and fro,
  She saw the gusty shadow sway.
But when the moon was very low,
  And wild winds bound within their cell,
The shadow of the poplar fell
Upon her bed, across her brow.
      She only said, "The night is dreary,
        He cometh not," she said;
      She said, "I am aweary, aweary,
        I would that I were dead!"

All day within the dreamy house,
  The doors upon their hinges creak'd;
The blue fly sung in the pane; the mouse
  Behind the mouldering wainscot shriek'd,
Or from the crevice peer'd about.
  Old faces glimmer'd thro' the doors,
  Old footsteps trod the upper floors,
Old voices called her from without.
      She only said, "My life is dreary,
        He cometh not," she said;

She said, "I am aweary, aweary,
　　I would that I were dead!"

The sparrow's chirrup on the roof,
　　The slow clock ticking, and the sound
Which to the wooing wind aloof
　　The poplar made, did all confound
Her sense; but most she loathed the hour
　　When the thick-moted sunbeam lay
　　Athwart the chambers, and the day
Was sloping toward his western bower.
　　　Then, said she, "I am very dreary,
　　　　He will not come," she said;
　　　She wept, "I am aweary, aweary,
　　　　Oh God, that I were dead!"

Song

A spirit haunts the year's last hours
Dwelling amid these yellowing bowers:
　　To himself he talks:
For at eventide, listening earnestly,
At his work you may hear him sob and sigh
　　In the walks;
　　Earthward he boweth the heavy stalks
Of the mouldering flowers:
　　Heavily hangs the broad sunflower
　　　Over its grave i' the earth so chilly;
　　Heavily hangs the hollyhock,
　　　Heavily hangs the tiger-lily.

The air is damp, and hush'd, and close,
As a sick man's room when he takes repose
　　An hour before death;

My very heart faints and my whole soul grieves
At the moist rich smell of the rotting leaves,
    And the breath
    Of the fading edges of box beneath,
And the year's last rose.
    Heavily hangs the broad sunflower
      Over its grave i' the earth so chilly;
    Heavily hangs the hollyhock,
      Heavily hangs the tiger-lily.

The Lotos-Eaters

"Courage!" he said, and pointed toward the land,
"This mounting wave will roll us shoreward soon."
In the afternoon they came unto a land
In which it seemed always afternoon.
All round the coast the languid air did swoon,
Breathing like one that hath a weary dream,
Full-faced above the valley stood the moon;
And like a downward smoke, the slender stream
Along the cliff to fall and pause and fall did seem.

A land of streams! some, like a downward smoke,
Slow-dropping veils of thinnest lawn, did go;
And some thro' wavering lights and shadows broke,
Rolling a slumbrous sheet of foam below.
They saw the gleaming river seaward flow
From the inner land: far off, three mountain-tops,
Three silent pinnacles of aged snow,
Stood sunset-flush'd: and, dew'd with showery drops,
Up-clomb the shadowy pine above the woven copse.

The charmed sunset linger'd low adown
In the red West: thro' mountain clefts the dale

Was seen far inland, and the yellow down
Border'd with palm, and many a winding vale
And meadow, set with slender galingale;
A land where all things always seem'd the same!
And round about the keel with faces pale,
Dark faces pale against that rosy flame,
The mild-eyed melancholy Lotos-eaters came.

Branches they bore of that enchanted stem,
Laden with flower and fruit, whereof they gave
To each, but whoso did receive of them,
And taste, to him the gushing of the wave
Far far away did seem to mourn and rave
On alien shores; and if his fellow spake,
His voice was thin, as voices from the grave;
And deep-asleep he seem'd, yet all awake,
And music in his ears his beating heart did make.

They sat them down upon the yellow sand,
Between the sun and moon upon the shore;
And sweet it was to dream of Fatherland,
Of child, and wife, and slave; but evermore
Most weary seem'd the sea, weary the oar,
Weary the wandering fields of barren foam.
Then some one said, "We will return no more;"
And all at once they sang, "Our island home
Is far beyond the wave; we will no longer roam.'

CHORIC SONG

There is sweet music here that softer falls
Than petals from blown roses on the grass,
Or night-dews on still waters between walls
Of shadowy granite, in a gleaming pass;
Music that gentlier on the spirit lies,
Than tir'd eyelids upon tir'd eyes;

Music that brings sweet sleep down from the blissful
    skies.
Here are cool mosses deep,
And thro' the moss the ivies creep,
And in the stream the long-leaved flowers weep,
And from the craggy ledge the poppy hangs in sleep.

Why are we weigh'd upon with heaviness,
And utterly consumed with sharp distress,
While all things else have rest from weariness?
All things have rest: why should we toil alone,
We only toil, who are the first of things,
And make perpetual moan,
Still from one sorrow to another thrown:
Nor ever fold our wings,
And cease from wanderings,
Nor steep our brows in slumber's holy balm;
Nor harken what the inner spirit sings,
"There is no joy but calm!"
Why should we only toil, the roof and crown of things?

Lo! in the middle of the wood,
The folded leaf is woo'd from out the bud
With winds upon the branch, and there
Grows green and broad, and takes no care,
Sun-steep'd at noon, and in the moon
Nightly dew-fed; and turning yellow
Falls, and floats adown the air.
Lo! sweeten'd with the summer light,
The full-juiced apple, waxing over-mellow,
Drops in a silent autumn night.
All its allotted length of days,
The flower ripens in its place,
Ripens and fades, and falls, and hath no toil,
Fast-rooted in the fruitful soil.

Hateful is the dark-blue sky,
Vaulted o'er the dark-blue sea.
Death is the end of life; ah, why
Should life all labour be?
Let us alone. Time driveth onward fast,
And in a little while our lips are dumb.
Let us alone. What is it that will last?
All things are taken from us, and become
Portions and parcels of the dreadful Past.
Let us alone. What pleasure can we have
To war with evil? Is there any peace
In ever climbing up the climbing wave?
All things have rest, and ripen toward the grave
In silence; ripen, fall and cease:
Give us long rest or death, dark death, or dreamful ease.

How sweet it were, hearing the downward stream,
With half-shut eyes ever to seem
Falling asleep in a half-dream!
To dream and dream, like yonder amber light,
Which will not leave the myrrh-bush on the height;
To hear each other's whisper'd speech;
Eating the Lotos day by day,
To watch the crisping ripples on the beach,
And tender curving lines of creamy spray;
To lend our hearts and spirits wholly
To the influence of mild-minded melancholy;
To muse and brood and live again in memory,
With those old faces of our infancy
Heap'd over with a mound of grass,
Two handfuls of white dust, shut in an urn of brass!

Dear is the memory of our wedded lives,
And dear the last embraces of our wives
And their warm tears: but all hath suffer'd change:

For surely now our household hearths are cold:
Our sons inherit us: our looks are strange:
And we should come like ghosts to trouble joy.
Or else the island princes over-bold
Have eat our substance, and the minstrel sings
Before them of the ten years' war in Troy,
And our great deeds, as half-forgotten things.
Is there confusion in the little isle?
Let what is broken so remain.
The Gods are hard to reconcile:
'Tis hard to settle order once again.
There *is* confusion worse than death,
Trouble on trouble, pain on pain,
Long labour unto aged breath,
Sore task to hearts worn out by many wars
And eyes grown dim with gazing on the pilot-stars.

But, propt on beds of amaranth and moly,
How sweet (while warm airs lull us, blowing lowly)
With half-dropt eyelid still,
Beneath a heaven dark and holy,
To watch the long bright river drawing slowly
His waters from the purple hill—
To hear the dewy echoes calling
From cave to cave thro' the thick-twined vine—
To watch the emerald-colour'd water falling
Thro' many a wov'n acanthus-wreath divine!
Only to hear and see the far-off sparkling brine,
Only to hear were sweet, stretch'd out beneath the pine.

The Lotos blooms below the barren peak:
The Lotos blows by every winding creek:
All day the wind breathes low with mellower tone:
Thro' every hollow cave and alley lone
Round and round the spicy downs the yellow Lotos-
    dust is blown.

We have had enough of action, and of motion we,
Roll'd to starboard, roll'd to larboard, when the surge
    was seething free,
Where the wallowing monster spouted his foam-foun-
    tains in the sea.
Let us swear an oath, and keep it with an equal mind,
In the hollow Lotos-land to live and lie reclined
On the hills like Gods together, careless of mankind.
For they lie beside their nectar, and the bolts are hur'd
Far below them in the valleys, and the clouds are lightly
    curl'd
Round their golden houses, girdled with the gleaming
    world:
Where they smile in secret, looking over wasted lands,
Blight and famine, plague and earthquake, roaring
    deeps and fiery sands,
Clanging fights, and flaming towns, and sinking ships,
    and praying hands.
But they smile, they find a music centred in a doleful
    song
Steaming up, a lamentation and an ancient tale of
    wrong,
Like a tale of little meaning tho' the words are strong;
Chanted from an ill-used race of men that cleave the
    soil,
Sow the seed, and reap the harvest with enduring toil,
Storing yearly little dues of wheat, and wine and oil;
Till they perish and they suffer—some, 'tis whisper'd—
    down in hell
Suffer endless anguish, others in Elysian valleys dwell,
Resting weary limbs at last on beds of asphodel.
Surely, surely, slumber is more sweet than toil, the shore
Than labour in the deep mid-ocean, wind and wave and
    oar;
Oh rest ye, brother mariners, we will not wander more.

Morte d'Arthur

So all day long the noise of battle roll'd
Among the mountains by the winter sea;
Until King Arthur's table, man by man,
Had fallen in Lyonnesse about their Lord,
King Arthur: then, because his wound was deep,
The bold Sir Bedivere uplifted him,
Sir Bedivere, the last of all his knights,
And bore him to a chapel nigh the field,
A broken chancel with a broken cross,
That stood on a dark strait of barren land.
On one side lay the Ocean, and on one
Lay a great water, and the moon was full.
    Then spake King Arthur to Sir Bedivere:
"The sequel of to-day unsolders all
The goodliest fellowship of famous knights
Whereof this world holds record. Such a sleep
They sleep—the men I loved. I think that we
Shall never more, at any future time,
Delight our souls with talk of knightly deeds,
Walking about the gardens and the halls
Of Camelot, as in the days that were.
I perish by this people which I made,—
Tho' Merlin sware that I should come again
To rule once more—but let what will be, be,
I am so deeply smitten thro' the helm
That without help I cannot last till morn.
Thou therefore take my brand Excalibur,
Which was my pride: for thou rememberest how
In those old days, one summer noon, an arm
Rose up from out the bosom of the lake,

Clothed in white samite, mystic, wonderful,
Holding the sword—and how I row'd across
And took it, and have worn it, like a king:
And, wheresoever I am sung or told
In aftertime, this also shall be known:
But now delay not: take Excalibur,
And fling him far into the middle mere:
Watch what thou seëst, and lightly bring me word."
    To him replied the bold Sir Bedivere:
"It is not meet, Sir King, to leave thee thus,
Aidless, alone, and smitten thro' the helm.
A little thing may harm a wounded man.
Yet I thy hest will all perform at full,
Watch what I see, and lightly bring thee word."
    So saying, from the ruin'd shrine he stept
And in the moon athwart the place of tombs,
Where lay the mighty bones of ancient men,
Old knights, and over them the sea-wind sang
Shrill, chill, with flakes of foam. He, stepping down
By zig-zag paths, and juts of pointed rock,
Came on the shining levels of the lake.
    There drew he forth the brand Excalibur,
And o'er him, drawing it, the winter moon,
Brightening the skirts of a long cloud, ran forth
And sparkled keen with frost against the hilt:
For all the haft twinkled with diamond sparks,
Myriads of topaz-lights, and jacinth-work
Of subtlest jewellery. He gazed so long
That both his eyes were dazzled, as he stood,
This way and that dividing the swift mind,
In act to throw: but at the last it seem'd
Better to leave Excalibur conceal'd
There in the many-knotted waterflags,
That whistled stiff and dry about the marge.
So strode he back slow to the wounded King.

Then spake King Arthur to Sir Bedivere:
"Hast thou perform'd my mission which I gave?
What is it thou hast seen? or what hast heard?"

And answer made the bold Sir Bedivere:
"I heard the ripple washing in the reeds,
And the wild water lapping on the crag."

To whom replied King Arthur, faint and pale:
"Thou hast betray'd thy nature and thy name,
Not rendering true answer, as beseem'd
Thy fealty, nor like a noble knight:
For surer sign had follow'd, either hand,
Or voice, or else a motion of the mere.
This is a shameful thing for men to lie.
Yet now, I charge thee, quickly go again
As thou art lief and dear, and do the thing
I bad thee, watch, and lightly bring me word."

Then went Sir Bedivere the second time
Across the ridge, and paced beside the mere,
Counting the dewy pebbles, fix'd in thought;
But when he saw the wonder of the hilt,
How curiously and strangely chased, he smote
His palms together, and he cried aloud,

"And if indeed I cast the brand away,
Surely a precious thing, one worthy note,
Should thus be lost for ever from the earth,
Which might have pleased the eyes of many men.
What good should follow this, if this were done?
What harm, undone? deep harm to disobey,
Seeing obedience is the bond of rule.
Were it well to obey then, if a king demand
An act unprofitable, against himself?
The King is sick, and knows not what he does.
What record, or what relic of my lord
Should be to aftertime, but empty breath
And rumours of a doubt? but were this kept,

Stored in some treasure-house of mighty kings,
Some one might show it at a joust of arms,
Saying, 'King Arthur's sword, Excalibur,
Wrought by the lonely maiden of the Lake.
Nine years she wrought it, sitting in the deeps
Upon the hidden bases of the hills.'
So might some old man speak in the aftertime
To all the people, winning reverence.
But now much honour and much fame were lost."

So spake he, clouded with his own conceit,
And hid Excalibur the second time,
And so strode back slow to the wounded King.

Then spoke King Arthur, breathing heavily:
"What is it thou hast seen? or what hast heard?"

And answer made the bold Sir Bedivere:
"I heard the water lapping on the crag,
And the long ripple washing in the reeds."

To whom replied King Arthur, much in wrath:
"Ah, miserable and unkind, untrue,
Unknightly, traitor-hearted! Woe is me!
Authority forgets a dying king,
Laid widow'd of the power in his eye
That bow'd the will. I see thee what thou art,
For thou, the latest-left of all my knights,
In whom should meet the offices of all,
Thou wouldst betray me for the precious hilt;
Either from lust of gold, or like a girl
Valuing the giddy pleasure of the eyes.
Yet, for a man may fail in duty twice,
And the third time may prosper, get thee hence:
But, if thou spare to fling Excalibur,
I will arise and slay thee with my hands."

Then quickly rose Sir Bedivere, and ran,
And, leaping down the ridges lightly, plunged
Among the bulrush-beds, and clutch'd the sword,

And strongly wheel'd and threw it. The great brand
Made lightnings in the splendour of the moon,
And flashing round and round, and whirl'd in an arch,
Shot like a streamer of the northern morn,
Seen where the moving isles of winter shock
By night, with noises of the northern sea.
So flash'd and fell the brand Excalibur:
But ere he dipt the surface, rose an arm
Clothed in white samite, mystic, wonderful,
And caught him by the hilt, and brandish'd him
Three times, and drew him under in the mere.
And lightly went the other to the King.

    Then spoke King Arthur, drawing thicker breath:
"Now see I by thine eyes that this is done.
Speak out: what is it thou hast heard, or seen?"

    And answer made the bold Sir Bedivere:
"Sir King, I closed mine eyelids, lest the gems
Should blind my purpose, for I never saw,
Nor shall see, here or elsewhere, till I die,
Not tho' I live three lives of mortal men,
So great a miracle as yonder hilt.
Then with both hands I flung him, wheeling him;
But when I look'd again, behold an arm,
Clothed in white samite, mystic, wonderful,
That caught him by the hilt, and brandish'd him
Three times, and drew him under in the mere."

    And answer made King Arthur, breathing hard:
"My end draws nigh; 'tis time that I were gone.
Make broad thy shoulders to receive my weight,
And bear me to the margin; yet I fear
My wound hath taken cold, and I shall die."

    So saying, from the pavement he half rose,
Slowly, with pain, reclining on his arm,
And looking wistfully with wide blue eyes
As in a picture. Him Sir Bedivere

Remorsefully regarded thro' his tears,
And would have spoken, but he found not words,
Then took with care, and kneeling on one knee,
O'er both his shoulders drew the languid hands,
And rising bore him thro' the place of tombs.

But, as he walk'd, King Arthur panted hard,
Like one that feels a nightmare on his bed
When all the house is mute. So sigh'd the King,
Muttering and murmuring at his ear, "Quick, quick!
I fear it is too late, and I shall die."
But the other swiftly strode from ridge to ridge,
Clothed with his breath, and looking, as he walk'd,
Larger than human on the frozen hills.
He heard the deep behind him, and a cry
Before. His own thought drove him, like a goad.
Dry clash'd his harness in the icy caves
And barren chasms, and all to left and right
The bare black cliff clang'd round him, as he based
His feet on juts of slippery crag that rang
Sharp-smitten with the dint of armed heels—
And on a sudden, lo! the level lake,
And the long glories of the winter moon.

Then saw they how there hove a dusky barge,
Dark as a funeral scarf from stem to stern,
Beneath them; and descending they were ware
That all the decks were dense with stately forms
Black-stoled, black-hooded, like a dream—by these
Three Queens with crowns of gold—and from them rose
A cry that shiver'd to the tingling stars,
And, as it were one voice, an agony
Of lamentation, like a wind, that shrills
All night in a waste land, where no one comes,
Or hath come, since the making of the world.

Then murmur'd Arthur, "Place me in the barge,"
And to the barge they came. There those three Queens

Put forth their hands, and took the King, and wept.
But she, that rose the tallest of them all
And fairest, laid his head upon her lap,
And loosed the shatter'd casque, and chafed his hands,
And call'd him by his name, complaining loud,
And dropping bitter tears against his brow
Striped with dark blood: for all his face was white
And colourless, and like the wither'd moon
Smote by the fresh beam of the springing east;
And all his greaves and cuisses dash'd with drops
Of onset; and the light and lustrous curls—
That made his forehead like a rising sun
High from the daïs-throne—were parch'd with dust;
Or, clotted into points and hanging loose,
Mix'd with the knightly growth that fringed his lips.
So like a shatter'd column lay the King;
Not like that Arthur who, with lance in rest,
From spur to plume a star of tournament,
Shot thro' the lists at Camelot, and charged
Before the eyes of ladies and of kings.

    Then loudly cried the bold Sir Bedivere,
"Ah! my Lord Arthur, whither shall I go?
Where shall I hide my forehead and my eyes?
For now I see the true old times are dead,
When every morning brought a noble chance,
And every chance brought out a noble knight.
Such times have been not since the light that led
The holy Elders with the gift of myrrh.
But now the whole Round Table is dissolved
Which was an image of the mighty world;
And I, the last, go forth companionless,
And the days darken round me, and the years,
Among new men, strange faces, other minds."

    And slowly answered Arthur from the barge:
"The old order changeth, yielding place to new,

And God fulfils Himself in many ways,
Lest one good custom should corrupt the world.
Comfort thyself: what comfort is in me?
I have lived my life, and that which I have done
May He within Himself make pure! but thou,
If thou shouldst never see my face again,
Pray for my soul. More things are wrought by prayer
Than this world dreams of. Wherefore, let thy voice
Rise like a fountain for me night and day.
For what are men better than sheep or goats
That nourish a blind life within the brain,
If, knowing God, they lift not hands of prayer
Both for themselves and those who call them friend?
For so the whole round earth is every way
Bound by gold chains about the feet of God.
But now farewell. I am going a long way
With these thou seëst—if indeed I go—
(For all my mind is clouded with a doubt)
To the island-valley of Avilion;
Where falls not hail, or rain, or any snow,
Nor ever wind blows loudly; but it lies
Deep-meadow'd, happy, fair with orchard-lawns
And bowery hollows crown'd with summer sea,
Where I will heal me of my grievous wound."
  So said he, and the barge with oar and sail
Moved from the brink, like some full-breasted swan
That, fluting a wild carol ere her death,
Ruffles her pure cold plume, and takes the flood
With swarthy webs. Long stood Sir Bedivere
Revolving many memories, till the hull
Look'd one black dot against the verge of dawn,
And on the mere the wailing died away.

Tithonus

The woods decay, the woods decay and fall,
The vapours weep their burthen to the ground,
Man comes and tills the field and lies beneath,
And after many a summer dies the swan.
Me only cruel immortality
Consumes: I wither slowly in thine arms,
Here at the quiet limit of the world,
A white-hair'd shadow roaming like a dream
The ever-silent spaces of the East,
Far-folded mists, and gleaming halls of morn.

  Alas! for this gray shadow, once a man—
So glorious in his beauty and thy choice,
Who madest him thy chosen that he seem'd
To his great heart none other than a God!
I ask'd thee, "Give me immortality."
Then didst thou grant mine asking with a smile,
Like wealthy men who care not how they give.
But thy strong Hours indignant work'd their wills,
And beat me down and marr'd and wasted me,
And tho' they could not end me, left me maim'd
To dwell in presence of immortal youth,
Immortal age beside immortal youth,
And all I was, in ashes. Can thy love,
Thy beauty, make amends, tho' even now,
Close over us, the silver star, thy guide,
Shines in those tremulous eyes that fill with tears
To hear me? Let me go: take back thy gift:
Why should a man desire in any way
To vary from the kindly race of men,

Or pass beyond the goal of ordinance
Where all should pause, as is most meet for all?

A soft air fans the cloud apart; there comes
A glimpse of that dark world where I was born.
Once more the old mysterious glimmer steals
From thy pure brows, and from thy shoulders pure,
And bosom beating with a heart renew'd.
Thy cheek begins to redden thro' the gloom,
Thy sweet eyes brighten slowly close to mine,
Ere yet they blind the stars, and the wild team
Which love thee, yearning for thy yoke, arise,
And shake the darkness from their loosen'd manes,
And beat the twilight into flakes of fire.

Lo! ever thus thou growest beautiful
In silence, then before thine answer given
Departest, and thy tears are on my cheek.

Why wilt thou ever scare me with thy tears,
And make me tremble lest a saying learnt,
In days far-off, on that dark earth, be true?
"The Gods themselves cannot recall their gifts."

Ay me! ay me! with what another heart
In days far-off, and with what other eyes
I used to watch—if I be he that watch'd—
The lucid outline forming round thee; saw
The dim curls kindle into sunny rings;
Changed with thy mystic change, and felt my blood
Glow with the glow that slowly crimson'd all
Thy presence and thy portals, while I lay,
Mouth, forehead, eyelids, growing dewy-warm
With kisses balmier than half-opening buds
Of April, and could hear the lips that kiss'd
Whispering I knew not what of wild and sweet,

Like that strange song I heard Apollo sing,
While Ilion like a mist rose into towers.

   Yet hold me not for ever in thine East:
How can my nature longer mix with thine?
Coldly thy rosy shadows bathe me, cold
Are all thy lights, and cold my wrinkled feet
Upon thy glimmering thresholds, when the steam
Floats up from those dim fields about the homes
Of happy men that have the power to die,
And grassy barrows of the happier dead.
Release me, and restore me to the ground;
Thou seëst all things, thou wilt see my grave:
Thou wilt renew thy beauty morn by morn;
I earth in earth forget these empty courts,
And thee returning on thy silver wheels.

FROM *The Vision of Sin*

[Song at the Ruin'd Inn, of a gray and gap-toothed man]

"Wrinkled ostler, grim and thin!
   Here is custom come your way;
Take my brute, and lead him in,
   Stuff his ribs with mouldy hay.

"Bitter barmaid, waning fast!
   See that sheets are on my bed;
What! the flower of life is past:
   It is long before you wed.

"Slip-shod waiter, lank and sour,
   At the Dragon on the heath!
Let us have a quiet hour,
   Let us hob-and-nob with Death.

"I am old, but let me drink;
  Bring me spices, bring me wine;
I remember, when I think,
  That my youth was half divine.

"Wine is good for shrivell'd lips,
  When a blanket wraps the day,
When the rotten woodland drips,
  And the leaf is stamp'd in clay.

"Sit thee down, and have no shame,
  Cheek by jowl, and knee by knee:
What care I for any name?
  What for order or degree?

"Let me screw thee up a peg:
  Let me loose thy tongue with wine:
Callest thou that thing a leg?
  Which is thinnest? thine or mine?

"Thou shalt not be saved by works:
  Thou hast been a sinner too:
Ruin'd trunks on wither'd forks,
  Empty scarecrows, I and you!

"Fill the cup, and fill the can:
  Have a rouse before the morn:
Every moment dies a man,
  Every moment one is born.

"We are men of ruin'd blood;
  Therefore comes it we are wise.
Fish are we that love the mud,
  Rising to no fancy-flies.

"Name and fame! to fly sublime
  Thro' the courts, the camps, the schools,
Is to be the ball of Time,
  Bandied by the hands of fools.

"Friendship!—to be two in one—
    Let the canting liar pack!
Well I know, when I am gone,
    How she mouths behind my back.

"Virtue!—to be good and just—
    Every heart, when sifted well,
Is a clot of warmer dust,
    Mix'd with cunning sparks of hell.

"O! we two as well can look
    Whited thought and cleanly life
As the priest, above his book
    Leering at his neighbour's wife.

"Fill the cup, and fill the can:
    Have a rouse before the morn:
Every moment dies a man,
    Every moment one is born.

"Drink, and let the parties rave:
    They are fill'd with idle spleen;
Rising, falling, like a wave,
    For they know not what they mean.

"He that roars for liberty
    Faster binds a tyrant's power;
And the tyrant's cruel glee
    Forces on the freer hour.

"Fill the can, and fill the cup:
    All the windy ways of men
Are but dust that rises up,
    And is lightly laid again.

"Greet her with applausive breath,
    Freedom, gaily doth she tread;
In her right a civic wreath,
    In her left a human head.

"No, I love not what is new;
  She is of an ancient house:
And I think we know the hue
  Of that cap upon her brows.

"Let her go! her thirst she slakes
  Where the bloody conduit runs,
Then her sweetest meal she makes
  On the first-born of her sons.

"Drink to lofty hopes that cool—
  Visions of a perfect State:
Drink we, last, the public fool,
  Frantic love and frantic hate.

"Chant me now some wicked stave,
  Till thy drooping courage rise,
And the glow-worm of the grave
  Glimmer in thy rheumy eyes.

"Fear not thou to loose thy tongue;
  Set thy hoary fancies free;
What is loathsome to the young
  Savours well to thee and me.

"Change, reverting to the years,
  When thy nerves could understand
What there is in loving tears,
  And the warmth of hand in hand.

"Tell me tales of thy first love—
  April hopes, the fools of chance;
Till the graves begin to move,
  And the dead begin to dance.

"Fill the can, and fill the cup:
  All the windy ways of men
Are but dust that rises up,
  And is lightly laid again.

"Trooping from their mouldy dens
  The chap-fallen circle spreads:
Welcome, fellow-citizens,
  Hollow hearts and empty heads!

"You are bones, and what of that?
  Every face, however full,
Padded round with flesh and fat,
  Is but modell'd on a skull.

"Death is king, and Vivat Rex!
  Tread a measure on the stones,
Madam—if I know your sex,
  From the fashion of your bones.

"No, I cannot praise the fire
  In your eye—nor yet your lip:
All the more do I admire
  Joints of cunning workmanship.

"Lo! God's likeness—the ground-plan—
  Neither modell'd, glazed, or framed:
Buss me thou rough sketch of man,
  Far too naked to be shamed!

"Drink to Fortune, drink to Chance,
  While we keep a little breath!
Drink to heavy Ignorance!
  Hob-and-nob with brother Death!

"Thou art mazed, the night is long,
  And the longer night is near:
What! I am not all as wrong
  As a bitter jest is dear.

"Youthful hopes, by scores, to all,
  When the locks are crisp and curl'd;
Unto me my maudlin gall
  And my mockeries of the world.

"Fill the cup, and fill the can!
　　Mingle madness, mingle scorn!
Dregs of life, and less of man:
　　Yet we will not die forlorn."

(Part IV)

Break, break, break

Break, break, break,
　　On thy cold gray stones, O Sea!
And I would that my tongue could utter
　　The thoughts that arise in me.

O well for the fisherman's boy,
　　That he shouts with his sister at play!
O well for the sailor lad,
　　That he sings in his boat on the bay!

And the stately ships go on
　　To their haven under the hill;
But O for the touch of a vanish'd hand,
　　And the sound of a voice that is still!

Break, break, break,
　　At the foot of thy crags, O Sea!
But the tender grace of a day that is dead
　　Will never come back to me.

FROM *The Princess*

SONGS

The splendour falls on castle walls
 And snowy summits old in story:
The long light shakes across the lakes,
 And the wild cataract leaps in glory.
Blow, bugle, blow, set the wild echoes flying,
Blow, bugle; answer, echoes, dying, dying, dying.

O hark, O hear! how thin and clear,
 And thinner, clearer, farther going!
O sweet and far from cliff and scar
 The horns of Elfland faintly blowing!
Blow, let us hear the purple glens replying:
Blow, bugle; answer, echoes, dying, dying, dying.

O love, they die in yon rich sky,
 They faint on hill or field or river:
Our echoes roll from soul to soul,
 And grow for ever and for ever.
Blow, bugle, blow, set the wild echoes flying,
And answer, echoes, answer, dying, dying, dying.

Tears, idle tears, I know not what they mean,
Tears from the depth of some divine despair
Rise in the heart, and gather to the eyes,
In looking on the happy Autumn-fields,
And thinking of the days that are no more.

Fresh as the first beam glittering on a sail,
That brings our friends up from the underworld,
Sad as the last which reddens over one
That sinks with all we love below the verge;
So sad, so fresh, the days that are no more.

Ah, sad and strange as in dark summer dawns
The earliest pipe of half-awaken'd birds
To dying ears, when unto dying eyes
The casement slowly grows a glimmering square;
So sad, so strange, the days that are no more.

Dear as remember'd kisses after death,
And sweet as those by hopeless fancy feign'd
On lips that are for others; deep as love,
Deep as first love, and wild with all regret;
O Death in Life, the days that are no more.

Ask me no more: the moon may draw the sea;
    The cloud may stoop from heaven and take shape,
    With fold to fold, of mountain or of cape;
But O too fond, when have I answer'd thee?
        Ask me no more.

Ask me no more: what answer should I give?
    I love not hollow cheek or faded eye:
    Yet O my friend, I will not have thee die!
Ask me no more, lest I should bid thee live;
        Ask me no more.

Ask me no more: thy fate and mine are seal'd:
    I strove against the stream and all in vain:
    Let the great river take me to the main:
No more, dear love, for at a touch I yield;
        Ask me no more.

Now sleeps the crimson petal, now the white;
Nor waves the cypress in the palace walk;
Nor winks the gold fin in the porphyry font:
The fire-fly wakens; waken thou with me.

Now droops the milk-white peacock like a ghost,
And like a ghost she glimmers on to me.

Now lies the Earth all Danaë to the stars,
And all thy heart lies open unto me.

Now slides the silent meteor on, and leaves
A shining furrow, as thy thoughts in me.

Now folds the lily all her sweetness up,
And slips into the bosom of the lake.
So fold thyself, my dearest, thou, and slip
Into my bosom and be lost in me.

FROM *In Memoriam A. H. H.*

OBIIT MDCCCXXXIII

II

Old Yew, which graspest at the stones
        That name the under-lying dead,
        Thy fibres net the dreamless head,
Thy roots are wrapt about the bones.

The seasons bring the flower again,
        And bring the firstling to the flock;
        And in the dusk of thee, the clock
Beats out the little lives of men.

O not for thee the glow, the bloom,
    Who changest not in any gale,
    Nor branding summer suns avail
To touch thy thousand years of gloom:

And gazing on thee, sullen tree,
    Sick for thy stubborn hardihood,
    I seem to fail from out my blood
And grow incorporate into thee.

VI

One writes, that "Other friends remain,"
    That "Loss is common to the race"—
    And common is the commonplace,
And vacant chaff well meant for grain.

That loss is common would not make
    My own less bitter, rather more:
    Too common! Never morning wore
To evening, but some heart did break.

O father, wheresoe'er thou be,
    Who pledgest now thy gallant son;
    A shot, ere half thy draught be done,
Hath still'd the life that beat from thee.

O mother, praying God will save
    Thy sailor,—while thy head is bow'd,
    His heavy-shotted hammock-shroud
Drops in his vast and wandering grave.

Ye know no more than I who wrought
    At that last hour to please him well:
    Who mused on all I had to tell,
And something written, something thought;

Expecting still his advent home;
    And ever met him on his way
    With wishes, thinking, "here to-day,"
Or "here to-morrow will he come."

O somewhere, meek, unconscious dove,
    That sittest ranging golden hair;
    And glad to find thyself so fair,
Poor child, that waitest for thy love!

For now her father's chimney glows
    In expectation of a guest;
    And thinking "this will please him best,"
She takes a riband or a rose;

For he will see them on to-night;
    And with the thought her colour burns;
    And, having left the glass, she turns
Once more to set a ringlet right;

And, even when she turn'd, the curse
    Had fallen, and her future Lord
    Was drown'd in passing thro' the ford,
Or kill'd in falling from his horse.

O what to her shall be the end?
    And what to me remains of good?
    To her, perpetual maidenhood,
And unto me no second friend.

VII

Dark house, by which once more I stand
    Here in the long unlovely street,
    Doors, where my heart was used to beat
So quickly, waiting for a hand,

A hand that can be clasp'd no more—
    Behold me, for I cannot sleep,
    And like a guilty thing I creep
At earliest morning to the door.

He is not here; but far away
    The noise of life begins again,
    And ghastly thro' the drizzling rain
On the bald street breaks the blank day.

XI

Calm is the morn without a sound,
    Calm as to suit a calmer grief,
    And only thro' the faded leaf
The chestnut pattering to the ground:

Calm and deep peace on this high wold,
    And on these dews that drench the furze,
    And all the silvery gossamers
That twinkle into green and gold:

Calm and still light on yon great plain
    That sweeps with all its autumn bowers,
    And crowded farms and lessening towers,
To mingle with the bounding main:

Calm and deep peace in this wide air,
    These leaves that redden to the fall;
    And in my heart, if calm at all,
If any calm, a calm despair:

Calm on the seas, and silver sleep,
    And waves that sway themselves in rest,
    And dead calm in that noble breast
Which heaves but with the heaving deep.

XV

To-night the winds begin to rise
  And roar from yonder dropping day:
  The last red leaf is whirl'd away,
The rooks are blown about the skies;

The forest crack'd, the waters curl'd,
  The cattle huddled on the lea;
  And wildly dash'd on tower and tree
The sunbeam strikes along the world:

And but for fancies, which aver
  That all thy motions gently pass
  Athwart a plane of molten glass,
I scarce could brook the strain and stir

That makes the barren branches loud;
  And but for fear it is not so,
  The wild unrest that lives in woe
Would dote and pore on yonder cloud

That rises upward always higher,
  And onward drags a labouring breast,
  And topples round the dreary west,
A looming bastion fringed with fire.

XXXIX

Old warder of these buried bones,
  And answering now my random stroke
  With fruitful cloud and living smoke,
Dark yew, that graspest at the stones

And dippest toward the dreamless head,
  To thee too comes the golden hour

When flower is feeling after flower;
But Sorrow—fixt upon the dead,

And darkening the dark graves of men,—
    What whisper'd from her lying lips?
    Thy gloom is kindled at the tips,
And passes into gloom again.

L

Be near me when my light is low,
    When the blood creeps, and the nerves prick
    And tingle; and the heart is sick,
And all the wheels of Being slow.

Be near me when the sensuous frame
    Is rack'd with pangs that conquer trust;
    And Time, a maniac scattering dust,
And Life, a Fury slinging flame.

Be near me when my faith is dry,
    And men the flies of latter spring,
    That lay their eggs, and sting and sing
And weave their petty cells and die.

Be near me when I fade away,
    To point the term of human strife,
    And on the low dark verge of life
The twilight of eternal day.

LXX

I cannot see the features right,
    When on the gloom I strive to paint
    The face I know; the hues are faint
And mix with hollow masks of night;

Cloud-towers by ghostly masons wrought,
    A gulf that ever shuts and gapes,
    A hand that points, and palled shapes
In shadowy thoroughfares of thought;

And crowds that stream from yawning doors,
    And shoals of pucker'd faces drive;
    Dark bulks that tumble half alive,
And lazy lengths on boundless shores;

Till all at once beyond the will
    I hear a wizard music roll,
    And thro' a lattice on the soul
Looks thy fair face and makes it still.

LXXII

Risest thou thus, dim dawn, again,
    And howlest, issuing out of night,
    With blasts that blow the poplar white,
And lash with storm the streaming pane?

Day, when my crown'd estate begun
    To pine in that reverse of doom,
    Which sicken'd every living bloom,
And blurr'd the splendour of the sun;

Who usherest in the dolorous hour
    With thy quick tears that make the rose
    Pull sideways, and the daisy close
Her crimson fringes to the shower;

Who might'st have heaved a windless flame
    Up the deep East, or, whispering, play'd
    A chequer-work of beam and shade
Along the hills, yet look'd the same,

As wan, as chill, as wild as now;
    Day, mark'd as with some hideous crime,
    When the dark hand struck down thro' time,
And cancell'd nature's best: but thou,

Lift as thou may'st thy burthen'd brows
    Thro' clouds that drench the morning star,
    And whirl the ungarner'd sheaf afar,
And sow the sky with flying boughs,

And up thy vault with roaring sound
    Climb thy thick noon, disastrous day;
    Touch thy dull goal of joyless gray,
And hide thy shame beneath the ground.

XCV

By night we linger'd on the lawn,
    For underfoot the herb was dry;
    And genial warmth; and o'er the sky
The silvery haze of summer drawn;

And calm that let the tapers burn
    Unwavering: not a cricket chirr'd;
    The brook alone far-off was heard,
And on the board the fluttering urn:

And bats went round in fragrant skies,
    And wheel'd or lit the filmy shapes
    That haunt the dusk, with ermine capes
And woolly breasts and beaded eyes;

While now we sang old songs that peal'd
    From knoll to knoll, where, couch'd at ease,
    The white kine glimmer'd, and the trees
Laid their dark arms about the field.

But when those others, one by one,
    Withdrew themselves from me and night,
    And in the house light after light
Went out, and I was all alone,

A hunger seized my heart; I read
    Of that glad year which once had been,
    In those fall'n leaves which kept their green,
The noble letters of the dead.

And strangely on the silence broke
    The silent-speaking words, and strange
    Was love's dumb cry defying change
To test his worth; and strangely spoke

The faith, the vigor, bold to dwell
    On doubts that drive the coward back,
    And keen thro' wordy snares to track
Suggestion to her inmost cell.

So word by word, and line by line,
    The dead man touch'd me from the past,
    And all at once it seem'd at last
The living soul was flash'd on mine,

And mine in this was wound, and whirl'd
    About empyreal heights of thought,
    And came on that which is, and caught
The deep pulsations of the world,

Æonian music measuring out
    The steps of Time—the shocks of Chance—
    The blows of Death. At length my trance
Was cancell'd, stricken thro' with doubt.

Vague words! but ah, how hard to frame
    In matter-moulded forms of speech,
    Or even for intellect to reach
Thro' memory that which I became:

Till now the doubtful dusk reveal'd
  The knolls once more where, couch'd at ease,
  The white kine glimmer'd, and the trees
Laid their dark arms about the field;

And suck'd from out the distant gloom
  A breeze began to tremble o'er
  The large leaves of the sycamore,
And fluctuate all the still perfume,

And gathering freshlier overhead,
  Rock'd the full-foliaged elms, and swung
  The heavy-folded rose, and flung
The lilies to and fro, and said,

"The dawn, the dawn," and died away;
  And East and West, without a breath,
  Mixt their dim lights, like life and death,
To broaden into boundless day.

C

I climb the hill: from end to end
  Of all the landscape underneath,
  I find no place that does not breathe
Some gracious memory of my friend;

No gray old grange, or lonely fold,
  Or low morass and whispering reed,
  Or simple stile from mead to mead,
Or sheepwalk up the windy wold;

Nor hoary knoll of ash and haw
  That hears the latest linnet trill,
  Nor quarry trench'd along the hill
And haunted by the wrangling daw;

Nor runlet tinkling from the rock;
　　　Nor pastoral rivulet that swerves
　　　To left and right thro' meadowy curves,
That feed the mothers of the flock;

But each has pleased a kindred eye,
　　　And each reflects a kindlier day;
　　　And, leaving these, to pass away,
I think once more he seems to die.

CI

Unwatch'd, the garden bough shall sway,
　　　The tender blossom flutter down,
　　　Unloved, that beech will gather brown,
This maple burn itself away;

Unloved, the sun-flower, shining fair,
　　　Ray round with flames her disk of seed,
　　　And many a rose-carnation feed
With summer spice the humming air;

Unloved, by many a sandy bar,
　　　The brook shall babble down the plain,
　　　At noon or when the lesser wain
Is twisting round the polar star;

Uncared for, gird the windy grove,
　　　And flood the haunts of hern and crake;
　　　Or into silver arrows break
The sailing moon in creek and cove;

Till from the garden and the wild
　　　A fresh association blow,
　　　And year by year the landscape grow
Familiar to the stranger's child;

As year by year the labourer tills
　　His wonted glebe, or lops the glades;
　　And year by year our memory fades
From all the circle of the hills.

CII

We leave the well-beloved place
　　Where first we gazed upon the sky;
　　The roofs, that heard our earliest cry,
Will shelter one of stranger race.

We go, but ere we go from home,
　　As down the garden-walks I move,
　　Two spirits of a diverse love
Contend for loving masterdom.

One whispers, "Here thy boyhood sung
　　Long since its matin song, and heard
　　The low love-language of the bird
In native hazels tassel-hung."

The other answers, "Yea, but here
　　Thy feet have stray'd in after hours
　　With thy lost friend among the bowers,
And this hath made them trebly dear."

These two have striven half the day,
　　And each prefers his separate claim,
　　Poor rivals in a losing game,
That will not yield each other way.

I turn to go: my feet are set
　　To leave the pleasant fields and farms;
　　They mix in one another's arms
To one pure image of regret.

CIII

On that last night before we went
　　From out the doors where I was bred,
　　I dream'd a vision of the dead,
Which left my after-morn content.

Methought I dwelt within a hall,
　　And maidens with me: distant hills
　　From hidden summits fed with rills
A river sliding by the wall.

The hall with harp and carol rang.
　　They sang of what is wise and good
　　And graceful. In the centre stood
A statue veil'd, to which they sang;

And which, tho' veil'd, was known to me,
　　The shape of him I loved, and love
　　For ever: then flew in a dove
And brought a summons from the sea:

And when they learnt that I must go
　　They wept and wail'd, but led the way
　　To where a little shallop lay
At anchor in the flood below;

And on by many a level mead,
　　And shadowing bluff that made the banks,
　　We glided winding under ranks
Of iris, and the golden reed;

And still as vaster grew the shore
　　And roll'd the floods in grander space,
　　The maidens gather'd strength and grace
And presence, lordlier than before;

And I myself, who sat apart
    And watch'd them, wax'd in every limb;
    I felt the thews of Anakim,
The pulses of a Titan's heart;

As one would sing the death of war,
    And one would chant the history
    Of that great race, which is to be,
And one the shaping of a star;

Until the forward-creeping tides
    Began to foam, and we to draw
    From deep to deep, to where we saw
A great ship lift her shining sides.

The man we loved was there on deck,
    But thrice as large as man he bent
    To greet us. Up the side I went,
And fell in silence on his neck:

Whereat those maidens with one mind
    Bewail'd their lot; I did them wrong:
    "We served thee here," they said, "so long,
And wilt thou leave us now behind?"

So rapt I was, they could not win
    An answer from my lips, but he
    Replying, "Enter likewise ye
And go with us": they enter'd in.

And while the wind began to sweep
    A music out of sheet and shroud,
    We steer'd her toward a crimson cloud
That landlike slept along the deep.

CXIX

Doors, where my heart was used to beat
    So quickly, not as one that weeps
    I come once more; the city sleeps;
I smell the meadow in the street;

I hear a chirp of birds; I see
    Betwixt the black fronts long-withdrawn
    A light-blue lane of early dawn,
And think of early days and thee,

And bless thee, for thy lips are bland,
    And bright the friendship of thine eye;
    And in my thoughts with scarce a sigh
I take the pressure of thine hand.

FROM *Maud*

I have led her home, my love, my only friend.
There is none like her, none.
And never yet so warmly ran my blood
And sweetly, on and on,
Calming itself to the long-wish'd-for end,
Full to the banks, close on the promised good.

None like her, none.
Just now the dry-tongued laurels' pattering talk
Seem'd her light foot along the garden walk,
And shook my heart to think she comes once more;
But even then I heard her close the door,
The gates of Heaven are closed, and she is gone.

There is none like her, none,
Nor will be when our summers have deceased.
O, art thou sighing for Lebanon
In the long breeze that streams to thy delicious East,
Sighing for Lebanon,
Dark cedar, tho' thy limbs have here increased,
Upon a pastoral slope as fair,
And looking to the South, and fed
With honey'd rain and delicate air,
And haunted by the starry head
Of her whose gentle will has changed my fate,
And made my life a perfumed altar-flame;
And over whom thy darkness must have spread
With such delight as theirs of old, thy great
Forefathers of the thornless garden, there
Shadowing the snow-limb'd Eve from whom she came.

(Part I, section xviii, stanzas 1–3)

See what a lovely shell,
Small and pure as a pearl,
Lying close to my foot,
Frail, but a work divine,
Made so fairily well
With delicate spire and whorl,
How exquisitely minute,
A miracle of design!

What is it? a learned man
Could give it a clumsy name.
Let him name it who can,
The beauty would be the same.

The tiny cell is forlorn,
Void of the little living will
That made it stir on the shore.

Did he stand at the diamond door
Of his house in a rainbow frill?
Did he push, when he was uncurl'd,
A golden foot or a fairy horn
Thro' his dim water-world?

Slight, to be crush'd with a tap
Of my finger-nail on the sand,
Small, but a work divine,
Frail, but a force to withstand,
Year upon year, the shock
Of cataract seas that snap
The three-decker's oaken spine
Athwart the ledges of rock,
Here on the Breton strand!

(*Part II, section ii, stanzas 1–4*)

FROM *Merlin and Vivien*

In Love, if Love be Love, if Love be ours,
Faith and unfaith can ne'er be equal powers:
Unfaith in aught is want of faith in all.

It is the little rift within the lute,
That by and by will make the music mute,
And ever widening slowly silence all.

The little rift within the lover's lute,
Or little pitted speck in garner'd fruit,
That rotting inward slowly moulders all.

It is not worth the keeping: let it go:
But shall it? answer, darling, answer, no.
And trust me not at all or all in all.

FROM *Pelleas and Ettarre*

A rose, but one, none other rose had I,
A rose, one rose, and this was wondrous fair,
One rose a rose that gladden'd earth and sky,
One rose, my rose, that sweeten'd all mine air—
I cared not for the thorns; the thorns were there.

One rose, a rose to gather by and by,
One rose, a rose to gather and to wear,
No rose but one—what other rose had I?
One rose, my rose; a rose that will not die,—
He dies who loves it,—if the worm be there.

Rizpah

Wailing, wailing, wailing, the wind over land and sea—
And Willy's voice in the wind, "O mother come out to
    me."
Why should he call me to-night, when he knows that
    I cannot go?
For the downs are as bright as day, and the full moon
    stares at the snow.

We should be seen, my dear; they would spy us out of
    the town.
The loud black nights for us, and the storm rushing over
    the down,
When I cannot see my own hand, but am led by the
    creak of the chain,

And grovel and grope for my son till I find myself
    drenched with the rain.

Anything fallen again? nay—what was there left to fall?
I have taken them home, I have number'd the bones, I
    have hidden them all.
What am I saying? and what are *you*? do you come as
    a spy?
Falls? what falls? who knows? As the tree falls so must
    it lie.

Who let her in? how long has she been? you—what
    have you heard?
Why did you sit so quiet? you never have spoken a
    word.
O—to pray with me—yes—a lady—none of their
    spies—
But the night has crept into my heart, and begun to
    darken my eyes.

Ah—you, that have lived so soft, what should *you* know
    of the night,
The blast and the burning shame and the bitter frost
    and the fright?
I have done it, while you were asleep—you were only
    made for the day.
I have gather'd my baby together—and now you may
    go your way.

Nay—for it's kind of you, madam, to sit by an old dying
    wife.
But say nothing hard of my boy, I have only an hour of
    life.
I kiss'd my boy in the prison, before he went out to die.
"They dared me to do it," he said, and he never has
    told me a lie.

I whipt him for robbing an orchard once when he was
but a child—

"The farmer dared me to do it," he said; he was always
so wild—

And idle—and couldn't be idle—my Willy—he never
could rest.

The King should have made him a soldier, he would
have been one of his best.

But he lived with a lot of wild mates, and they never
would let him be good;

They swore that he dare not rob the mail, and he swore
that he would;

And he took no life, but he took one purse, and when
all was done

He flung it among his fellows—"I'll none of it," said my
son.

I came into court to the judge and the lawyers. I told
them my tale,

God's own truth—but they kill'd him, they kill'd him for
robbing the mail.

They hang'd him in chains for a show—we had always
borne a good name—

To be hang'd for a thief—and then put away—isn't
that enough shame?

Dust to dust—low down—let us hide! but they set him
so high

That all the ships of the world could stare at him, pass-
ing by.

God 'ill pardon the hell-black raven and horrible fowls
of the air,

But not the black heart of the lawyer who kill'd him
and hang'd him there.

And the jailer forced me away. I had bid him my last
good-bye;

They had fasten'd the door of his cell. "O mother!" I
heard him cry.
I couldn't get back tho' I tried, he had something
further to say,
And now I shall never know it. The jailer forced me
away.

Then since I couldn't but hear that cry of my boy that
was dead,
They seized me and shut me up: they fasten'd me down
on my bed.
"Mother, O mother!"—he call'd in the dark to me year
after year—
They beat me for that, they beat me—you know that
I couldn't but hear;
And then at the last they found I had grown so stupid
and still
They let me abroad again—but the creatures had
worked their will.

Flesh of my flesh was gone, but bone of my bone was
left—
I stole them all from the lawyers—and you, will you
call it a theft?—
My baby, the bones that had suck'd me, the bones that
had laugh'd and had cried—
Theirs? O no! they are mine—not theirs—they had
moved in my side.

Do you think I was scared by the bones? I kiss'd 'em, I
buried 'em all—
I can't dig deep, I am old—in the night by the church-
yard wall.
My Willy 'ill rise up whole when the trumpet of judg-
ment 'ill sound;
But I charge you never to say that I laid him in holy
ground.

They would scratch him up—they would hang him
again on the cursed tree.
Sin? O yes, we are sinners, I know—let all that be,
And read me a Bible verse of the Lord's goodwill
toward men—
"Full of compassion and mercy, the Lord"—let me hear
it again;
"Full of compassion and mercy—long-suffering." Yes,
O, yes!
For the lawyer is born but to murder—the Saviour lives
but to bless.
He'll never put on the black cap except for the worst of
the worst,
And the first may be last—I have heard it in church—
and the last may be first.
Suffering—O, long-suffering—yes, as the Lord must
know,
Year after year in the mist and the wind and the shower
and the snow.

Heard, have you? what? they have told you he never
repented his sin.
How do they know it? are *they* his mother? are *you* of
his kin?
Heard! have you ever heard, when the storm on the
downs began,
The wind that 'ill wail like a child and the sea that 'ill
moan like a man?

Election, Election, and Reprobation—it's all very well.
But I go to-night to my boy, and I shall not find him in
hell.
For I cared so much for my boy that the Lord has look'd
into my care,
And He means me I'm sure to be happy with Willy, I
know not where.

And if *he* be lost—but to save *my* soul, that is all your
  desire—
Do you think that I care for *my* soul if my boy be gone
  to the fire?
I have been with God in the dark—go, go, you may
  leave me alone—
You never have borne a child—you are just as hard as
  a stone.

Madam, I beg your pardon! I think that you mean to be
  kind,
But I cannot hear what you say for my Willy's voice in
  the wind—
The snow and the sky so bright—he used but to call in
  the dark,
And he calls to me now from the church and not from
  the gibbet—for hark!
Nay—you can hear it yourself—it is coming—shaking
  the walls—
Willy—the moon's in a cloud—Good-night. I am going.
  He calls.

The Voyage of Maeldune

(*Founded on an Irish Legend.* A. D. 700)

I was the chief of the race—he had stricken my father
  dead—
But I gather'd my fellows together, I swore I would
  strike off his head.
Each of them look'd like a king, and was noble in birth
  as in worth,
And each of them boasted he sprang from the oldest
  race upon earth.

Each was as brave in the fight as the bravest hero of
    song,
And each of them liefer had died than have done one
    another a wrong.
He lived on an isle in the ocean—we sail'd on a Friday
    morn—
He that had slain my father the day before I was born.

And we came to the isle in the ocean, and there on the
    shore was he.
But a sudden blast blew us out and away thro' a bound-
    less sea.

And we came to the Silent Isle that we never had
    touch'd at before,
Where a silent ocean always broke on a silent shore,
And the brooks glitter'd on in the light without sound,
    and the long waterfalls
Pour'd in a thunderless plunge to the base of the moun-
    tain walls,
And the poplar and cypress unshaken by storm flour-
    ish'd up beyond sight,
And the pine shot aloft from the crag to an unbelievable
    height,
And high in the heaven above it there flicker'd a song-
    less lark,
And the cock couldn't crow, and the bull couldn't low,
    and the dog couldn't bark.
And round it we went, and thro' it, but never a mur-
    mur, a breath—
It was all of it fair as life, it was all of it quiet as death,
And we hated the beautiful Isle, for whenever we strove
    to speak
Our voices were thinner and fainter than any flitter-
    mouse-shriek;

And the men that were mighty of tongue and could raise
    such a battle-cry

That a hundred who heard it would rush on a thousand
    lances and die—

O they to be dumb'd by the charm!—so fluster'd with
    anger were they

They almost fell on each other; but after we sail'd away.

And we came to the Isle of Shouting; we landed, a score
    of wild birds

Cried from the topmost summit with human voices and
    words.

Once in an hour they cried, and whenever their voices
    peal'd

The steer fell down at the plow and the harvest died
    from the field,

And the men dropt dead in the valleys and half of the
    cattle went lame,

And the roof sank in on the hearth, and the dwelling
    broke into flame;

And the shouting of these wild birds ran into the hearts
    of my crew,

Till they shouted along with the shouting and seized one
    another and slew.

But I drew them the one from the other; I saw that we
    could not stay,

And we left the dead to the birds, and we sail'd with our
    wounded away.

And we came to the Isle of Flowers; their breath met us
    out on the seas,

For the Spring and the middle Summer sat each on the
    lap of the breeze;

And the red passion-flower to the cliffs, and the dark
    blue clematis, clung,

And starr'd with a myriad blossom the long convolvulus
  hung;
And the topmost spire of the mountain was lilies in lieu
  of snow,
And the lilies like glaciers winded down, running out
  below
Thro' the fire of the tulip and poppy, the blaze of gorse,
  and the blush
Of millions of roses that sprang without leaf or a thorn
  from the bush;
And the whole isle-side flashing down from the peak
  without ever a tree
Swept like a torrent of gems from the sky to the blue of
  the sea.
And we roll'd upon capes of crocus and vaunted our kith
  and our kin,
And we wallow'd in beds of lilies, and chanted the
  triumph of Finn,
Till each like a golden image was pollen'd from head
  to feet
And each was as dry as a cricket, with thirst in the
  middle-day heat.
Blossom and blossom, and promise of blossom, but never
  a fruit!
And we hated the Flowering Isle, as we hated the isle
  that was mute,
And we tore up the flowers by the million and flung
  them in bight and bay,
And we left but a naked rock, and in anger we sail'd away.

And we came to the Isle of Fruits; all round from the
  cliffs and the capes,
Purple or amber, dangled a hundred fathom of grapes,
And the warm melon lay like a little sun on the tawny
  sand,

And the fig ran up from the beach and rioted over the
    land,
And the mountain arose like a jewell'd throne thro' the
    fragrant air,
Glowing with all-color'd plums and with golden masses
    of pear,
And the crimson and scarlet of berries that flamed upon
    bine and vine,
But in every berry and fruit was the poisonous pleasure
    of wine;
And the peak of the mountain was apples, the hugest
    that ever were seen,
And they prest, as they grew, on each other, with hardly
    a leaflet between,
And all of them redder than rosiest health or than utter-
    est shame,
And setting, when Even descended, the very sunset
    aflame.
And we stay'd three days, and we gorged and we mad-
    den'd, till every one drew
His sword on his fellow to slay him, and ever they struck
    and they slew;
And myself, I had eaten but sparely, and fought till I
    sunder'd the fray,
Then I bad them remember my father's death, and we
    sail'd away

And we came to the Isle of Fire; we were lured by the
    light from afar,
For the peak sent up one league of fire to the Northern
    Star;
Lured by the glare and the blare, but scarcely could
    stand upright,
For the whole isle shudder'd and shook like a man in a
    mortal affright.

We were giddy besides with the fruits we had gorged,
and so crazed that at last
There were some leap'd into the fire; and away we
sailed, and we past
Over that undersea isle, where the water is clearer than
air.
Down we look'd—what a garden! O bliss, what a Par-
adise there!
Towers of a happier time, low down in a rainbow deep
Silent palaces, quiet fields of eternal sleep!
And three of the gentlest and best of my people,
whate'er I could say,
Plunged head down in the sea, and the Paradise trem-
bled away.

And we came to the Bounteous Isle, where the heavens
lean low on the land,
And ever at dawn from the cloud glitter'd o'er us a sun-
bright hand,
Then it open'd and dropt at the side of each man, as he
rose from his rest,
Bread enough for his need till the labourless day dipt
under the west;
And we wander'd about it and thro' it. O never was time
so good!
And we sang of the triumphs of Finn, and the boast of
our ancient blood,
And we gazed at the wandering wave as we sat by the
gurgle of springs,
And we chanted the songs of the Bards and the glories
of fairy kings.
But at length we began to be weary, to sigh, and to
stretch and yawn,
Till we hated the Bounteous Isle and the sun-bright
hand of the dawn,

For there was not an enemy near, but the whole green
Isle was our own,
And we took to playing at ball, and we took to throw-
ing the stone,
And we took to playing at battle, but that was a perilous
play,
For the passion of battle was in us, we slew and we
sail'd away.

And we came to the Isle of Witches and heard their
musical cry—
"Come to us, O come, come!" in the stormy red of a sky
Dashing the fires and the shadows of dawn on the beau-
tiful shapes,
For a wild witch naked as heaven stood on each of the
loftiest capes,
And a hundred ranged on the rock like white sea-birds
in a row,
And a hundred gamboll'd and pranced on the wrecks in
the sand below,
And a hundred splash'd from the ledges, and bosom'd
the burst of the spray,
But I knew we should fall on each other, and hastily
sail'd away.

And we came in an evil time to the Isle of the Double
Towers,
One was of smooth-cut stone, one carved all over with
flowers,
But an earthquake always moved in the hollows under
the dells,
And they shock'd on each other and butted each other
with clashing of bells,
And the daws flew out of the towers and jangled and
wrangled in vain,

And the clash and boom of the bells rang into the heart
and the brain,

Till the passion of battle was on us, and all took sides
with the towers,

There were some for the clean-cut stone, there were
more for the carven flowers,

And the wrathful thunder of God peal'd over us all the
day,

For the one half slew the other, and after we sail'd
away.

And we came to the Isle of a Saint who had sail'd with
Saint Brendan of yore,

He had lived ever since on the isle and his winters were
fifteen score,

And his voice was low as from other worlds, and his
eyes were sweet,

And his white hair sank to his heels, and his white beard
fell to his feet,

And he spake to me: "O Maeldune, let be this purpose
of thine!

Remember the words of the Lord when he told us,
'Vengeance is mine!'

His fathers have slain thy fathers in war or in single
strife,

Thy fathers have slain his fathers, each taken a life for
a life,

Thy father had slain his father, how long shall the
murder last?

Go back to the Isle of Finn and suffer the Past to be
Past."

And we kiss'd the fringe of his beard, and we pray'd
as we heard him pray,

And the holy man he assoil'd us, and sadly we sail'd
away.

And we came to the isle we were blown from, and there
    on the shore was he,
The man that had slain my father. I saw him and let
    him be.
O, weary was I of the travel, the trouble, the strife, and
    the sin,
When I landed again with a tithe of my men, on the Isle
    of Finn!

The Daisy

Written at Edinburgh

O love, what hours were thine and mine,
In lands of palm and southern pine;
    In lands of palm, of orange-blossom,
Of olive, aloe, and maize and vine.

What Roman strength Turbìa show'd
In ruin, by the mountain road;
    How like a gem, beneath, the city
Of little Monaco, basking, glow'd.

How richly down the rocky dell
The torrent vineyard streaming fell
    To meet the sun and sunny waters,
That only heaved with a summer swell.

What slender campanili grew
By bays, the peacock's neck in hue;
    Where, here and there, on sandy beaches
A milky-bell'd amaryllis blew.

How young Columbus seem'd to rove,
Yet present in his natal grove,

Now watching high on mountain cornice,
And steering, now, from a purple cove,

Now pacing mute by ocean's rim;
Till, in a narrow street and dim,
   I stay'd the wheels at Cogoletto,
And drank, and loyally drank to him.

Nor knew we well what pleased us most,
Not the clipt palm of which they boast;
   But distant colour, happy hamlet,
A moulder'd citadel on the coast,

Of tower, or high hill-convent, seen
A light amid its olives green;
   Or olive-hoary cape in ocean;
Or rosy blossom in hot ravine,

Where oleanders flush'd the bed
Of silent torrents, gravel-spread;
   And, crossing, oft we saw the glisten
Of ice, far up on a mountain head.

We loved that hall, tho' white and cold,
Those niched shapes of noble mould,
   A princely people's awful princes,
The grave, severe Genovese of old.

At Florence too what golden hours,
In those long galleries, were ours;
   What drives about the fresh Cascinè,
Or walks in Boboli's ducal bowers.

In bright vignettes, and each complete,
Of tower or duomo, sunny-sweet,
   Or palace, how the city glitter'd,
Thro' cypress avenues, at our feet.

But when we crost the Lombard plain
Remember what a plague of rain;
   Of rain at Reggio, rain at Parma;
At Lodi, rain, Piacenza, rain.

And stern and sad (so rare the smiles
Of sunlight) look'd the Lombard piles;
   Porch-pillars on the lion resting,
And sombre, old, colonnaded aisles.

O Milan, O the chanting quires,
The giant windows' blazon'd fires,
   The height, the space, the gloom, the glory!
A mount of marble, a hundred spires!

I climb'd the roofs at break of day
Sun-smitten Alps before me lay.
   I stood among the silent statues,
And statued pinnacles, mute as they.

How faintly-flush'd, how phantom-fair,
Was Monte Rosa, hanging there
   A thousand shadowy-pencill'd valleys
And snowy dells in a golden air.

Remember how we came at last
To Como; shower and storm and blast
   Had blown the lake beyond his limit,
And all was flooded; and how we past

From Como, when the light was gray,
And in my head, for half the day,
   The rich Virgilian rustic measure
Of Lari Maxume, all the way,

Like ballad-burthen music, kept,
As on the Lariano crept

To that fair port below the castle
Of Queen Theodolind, where we slept;

Or hardly slept, but watch'd awake
A cypress in the moonlight shake,
    The moonlight touching o'er a terrace
One tall Agavè above the lake.

What more? we took our last adieu,
And up the snowy Spulgen drew,
    But ere we reach'd the highest summit
I pluck'd a daisy, I gave it you.

It told of England then to me,
And now it tells of Italy.
    O love, we two shall go no longer
To lands of summer across the sea;

So dear a life your arms enfold
Whose crying is a cry for gold:
    Yet here to-night in this dark city,
When ill and weary, alone and cold,

I found, tho' crushed to hard and dry,
This nurseling of another sky
    Still in the little book you lent me,
And where you tenderly laid it by:

And I forgot the clouded Forth,
The gloom that saddens Heaven and Earth,
    The bitter east, the misty summer
And gray metropolis of the North.

Perchance, to lull the throbs of pain,
Perchance, to charm a vacant brain,
    Perchance, to dream you still beside me,
My fancy fled to the South again.

To Virgil

WRITTEN AT THE REQUEST OF THE
MANTUANS FOR THE NINETEENTH
CENTENARY OF VIRGIL'S DEATH

Roman Virgil, thou that singest
    Ilion's lofty temples robed in fire,
Ilion falling, Rome arising,
    wars, and filial faith, and Dido's pyre;

Landscape-lover, lord of language
    more than he that sang the "Works and Days,"
All the chosen coin of fancy
    flashing out from many a golden phrase;

Thou that singest wheat and woodland,
    tilth and vineyard, hive and horse and herd;
All the charm of all the Muses
    often flowering in a lonely word;

Poet of the happy Tityrus
    piping underneath his beechen bowers;
Poet of the poet-satyr
    whom the laughing shepherd bound with flowers;

Chanter of the Pollio, glorying
    in the blissful years again to be,
Summers of the snakeless meadow,
    unlaborious earth and oarless sea;

Thou that seest Universal
    Nature moved by Universal Mind;

Thou majestic in thy sadness
    at the doubtful doom of human kind;

Light among the vanish'd ages;
    star that gildest yet this phantom shore;
Golden branch amid the shadows,
    kings and realms that pass to rise no more;

Now thy Forum roars no longer,
    fallen every purple Cæsar's dome—
Tho' thine ocean-roll of rhythm
    sound forever of Imperial Rome—

Now the Rome of slaves hath perish'd,
    and the Rome of freemen holds her place,
I, from out the Northern Island
    sunder'd once from all the human race,

I salute thee, Mantovano,
    I that loved thee since my day began,
Wielder of the stateliest measure
    ever moulded by the lips of man.

To E. FitzGerald

Old Fitz, who from your suburb grange,
    Where once I tarried for a while,
Glance at the wheeling Orb of change,
    And greet it with a kindly smile;
Whom yet I see as there you sit
    Beneath your sheltering garden-tree,
And while your doves about you flit,
    And plant on shoulder, hand and knee,
Or on your head their rosy feet.

As if they knew your diet spares
Whatever moved in that full sheet
   Let down to Peter at his prayers;
Who live on milk and meal and grass;
   And once for ten long weeks I tried
Your table of Pythagoras,
   And seem'd at first "a thing enskied"
(As Shakespeare has it) airy-light
   To float above the ways of men,
Then fell from that half-spiritual height
   Chill'd, till I tasted flesh again
One night when earth was winter-black,
   And all the heavens flash'd in frost;
And on me, half-asleep, came back
   That wholesome heat the blood had lost,
And set me climbing icy capes
   And glaciers, over which there roll'd
To meet me long-arm'd vines with grapes
   Of Eshcol hugeness; for the cold
Without, and warmth within me, wrought
   To mould the dream; but none can say
That Lenten fare makes Lenten thought,
   Who reads your golden Eastern lay,
Than which I know no version done
   In English more divinely well;
A planet equal to the sun
   Which cast it, that large infidel
Your Omar; and your Omar drew
   Full-handed plaudits from our best
In modern letters, and from two,
   Old friends outvaluing all the rest,
Two voices heard on earth no more;
   But we old friends are still alive,
And I am nearing seventy-four,
   While you have touch'd at seventy-five,

And so I send a birthday line
    Of greeting; and my son, who dipt
In some forgotten book of mine
    With sallow scraps of manuscript,
And dating many a year ago,
    Has hit on this, which you will take
My Fitz, and welcome, as I know
    Less for its own than for the sake
Of one recalling gracious times,
    When, in our younger London days,
You found some merit in my rhymes,
    And I more pleasure in your praise.

Edward FitzGerald

(1809–1883)

Rubáiyát of Omar Khayyám of Naishápúr

Wake! For the Sun who scattered into flight
The Stars before him from the Field of Night,
   Drives Night along with them from Heav'n, and
    strikes
The Sultán's Turret with a Shaft of Light.

Before the phantom of False morning died,
Methought a Voice within the Tavern cried,
   "When all the Temple is prepared within,
Why nods the drowsy Worshipper outside?"

And, as the Cock crew, those who stood before
The Tavern shouted—"Open then the door!
   You know how little while we have to stay,
And, once departed, may return no more."

Now the New Year reviving old Desires,
The thoughtful Soul to Solitude retires,
   Where the WHITE HAND OF MOSES on the Bough
Puts out, and Jesus from the Ground suspires.

Iram indeed is gone with all his Rose,
And Jamshyd's Sev'n-ringed Cup where no one knows;
   But still a Ruby kindles in the Vine,
And many a Garden by the Water blows.

And David's lips are lockt; but in divine
High-piping Pehleví, with "Wine! Wine! Wine!
     Red Wine!"—the Nightingale cries to the Rose
That sallow cheek of hers to incarnadine.

Come, fill the Cup, and in the fire of Spring
Your Winter-garment of Repentance fling:
     The Bird of Time has but a little way
To flutter—and the Bird is on the Wing.

Whether at Naishápúr or Babylon,
Whether the Cup with sweet or bitter run,
     The Wine of Life keeps oozing drop by drop,
The Leaves of Life keep falling one by one.

Each Morn a thousand Roses brings, you say;
Yes, but where leaves the Rose of Yesterday?
     And this first Summer month that brings the Rose
Shall take Jamshyd and Kaikobád away.

Well, let it take them! What have we to do
With Kaikobád the Great, or Kaikhosrú?
     Let Zál and Rustum bluster as they will,
Or Hátim call to Supper—heed not you.

With me along the strip of Herbage strown
That just divides the desert from the sown,
     Where name of Slave and Sultán is forgot—
And Peace to Mahmúd on his golden Throne!

A Book of Verses underneath the Bough,
A Jug of Wine, a Loaf of Bread—and Thou
     Beside me singing in the Wilderness—
Oh, Wilderness were Paradise enow!

Some for the Glories of This World; and some
Sigh for the Prophet's Paradise to come;
     Ah, take the Cash, and let the Credit go,
Nor heed the rumble of a distant Drum!

Look to the blowing Rose about us—"Lo,
Laughing," she says, "into the world I blow,
    At once the silken tassel of my Purse
Tear, and its Treasure on the Garden throw."

And those who husbanded the Golden grain,
And those who flung it to the winds like Rain,
    Alike to no such aureate Earth are turned
As, buried once, Men want dug up again.

The Worldly Hope men set their Hearts upon
Turns Ashes—or it prospers; and anon,
    Like Snow upon the Desert's dusty Face,
Lighting a little hour or two—is gone.

Think, in this battered Caravanserai
Whose Portals are alternate Night and Day,
    How Sultán after Sultán with his Pomp
Abode his destined Hour, and went his way.

They say the Lion and the Lizard keep
The Courts where Jamshyd gloried and drank deep:
    And Bahrám, that great Hunter—the Wild Ass
Stamps o'er his Head, but cannot break his Sleep.

I sometimes think that never blows so red
The Rose as where some buried Cæsar bled;
    That every Hyacinth the Garden wears
Dropt in her Lap from some once lovely Head.

And this reviving Herb whose tender Green
Fledges the River-Lip on which we lean—
    Ah, lean upon it lightly! for who knows
From what once lovely Lip it springs unseen!

Ah, my Belovéd, fill the cup that clears
TO-DAY of past Regrets and future Fears:
    To-morrow!—Why, To-morrow I may be
Myself with Yesterday's Sev'n thousand Years.

For some we loved, the loveliest and the best
That from his Vintage rolling Time hath prest,
    Have drunk their Cup a Round or two before,
And one by one crept silently to rest.

And we, that now make merry in the Room
They left, and Summer dresses in new bloom,
    Ourselves must we beneath the Couch of Earth
Descend—ourselves to make a Couch—for whom?

Ah, make the most of what we yet may spend,
Before we too into the Dust descend;
    Dust into Dust, and under Dust, to lie,
Sans Wine, sans Song, sans Singer, and—sans End!

Alike for those who for TO-DAY prepare,
And those that after some TO-MORROW stare,
    A Muezzín from the Tower of Darkness cries,
"Fools! your Reward is neither Here nor There."

Why, all the Saints and Sages who discussed
Of the Two Worlds so wisely—they are thrust
    Like foolish Prophets forth; their Words to Scorn
Are scatter'd, and their Mouths are stopt with Dust.

Myself when young did eagerly frequent
Doctor and Saint, and heard great argument
    About it and about: but evermore
Came out by the same door where in I went.

With them the seed of Wisdom did I sow,
And with mine own hand wrought to make it grow;
    And this was all the Harvest that I reap'd—
"I came like Water, and like Wind I go."

Into this Universe, and *Why* not knowing,
Nor *Whence*, like Water willy-nilly flowing;
    And out of it, as Wind along the Waste,
I know not *Whither*, willy-nilly blowing.

What, without asking, hither hurried *Whence?*
And, without asking, *Whither* hurried hence!
   Oh, many a Cup of this forbidden Wine
Must drown the memory of that insolence!

Up from Earth's Centre through the Seventh Gate
I rose, and on the Throne of Saturn sate;
   And many a Knot unravel'd by the Road;
But not the Master-knot of Human Fate.

There was the Door to which I found no Key;
There was the Veil through which I might not see:
   Some little talk awhile of ME AND THEE
There was—and then no more of THEE AND ME.

Earth could not answer; nor the Seas that mourn
In flowing Purple, of their Lord forlorn;
   Nor rolling Heaven, with all his Signs revealed
And hidden by the sleeve of Night and Morn.

Then of the THEE IN ME who works behind
The Veil, I lifted up my hands to find
   A Lamp amid the Darkness; and I heard,
As from Without— "THE ME WITHIN THEE BLIND!"

Then to the Lip of this poor earthen Urn
I lean'd, the Secret of my Life to learn:
   And Lip to Lip it murmur'd—"While you live,
Drink!—for, once dead, you never shall return."

I think the Vessel, that with fugitive
Articulation answer'd, once did live,
   And drink; and Ah! the passive Lip I kiss'd,
How many Kisses might it take—and give!

For I remember stopping by the way
To watch a Potter thumping his wet Clay:
   And with its all-obliterated Tongue
It murmured—"Gently, Brother, gently pray!"

And has not such a Story from of Old
Down Man's successive generations roll'd,
     Of such a clod of saturated Earth
Cast by the Maker into Human mould?

And not a drop that from our Cups we throw
For Earth to drink of, but may steal below
     To quench the fire of Anguish in some Eye
There hidden—far beneath, and long ago.

As then the Tulip for her morning sup
Of Heav'nly Vintage from the soil looks up,
     Do you devoutly do the like, till Heav'n
To Earth invert you—like an empty Cup.

Perplext no more with Human or Divine,
To-morrow's tangle to the winds resign,
     And lose your fingers in the tresses of
The Cypress-slender Minister of Wine.

And if the Wine you drink, the Lip you press,
End in what All begins and ends in—Yes;
     Think then you are TO-DAY what YESTERDAY
You were—TO-MORROW you shall not be less.

So when the Angel of the darker Drink
At last shall find you by the river-brink,
     And, offering his Cup, invite your Soul
Forth to your Lips to quaff—you shall not shrink.

Why, if the Soul can fling the Dust aside,
And naked on the Air of Heaven ride,
     Were't not a Shame—were't not a Shame for him
In this clay carcase crippled to abide?

'Tis but a Tent where takes his one-day's rest
A Sultán to the realm of Death addrest;
     The Sultán rises, and the dark Ferrásh
Strikes, and prepares it for another Guest.

And fear not lest Existence closing your
Account, and mine, should know the like no more;
  The Eternal Sákí from that Bowl has pour'd
Millions of Bubbles like us, and will pour.

When You and I behind the Veil are past,
Oh but the long, long while the World shall last,
  Which of our Coming and Departure heeds
As the SEA's SELF should heed a pebble-cast.

A Moment's Halt—a momentary taste
Of BEING from the Well amid the Waste—
  And Lo!—the phantom Caravan has reach'd
The NOTHING it set out from—Oh, make haste!

Would you that spangle of Existence spend
About THE SECRET—quick about it, Friend!
  A Hair perhaps divides the False and True—
And upon what, prithee, may Life depend?

A Hair perhaps divides the False and True;
Yes; and a single Alif were the clue—
  Could you but find it—to the Treasure-house,
And peradventure to THE MASTER too;

Whose secret Presence, through Creation's veins
Running Quicksilver-like eludes your pains;
  Taking all shapes from Máh to Máhi; and
They change and perish all—but He remains;

A moment guess'd—then back behind the Fold
Immerst of Darkness round the Drama roll'd
  Which, for the Pastime of Eternity,
He does Himself contrive, enact, behold.

But if in vain, down on the stubborn floor
Of Earth, and up to Heav'n's unopening door,
  You gaze TO-DAY, while You are You—how then
TO-MORROW, You when shall be You no more?

Waste not your Hour, nor in the vain pursuit
Of This and That endeavour and dispute;
   Better be jocund with the fruitful Grape
Then sadden after none, or bitter, Fruit.

You know, my Friends, with what a brave Carouse
I made a Second Marriage in my house;
   Divorced old barren Reason from my Bed,
And took the Daughter of the Vine to Spouse.

For "is" and "is-not" though with Rule and Line,
And "up-and-down" by Logic I define,
   Of all that one should care to fathom, I
Was never deep in anything but—Wine.

Ah, but my Computations, People say,
Reduced the Year to better reckoning?—Nay,
   'Twas only striking from the Calendar
Unborn To-morrow, and dead Yesterday.

And lately, by the Tavern Door agape,
Came shining through the Dusk an Angel Shape
   Bearing a Vessel on his Shoulder; and
He bid me taste of it; and 'twas—the Grape!

The Grape that can with Logic absolute
The Two-and-Seventy jarring Sects confute:
   The sovereign Alchemist that in a trice
Life's leaden metal into Gold transmute:

The mighty Mahmúd, Allah-breathing Lord,
That all the misbelieving and black Horde
   Of Fears and Sorrows that infest the Soul
Scatters before him with his whirlwind Sword.

Why, be this Juice the growth of God, who dare
Blaspheme the twisted tendril as a Snare?
   A Blessing, we should use it, should we not?
And if a Curse—why, then, Who set it there?

I must abjure the Balm of Life, I must,
Scared by some After-reckoning ta'en on trust,
    Or lured with Hope of some Diviner Drink,
To fill the Cup—when crumbled into Dust!

O threats of Hell and Hopes of Paradise!
One thing at least is certain,—*This* Life flies;
    One thing is certain and the rest is Lies;·
The Flower that once has blown for ever dies.

Strange, is it not? that of the myriads who
Before us passed the door of Darkness through
    Not one returns to tell us of the Road
Which to discover we must travel too.

The Revelations of Devout and Learn'd
Who rose before us, and as Prophets burn'd,
    Are all but Stories, which, awoke from Sleep
They told their fellows, and to Sleep return'd.

I sent my Soul through the Invisible,
Some letter of that After-life to spell:
    And by and by my Soul return'd to me,
And answered "I Myself am Heav'n and Hell":

Heav'n but the Vision of fulfill'd Desire,
And Hell the Shadow from a Soul on fire,
    Cast on the Darkness into which Ourselves,
So late emerged from, shall so soon expire.

We are no other than a moving row
Of Magic Shadow-shapes that come and go
    Round with this Sun-illumined Lantern held
In Midnight by the Master of the Show;

But helpless Pieces of the Game He plays
Upon this Chequer-board of Nights and Days;
    Hither and thither moves, and checks, and slays,
And one by one back in the Closet lays.

The Ball no question makes of Ayes and Noes,
But Here or There as strikes the Player goes;
   And He that tossed you down into the Field,
He knows about it all—HE knows—HE knows!

The Moving Finger writes; and, having writ,
Moves on: nor all your Piety nor Wit
   Shall lure it back to cancel half a Line,
Nor all your Tears wash out a Word of it.

And that inverted Bowl they call the Sky,
Whereunder crawling coop'd we live and die,
   Lift not your hands to *It* for help—for It
As impotently rolls as you or I.

With Earth's first Clay They did the Last Man knead,
And there of the Last Harvest sowed the Seed:
   And the first Morning of Creation wrote
What the Last Dawn of Reckoning shall read.

YESTERDAY *This* Day's Madness did prepare;
TO-MORROW's Silence, Triumph, or Despair:
   Drink! for you know not whence you came, nor why:
Drink! for you know not why you go, nor where.

I tell you this—When, started from the Goal,
Over the flaming shoulders of the Foal
   Of Heav'n Parwín and Mushtarí they flung,
In my predestined Plot of Dust and Soul

The Vine had struck a fibre: which about
If clings my Being—let the Dervish flout;
   Of my Base metal may be filed a Key,
That shall unlock the Door he howls without.

And this I know: whether the one True Light
Kindle to Love, or Wrath-consume me quite,
   One Flash of It within the Tavern caught
Better than in the Temple lost outright.

What! out of senseless Nothing to provoke
A conscious Something to resent the yoke
   Of unpermitted Pleasure, under pain
Of Everlasting Penalties, if broke!

What! from his helpless Creature be repaid
Pure Gold for what he lent him dross-allayed—
   Sue for a Debt we never did contract,
And cannot answer—Oh the sorry trade!

Oh Thou, who didst with pitfall and with gin
Beset the Road I was to wander in,
   Thou wilt not with Predestined Evil round
Enmesh, and then impute my Fall to Sin!

Oh Thou, who Man of baser Earth didst make
And ev'n with Paradise devise the Snake:
   For all the Sin wherewith the Face of Man
Is blacken'd—Man's Forgiveness give—and take!

.   .   .   .   .   .

As under cover of departing Day
Slunk hunger-stricken Ramazán away,
   Once more within the Potter's house alone
I stood, surrounded by the Shapes of Clay.

Shapes of all Sorts and Sizes, great and small,
That stood along the floor and by the wall;
   And some loquacious Vessels were; and some
Listen'd perhaps, but never talk'd at all.

Said one among them—"Surely not in vain
My substance of the common Earth was ta'en
   And to this Figure moulded, to be broke,
Or trampled back to shapeless Earth again."

Then said a Second—"Ne'er a peevish Boy
Would break the Bowl from which he drank in joy;

And He that with his hand the Vessel made
Will surely not in after Wrath destroy."

After a momentary silence spake
Some Vessel of a more ungainly Make;
   "They sneer at me for leaning all awry:
What! did the Hand then of the Potter shake?"

Whereat some one of the loquacious Lot—
I think a Súfi pipkin—waxing hot—
   "All this of Pot and Potter—Tell me, then,
Who is the Potter, pray, and who the Pot?"

"Why," said another, "Some there are who tell
Of one who threatens he will toss to Hell
   The luckless Pots he marr'd in making—Pish!
He's a Good Fellow, and 'twill all be well."

"Well," murmur'd one, "Let whoso make or buy,
My Clay with long Oblivion is gone dry:
   But fill me with the old familiar Juice,
Methinks I might recover by and by."

So while the Vessels one by one were speaking,
The little Moon look'd in that all were seeking:
   And then they jogg'd each other, "Brother! Brother!
Now for the Porter's shoulder-knot a-creaking!"

    ·   ·   ·   ·   ·

Ah, with the Grape my fading Life provide,
And wash the Body whence the Life has died,
   And lay me, shrouded in the living Leaf,
By some not unfrequented Garden-side.

That ev'n my buried Ashes such a snare
Of Vintage shall fling up into the Air
   As not a True-believer passing by
But shall be overtaken unaware.

Indeed the Idols I have loved so long
Have done my credit in this World much wrong:
    Have drown'd my Glory in a shallow Cup,
And sold my Reputation for a Song.

Indeed, indeed, Repentance oft before
I swore—but was I sober when I swore?
    And then and then came Spring, and Rose-in-hand
My thread-bare Penitence apieces tore.

And much as Wine has play'd the Infidel,
And robb'd me of my Robe of Honour—Well,
    I wonder often what the Vintners buy
One half so precious as the stuff they sell.

Yet Ah, that Spring should vanish with the Rose!
That Youth's sweet-scented manuscript should close!
    The Nightingale that in the branches sang,
Ah whence, and whither flown again, who knows!

Would but the Desert of the Fountain yield
One glimpse—if dimly, yet indeed, reveal'd,
    To which the fainting Traveller might spring,
As springs the trampled herbage of the field!

Would but some wingèd Angel ere too late
Arrest the yet unfolded Roll of Fate,
    And make the stern Recorder otherwise
Enregister, or quite obliterate!

Ah Love! could you and I with Him conspire
To grasp this sorry Scheme of Things entire,
    Would not we shatter it to bits—and then
Re-mould it nearer to the Heart's Desire!

.   .   .   .   .   .

Yon rising Moon that looks for us again—
How oft hereafter will she wax and wane;

How oft hereafter rising look for us
Through this same Garden—and for *one* in vain!

And when like her, oh Sákí, you shall pass
Among the Guests Star-scatter'd on the Grass,
    And in your joyous errand reach the spot
Where I made One—turn down an empty Glass!

TAMÁM

Edward Lear

(1812–1888)

By Way of Preface

"How pleasant to know Mr. Lear!"
  Who has written such volumes of stuff!
Some think him ill-tempered and queer,
  But a few think him pleasant enough.

His mind is concrete and fastidious,
  His nose is remarkably big;
His visage is more or less hideous,
  His beard it resembles a wig.

He has ears, and two eyes, and ten fingers,
  Leastways if you reckon two thumbs;
Long ago he was one of the singers,
  But now he is one of the dumbs.

He sits in a beautiful parlour,
  With hundreds of books on the wall;
He drinks a great deal of Marsala,
  But never gets tipsy at all.

He has many friends, laymen and clerical,
  Old Foss is the name of his cat:
His body is perfectly spherical,
  He weareth a runcible hat.

When he walks in a waterproof white,
  The children run after him so!

Calling out, "He's come out in his night-
   Gown, that crazy old Englishman, oh!"

He weeps by the side of the ocean,
   He weeps on the top of the hill;
He purchases pancakes and lotion,
   And chocolate shrimps from the mill.

He reads but he cannot speak Spanish,
   He cannot abide ginger-beer:
Ere the days of his pilgrimage vanish,
   How pleasant to know Mr. Lear!

The Dong with a Luminous Nose

When awful darkness and silence reign
Over the great Gromboolian plain,
   Through the long, long wintry nights;
When the angry breakers roar
As they beat on the rocky shore;
   When Storm-clouds brood on the towering heights
Of the Hills of the Chankly Bore,—

Then, through the vast and gloomy dark
There moves what seems a fiery spark,—
   A lonely spark with silvery rays
   Piercing the coal-black night,—
   A Meteor strange and bright:
Hither and thither the vision strays,
   A single lurid light.

Slowly it wanders, pauses, creeps,—
Anon it sparkles, flashes, and leaps;
And ever as onward it gleaming goes
A light on the Bong-tree stems it throws.

And those who watch at that midnight hour
From Hall or Terrace or lofty Tower,
Cry, as the wild light passes along,—
        "The Dong! the Dong!
    The wandering Dong through the forest goes!
        The Dong! the Dong!
    The Dong with a luminous Nose!"

        Long years ago
    The Dong was happy and gay,
Till he fell in love with a Jumbly Girl
    Who came to those shores one day.
For the Jumblies came in a sieve, they did,—
Landing at eve near the Zemmery Fidd
    Where the Oblong Oysters grow,
    And the rocks are smooth and gray.
And all the woods and the valleys rang
With the Chorus they daily and nightly sang,—
        "Far and few, far and few,
        Are the lands where the Jumblies live;
        Their heads are green, and their hands are
            blue,
        And they went to sea in a sieve."

Happily, happily passed those days!
        While the cheerful Jumblies staid;
    They danced in circlets all night long,
    To the plaintive pipe of the lively Dong,
        In moonlight, shine, or shade.
For day and night he was always there
By the side of the Jumbly Girl so fair,
With her sky-blue hands and her sea-green hair;
Till the morning came of that hateful day
When the Jumblies sailed in their sieve away,
And the Dong was left on the cruel shore
Gazing, gazing for evermore,—

Ever keeping his weary eyes on
That pea-green sail on the far horizon,—
Singing the Jumbly Chorus still
As he sate all day on the grassy hill,—
      "Far and few, far and few,
      Are the lands where the Jumblies live;
      Their heads are green, and their hands are
        blue,
      And they went to sea in a sieve."

But when the sun was low in the West,
    The Dong arose and said,—
"What little sense I once possessed
    Has quite gone out of my head!"
And since that day he wanders still
By lake and forest, marsh and hill,
Singing, "O somewhere, in valley or plain,
Might I find my Jumbly Girl again!
For ever I'll seek by lake and shore
Till I find my Jumbly Girl once more!"

    Playing a pipe with silvery squeaks,
    Since then his Jumbly Girl he seeks;
    And because by night he could not see,
    He gathered the bark of the Twangum Tree
      On the flowery plain that grows.
      And he wove him a wondrous Nose,—
    A Nose as strange as a Nose could be!
Of vast proportions and painted red,
And tied with cords to the back of his head.
    In a hollow rounded space it ended
    With a luminous Lamp within suspended,
      All fenced about
      With a bandage stout
      To prevent the wind from blowing it out;

And with holes all round to send the light
In gleaming rays on the dismal night.

And now each night, and all night long,
Over those plains still roams the Dong;
And above the wail of the Chimp and Snipe
You may hear the squeak of his plaintive pipe,
While ever he seeks, but seeks in vain,
To meet with his Jumbly Girl again;
Lonely and wild, all night he goes,—
The Dong with a luminous Nose!
And all who watch at the midnight hour,
From Hall or Terrace or lofty Tower,
Cry, as they trace the Meteor bright,
Moving along through the dreary night,—
    "This is the hour when forth he goes,
    The Dong with a luminous Nose!
    Yonder, over the plain he goes,—
        He goes!
        He goes,—
    The Dong with a luminous Nose!"

Henry Wadsworth Longfellow

(1807–1882)

Snow-Flakes

Out of the bosom of the Air,
　Out of the cloud-folds of her garments shaken,
Over the woodlands brown and bare,
　Over the harvest-fields forsaken,
　　Silent, and soft, and slow
　　Descends the snow.

Even as our cloudy fancies take
　Suddenly shape in some divine expression,
Even as the troubled heart doth make
　In the white countenance confession,
　　The troubled sky reveals
　　The grief it feels.

This is the poem of the air,
　Slowly in silent syllables recorded;
This is the secret of despair,
　Long in its cloudy bosom hoarded,
　　Now whispered and revealed
　　To wood and field.

FROM *Evangeline*

[*The Lakes of the Atchafalaya*]

Thus ere another noon they emerged from the shades;
and before them
Lay, in the golden sun, the lakes of the Atchafalaya.
Water-lilies in myriads rocked on the slight undulations
Made by the passing oars, and, resplendent in beauty,
the lotus
Lifted her golden crown above the heads of the boat-
men.
Faint was the air with the odorous breath of magnolia
blossoms,
And with the heat of noon; and numberless sylvan is-
lands,
Fragrant and thickly embowered with blossoming hedges
of roses,
Near to whose shores they glided along, invited to slum-
ber.
Soon by the fairest of these their weary oars were sus-
pended.
Under the boughs of Wachita willows, that grew by the
margin,
Safely their boat was moored; and scattered about on
the greensward,
Tired with their midnight toil, the weary travellers
slumbered.
Over them vast and high extended the cope of a cedar.
Swinging from its great arms, the trumpet-flower and
the grapevine
Hung their ladder of ropes aloft like the ladder of Jacob,

On whose pendulous stairs the angels ascending, de-
    scending,
Were the swift humming-birds, that flitted from blossom
    to blossom.
Such was the vision Evangeline saw as she slumbered
    beneath it.
Filled was her heart with love, and the dawn of an
    opening heaven
Lighted her soul in sleep with the glory of regions ce-
    lestial.

(Part II, section ii, lines 66–87)

My Lost Youth

Often I think of the beautiful town
    That is seated by the sea;
Often in thought go up and down
The pleasant streets of that dear old town,
    And my youth comes back to me.
        And a verse of a Lapland song
        Is haunting my memory still:
        "A boy's will is the wind's will,
And the thoughts of youth are long, long thoughts."

I can see the shadowy lines of its trees,
    And catch, in sudden gleams,
The sheen of the far-surrounding seas,
And islands that were the Hesperides
    Of all my boyish dreams.
        And the burden of that old song,
        It murmurs and whispers still:
        "A boy's will is the wind's will,
And the thoughts of youth are long, long thoughts."

I remember the black wharves and the slips,
   And the sea-tides tossing free;
And Spanish sailors with bearded lips,
And the beauty and mystery of the ships,
   And the magic of the sea.
      And the voice of that wayward song
      Is singing and saying still:
      "A boy's will is the wind's will,
And the thoughts of youth are long, long thoughts."

I remember the bulwarks by the shore,
   And the fort upon the hill;
The sunrise gun, with its hollow roar,
The drum-beat repeated o'er and o'er,
   And the bugle wild and shrill.
      And the music of that old song
      Throbs in my memory still:
      "A boy's will is the wind's will,
And the thoughts of youth are long, long thoughts."

I remember the sea-fight far away,
   How it thundered o'er the tide!
And the dead captains, as they lay
In their graves, o'erlooking the tranquil bay,
   Where they in battle died.
      And the sound of that mournful song
      Goes through me with a thrill:
      "A boy's will is the wind's will,
And the thoughts of youth are long, long thoughts."

I can see the breezy dome of groves,
   The shadows of Deering's Woods;
And the friendships old and the early loves
Come back with a Sabbath sound, as of doves
   In quiet neighborhoods.
      And the verse of that sweet old song,

It flutters and murmurs still:
"A boy's will is the wind's will,
And the thoughts of youth are long, long thoughts."

I remember the gleams and glooms that dart
  Across the school-boy's brain;
The song and the silence in the heart,
That in part are prophecies, and in part
  Are longings wild and vain.
    And the voice of that fitful song
    Sings on, and is never still:
    "A boy's will is the wind's will,
And the thoughts of youth are long, long thoughts."

There are things of which I may not speak;
  There are dreams that cannot die;
There are thoughts that make the strong heart weak,
And bring a pallor into the cheek,
  And a mist before the eye,
    And the words of that fatal song
    Come over me like a chill:
    "A boy's will is the wind's will,
And the thoughts of youth are long, long thoughts."

Strange to me now are the forms I meet
  When I visit the dear old town;
But the native air is pure and sweet,
And the trees that o'ershadow each well-known street,
  As they balance up and down,
    Are singing the beautiful song,
    Are sighing and whispering still:
    "A boy's will is the wind's will,
And the thoughts of youth are long, long thoughts."

And Deering's Woods are fresh and fair,
  And with joy that is almost pain
My heart goes back to wander there,

And among the dreams of the days that were,
I find my lost youth again.
And the strange and beautiful song,
The groves are repeating it still:
"A boy's will is the wind's will,
And the thoughts of youth are long, long thoughts."

FROM *Kéramos*

[*The Potter's Song*]

Turn, turn, my wheel! Turn round and round
Without a pause, without a sound:
So spins the flying world away!
This clay, well mixed with marl and sand,
Follows the motion of my hand;
For some must follow, and some command,
Though all are made of clay!

Turn, turn my wheel! All things must change
To something new, to something strange;
Nothing that is can pause or stay;
The moon will wax, the moon will wane,
The mist and cloud will turn to rain,
The rain to mist and cloud again,
To-morrow be to-day.

Turn, turn, my wheel! All life is brief;
What now is bud will soon be leaf,
What now is leaf will soon decay;
The wind blows east, the wind blows west;
The blue eggs in the robin's nest
Will soon have wings and beak and breast,
And flutter and fly away.

Turn, turn my wheel! This earthen jar
A touch can make, a touch can mar;
　　And shall it to the Potter say,
What makest thou? Thou hast no hand?
As men who think to understand
A world by their Creator planned,
　　Who wiser is than they.

Turn, turn, my wheel! 'Tis nature's plan
The child should grow into the man,
　　The man grow wrinkled, old, and gray.
In youth the heart exults and sings,
The pulses leap, the feet have wings;
In age the cricket chirps, and brings
　　The harvest-home of day.

Turn, turn, my wheel! The human race,
Of every tongue, of every place,
　　Caucasian, Coptic, or Malay,
All that inhabit this great earth,
Whatever be their rank or worth,
Are kindred and allied by birth,
　　And made of the same clay.

Turn, turn, my wheel! What is begun
At daybreak must at dark be done,
　　To-morrow will be another day;
To-morrow the hot furnace flame
Will search the heart and try the frame,
And stamp with honor or with shame
　　These vessels made of clay.

Stop, stop, my wheel! Too soon, too soon
The noon will be the afternoon,
　　Too soon to-day be yesterday;
Behind us in our path we cast

The broken potsherds of the past,
And all are ground to dust at last,
    And trodden into clay!

The Golden Mile-Stone

Leafless are the trees; their purple branches
Spread themselves abroad, like reefs of coral,
        Rising silent
In the Red Sea of the winter sunset.

From the hundred chimneys of the village,
Like the Afreet in the Arabian story,
        Smoky columns
Tower aloft into the air of amber.

At the window winks the flickering firelight;
Here and there the lamps of evening glimmer,
        Social watch-fires
Answering one another through the darkness.

On the hearth the lighted logs are glowing,
And like Ariel in the cloven pine-tree
        For its freedom
Groans and sighs the air imprisoned in them.

By the fireside there are old men seated,
Seeing ruined cities in the ashes,
        Asking sadly
Of the Past what it can ne'er restore them.

By the fireside there are youthful dreamers,
Building castles fair, with stately stairways,
        Asking blindly
Of the Future what it cannot give them.

By the fireside tragedies are acted
In whose scenes appear two actors only,
    Wife and husband,
And above them God the sole spectator.

By the fireside there are peace and comfort,
Wives and children, with fair, thoughtful faces,
    Waiting, watching
For a well-known footstep in the passage.

Each man's chimney is his Golden Mile-Stone;
Is the central point from which he measures
    Every distance
Through the gateways of the world around him.

In his farthest wanderings still he sees it;
Hears the talking flame, the answering night-wind
    As he heard them
When he sat with those who were, but are not.

Happy he whom neither wealth nor fashion,
Nor the march of the encroaching city,
    Drives an exile
From the hearth of his ancestral homestead.

We may build more splendid habitations,
Fill our rooms with paintings and with sculptures,
    But we cannot
Buy with gold the old associations!

To the Driving Cloud

Gloomy and dark art thou, O chief of the mighty
    Omahas;
Gloomy and dark as the driving cloud, whose name thou
    hast taken!

Wrapped in thy scarlet blanket, I see thee stalk through
the city's

Narrow and populous streets, as once by the margin
of rivers

Stalked those birds unknown, that have left us only
their footprints.

What, in a few short years, will remain of thy race but
the footprints?

How canst thou walk these streets, who has trod the
green turf of the prairies?

How canst thou breathe this air, who hast breathed the
sweet air of the mountains?

Ah! 'tis in vain that with lordly looks of disdain thou
dost challenge

Looks of disdain in return, and question these walls
and these pavements,

Claiming the soil for thy hunting-grounds, while down-
trodden millions

Starve in the garrets of Europe, and cry from its caverns
that they, too,

Have been created heirs of the earth, and claim its
division!

Back, then, back to thy woods in the regions west of
the Wabash!

There as a monarch thou reignest. In autumn the leaves
of the maple

Pave the floors of thy palace-halls with gold, and in
summer

Pine-trees waft through its chambers the odorous breath
of their branches.

There thou art strong and great, a hero, a tamer of
horses!

There thou chasest the stately stag on the banks of the
Elkhorn,

Or by the roar of the Running-Water, or where the
  Omaha
Calls thee, and leaps through the wild ravine like a
  brave of the Blackfeet!

Hark! what murmurs arise from the heart of those moun-
  tainous deserts?
Is it the cry of the Foxes and Crows, or the mighty
  Behemoth,
Who, unharmed, on his tusks once caught the bolts of
  the thunder,
And now lurks in his lair to destroy the race of the red
  man?
Far more fatal to thee and thy race than the Crows and
  the Foxes,
Far more fatal to thee and thy race than the tread of
  Behemoth,
Lo! the big thunder-canoe, that steadily breasts the
  Missouri's
Merciless current! and yonder, afar on the prairies, the
  camp-fires
Gleam through the night; and the cloud of dust in the
  gray of the daybreak
Marks not the buffalo's track, nor the Mandan's dexter-
  ous horse-race;
It is a caravan, whitening the desert where dwell the
  Camanches!
Ha! how the breath of these Saxons and Celts, like the
  blast of the east-wind,
Drifts evermore to the west the scanty smokes of thy
  wigwams!

In the Churchyard at Cambridge

In the village churchyard she lies,
Dust is in her beautiful eyes,
   No more she breathes, nor feels, nor stirs;
At her feet and at her head
Lies a slave to attend the dead,
   But their dust is white as hers.

Was she a lady of high degree,
So much in love with the vanity
   And foolish pomp of this world of ours?
Or was it Christian charity,
And lowliness and humility,
   The richest and rarest of all dowers?

Who shall tell us? No one speaks;
No color shoots into those cheeks,
   Either of anger or of pride,
At the rude question we have asked;
Nor will the mystery be unmasked
   By those who are sleeping at her side.

Hereafter?—And do you think to look
On the terrible pages of that Book
   To find her failings, faults, and errors?
Ah, you will then have other cares,
In your own shortcomings and despairs,
   In your own secret sins and terrors!

The Children's Hour

Between the dark and the daylight,
  When the night is beginning to lower,
Comes a pause in the day's occupations,
  That is known as the Children's Hour.

I hear in the chamber above me
  The patter of little feet,
The sound of a door that is opened,
  And voices soft and sweet.

From my study I see in the lamplight,
  Descending the broad hall stair,
Grave Alice, and laughing Allegra,
  And Edith with golden hair.

A whisper, and then a silence:
  Yet I know by their merry eyes
They are plotting and planning together
  To take me by surprise.

A sudden rush from the stairway,
  A sudden raid from the hall!
By three doors left unguarded
  They enter my castle wall!

They climb up into my turret
  O'er the arms and back of my chair;
If I try to escape, they surround me;
  They seem to be everywhere.

They almost devour me with kisses,
  Their arms about me entwine,

Till I think of the Bishop of Bingen
   In his Mouse-Tower on the Rhine!

Do you think, O blue-eyed banditti,
   Because you have scaled the wall,
Such an old mustache as I am
   Is not a match for you all!

I have you fast in my fortress,
   And will not let you depart,
But put you down into the dungeon
   In the round-tower of my heart.

And there will I keep you forever,
   Yes, forever and a day,
Till the walls shall crumble to ruin,
   And moulder in dust away!

Hawthorne

(May 23, 1864)

How beautiful it was, that one bright day
   In the long week of rain!
Though all its splendor could not chase away
   The omnipresent pain.

The lovely town was white with apple-blooms,
   And the great elms o'erhead
Dark shadows wove on their aerial looms
   Shot through with golden thread.

Across the meadows, by the gray old manse,
   The historic river flowed:
I was as one who wanders in a trance,
   Unconscious of his road.

The faces of familiar friends seemed strange;
  Their voices I could hear,
And yet the words they uttered seemed to change
  Their meaning to my ear.

For the one face I looked for was not there,
  The one low voice was mute;
Only an unseen presence filled the air,
  And baffled my pursuit.

Now I look back, and meadow, manse, and stream
  Dimly my thought defines;
I only see—a dream within a dream—
  The hill-top hearsed with pines.

I only hear above his place of rest
  Their tender undertone,
The infinite longings of a troubled breast,
  The voice so like his own.

There in seclusion and remote from men
  The wizard hand lies cold,
Which at its topmost speed let fall the pen,
  And left the tale half told.

Ah! who shall lift that wand of magic power,
  And the lost clew regain?
The unfinished window in Aladdin's tower
  Unfinished must remain!

Belisarius

I am poor and old and blind;
The sun burns me, and the wind
    Blows through the city gate,
And covers me with dust

From the wheels of the august
    Justinian the Great.

It was for him I chased
The Persians o'er wild and waste,
    As General of the East;
Night after night I lay
In their camps of yesterday;
    Their forage was my feast.

For him, with sails of red,
And torches at mast-head,
    Piloting the great fleet,
I swept the Afric coasts
And scattered the Vandal hosts,
    Like dust in a windy street.

For him I won again
The Ausonian realm and reign,
    Rome and Parthenope;
And all the land was mine
From the summits of Apennine
    To the shores of either sea.

For him, in my feeble age,
I dared the battle's rage,
    To save Byzantium's state,
When the tents of Zabergan
Like snow-drifts overran
    The road of the Golden Gate.

And for this, for this, behold!
Infirm and blind and old,
    With gray, uncovered head,
Beneath the very arch
Of my triumphal march,
    I stand and beg my bread!

Methinks I still can hear,
Sounding distinct and near,
    The Vandal monarch's cry,
As, captive and disgraced,
With majestic step he paced,—
    "All, all is Vanity!"

Ah! vainest of all things
Is the gratitude of kings;
    The plaudits of the crowd
Are but the clatter of feet
At midnight in the street,
    Hollow and restless and loud.

But the bitterest disgrace
Is to see forever the face
    Of the Monk of Ephesus!
The unconquerable will
This, too, can bear;—I still
    Am Belisarius!

Santa Teresa's Book-Mark

(*Letrilla que Llevaba por Registro en su Breviario*, by Santa
Teresa de Avila)

Let nothing disturb thee,
Nothing affright thee;
All things are passing;
God never changeth;
Patient endurance
Attaineth to all things;
Who God possesseth
In nothing is wanting;
Alone God sufficeth.

Oliver Wendell Holmes

(1809–1894)

The Poet's Lot

What is a poet's love?—
  To write a girl a sonnet,
To get a ring, or some such thing,
  And fustianize upon it.

What is a poet's fame?—
  Sad hints about his reason,
And sadder praise from garreteers,
  To be returned in season.

Where go the poet's lines?—
  Answer, ye evening tapers!
Ye auburn locks, ye golden curls,
  Speak from your folded papers!

Child of the ploughshare, smile;
  Boy of the counter, grieve not,
Though muses round thy trundle-bed
  Their broidered tissue weave not.

The poet's future holds
  No civic wreath above him;
Nor slated roof, nor varnished chaise,
  Nor wife nor child to love him.

Maid of the village inn,
  Who workest woe on satin,

(The grass in black, the graves in green,
   The epitaph in Latin,)

Trust not to them who say,
   In stanzas, they adore thee;
O rather sleep in churchyard clay,
   With urn and cherub o'er thee!

A Poem for the Meeting of the American Medical Association

AT NEW YORK, MAY 5, 1853

I hold a letter in my hand,—
   A flattering letter—more's the pity,—
By some contriving junto planned,
   And signed *per order of Committee;*
It touches every tenderest spot,—
   My patriotic predilections,
My well-known—something—don't ask what,
   My poor old songs, my kind affections.

They make a feast on Thursday next,
   And hope to make the feasters merry;
They own they're something more perplexed
   For poets than for port and sherry;—
They want the men of—(word torn out);
   Our friends will come with anxious faces
(To see our blankets off, no doubt,
   And trot us out and show our paces).

They hint that papers by the score
   Are rather musty kind of rations;

They don't exactly mean a bore,
    But only trying to the patience;
That such as—you know who I mean—
    Distinguished for their—what d' ye call 'em—
Should bring the dews of Hippocrene
    To sprinkle on the faces solemn.

—The same old story; that's the chaff
    To catch the birds that sing the ditties;
Upon my soul, it makes me laugh
    To read these letters from Committees!
They're all *so* loving and *so* fair,—
    All for *your* sake such kind compunction,—
'T would save your carriage half its wear
    To touch its wheels with such an unction!

Why, who am I, to lift me here
    And beg such learned folk to listen—
To ask a smile, or coax a tear
    Beneath these stoic lids to glisten?
As well might some arterial thread
    Ask the whole frame to feel it gushing,
While throbbing fierce from heel to head
    The vast aortic tide was rushing.

As well some hair-like nerve might strain
    To set its special streamlet going,
While through the myriad-channelled brain
    The burning flood of thought was flowing;
Or trembling fibre strive to keep
    The springing haunches gathered shorter,
While the scourged racer, leap on leap,
    Was stretching through the last hot quarter!

Ah me! you take the bud that came
    Self-sown in your poor garden's borders,
And hand it to the stately dame

That florists breed for, all she orders;
  She thanks you—it was kindly meant—
    (A pale affair, not worth the keeping,)—
Good morning;—and your bud is sent
  To join the tea-leaves used for sweeping.

Not always so, kind hearts and true,—
  For such I know are round me beating;
Is not the bud I offer you,—
  Fresh gathered for the hour of meeting,—
Pale though its outer leaves may be,
  Rose-red in all its inner petals,
Where the warm life we cannot see—
  The life of love that gave it—settles.

We meet from regions far away,
  Like rills from distant mountains streaming;
The sun is on Francisco's bay,
  O'er Chesapeake the lighthouse gleaming;
While summer girds the still bayou
  In chains of bloom, her bridal token,
Monadnock sees the sky grow blue,
  His crystal bracelet yet unbroken.

Yet Nature bears the selfsame heart
  Beneath her russet-mantled bosom,
As where with burning lips apart
  She breathes, and white magnolias blossom;
The selfsame founts her chalice fill
  With showery sunlight running over,
On fiery plain and frozen hill,
  On myrtle-beds and fields of clover.

I give you *Home!* its crossing lines
  United in one golden suture,
And showing every day that shines
  The present growing to the future,—

A flag that bears a hundred stars
   In one bright ring, with love for centre,
Fenced round with white and crimson bars,
   No prowling treason dares to enter!

O brothers, home may be a word
   To make affection's living treasure—
The wave an angel might have stirred—
   A stagnant pool of selfish pleasure;
HOME! It is where the day-star springs
   And where the evening sun reposes,
Where'er the eagle spreads his wings,
   From northern pines to southern roses!

Daily Trials

BY A SENSITIVE MAN

   O, there are times
When all this fret and tumult that we hear
Do seem more stale than to the sexton's ear
   His own dull chimes.

   Ding dong! ding dong!
The world is in a simmer like a sea
Over a pent volcano,—woe is me
   All the day long!

   From crib to shroud!
Nurse o'er our cradles screameth lullaby,
And friends in boots tramp round us as we die,
   Snuffling aloud.

   At morning's call
The small-voiced pug-dog welcomes in the sun,

And flea-bit mongrels, wakening one by one,
  Give answer all.

    When evening dim
Draws round us, then the lonely caterwaul,
Tart solo, sour duet, and general squall,—
    These are our hymn.

    Women, with tongues
Like polar needles, ever on the jar;
Men, plugless word-spouts, whose deep fountains are
    Within their lungs.

    Children, with drums
Strapped round them by the fond paternal ass;
Peripatetics with a blade of grass
    Between their thumbs.

    Vagrants, whose arts
Have caged some devil in their mad machine,
Which grinding, squeaks, with husky groans between,
    Come out by starts.

    Cockneys that kill
Thin horses of a Sunday,—men, with clams,
Hoarse as young bisons roaring for their dams
    From hill to hill.

    Soldiers, with guns,
Making a nuisance of the blessed air,
Child-crying bellmen, children in despair,
    Screeching for buns.

    Storms, thunders, waves!
Howl, crash, and bellow till ye get your fill;
Ye sometimes rest; men never can be still
    But in their graves.

The Chambered Nautilus

This is the ship of pearl, which, poets feign,
    Sails the unshadowed main,—
    The venturous bark that flings
On the sweet summer wind its purpled wings
In gulfs enchanted, where the Siren sings,
    And coral reefs lie bare,
Where the cold sea-maids rise to sun their streaming
    hair.

Its webs of living gauze no more unfurl;
    Wrecked is the ship of pearl!
    And every chambered cell,
Where its dim dreaming life was wont to dwell,
As the frail tenant shaped his growing shell,
    Before thee lies revealed,—
Its irised ceiling rent, its sunless crypt unsealed!

Year after year beheld the silent toil
    That spread his lustrous coil;
    Still, as the spiral grew,
He left the past year's dwelling for the new,
Stole with soft step its shining archway through,
    Built up its idle door,
Stretched in his last-found home, and knew the old no
    more.

Thanks for the heavenly message brought by thee,
    Child of the wandering sea,
    Cast from her lap, forlorn!
From thy dead lips a clearer note is born
Than ever Triton blew from wreathèd horn!

While on mine ear it rings,
Through the deep caves of thought I hear a voice that
     sings:—

Build thee more stately mansions, O my soul,
  As the swift seasons roll!
  Leave thy low-vaulted past!
Let each new temple, nobler than the last,
Shut thee from heaven with a dome more vast,
  Till thou at length art free,
Leaving thine outgrown shell by life's unresting sea!

James Russell Lowell

(1819–1891)

FROM *The Biglow Papers*

MR. HOSEA BIGLOW TO THE EDITOR
OF THE ATLANTIC MONTHLY

Beaver roars hoarse with meltin' snows,
  An' rattles di'mon's from his granite;
Time wuz, he snatched away my prose,
  An' into psalms or satires ran it;
But he, nor all the rest thet once
  Started my blood to country-dances,
Can't set me goin' more 'n a dunce
  Thet hain't no use for dreams an' fancies.

Rat-tat-tat-tattle thru the street
  I hear the drummers makin' riot,
An' I set thinkin' o' the feet
  Thet follered once an' now are quiet,—
White feet ez snowdrops innercent,
  Thet never knowed the paths o' Satan,
Whose comin' step ther' 's ears thet won't,
  No, not lifelong, leave off awaitin'.

Why, hain't I held 'em on my knee?
  Did n't I love to see 'em growin',
Three likely lads ez wal could be,
  Hahnsome an' brave an' not tu knowin'?
I set an' look into the blaze

Whose natur', jes' like theirn, keeps climbin',
  Ez long 'z it lives, in shinin' ways,
    An' half despise myself for rhymin'.

Wut's words to them whose faith an' truth
  On War's red techstone rang true metal,
Who ventured life an' love an' youth
  For the gret prize o' death in battle?
To him who, deadly hurt, agen
  Flashed on afore the charge's thunder,
Tippin' with fire the bolt of men
  Thet rived the Rebel line asunder?

'T ain't right to hev the young go fust,
  All throbbin' full o' gifts an' graces,
Leavin' life's paupers dry ez dust
  To try an' make b'lieve fill their places:
Nothin' but tell us wut we miss,
  Ther''s gaps our lives can't never fay in,
An' *thet* world seems so fur from this
  Lef' for us loafers to grow gray in!

My eyes cloud up for rain; my mouth
  Will take to twitchin' roun' the corners;
I pity mothers, tu, down South,
  For all they sot among the scorners:
I'd sooner take my chance to stan'
  At Jedgment where your meanest slave is,
Than at God's bar hol' up a han'
  Ez drippin' red ez yourn, Jeff Davis!

Come, Peace! not like a mourner bowed
  For honor lost an' dear ones wasted,
But proud, to meet a people proud,
  With eyes thet tell o' triumph tasted!
Come, with han' grippin' on the hilt,
  An' step thet proves ye Victory's daughter!

Longin' for you, our sperits wilt
    Like shipwrecked men's on rafs for water.

Come, while our country feels the lift
    Of a gret instinct shoutin' "Forwards!"
An' knows thet freedom ain't a gift
    Thet tarries long in han's o' cowards!
Come, sech ez mothers prayed for, when
    They kissed their cross with lips thet quivered,
An' bring fair wages for brave men,
    A nation saved, a race delivered!

(Second Series, x, lines 105–168)

The Origin of Didactic Poetry

When wise Minerva still was young
    And just the least romantic,
Soon after from Jove's head she flung
    That preternatural antic,
'T is said, to keep from idleness
    Or flirting, those twin curses,
She spent her leisure, more or less,
    In writing po——, no, verses.

How nice they were! to rhyme with *far*
    A kind *star* did not tarry;
The metre, too, was regular
    As schoolboy's dot and carry;
And full they were of pious plums,
    So extra-super-moral,—
For sucking Virtue's tender gums
    Most tooth-enticing coral.

A clean, fair copy she prepares,
    Makes sure of moods and tenses,
With her own hand,—for prudence spares
    A man-(or woman-)-uensis;
Complete, and tied with ribbons proud,
    She hinted soon how cosy a
Treat it would be to read them loud
    After next day's Ambrosia.

The Gods thought not it would amuse
    So much as Homer's Odyssees,
But could not very well refuse
    The properest of Goddesses;
So all sat round in attitudes
    Of various dejection,
As with a *hem!* the queen of prudes
    Began her grave prelection.

At the first pause Zeus said, "Well sung!—
    I mean—ask Phœbus,—*he* knows."
Says Phœbus, "Zounds! a wolf's among
    Admetus's merinos!
Fine! very fine! but I must go;
    They stand in need of me there;
Excuse me!" snatched his stick, and so
    Plunged down the gladdened ether.

With the next gap, Mars said, "For me
    Don't wait,—naught could be finer,
But I'm engaged at half past three,—
    A fight in Asia Minor!"
Then Venus lisped, "I'm sorely tried,
    These duty-calls are vip'rous;
But I *must* go; I have a bride
    To see about in Cyprus."

Then Bacchus,—"I must say good bye,
  Although my peace it jeopards;
I meet a man at four, to try
  A well-broke pair of leopards."
His words woke Hermes. "Ah!" he said,
  "I *so* love moral theses!"
Then winked at Hebe, who turned red,
  And smoothed her apron's creases.

Just then Zeus snored,—the Eagle drew
  His head the wing from under;
Zeus snored,—o'er startled Greece there flew
  The many-volumed thunder.
Some augurs counted nine, some, ten;
  Some said 't was war, some, famine,
And all, that other-minded men
  Would get a precious ——.

Proud Pallas sighed, "It will not do;
  Against the Muse I've sinned, oh!"
And her torn rhymes sent flying through
  Olympus's back window.
Then, packing up a peplus clean,
  She took the shortest path thence,
And opened, with a mind serene,
  A Sunday-school in Athens.

The verses? Some in ocean swilled,
  Killed every fish that bit to 'em;
Some Galen caught, and, when distilled,
  Found morphine the residuum;
But some that rotted on the earth
  Sprang up again in copies,
And gave two strong narcotics birth,
  Didactic verse and poppies.

Years after, when a poet asked
  The Goddess's opinion,
As one whose soul its wings had tasked
  In Art's clear-aired dominion,
"Discriminate," she said, "betimes;
  The Muse is unforgiving;
Put all your beauty in your rhymes,
  Your morals in your living."

An Oriental Apologue

Somewhere in India, upon a time,
(Read it not Injah, or you spoil the verse,)
  There dwelt two saints whose privilege sublime
It was to sit and watch the world grow worse,
  Their only care (in that delicious clime)
At proper intervals to pray and curse;
  Pracrit the dialect each prudent brother
  Used for himself, Damnonian for the other.

One half the time of each was spent in praying
For blessings on his own unworthy head,
  The other half in fearfully portraying
Where certain folks would go when they were dead;
  This system of exchanges—there's no saying
To what more solid barter 't would have led,
  But that a river, vext with boils and swellings
  At rainy times, kept peace between their dwellings.

So they two played at wordy battledore
And kept a curse forever in the air,
  Flying this way or that from shore to shore;
Nor other labor did this holy pair,
  Clothed and supported from the lavish store

Which crowds lanigerous brought with daily care;
   They toiled not, neither did they spin; their bias
   Was tow'rd the harder task of being pious.

Each from his hut rushed six score times a day,
Like a great canon of the Church full-rammed
   With cartridge theologic, (so to say,)
Touched himself off, and then, recoiling, slammed
   His hovel's door behind him in a way
That to his foe said plainly,—*you'll* be damned;
   And so like Potts and Wainwright, shrill and strong
   The two D——D'd each other all day long.

One was a dancing Dervise, a Mohammedan,
The other was a Hindoo, a gymnosophist;
   One kept his whatd'yecallit and his Ramadan,
Laughing to scorn the sacred rites and laws of his
   Transfluvial rival, who, in turn, called Ahmed an
Old top, and, as a clincher, shook across a fist
   With nails six inches long, yet lifted not
   His eyes from off his navel's mystic knot.

"Who whirls not round six thousand times an hour
Will go," screamed Ahmed, "to the evil place;
   May he eat dirt, and may the dog and Giaour
Defile the graves of him and all his race;
   Allah loves faithful souls and gives them power
To spin till they are purple in the face;
   Some folks get you know what, but he that pure is
   Earns Paradise and ninety thousand houries."

"Upon the silver mountain, South by East,
Sits Brahma fed upon the sacred bean;
   He loves those men whose nails are still increased,
Who all their lives keep ugly, foul, and lean;
   'T is of his grace that not a bird or beast
Adorned with claws like mine was ever seen;

The suns and stars are Brahma's thoughts divine
Even as these trees I seem to see are mine."

"Thou seem'st to see, indeed!" roared Ahmed back;
'Were I but once across this plaguy stream,
   With a stout sapling in my hand, one whack
On those lank ribs would rid thee of that dream!
   Thy Brahma-blasphemy is ipecac
To my soul's stomach; couldst thou grasp the scheme
   Of true redemption, thou wouldst know that Deity
   Whirls by a kind of blessed spontaneity.

"And this it is which keeps our earth here going
With all the stars."—"Oh, vile! but there's a place
   Prepared for such; to think of Brahma throwing
Worlds like a juggler's balls up into Space!
   Why, not so much as a smooth lotos blowing
Is e'er allowed that silence to efface
   Which broods round Brahma, and our earth, 't is
      known,
   Rests on a tortoise, moveless as this stone."

So they kept up their banning amœbæan,
When suddenly came floating down the stream
   A youth whose face like an incarnate pæan
Glowed, 't was so full of grandeur and of gleam;
   "If there be gods, then, doubtless, this must be one,"
Thought both at once, and then began to scream,
   "Surely, whate'er immortals know, thou knowest,
   Decide between us twain before thou goest!"

The youth was drifting in a slim canoe
Most like a huge white water-lily's petal,
   But neither of our theologians knew
Whereof 't was made; whether of heavenly metal
   Seldseen, or of a vast pearl split in two
And hollowed, was a point they could not settle;

'T was good debate-seed, though, and bore large frui*
In after years of many a tart dispute.

There were no wings upon the stranger's shoulders,
And yet he seemed so capable of rising
    That, had he soared like thistledown, beholders
Had thought the circumstance noways surprising;
    Enough that he remained, and, when the scolders
Hailed him as umpire in their vocal prize-ring,
    The painter of his boat he lightly threw
    Around a lotos-stem, and brought her to.

The strange youth had a look as if he might
Have trod far planets where the atmosphere
    (Of nobler temper) steeps the face with light,
Just as our skins are tanned and freckled here;
    His air was that of a cosmopolite
In the wide universe from sphere to sphere;
    Perhaps he was (his face had such grave beauty)
    An officer of Saturn's guards off duty.

Both saints began to unfold their tales at once,
Both wished their tales, like simial ones, prehensile,
    That they might seize his ear; *fool! knave!* and *dunce!*
Flew zigzag back and forth, like strokes of pencil
    In a child's fingers; voluble as duns,
They jabbered like the stones on that immense hill
    In the Arabian Nights; until the stranger
    Began to think his ear-drums in some danger.

In general those who nothing have to say
Contrive to spend the longest time in doing it;
    They turn and vary it in every way,
Hashing it, stewing it, mincing it, *ragouting* it;
    Sometimes they keep it purposely at bay,
Then let it slip to be again pursuing it;

They drone it, groan it, whisper it and shout it,
Refute it, flout it, swear to 't, prove it, doubt it.

Our saints had practised for some thirty years;
Their talk, beginning with a single stem,
  Spread like a banyan, sending down live piers,
Colonies of digression, and, in them,
  Germs of yet new dispersion; once by the ears,
They could convey damnation in a hem,
  And blow the pinch of premise-priming off
  Long syllogistic batteries, with a cough.

Each had a theory that the human ear
A providential tunnel was, which led
  To a huge vacuum (and surely here
They showed some knowledge of the general head),
  For cant to be decanted through, a mere
Auricular canal or mill-race fed
  All day and night, in sunshine and in shower,
  From their vast heads of milk-and-water-power.

The present being a peculiar case,
Each with unwonted zeal the other scouted,
  Put his spurred hobby through its every pace,
Pished, pshawed, poohed, horribled, bahed, jeered,
        sneered, flouted,
  Sniffed, nonsensed, infideled, fudged, with his face
Looked scorn too nicely shaded to be shouted,
  And, with each inch of person and of vesture,
  Contrived to hint some most disdainful gesture.

At length, when their breath's end was come about,
And both could now and then just gasp "impostor!"
  Holding their heads thrust menacingly out,
As staggering cocks keep up their fighting posture,
  The stranger smiled and said, "Beyond a doubt
'T is fortunate, my friends, that you have lost your

United parts of speech, or it had been
Impossible for me to get between.

"Produce! says Nature,—what have you produced?
A new strait-waistcoat for the human mind;
　Are you not limbed, nerved, jointed, arteried, juiced,
As other men? yet, faithless to your kind,
　Rather like noxious insects you are used
To puncture life's fair fruit, beneath the rind
　Laying your creed-eggs, whence in time there spring
　Consumers new to eat and buzz and sting.

"Work! you have no conception how 't will sweeten
Your views of Life and Nature, God and Man;
　Had you been forced to earn what you have eaten,
Your heaven had shown a less dyspeptic plan;
　At present your whole function is to eat ten
And talk ten times as rapidly as you can;
　Were your shape true to cosmogonic laws,
　You would be nothing but a pair of jaws.

"Of all the useless beings in creation
The earth could spare most easily you bakers
　Of little clay gods, formed in shape and fashion
Precisely in the image of their makers;
　Why, it would almost move a saint to passion,
To see these blind and deaf, the hourly breakers
　Of God's own image in their brother men,
　Set themselves up to tell the how, where, when,

"Of God's existence; one's digestion's worse—
So makes a god of vengeance and of blood;
　Another,—but no matter, they reverse
Creation's plan, out of their own vile mud
　Pat up a god, and burn, drown, hang, or curse
Whoever worships not; each keeps his stud

Of texts which wait with saddle on and bridle
To hunt down atheists to their ugly idol.

"This, I perceive, has been your occupation;
You should have been more usefully employed;
   All men are bound to earn their daily ration,
Where States make not that primal contract void
   By cramps and limits; simple devastation
Is the worm's task, and what he has destroyed
   His monument; creating is man's work
   And that, too, something more than mist and murk."

So having said, the youth was seen no more,
And straightway our sage Brahmin, the philosopher,
   Cried, "That was aimed at thee, thou endless bore,
Idle and useless as the growth of moss over
   A rotting tree-trunk!" "I would square that score
Full soon," replied the Dervise, "could I cross over
   And catch thee by the beard. Thy nails I'd trim
   And make thee work, as was advised by him."

"Work? Am I not at work from morn till night
Sounding the deeps of oracles umbilical
   Which for man's guidance never come to light,
With all their various aptitudes, until I call?"
   "And I, do I not twirl from left to right
For conscience' sake? Is that no work? Thou silly gull,
   He had thee in his eye; 'twas Gabriel
   Sent to reward my faith, I know him well."

" 'T was Vishnu, thou vile whirligig!" and so
The good old quarrel was begun anew;
   One would have sworn the sky was black as sloe,
Had but the other dared to call it blue;
   Nor were the followers who fed them slow
To treat each other with their curses, too,

Each hating t' other (moves it tears or laughter?)
Because he thought him sure of hell hereafter.

At last some genius built a bridge of boats
Over the stream, and Ahmed's zealots filed
    Across, upon a mission to (cut throats
And) spread religion pure and undefiled;
    They sowed the propagandist's wildest oats,
Cutting off all, down to the smallest child,
    And came back, giving thanks for such fat mercies,
    To find their harvest gone past prayers or curses.

All gone except their saint's religious hops,
Which he kept up with more than common flourish;
    But these, however satisfying crops
For the inner man, were not enough to nourish
    The body politic, which quickly drops
Reserve in such sad junctures, and turns currish;
    So Ahmed soon got cursed for all the famine
    Where'er the popular voice could edge a damn in.

At first he pledged a miracle quite boldly,
And, for a day or two, they growled and waited;
    But, finding that this kind of manna coldly
Sat on their stomachs, they erelong berated
    The saint for still persisting in that old lie,
Till soon the whole machine of saintship grated,
    Ran slow, creaked, stopped, and, wishing him in
        Tophet,
    They gathered strength enough to stone the prophet.

Some stronger ones contrived (by eating leather,
Their weaker friends, and one thing or another)
    The winter months of scarcity to weather;
Among these was the late saint's younger brother,
    Who, in the spring, collecting them together,
Persuaded them that Ahmed's holy pother

Had wrought in their behalf, and that the place
Of Saint should be continued to his race.

Accordingly 't was settled on the spot
That Allah favored that peculiar breed;
  Beside, as all were satisfied, 't would not
Be quite respectable to have the need
  Of public spiritual food forgot;
And so the tribe, with proper forms, decreed
  That he, and, failing him, his next of kin,
  Forever for the people's good should spin.

Sixty-eighth Birthday

As life runs on, the road grows strange
With faces new, and near the end
The milestones into headstones change,
'Neath every one a friend.

Auspex

My heart, I cannot still it,
Nest that had song-birds in it;
And when the last shall go,
The dreary days, to fill it,
Instead of lark or linnet,
Shall whirl dead leaves and snow.

Had they been swallows only,
Without the passion stronger
That skyward longs and sings,—

Woe's me, I shall be lonely
When I can feel no longer
The impatience of their wings!

A moment, sweet delusion,
Like birds the brown leaves hover;
But it will not be long
Before their wild confusion
Fall wavering down to cover
The poet and his song.

Robert Browning

(1812–1889)

Love Among the Ruins

Where the quiet-coloured end of evening smiles
    Miles and miles
On the solitary pastures where our sheep
    Half-asleep
Tinkle homeward thro' the twilight, stray or stop
    As they crop—
Was the site once of a city great and gay,
    (So they say)
Of our country's very capital, its prince
    Ages since
Held his court in, gathered councils, wielding far
    Peace or war.

Now,—the country does not even boast a tree,
    As you see,
To distinguish slopes of verdure, certain rills
    From the hills
Intersect and give a name to, (else they run
    Into one,)
Where the domed and daring palace shot its spires
    Up like fires
O'er the hundred-gated circuit of a wall
    Bounding all,
Made of marble, men might march on nor be pressed,
    Twelve abreast.

And such plenty and perfection, see, of grass
      Never was!
Such a carpet as, this summer-time, o'erspreads
      And embeds
Every vestige of the city, guessed alone,
      Stock or stone—
Where a multitude of men breathed joy and woe
      Long ago;
Lust of glory pricked their hearts up, dread of shame
      Struck them tame;
And that glory and that shame alike, the gold
      Bought and sold.

Now,—the single little turret that remains
      On the plains,
By the caper overrooted, by the gourd
      Overscored,
While the patching houseleek's head of blossom winks
      Through the chinks—
Marks the basement whence a tower in ancient time
      Sprang sublime,
And a burning ring, all round, the chariots traced
      As they raced,
And the monarch and his minions and his dames
      Viewed the games.

And I know, while thus the quiet-coloured eve
      Smiles to leave
To their folding, all our many-tinkling fleece
      In such peace,
And the slopes and rills in undistinguished grey
      Melt away—
That a girl with eager eyes and yellow hair
      Waits me there
In the turret whence the charioteers caught soul
      For the goal,

When the king looked, where she looks now, breathless,
        dumb
      Till I come.

But he looked upon the city, every side,
      Far and wide,
All the mountains topped with temples, all the glades'
      Colonnades,
All the causeys, bridges, aqueducts,—and then,
      All the men!
When I do come, she will speak not, she will stand,
      Either hand
On my shoulder, give her eyes the first embrace
      Of my face,
Ere we rush, ere we extinguish sight and speech
      Each on each.

In one year they sent a million fighters forth
      South and North,
And they built their gods a brazen pillar high
      As the sky,
Yet reserved a thousand chariots in full force—
      Gold, of course.
Oh, heart! oh, blood that freezes, blood that burns!
      Earth's returns
For whole centuries of folly, noise and sin!
      Shut them in,
With their triumphs and their glories and the rest!
      Love is best.

Two in the Campagna

      I wonder do you feel to-day
        As I have felt, since, hand in hand,
      We sat down on the grass, to stray

In spirit better through the land,
This morn of Rome and May?

For me, I touched a thought, I know,
    Has tantalised me many times,
(Like turns of thread the spiders throw
    Mocking across our path) for rhymes
To catch at and let go.

Help me to hold it! First it left
    The yellowing fennel, run to seed
There, branching from the brickwork's cleft,
    Some old tomb's ruin: yonder weed
Took up the floating weft,

Where one small orange cup amassed
    Five beetles,—blind and green they grope
Among the honey-meal; and last,
    Everywhere on the grassy slope
I traced it. Hold it fast!

The champaign with its endless fleece
    Of feathery grasses everywhere!
Silence and passion, joy and peace,
    An everlasting wash of air—
Rome's ghost since her decease.

Such life there, through such lengths of hours,
    Such miracles performed in play,
Such primal naked forms of flowers,
    Such letting nature have her way
While heaven looks from its towers.

How say you? Let us, O my dove,
    Let us be unashamed of soul,
As earth lies bare to heaven above!
    How is it under our control
To love or not to love?

I would that you were all to me,
　You that are just so much, no more—
Nor yours, nor mine, nor slave nor free!
　Where does the fault lie? what the core
Of the wound, since wound must be?

I would I could adopt your will,
　See with your eyes, and set my heart
Beating by yours, and drink my fill
　At your soul's springs,—your part my part
In life, for good and ill.

No. I yearn upward, touch you close,
　Then stand away. I kiss your cheek,
Catch your soul's warmth,—I pluck the rose
　And love it more than tongue can speak—
Then the good minute goes.

Already how am I so far
　Out of that minute? Must I go
Still like the thistle-ball, no bar,
　Onward, whenever light winds blow,
Fixed by no friendly star?

Just when I seemed about to learn!
　Where is the thread now? Off again!
The old trick! Only I discern—
　Infinite passion, and the pain
Of finite hearts that yearn.

My Last Duchess

FERRARA

That's my last Duchess painted on the wall,
Looking as if she were alive. I call
That piece a wonder, now: Frà Pandolf's hands
Worked busily a day, and there she stands.
Will't please you sit and look at her? I said
"Frà Pandolf" by design, for never read
Strangers like you that pictured countenance,
The depth and passion of its earnest glance,
But to myself they turned (since none puts by
The curtain I have drawn for you, but I)
And seemed as they would ask me, if they durst,
How such a glance came there; so, not the first
Are you to turn and ask thus. Sir, 'twas not
Her husband's presence only, called that spot
Of joy into the Duchess' cheek: perhaps
Frà Pandolf chanced to say "Her mantle laps
Over my Lady's wrist too much," or "Paint
Must never hope to reproduce the faint
Half-flush that dies along her throat": such stuff
Was courtesy, she thought, and cause enough
For calling up that spot of joy. She had
A heart—how shall I say?—too soon made glad,
Too easily impressed; she liked whate'er
She looked on, and her looks went everywhere.
Sir, 'twas all one! My favour at her breast,
The dropping of the daylight in the West,
The bough of cherries some officious fool
Broke in the orchard for her, the white mule

She rode with round the terrace—all and each
Would draw from her alike the approving speech,
Or blush, at least. She thanked men,—good! but
    thanked
Somehow—I know not how—as if she ranked
My gift of a nine-hundred-years-old name
With anybody's gift. Who'd stoop to blame
This sort of trifling? Even had you skill
In speech—(which I have not)—to make your will
Quite clear to such an one, and say "Just this
Or that in you disgusts me; here you miss,
Or there exceed the mark"—and if she let
Herself be lessoned so, nor plainly set
Her wits to yours, forsooth, and made excuse,
—E'en then would be some stooping, and I choose
Never to stoop. Oh, Sir, she smiled, no doubt
Whene'er I passed her; but who passed without
Much the same smile? This grew; I gave commands;
Then all smiles stopped together. There she stands
As if alive. Will't please you rise? We'll meet
The company below, then. I repeat,
The Count your master's known munificence
Is ample warrant that no just pretence
Of mine for dowry will be disallowed;
Though his fair daughter's self, as I avowed
At starting, is my object. Nay, we'll go
Together down, Sir! Notice Neptune, tho',
Taming a sea-horse, thought a rarity,
Which Claus of Innsbruck cast in bronze for me!

The Englishman in Italy

PIANO DI SORRENTO

Fortù, Fortù, my beloved one,
  Sit here by my side,
On my knees put up both little feet!
  I was sure, if I tried,
I could make you laugh spite of Scirocco:
  Now, open your eyes,
Let me keep you amused till he vanish
  In black from the skies,
With telling my memories over
  As you tell your beads;
All the Plain saw me gather, I garland
  —The flowers or the weeds.

Time for rain! for your long hot dry Autumn
  Had net-worked with brown
The white skin of each grape on the bunches,
  Marked like a quail's crown,
Those creatures you make such account of,
  Whose heads,—speckled white
Over brown like a great spider's back,
  As I told you last night,—
Your mother bites off for her supper.
  Red-ripe as could be,
Pomegranates were chapping and splitting
  In halves on the tree:
And betwixt the loose walls of great flintstone,
  Or in the thick dust
On the path, or straight out of the rockside,
  Wherever could thrust

Some burnt sprig of bold hardy rock-flower
   Its yellow face up,
For the prize were great butterflies fighting,
   Some five for one cup.
So I guessed, ere I got up this morning,
   What change was in store,
By the quick rustle-down of the quail-nets
   Which woke me before
I could open my shutter, made fast
   With a bough and a stone,
And look thro' the twisted dead vine-twigs,
   Sole lattice that's known.
Quick and sharp rang the rings down the net-poles,
   While, busy beneath,
Your priest and his brother tugged at them,
   The rain in their teeth.
And out upon all the flat house-roofs
   Where split figs lay drying,
The girls took the frails under cover:
   Nor use seemed in trying
To get out the boats and go fishing,
   For, under the cliff,
Fierce the black water frothed o'er the blind-rock.
   No seeing our skiff
Arrive about noon from Amalfi,
   —Our fisher arrive,
And pitch down his basket before us,
   All trembling alive
With pink and grey jellies, your sea-fruit;
   You touch the strange lumps,
And mouths gape there, eyes open, all manner
   Of horns and of humps,
Which only the fisher looks grave at,
   While round him like imps
Cling screaming the children as naked

And brown as his shrimps;
Himself too as bare to the middle
   —You see round his neck
The string and its brass coin suspended,
   That saves him from wreck.
But to-day not a boat reached Salerno,
   So back, to a man,
Came our friends, with whose help in the vineyards
   Grape-harvest began.
In the vat, half-way up in our house-side,
   Like blood the juice spins,
While your brother all bare-legged is dancing
   Till breathless he grins
Dead-beaten, in effort on effort
   To keep the grapes under,
Since still when he seems all but master,
   In pours the fresh plunder
From girls who keep coming and going
   With basket on shoulder,
And eyes shut against the rain's driving;
   Your girls that are older,—
For under the hedges of aloe,
   And where, on its bed
Of the orchard's black mould, the love-apple
   Lies pulpy and red,
All the young ones are kneeling and filling
   Their laps with the snails
Tempted out by this first rainy weather,—
   Your best of regales,
As to-night will be proved to my sorrow,
   When, supping in state,
We shall feast our grape-gleaners (two dozen,
   Three over one plate)
With lasagne so tempting to swallow
   In slippery ropes,

And gourds fried in great purple slices,
    That colour of popes.
Meantime, see the grape bunch they've brought you:
    The rain-water slips
O'er the heavy blue bloom on each globe
    Which the wasp to your lips
Still follows with fretful persistence:
    Nay, taste, while awake,
This half of a curd-white smooth cheese-ball,
    That peels, flake by flake,
Like an onion, each smoother and whiter;
    Next, sip this weak wine
From the thin green glass flask, with its stopper,
    A leaf of the vine;
And end with the prickly-pear's red flesh
    That leaves thro' its juice
The stony black seeds on your pearl-teeth.
    Scirocco is loose!
Hark, the quick, whistling pelt of the olives
    Which, thick in one's track,
Tempt the stranger to pick up and bite them,
    Tho' not yet half black!
How the old twisted olive trunks shudder,
    The medlars let fall
Their hard fruit, and the brittle great fig-trees
    Snap off, figs and all,
For here comes the whole of the tempest!
    No refuge, but creep
Back again to my side and my shoulder,
    And listen or sleep.

O how will your country show next week,
    When all the vine-boughs
Have been stripped of their foliage to pasture
    The mules and the cows?

Last eve, I rode over the mountains;
    Your brother, my guide,
Soon left me, to feast on the myrtles
    That offered, each side,
Their fruit-balls, black, glossy, and luscious,—
    Or strip from the sorbs
A treasure, or, rosy and wondrous,
    Those hairy gold orbs!
But my mule picked his sure sober path out,
    Just stopping to neigh
When he recognized down in the valley
    His mates on their way
With the faggots and barrels of water;
    And soon we emerged
From the plain, where the woods could scarce follow;
    And still as we urged
Our way, the woods wondered, and left us,
    As up still we trudged
Though the wild path grew wilder each instant,
    And place was e'en grudged
'Mid the rock-chasms, and piles of loose stones
    Like the loose broken teeth
Of some monster which climbed there to die
    From the ocean beneath—
Place was grudged to the silver-grey fume-weed
    That clung to the path,
And dark rosemary, ever a-dying,
    That, 'spite the wind's wrath,
So loves the salt rock's face to seaward,
    And lentisks as staunch
To the stone where they root and bear berries,
    And . . . what shows a branch
Coral-coloured, transparent, with circlets
    Of pale seagreen leaves;
Over all trod my mule with the caution

Of gleaners o'er sheaves,
Still, foot after foot like a lady,
 Till, round after round,
He climbed to the top of Calvano,
 And God's own profound
Was above me, and round the mountains,
 And under, the sea,
And within me my heart to bear witness
 What was and shall be.
Oh heaven, and the terrible crystal!
 No rampart excludes
Your eye from the life to be lived
 In the blue solitudes.
Oh, those mountains, their infinite movement!
 Still moving with you;
For, ever some new head and breast of them
 Thrusts into view
To observe the intruder; you see it
 If quickly you turn
And, before they escape you, surprise them.
 They grudge you should learn
How the soft plains they look on, lean over,
 And love (they pretend)
—Cower beneath them; the flat sea-pine crouches,
 The wild fruit-trees bend,
E'en the myrtle-leaves curl, shrink and shut:
 All is silent and grave:
'Tis a sensual and timorous beauty,
 How fair! but a slave.
So, I turned to the sea; and there slumbered
 As greenly as ever
Those isles of the siren, your Galli;
 No ages can sever
The Three, nor enable their sister
 To join them,—half way

On the voyage, she looked at Ulysses—
    No farther to-day;
Tho' the small one, just launched in the wave,
    Watches breast-high and steady
From under the rock, her bold sister
    Swum half-way already.
Fortù, shall we sail there together
    And see from the sides
Quite new rocks show their faces, new haunts
    Where the siren abides?
Shall we sail round and round them, close over
    The rocks, tho' unseen,
That ruffle the grey glassy water
    To glorious green?
Then scramble from splinter to splinter,
    Reach land and explore,
On the largest, the strange square black turret
    With never a door,
Just a loop to admit the quick lizards;
    Then, stand there and hear
The birds' quiet singing, that tells us
    What life is, so clear?
—The secret they sang to Ulysses,
    When, ages ago,
He heard and he knew this life's secret
    I hear and I know!

Ah, see! The sun breaks o'er Calvano;
    He strikes the great gloom
And flutters it o'er the mount's summit
    In airy gold fume.
All is over. Look out, see the gipsy,
    Our tinker and smith,
Has arrived, set up bellows and forge,
    And down-squatted forthwith

To his hammering, under the wall there;
   One eye keeps aloof
The urchins that itch to be putting
   His jews'-harps to proof,
While the other, thro' locks of curled wire,
   Is watching how sleek
Shines the hog, come to share in the windfall
   —Chew, abbot's own cheek!

All is over. Wake up and come out now,
   And down let us go,
And see the fine things got in order
   At church for the show
Of the Sacrament, set forth this evening.
   To-morrow's the Feast
Of the Rosary's Virgin, by no means
   Of Virgins the least,
As you'll hear in the off-hand discourse
   Which (all nature, no art)
The Dominican brother, these three weeks,
   Was getting by heart.

Not a post nor a pillar but is dizened
   With red and blue papers;
All the roof waves with ribbons, each altar
   A-blaze with long tapers;
But the great masterpiece is the scaffold
   Rigged glorious to hold
All the fiddlers and fifers and drummers,
   And trumpeters bold,
Not afraid of Bellini nor Auber,
   Who, when the priest's hoarse,
Will strike us up something that's brisk
   For the feast's second course.

And then will the flaxen-wigged Image
   Be carried in pomp
Thro' the plain, while in gallant procession

The priests mean to stomp.
And all round the glad church lie old bottles
    With gunpowder stopped,
Which will be, when the Image re-enters,
    Religiously popped;
And at night from the crest of Calvano
    Great bonfires will hang,
On the plain will the trumpets join chorus,
    And more poppers bang.
At all events, come—to the garden
    As far as the wall;
See me tap with a hoe on the plaster
    Till out there shall fall
A scorpion with wide angry nippers!

    —"Such trifles!" you say?
Fortù, in my England at home,
    Men meet gravely to-day
And debate, if abolishing Corn-laws
    Be righteous and wise
—If 'twere proper, Scirocco should vanish
    In black from the skies!

Waring

I

What's become of Waring
Since he gave us all the slip,
Chose land-travel or seafaring,
Boots and chest or staff and scrip,
Rather than pace up and down
Any longer London town?

Who'd have guessed it from his lip
Or his brow's accustomed bearing,
On the night he thus took ship
Or started landward?—little caring
For us, it seems, who supped together
(Friends of his too, I remember)
And walked home thro' the merry weather,
The snowiest in all December.
I left his arm that night myself
For what's-his-name's, the new prose-poet
Who wrote the book there, on the shelf—
How, forsooth, was I to know it
If Waring meant to glide away
Like a ghost at break of day?
Never looked he half so gay!

He was prouder than the devil:
How he must have cursed our revel!
Ay and many other meetings,
Indoor visits, outdoor greetings,
As up and down he paced this London,
With no work done, but great works undone,
Where scarce twenty knew his name.
Why not, then, have earlier spoken,
Written, bustled? Who's to blame
If your silence kept unbroken?
"True, but there were sundry jottings,
Stray-leaves, fragments, blurrs and blottings,
Certain first steps were achieved
Already which"—(is that your meaning?)
"Had well borne out whoe'er believed
In more to come!" But who goes gleaning
Hedgeside chance-blades, while full-sheaved
Stand cornfields by him? Pride, o'erweening
Pride alone, puts forth such claims
O'er the day's distinguished names.

Meantime, how much I loved him,
I find out now I've lost him.
I who cared not if I moved him,
Who could so carelessly accost him,
Henceforth never shall get free
Of his ghostly company,
His eyes that just a little wink
As deep as I go into the merit
Of this and that distinguished spirit—
His cheeks' raised colour, soon to sink,
As long as I dwell on some stupendous
And tremendous (Heaven defend us!)
Monstr'-inform'-ingens-horrend-ous
Demoniaco-seraphic
Penman's latest piece of graphic.
Nay, my very wrist grows warm
With his dragging weight of arm.
E'en so, swimmingly appears,
Through one's after-supper musings,
Some lost lady of old years
With her beauteous vain endeavour
And goodness unrepaid as ever;
The face, accustomed to refusings,
We, puppies that we were . . . Oh never
Surely, nice of conscience, scrupled
Being aught like false, forsooth, to?
Telling aught but honest truth to?
What a sin, had we centupled
Its possessor's grace and sweetness!
No! she heard in its completeness
Truth, for truth's a weighty matter,
And truth at issue, we can't flatter!
Well, 'tis done with; she's exempt
From damning us thro' such a sally;
And so she glides, as down a valley,

Taking up with her contempt,
Past our reach; and in, the flowers
Shut her unregarded hours.

Oh, could I have him back once more,
This Waring, but one half-day more!
Back, with the quiet face of yore,
So hungry for acknowledgment
Like mine! I'd fool him to his bent.
Feed, should not he, to heart's content?
I'd say, "To only have conceived,
Planned your great works, apart from progress,
Surpasses little works achieved!"
I'd lie so, I should be believed.
I'd make such havoc of the claims
Of the day's distinguished names
To feast him with, as feasts an ogress
Her feverish sharp-toothed gold-crowned child!
Or as one feasts a creature rarely
Captured here, unreconciled
To capture; and completely gives
Its pettish humours license, barely
Requiring that it lives.

Ichabod, Ichabod,
The glory is departed!
Travels Waring East away?
Who, of knowledge, by hearsay,
Reports a man upstarted
Somewhere as a god,
Hordes grown European-hearted,
Millions of the wild made tame
On a sudden at his fame?
In Vishnu-land what Avatar?
Or who in Moscow, toward the Czar,
With the demurest of footfalls

Over the Kremlin's pavement bright
With serpentine and syenite,
Steps, with five other Generals
That simultaneously take snuff.
For each to have pretext enough
And kerchiefwise unfold his sash
Which, softness' self, is yet the stuff
To hold fast where a steel chain snaps,
And leave the grand white neck no gash?
Waring in Moscow, to those rough
Cold northern natures born perhaps,
Like the lambwhite maiden dear
From the circle of mute kings
Unable to repress the tear,
Each as his sceptre down he flings,
To Dian's fane at Taurica,
Where now a captive priestess, she alway
Mingles her tender grave Hellenic speech
With theirs, tuned to the hailstone-beaten beach
As pours some pigeon, from the myrrhy lands
Rapt by the whirlblast to fierce Scythian strands
Where breed the swallows, her melodious cry
Amid their barbarous twitter!
In Russia? Never! Spain were fitter!
Ay, most likely 'tis in Spain
That we and Waring meet again
Now, while he turns down that cool narrow lane
Into the blackness, out of grave Madrid
All fire and shine, abrupt as when there's slid
Its stiff gold blazing pall
From some black coffin-lid.
Or, best of all,
I love to think
The leaving us was just a feint;
Back here to London did he slink,

And now works on without a wink
Of sleep, and we are on the brink
Of something great in fresco-paint:
Some garret's ceiling, walls and floor,
Up and down and o'er and o'er
He splashes, as none splashed before
Since great Caldara Polidore.
Or Music means this land of ours
Some favour yet, to pity won
By Purcell from his Rosy Bowers,—
"Give me my so-long promised son,
Let Waring end what I begun!"
Then down he creeps and out he steals
Only when the night conceals
His face; in Kent 'tis cherry-time,
Or hops are picking: or at prime
Of March he wanders as, too happy,
Years ago when he was young,
Some mild eve when woods grew sappy
And the early moths had sprung
To life from many a trembling sheath
Woven the warm boughs beneath;
While small birds said to themselves
What should soon be actual song,
And young gnats, by tens and twelves,
Made as if they were the throng
That crowd around and carry aloft
The sound they have nursed, so sweet and pure,
Out of a myriad noises soft,
Into a tone that can endure
Amid the noise of a July noon
When all God's creatures crave their boon,
All at once, and all in tune,
And get it, happy as Waring then,
Having first within his ken

What a man might do with men:
And far too glad, in the even-glow,
To mix with the world he meant to take
Into his hand, he told you, so—
And out of it his world to make,
To contract and to expand
As he shut or oped his hand.
Oh Waring, what's to really be?
A clear stage and a crowd to see!
Some Garrick, say, out shall not he
The heart of Hamlet's mystery pluck?
Or, where most unclean beasts are rife,
Some Junius—am I right?—shall tuck
His sleeve, and forth with flaying-knife!
Some Chatterton shall have the luck
Of calling Rowley into life!
Some one shall somehow run amuck
With this old world for want of strife
Sound asleep. Contrive, contrive
To rouse us, Waring! Who's alive?
Our men scarce seem in earnest now.
Distinguished names!—but 'tis, somehow,
As if they played at being names
Still more distinguished, like the games
Of children. Turn our sport to earnest
With a vision of the sternest!
Bring the real times back, confessed
Still better than our very best!

II

"When I last saw Waring . . ."
(How all turned to him who spoke!
You saw Waring? Truth or joke?
In land-travel or sea-faring?)

"We were sailing by Triest
Where a day or two we harboured:
A sunset was in the West,
When, looking over the vessel's side,
One of our company espied
A sudden speck to larboard.
And as a sea-duck flies and swims
At once, so came the light craft up,
With its sole lateen sail that trims
And turns (the water round its rims
Dancing, as round a sinking cup)
And by us like a fish it curled,
And drew itself up close beside,
Its great sail on the instant furled,
And o'er its thwarts a shrill voice cried,
(A neck as bronzed as a Lascar's)
'Buy wine of us, you English Brig?
Or fruit, tobacco and cigars?
A pilot for you to Triest?
Without one, look you ne'er so big,
They'll never let you up the bay!
We natives should know best.'
Our captain said, 'The 'long-shore thieves
Are laughing at us in their sleeves.'

"In truth, the boy leaned laughing back;
And one, half-hidden by his side
Under the furled sail, soon I spied,
With great grass hat and kerchief black,
Who looked up with his kingly throat,
Said somewhat, while the other shook
His hair back from his eyes to look
Their longest at us; then the boat,
I know not how, turned sharply round,
Laying her whole side on the sea

As a leaping fish does; from the lee
Into the weather, cut somehow
Her sparkling path beneath our bow
And so went off, as with a bound,
Into the rosy and golden half
O' the sky, to overtake the sun
And reach the shore, like the sea-calf
Its singing cave; yet I caught one
Glance ere away the boat quite passed,
And neither time nor toil could mar
Those features: so I saw the last
Of Waring!"—You? Oh, never star
Was lost here but it rose afar!
Look East, where whole new thousands are!
In Vishnu-land what Avatar?

The Last Ride Together

I said—Then, dearest, since 'tis so,
Since now at length my fate I know,
Since nothing all my love avails,
Since all, my life seemed meant for, fails,
    Since this was written and needs must be—
My whole heart rises up to bless
Your name in pride and thankfulness!
Take back the hope you gave,—I claim
Only a memory of the same,
—And this beside, if you will not blame,
    Your leave for one more last ride with me.

My mistress bent that brow of hers;
Those deep dark eyes where pride demurs
When pity would for softening through,

Fixed me a breathing-while or two
    With life or death in the balance: right!
The blood replenished me again;
My last thought was at least not vain:
I and my mistress, side by side
Shall be together, breathe and ride,
So, one day more am I deified.
    Who knows but the world may end tonight?

Hush! if you saw some western cloud
All billowy-bosomed, over-bowed
By many benedictions—sun's
And moon's and evening-star's at once—
    And so, you, looking and loving best,
Conscious grew, your passion drew
Cloud, sunset, moonrise, star-shine too,
Down on you, near and yet more near,
Till flesh must fade for heaven was here!—
    Thus lay she a moment on my breast.

Then we began to ride. My soul
Smoothed itself out, a long-cramped scroll
Freshening and fluttering in the wind.
Past hopes already lay behind.
    What need to strive with a life awry?
Had I said that, had I done this,
So might I gain, so might I miss.
Might she have loved me? just as well
She might have hated, who can tell!
Where had I been now if the worst befell?
    And here we are riding, she and I.

Fail I alone, in words and deeds?
Why, all men strive and who succeeds?
We rode; it seemed my spirit flew,
Saw other regions, cities new,

As the world rushed by on either side.
I thought,—All labour, yet no less
Bear up beneath their unsuccess.
Look at the end of the work, contrast
The petty done, the undone vast,
This present of theirs with the hopeful past!
   I hoped she would love me; here we ride.

What hand and brain went ever paired?
What heart alike conceived and dared?
What act proved all its thought had been?
What will but felt the fleshly screen?
   We ride and I see her bosom heave.
There's many a crown for those who can reach.
Ten lines, a statesman's life in each!
The flag stuck on a heap of bones,
A soldier's doing! what atones?
They scratch his name on the Abbey-stones.
   My riding is better, by their leave.

What does it all mean, poet? Well,
Your brains beat into rhythm, you tell
What we felt only; you expressed
You hold things beautiful the best,
   And pace them in rhyme so, side by side.
'Tis something, nay 'tis much: but then,
Have you yourself what's best for men?
Are you—poor, sick, old ere your time—
Nearer one whit your own sublime
Than we who never have turned a rhyme?
   Sing, riding's a joy? For me, I ride.

And you, great sculptor—so, you gave
A score of years to Art, her slave,
And that's your Venus, whence we turn
To yonder girl that fords the burn!

You acquiesce, and shall I repine?
What, man of music, you grown grey
With notes and nothing else to say,
Is this your sole praise from a friend,
"Greatly his opera's strains intend,
"Put in music we know how fashions end!"
 I gave my youth; but we ride, in fine.

Who knows what's fit for us? Had fate
Proposed bliss here should sublimate
My being—had I signed the bond—
Still one must lead some life beyond,
 Have a bliss to die with, dim-descried.
This foot once planted on the goal,
This glory-garland round my soul,
Could I descry such? Try and test!
I sink back shuddering from the quest.
Earth being so good, would heaven seem best?
 Now, heaven and she are beyond this ride.

And yet—she has not spoke so long!
What if heaven be that, fair and strong
At life's best, with our eyes upturned
Whither life's flower is first discerned,
 We, fixed so, ever should so abide?
What if we still ride on, we two
With life for ever old yet new,
Changed not in kind but in degree,
The instant made eternity,—
And heaven just prove that I and she
 Ride, ride together, for ever ride?

Andrea del Sarto

CALLED "THE FAULTLESS PAINTER"

But do not let us quarrel any more,
No, my Lucrezia; bear with me for once:
Sit down and all shall happen as you wish.
You turn your face, but does it bring your heart?
I'll work then for your friend's friend, never fear,
Treat his own subject after his own way,
Fix his own time, accept too his own price,
And shut the money into this small hand
When next it takes mine. Will it? tenderly?
Oh, I'll content him,—but to-morrow, Love!
I often am much wearier than you think,
This evening more than usual, and it seems
As if—forgive now—should you let me sit
Here by the window with your hand in mine
And look a half-hour forth on Fiesole,
Both of one mind, as married people use,
Quietly, quietly, the evening through,
I might get up to-morrow to my work
Cheerful and fresh as ever. Let us try.
To-morrow, how you shall be glad for this!
Your soft hand is a woman of itself,
And mine the man's bared breast she curls inside.
Don't count the time lost, either; you must serve
For each of the five pictures we require:
It saves a model. So! keep looking so—
My serpentining beauty, rounds on rounds!
—How could you ever prick those perfect ears,
Even to put the pearl there! oh, so sweet—

My face, my moon, my everybody's moon,
Which everybody looks on and calls his,
And, I suppose, is looked on by in turn,
While she looks—no one's: very dear, no less.
You smile? why, there's my picture ready made,
There's what we painters call our harmony!
A common greyness silvers everything,—
All in a twilight, you and I alike
—You, at the point of your first pride in me
(That's gone, you know),—but I, at every point;
My youth, my hope, my art, being all toned down
To yonder sober pleasant Fiesole.
There's the bell chinking from the chapel-top;
That length of convent-wall across the way
Holds the trees safer, huddled more inside;
The last monk leaves the garden; days decrease
And autumn grows, autumn in everything.
Eh? the whole seems to fall into a shape
As if I saw alike my work and self
And all that I was born to be and do,
A twilight-piece. Love, we are in God's hand.
How strange now, looks the life he makes us lead!
So free we seem, so fettered fast we are!
I feel He laid the fetter: let it lie!
This chamber for example—turn your head—
All that's behind us! you don't understand
Nor care to understand about my art,
But you can hear at least when people speak;
And that cartoon, the second from the door
—It is the thing, Love! so such things should be—
Behold Madonna, I am bold to say.
I can do with my pencil what I know,
What I see, what at bottom of my heart
I wish for, if I ever wish so deep—
Do easily, too—when I say, perfectly,

I do not boast, perhaps: yourself are judge
Who listened to the Legate's talk last week,
And just as much they used to say in France.
At any rate 'tis easy, all of it!
No sketches first, no studies, that's long past—
I do what many dream of all their lives
—Dream? strive to do, and agonize to do,
And fail in doing. I could count twenty such
On twice your fingers, and not leave this town,
Who strive—you don't know how the others strive
To paint a little thing like that you smeared
Carelessly passing with your robes afloat,—
Yet do much less, so much less, Someone says,
(I know his name, no matter) so much less!
Well, less is more, Lucrezia: I am judged.
There burns a truer light of God in them,
In their vexed, beating, stuffed and stopped-up brain,
Heart, or whate'er else, than goes on to prompt
This low-pulsed forthright craftsman's hand of mine.
Their works drop groundward, but themselves, I know,
Reach many a time a heaven that's shut to me,
Enter and take their place there sure enough,
Though they come back and cannot tell the world.
My works are nearer heaven, but I sit here.
The sudden blood of these men! at a word—
Praise them, it boils, or blame them, it boils too.
I, painting from myself and to myself,
Know what I do, am unmoved by men's blame
Or their praise either. Somebody remarks
Morello's outline there is wrongly traced,
His hue mistaken; what of that? or else,
Rightly traced and well ordered, what of that?
Speak as they please, what does the mountain care?
Ah, but a man's reach should exceed his grasp,
Or what's a heaven for? All is silver-grey

Placid and perfect with my art: the worse!
I know both what I want and what might gain,
And yet how profitless to know, to sigh
"Had I been two, another and myself.
Our head would have o'erlooked the world!" No doubt.
Yonder's a work, now, of that famous youth,
The Urbinate who died five years ago.
('Tis copied, George Vasari sent it me.)
Well, I can fancy how he did it all,
Pouring his soul, with kings and popes to see,
Reaching, that heaven might so replenish him,
Above and through his art—for it gives way;
That arm is wrongly put—and there again—
A fault to pardon in the drawing's lines,
Its body, so to speak: its soul is right,
He means right—that, a child may understand.
Still, what an arm! and I could alter it;
But all the play, the insight and the stretch—
Out of me, out of me! And wherefore out?
Had you enjoined them on me, given me soul,
We might have risen to Rafael, I and you!
Nay, Love, you did give all I asked, I think—
More than I merit, yes, by many times.
But had you—oh, with the same perfect brow,
And perfect eyes, and more than perfect mouth,
And the low voice my soul hears, as a bird
The fowler's pipe, and follows to the snare—
Had you, with these the same, but brought a mind!
Some women do so. Had the mouth there urged
"God and the glory! never care for gain.
The present by the future, what is that?
Live for fame, side by side with Agnolo!
Rafael is waiting: up to God all three!"
I might have done it for you. So it seems:
Perhaps not. All is as God overrules.
Beside, incentives come from the soul's self;

The rest avail not. Why do I need you?
What wife had Rafael, or has Agnolo?
In this world, who can do a thing, will not;
And who would do it, cannot, I perceive:
Yet the will's somewhat—somewhat, too, the power—
And thus we half-men struggle. At the end,
God, I conclude, compensates, punishes.
'Tis safer for me, if the award be strict,
That I am something underrated here,
Poor this long while, despised, to speak the truth.
I dared not, do you know, leave home all day,
For fear of chancing on the Paris lords.
The best is when they pass and look aside;
But they speak sometimes; I must bear it all.
Well may they speak! That Francis, that first time,
And that long festal year at Fontainebleau!
I surely then could sometimes leave the ground,
Put on the glory, Rafael's daily wear,
In that humane great monarch's golden look,—
One finger in his beard or twisted curl
Over his mouth's good mark that made the smile,
One arm about my shoulder, round my neck,
The jingle of his gold chain in my ear,
I painting proudly with his breath on me,
All his court round him, seeing with his eyes,
Such frank French eyes, and such a fire of souls
Profuse, my hand kept plying by those hearts,—
And, best of all, this, this, this face beyond,
This in the background, waiting on my work,
To crown the issue with a last reward!
A good time, was it not, my kingly days?
And had you not grown restless . . . but I know—
'Tis done and past; 'twas right, my instinct said;
Too live the life grew, golden and not grey,
And I'm the weak-eyed bat no sun should tempt

Out of the grange whose four walls make his world.
How could it end in any other way?
You called me, and I came home to your heart.
The triumph was—to reach and stay there; since
I reached it ere the triumph, what is lost?
Let my hands frame your face in your hair's gold,
You beautiful Lucrezia that are mine!
"Rafael did this, Andrea painted that;
The Roman's is the better when you pray,
But still the other's Virgin was his wife—"
Men will excuse me. I am glad to judge
Both pictures in your presence; clearer grows
My better fortune, I resolve to think.
For, do you know, Lucrezia, as God lives,
Said one day Agnolo, his very self,
To Rafael . . . I have known it all these years . . .
(When the young man was flaming out his thoughts
Upon a palace-wall for Rome to see,
Too lifted up in heart because of it)
"Friend, there's a certain sorry little scrub
Goes up and down our Florence, none cares how,
Who, were he set to plan and execute
As you are, pricked on by your popes and kings,
Would bring the sweat into that brow of yours!"
To Rafael's!—And indeed the arm is wrong.
I hardly dare . . . yet, only you to see,
Give the chalk here—quick, thus the line should go!
Ay, but the soul! he's Rafael! rub it out!
Still, all I care for, if he spoke the truth,
(What he? why, who but Michel Agnolo?
Do you forget already words like those?)
If really there was such a chance, so lost,—
Is, whether you're—not grateful—but more pleased.
Well, let me think so. And you smile indeed!
This hour has been an hour! Another smile?

If you would sit thus by me every night
I should work better, do you comprehend?
I mean that I should earn more, give you more.
See, it is settled dusk now; there's a star;
Morello's gone, the watch-lights show the wall,
The cue-owls speak the name we call them by.
Come from the window, love,—come in, at last,
Inside the melancholy little house
We built to be so gay with. God is just.
King Francis may forgive me: oft at nights
When I look up from painting, eyes tired out,
The walls become illumined, brick from brick
Distinct, instead of mortar, fierce bright gold,
That gold of his I did cement them with!
Let us but love each other. Must you go?
That Cousin here again? he waits outside?
Must see you—you, and not with me? Those loans?
More gaming debts to pay? you smiled for that?
Well, let smiles buy me! have you more to spend?
While hand and eye and something of a heart
Are left me, work's my ware, and what's it worth?
I'll pay my fancy. Only let me sit
The grey remainder of the evening out,
Idle, you call it, and muse perfectly
How I could paint, were I but back in France,
One picture, just one more—the Virgin face,
Not yours this time! I want you at my side
To hear them—that is, Michel Agnolo—
Judge all I do and tell you of its worth
Will you? To-morrow, satisfy your friend.
I take the subjects for his corridor,
Finish the portrait out of hand—there, there,
And throw him in another thing or two
If he demurs; the whole should prove enough
To pay for this same Cousin's freak. Beside,

What's better and what's all I care about,
Get you the thirteen scudi for the ruff!
Love, does that please you? Ah, but what does he,
The Cousin! what does he to please you more?

    I am grown peaceful as old age to-night.
I regret little, I would change still less.
Since there my past life lies, why alter it?
The very wrong to Francis!—it is true
I took his coin, was tempted and complied,
And built this house and sinned, and all is said.
My father and my mother died of want.
Well, had I riches of my own? you see
How one gets rich! Let each one bear his lot.
They were born poor, lived poor, and poor they died:
And I have laboured somewhat in my time
And not been paid profusely. Some good son
Paint my two hundred pictures—let him try!
No doubt, there's something strikes a balance. Yes,
You loved me quite enough, it seems to-night.
This must suffice me here. What would one have?
In heaven, perhaps, new chances, one more chance—
Four great walls in the New Jerusalem
Meted on each side by the angel's reed,
For Leonard, Rafael, Agnolo and me
To cover—the three first without a wife,
While I have mine! So—still they overcome
Because there's still Lucrezia,—as I choose.

Again the Cousin's whistle! Go, my Love.

Bishop Blougram's Apology

No more wine? Then we'll push back chairs and talk.
A final glass for me, though; cool, i'faith!
We ought to have our Abbey back, you see.
It's different, preaching in basilicas,
And doing duty in some masterpiece
Like this of brother Pugin's, bless his heart!
I doubt if they're half baked, those chalk rosettes,
Ciphers and stucco-twiddlings everywhere;
It's just like breathing in a lime-kiln: eh?
These hot long ceremonies of our church
Cost us a little—oh, they pay the price,
You take me—amply pay it! Now, we'll talk.

So, you despise me, Mr. Gigadibs.
No deprecation,—nay, I beg you, sir!
Beside 'tis our engagement; don't you know,
I promised, if you'd watch a dinner out,
We'd see truth dawn together?—truth that peeps
Over the glasses' edge when dinner's done,
And body gets its sop and holds its noise
And leaves soul free a little. Now's the time:
Truth's break of day! You do despise me then.
And if I say, "despise me,"—never fear!
I know you do not in a certain sense—
Not in my arm-chair, for example: here,
I well imagine you respect my place
(*Status, entourage,* worldly circumstance)
Quite to its value—very much indeed:
—Are up to the protesting eyes of you
In pride at being seated here for once—

You'll turn it to such capital account!
When somebody, through years and years to come,
Hints of the bishop,—names me—that's enough:
"Blougram? I knew him"—(into it you slide)
"Dined with him once, a Corpus Christi Day,
All alone, we two; he's a clever man:
And after dinner,—why, the wine you know,—
Oh, there was wine, and good!—what with the
        wine . . .
'Faith, we began upon all sorts of talk!
He's no bad fellow, Blougram; he had seen
Something of mine he relished, some review:
He's quite above their humbug in his heart,
Half-said as much, indeed—the thing's his trade.
I warrant, Blougram's sceptical at times:
How otherwise? I liked him, I confess!"
Che che, my dear sir, as we say at Rome,
Don't you protest now! It's fair give and take;
You have had your turn and spoken your home-truths:
The hand's mine now, and here you follow suit.

    Thus much conceded, still the first fact stays—
You do despise me; your ideal of life
Is not the bishop's: you would not be I.
You would like better to be Goethe, now,
Or Buonaparte—or, bless me, lower still,
Count D'Orsay,—so you did what you preferred,
Spoke as you thought, and, as you cannot help,
Believed or disbelieved, no matter what,
So long as on that point, whate'er it was,
You loosed your mind, were whole and sole yourself.
—That, my ideal never can include,
Upon that element of truth and worth
Never be based! for say they make me Pope—
(They can't—suppose it for our argument!)

BISHOP BLOUGRAM'S APOLOGY 163

Why, there I'm at my tether's end, I've reached
My height, and not a height which pleases you:
An unbelieving Pope won't do, you say.
It's like those eerie stories nurses tell,
Of how some actor on a stage played Death,
With pasteboard crown, sham orb, and tinselled dart,
And called himself the monarch of the world;
Then, going in the tire-room afterward,
Because the play was done, to shift himself,
Got touched upon the sleeve familiarly,
The moment he had shut the closet door,
By Death himself. Thus God might touch a Pope
At unawares, ask what his baubles mean,
And whose part he presumed to play just now.
Best be yourself, imperial, plain and true!

So, drawing comfortable breath again,
You weigh and find, whatever more or less
I boast of my ideal realized
Is nothing in the balance when opposed
To your ideal, your grand simple life,
Of which you will not realize one jot.
I am much, you are nothing; you would be all,
I would be merely much: you beat me there.

No, friend, you do not beat me: hearken why!
The common problem, yours, mine, every one's,
Is—not to fancy what were fair in life
Provided it could be,—but, finding first
What may be, then find how to make it fair
Up to our means: a very different thing!
No abstract intellectual plan of life
Quite irrespective of life's plainest laws,
But one, a man, who is man and nothing more,
May lead within a world which (by your leave)
Is Rome or London, not Fool's-paradise.

Embellish Rome, idealize away,
Make Paradise of London if you can,
You're welcome, nay, you're wise.

                                    A simile!
We mortals cross the ocean of this world
Each in his average cabin of a life;
The best's not big, the worst yields elbow-room.
Now for our six months' voyage—how prepare?
You come on shipboard with a landsman's list
Of things he calls convenient: so they are!
An India screen is pretty furniture,
A piano-forte is a fine resource,
All Balzac's novels occupy one shelf,
The new edition fifty volumes long;
And little Greek books with the funny type
They get up well at Leipsic, fill the next:
Go on! slabbed marble, what a bath it makes!
And Parma's pride, the Jerome, let us add!
'Twere pleasant could Correggio's fleeting glow
Hang full in face of one where'er one roams,
Since he more than the others brings with him
Italy's self,—the marvellous Modenese!—
Yet was not on your list before, perhaps.
—Alas, friend, here's the agent . . . is't the name?
The captain, or whoever's master here—
You see him screw his face up; what's his cry
Ere you set foot on shipboard? "Six feet square!"
If you won't understand what six feet mean,
Compute and purchase stores accordingly—
And if in pique because he overhauls
Your Jerome, piano, bath, you come on board
Bare—why, you cut a figure at the first
While sympathetic landsmen see you off;
Not afterward, when long ere half seas over,

You peep up from your utterly naked boards
Into some snug and well-appointed berth,
Like mine, for instance (try the cooler jug—
Put back the other, but don't jog the ice!)
And mortified you mutter, "Well and good;
He sits enjoying his sea-furniture;
'Tis stout and proper, and there's store of it:
Though I've the better notion, all agree,
Of fitting rooms up. Hang the carpenter,
Neat ship-shape fixings and contrivances—
I would have brought my Jerome, frame and all!"
And meantime you bring nothing: never mind—
You've proved your artist-nature: what you don't,
You might bring, so despise me, as I say.

Now come, let's backward to the starting-place.
See my way: we're two college friends, suppose.
Prepare together for our voyage, then;
Each note and check the other in his work,—
Here's mine, a bishop's outfit; criticise!
What's wrong? why won't you be a bishop too?

Why, first, you don't believe, you don't and can't,
(Not statedly, that is, and fixedly
And absolutely and exclusively)
In any revelation called divine.
No dogmas nail your faith; and what remains
But say so, like the honest man you are?
First, therefore, overhaul theology!
Nay, I too, not a fool, you please to think,
Must find believing every whit as hard:
And if I do not frankly say as much,
The ugly consequence is clear enough.

Now, wait, my friend: well, I do not believe—
If you'll accept no faith that is not fixed,

Absolute and exclusive, as you say.
You're wrong—I mean to prove it in due time.
Meanwhile, I know where difficulties lie
I could not, cannot solve, nor ever shall,
So give up hope accordingly to solve—
(To you, and over the wine). Our dogmas then
With both of us, though in unlike degree,
Missing full credence—overboard with them!
I mean to meet you on your own premise:
Good, there go mine in company with yours!

And now what are we? unbelievers both,
Calm and complete, determinately fixed
To-day, to-morrow, and for ever, pray?
You'll guarantee me that? Not so, I think!
In no wise! all we've gained is, that belief,
As unbelief before, shakes us by fits,
Confounds us like its predecessor. Where's
The gain? how can we guard our unbelief,
Make it bear fruit to us?—the problem here.
Just when we are safest, there's a sunset-touch,
A fancy from a flower-bell, some one's death,
A chorus-ending from Euripides,—
And that's enough for fifty hopes and fears
As old and new at once as nature's self,
To rap and knock and enter in our soul,
Take hands and dance there, a fantastic ring,
Round the ancient idol, on his base again,—
The grand Perhaps! we look on helplessly.
There the old misgivings, crooked questions are—
This good God,—what he could do, if he would,
Would, if he could—then must have done long since
If so, when, where, and how? some way must be,—
Once feel about, and soon or late you hit

Some sense, in which it might be, after all.
Why not, "The Way, the Truth, the Life?"

                       —That way
Over the mountain, which who stands upon
Is apt to doubt if it be meant for a road;
While, if he views it from the waste itself,
Up goes the line there, plain from base to brow,
Not vague, mistakable! what's a break or two
Seen from the unbroken desert either side?
And then (to bring in fresh philosophy)
What if the breaks themselves should prove at last
The most consummate of contrivances
To train a man's eye, teach him what is faith?
And so we stumble at truth's very test!
All we have gained then by our unbelief
Is a life of doubt diversified by faith,
For one of faith diversified by doubt:
We called the chess-board white,—we call it black.

"Well," you rejoin, "the end's no worse, at least;
We've reason for both colours on the board:
Why not confess, then, where I drop the faith
And you the doubt, that I'm as right as you?"

Because, friend, in the next place, this being so,
And both things even,—faith and unbelief
Left to a man's choice,—we'll proceed a step,
Returning to our image, which I like.

A man's choice, yes—but a cabin-passenger's—
The man made for the special life o' the world —
Do you forget him? I remember though!
Consult our ship's conditions and you find
One and but one choice suitable to all;

The choice, that you unluckily prefer
Turning things topsy-turvy—they or it
Going to the ground. Belief or unbelief
Bears upon life, determines its whole course,
Begins at its beginning. See the world
Such as it is,—you made it not, nor I;
I mean to take it as it is,—and you
Not so you'll take it,—though you get nought else.
I know the special kind of life I like,
What suits the most my idiosyncrasy,
Brings out the best of me and bears me fruit
In power, peace, pleasantness, and length of days.
I find that positive belief does this
For me, and unbelief, no whit of this.
—For you, it does, however?—that, we'll try.
'Tis clear, I cannot lead my life, at least,
Induce the world to let me peaceably,
Without declaring at the outset, "Friends,
I absolutely and peremptorily
Believe!"—I say, faith is my waking life:
One sleeps, indeed, and dreams at intervals,
We know, but waking's the main point with us,
And my provision's for life's waking part.
Accordingly, I use heart, head and hand
All day, I build, scheme, study, and make friends;
And when night overtakes me, down I lie,
Sleep, dream a little, and get done with it,
The sooner the better, to begin afresh.
What's midnight doubt before the dayspring's faith?
You, the philosopher, that disbelieve,
That recognize the night, give dreams their weight—
To be consistent you should keep your bed,
Abstain from healthy acts that prove you man,
For fear you drowse perhaps at unawares!
And certainly at night you'll sleep and dream,

Live through the day and bustle as you please.
And so you live to sleep as I to wake,
To unbelieve as I to still believe?
Well, and the common sense o' the world calls you
Bed-ridden,—and its good things come to me.
Its estimation, which is half the fight,
That's the first cabin-comfort I secure—
The next . . . but you perceive with half an eye!
Come, come, it's best believing, if we may;
You can't but own that!

                    Next, concede again,
If once we choose belief, on all accounts
We can't be too decisive in our faith,
Conclusive and exclusive in its terms,
To suit the world which gives us the good things.
In every man's career are certain points
Whereon he dares not be indifferent;
The world detects him clearly, if he dare,
As baffled at the game, and losing life.
He may care little or he may care much
For riches, honour, pleasure, work, repose,
Since various theories of life and life's
Success are extant which might easily
Comport with either estimate of these;
And whoso chooses wealth or poverty,
Labour or quiet, is not judged a fool
Because his fellows would choose otherwise:
We let him choose upon his own account
So long as he's consistent with his choice.
But certain points, left wholly to himself,
When once a man has arbitrated on,
We say he must succeed there or go hang.
Thus, he should wed the woman he loves most
Or needs most, whatsoe'er the love or need—

For he can't wed twice. Then, he must avouch,
Or follow, at the least, sufficiently,
The form of faith his conscience holds the best,
Whate'er the process of conviction was:
For nothing can compensate his mistake
On such a point, the man himself being judge:
He cannot wed twice, nor twice lose his soul.

Well now, there's one great form of Christian faith
I happened to be born in—which to teach
Was given me as I grew up, on all hands,
As best and readiest means of living by;
The same on examination being proved
The most pronounced moreover, fixed, precise,
And absolute form of faith in the whole world—
Accordingly, most potent of all forms
For working on the world. Observe, my friend!
Such as you know me, I am free to say,
In these hard latter days which hamper one,
Myself—by no immoderate exercise
Of intellect and learning, but the tact
To let external forces work for me,
—Bid the street's stones be bread and they are bread;
Bid Peter's creed, or rather, Hildebrand's,
Exalt me o'er my fellows in the world
And make my life an ease and joy and pride;
It does so,—which for me's a great point gained,
Who have a soul and body that exact
A comfortable care in many ways.
There's power in me and will to dominate
Which I must exercise, they hurt me else:
In many ways I need mankind's respect,
Obedience, and the love that's born of fear:
While at the same time, there's a taste I have,
A toy of soul, a titillating thing,

Refuses to digest these dainties crude.
The naked life is gross till clothed upon:
I must take what men offer, with a grace
As though I would not, could I help it, take!
An uniform I wear though over-rich—
Something imposed on me, no choice of mine;
No fancy-dress worn for pure fancy's sake
And despicable therefore! now folk kneel
And kiss my hand—of course the Church's hand.
Thus I am made, thus life is best for me,
And thus that it should be I have procured;
And thus it could not be another way,
I venture to imagine.

         You'll reply—
So far my choice, no doubt, is a success;
But were I made of better elements,
With nobler instincts, purer tastes, like you,
I hardly would account the thing success
Though it did all for me I say.

           But, friend,
We speak of what is; not of what might be,
And how 'twere better if 'twere otherwise.
I am the man you see here plain enough:
Grant I'm a beast, why, beasts must lead beasts' lives!
Suppose I own at once to tail and claws;
The tailless man exceeds me; but being tailed
I'll lash out lion fashion, and leave apes
To dock their stump and dress their haunches up.
My business is not to remake myself,
But make the absolute best of what God made.
Or—our first simile—though you prove me doomed
To a viler berth still, to the steerage-hole,
The sheep-pen or the pig-sty, I should strive
To make what use of each were possible;

And as this cabin gets upholstery,
That hutch should rustle with sufficient straw.

But, friend, I don't acknowledge quite so fast
I fail of all your manhood's lofty tastes
Enumerated so complacently,
On the mere ground that you forsooth can find
In this particular life I choose to lead
No fit provision for them. Can you not?
Say you, my fault is I address myself
To grosser estimators than I should judge?
And that's no way of holding up the soul,
Which, nobler, needs men's praise perhaps, yet knows
One wise man's verdict outweighs all the fools'—
Would like the two, but, forced to choose, takes that.
I pine among my million imbeciles
(You think) aware some dozen men of sense
Eye me and know me, whether I believe
In the last winking Virgin, as I vow,
And am a fool, or disbelieve in her
And am a knave,—approve in neither case,
Withhold their voices though I look their way:
Like Verdi when, at his worst opera's end
(The thing they gave at Florence,—what's its name?)
While the mad houseful's plaudits near out-bang
His orchestra of salt-box, tongs and bones,
He looks through all the roaring and the wreaths
Where sits Rossini patient in his stall.

Nay, friend, I meet you with an answer here—
For even your prime men who appraise their kind
Are men still, catch a wheel within a wheel,
See more in a truth than the truth's simple self,
Confuse themselves. You see lads walk the street
Sixty the minute; what's to note in that?
You see one lad o'erstride a chimney-stack;

Him you must watch—he's sure to fall, yet stands!
Our interest's on the dangerous edge of things.
The honest thief, the tender murderer,
The superstitious atheist, demirep
That loves and saves her soul in new French books—
We watch while these in equilibrium keep
The giddy line midway: one step aside,
They're classed and done with. I, then, keep the line
Before your sages,—just the men to shrink
From the gross weights, coarse scales, and labels broad
You offer their refinement. Fool or knave?
Why needs a bishop be a fool or knave
When there's a thousand diamond weights between?
So I enlist them. Your picked twelve, you'll find,
Profess themselves indignant, scandalized
At thus being held unable to explain
How a superior man who disbelieves
May not believe as well: that's Schelling's way!
It's through my coming in the tail of time,
Nicking the minute with a happy tact.
Had I been born three hundred years ago
They'd say, "What's strange? Blougram of course be-
     lieves";
And, seventy years since, "disbelieves of course."
But now, "He may believe; and yet, and yet
How can he?"—All eyes turn with interest.
Whereas, step off the line on either side—
You, for example, clever to a fault,
The rough and ready man who write apace,
Read somewhat seldomer, think perhaps even less—
You disbelieve! Who wonders and who cares?
Lord So-and-So—his coat bedropped with wax,
All Peter's chains about his waist, his back
Brave with the needlework of Noodledom—
Believes! Again, who wonders and who cares?

But I, the man of sense and learning too,
The able to think yet act, the this, the that,
I, to believe at this late time of day!
Enough; you see, I need not fear contempt.

    —Except it's yours! Admire me as these may,
You don't. But whom at least do you admire?
Present your own perfection, your ideal,
Your pattern man for a minute—oh, make haste,
Is it Napoleon you would have us grow?
Concede the means; allow his head and hand,
(A large concession, clever as you are)
Good!—In our common primal element
Of unbelief (we can't believe, you know—
We're still at that admission, recollect!)
Where do you find—apart from, towering o'er
The secondary temporary aims
Which satisfy the gross taste you despise—
Where do you find his star?—his crazy trust
God knows through what or in what? it's alive
And shines and leads him and that's all we want.
Have we aught in our sober night shall point
Such ends as his were, and direct the means
Of working out our purpose straight as his,
Nor bring a moment's trouble on success,
With after-care to justify the same?
—Be a Napoleon and yet disbelieve—
Why, the man's mad, friend, take his light away!
What's the vague good o' the world for which you dare
With comfort to yourself blow millions up?
We neither of us see it! we do see
The blown-up millions—spatter of their brains
And writhing of their bowels and so forth,
In that bewildering entanglement
Of horrible eventualities

Past calculation to the end of time!
Can I mistake for some clear word of God
(Which were my ample warrant for it all)
His puff of hazy instincts, idle talk,
"The State, that's I," quack-nonsense about kings,
And (when one beats the man to his last hold)
The vague idea of setting things to rights,
Policing people efficaciously,
More to their profit, most of all to his own;
The whole to end that dismallest of ends
By an Austrian marriage, cant to us the Church,
And resurrection of the old *régime?*
Would I, who hope to live a dozen years,
Fight Austerlitz for reasons such and such?
No: for, concede me but the merest chance
Doubt may be wrong—there's judgment, life to come!
With just that chance, I dare not. Doubt proves right?
This present life is all?—you offer me
Its dozen noisy years with not a chance
That wedding an archduchess, wearing lace,
And getting called by divers new-coined names,
Will drive off ugly thoughts and let me dine,
Sleep, read and chat in quiet as I like!
Therefore, I will not.

             Take another case;
Fit up the cabin yet another way.
What say you to the poet? shall we write
Hamlet, Othello—make the world our own,
Without a risk to run of either sort?
I can't!—to put the strongest reason first.
"But try," you urge, "the trying shall suffice:
The aim, if reached or not, makes great the life:
Try to be Shakespeare, leave the rest to fate!"
Spare my self-knowledge—there's no fooling me!

If I prefer remaining my poor self,
I say so not in self-dispraise but praise.
If I'm a Shakespeare, let the well alone;
Why should I try to be what now I am?
If I'm no Shakespeare, as too probable,—
His power and consciousness and self-delight
And all we want in common, shall I find—
Trying for ever? while on points of taste
Wherewith, to speak it humbly, he and I
Are dowered alike—I'll ask you, I or he,
Which in our two lives realizes most?
Much, he imagined—somewhat, I possess.
He had the imagination; stick to that!
Let him say "In the face of my soul's works
Your world is worthless and I touch it not
Lest I should wrong them"—I'll withdraw my plea.
But does he say so? look upon his life!
Himself, who only can, gives judgment there.
He leaves his towers and gorgeous palaces
To build the trimmest house in Stratford town;
Saves money, spends it, owns the worth of things,
Giulio Romano's pictures, Dowland's lute;
Enjoys a show, respects the puppets, too,
And none more, had he seen its entry once,
Than "Pandulph, of fair Milan cardinal."
Why then should I who play that personage,
The very Pandulph Shakespeare's fancy made,
Be told that had the poet chanced to start
From where I stand now (some degree like mine
Being just the goal he ran his race to reach)
He would have run the whole race back, forsooth,
And left being Pandulph, to begin write plays?
Ah, the earth's best can be but the earth's best!
Did Shakespeare live, he could but sit at home
And get himself in dreams the Vatican,

Greek busts, Venetian paintings, Roman walls,
And English books, none equal to his own,
Which I read, bound in gold (he never did).
—Terni's fall, Naples' bay and Gothard's top—
Eh, friend? I could not fancy one of these;
But, as I pour this claret, there they are:
I've gained them—crossed St. Gothard last July
With ten mules to the carriage and a bed
Slung inside; is my hap the worse for that?
We want the same things, Shakespeare and myself,
And what I want, I have: he, gifted more,
Could fancy he too had them when he liked,
But not so thoroughly that, if fate allowed,
He would not have them also in my sense.
We play one game; I send the ball aloft
No less adroitly that of fifty strokes
Scarce five go o'er the wall so wide and high
Which sends them back to me: I wish and get.
He struck balls higher and with better skill,
But at a poor fence level with his head,
And hit—his Stratford house, a coat of arms,
Successful dealings in his grain and wool,—
While I receive heaven's incense in my nose
And style myself the cousin of Queen Bess.
Ask him, if this life's all, who wins the game?

Believe—and our whole argument breaks up.
Enthusiasm's the best thing, I repeat;
Only, we can't command it; fire and life
Are all, dead matter's nothing, we agree:
And be it a mad dream or God's very breath,
The fact's the same,—belief's fire, once in us,
Makes of all else mere stuff to show itself:
We penetrate our life with such a glow
As fire lends wood and iron—this turns steel,

That burns to ash—all's one, fire proves its power
For good or ill, since men call flare success.
But paint a fire, it will not therefore burn.
Light one in me, I'll find it food enough!
Why, to be Luther—that's a life to lead,
Incomparably better than my own.
He comes, reclaims God's earth for God, he says,
Sets up God's rule again by simple means,
Re-opens a shut book, and all is done.
He flared out in the flaring of mankind;
Such Luther's luck was: how shall such be mine?
If he succeeded, nothing's left to do:
And if he did not altogether—well,
Strauss is the next advance. All Strauss should be
I might be also. But to what result?
He looks upon no future: Luther did.
What can I gain on the denying side?
Ice makes no conflagration. State the facts,
Read the text right, emancipate the world—
The emancipated world enjoys itself
With scarce a thank-you: Blougram told it first
It could not owe a farthing,—not to him
More than St. Paul! 'twould press its pay, you think?
Then add there's still that plaguy hundredth chance
Strauss may be wrong. And so a risk is run—
For what gain? not for Luther's, who secured
A real heaven in his heart throughout his life,
Supposing death a little altered things!

   "Ay, but since really I lack faith," you cry,
"I run the same risk really on all sides,
In cool indifference as bold unbelief.
As well be Strauss as swing 'twixt Paul and him.
It's not worth having, such imperfect faith,

Nor more available to do faith's work
Than unbelief like mine. Whole faith, or none!"

Softly, my friend! I must dispute that point.
Once own the use of faith, I'll find you faith.
We're back on Christian ground. You call for faith:
I show you doubt, to prove that faith exists.
The more of doubt, the stronger faith, I say,
If faith o'ercomes doubt. How I know it does?
By life and man's free will, God gave for that!
To mould life as we choose it, shows our choice:
That's our one act, the previous work's his own.
You criticize the soil? it reared this tree—
This broad life and whatever fruit it bears!
What matter though I doubt at every pore,
Head-doubts, heart-doubts, doubts at my fingers' ends,
Doubts in the trivial work of every day,
Doubts at the very bases of my soul
In the grand moments when she probes herself—
If finally I have a life to show,
The thing I did, brought out in evidence
Against the thing done to me underground
By hell and all its brood, for aught I know?
I say, whence sprang this? shows it faith or doubt?
All's doubt in me; where's break of faith in this?
It is the idea, the feeling and the love
God means mankind should strive for and show forth,
Whatever be the process to that end,—
And not historic knowledge, logic sound,
And metaphysical acumen, sure!
"What think ye of Christ," friend? when all's done and
    said,
Like you this Christianity or not?
It may be false, but will you wish it true?

Has it your vote to be so if it can?
Trust you an instinct silenced long ago
That will break silence and enjoin you love
What mortified philosophy is hoarse,
And all in vain, with bidding you despise?
If you desire faith—then you've faith enough:
What else seeks God—nay, what else seek ourselves?
You form a notion of me, we'll suppose,
On hearsay; it's a favourable one:
"But still" (you add), "there was no such good man,
Because of contradiction in the facts.
One proves, for instance, he was born in Rome,
This Blougram; yet throughout the tales of him
I see he figures as an Englishman."
Well, the two things are reconcileable.
But would I rather you discovered that,
Subjoining—"Still, what matter though they be?
Blougram—concerns me naught, born here or there."

    Pure faith indeed—you know not what you ask!
Naked belief in God the Omnipotent,
Omniscient, Omnipresent, sears too much
The sense of conscious creatures to be borne.
It were the seeing him, no flesh shall dare.
Some think, Creation's meant to show him forth:
I say, it's meant to hide him all it can,
And that's what all the blessed evil's for.
It's use in Time is to environ us,
Our breath, our drop of dew, with shield enough
Against that sight till we can bear its stress.
Under a vertical sun, the exposed brain
And lidless eye and disemprisoned heart
Less certainly would wither up at once
Than mind, confronted with the truth of him.
But time and earth case-harden us to live;

The feeblest sense is trusted most; the child
Feels God a moment, ichors o'er the place,
Plays on and grows to be a man like us.
With me, faith means perpetual unbelief
Kept quiet like the snake 'neath Michael's foot
Who stands calm just because he feels it writhe.
Or, if that's too ambitious,—here's my box—
I need the excitation of a pinch
Threatening the torpor of the inside-nose
Nigh on the imminent sneeze that never comes.
"Leave it in peace" advise the simple folk:
Make it aware of peace by itching-fits,
Say I—let doubt occasion still more faith!

You'll say, once all believed, man, woman, child,
In that dear middle-age these noodles praise.
How you'd exult if I could put you back
Six hundred years, blot out cosmogony,
Geology, ethnology, what not,
(Greek endings, each the little passing-bell
That signifies some faith's about to die),
And set you square with Genesis again,—
When such a traveller told you his last news,
He saw the ark a-top of Ararat
But did not climb there since 'twas getting dusk
And robber-bands infest the mountain's foot!
How should you feel, I ask, in such an age,
How act? As other people felt and did;
With soul more blank than this decanter's knob,
Believe—and yet lie, kill, rob, fornicate,
Full in belief's face, like the beast you'd be!

No, when the fight begins within himself,
A man's worth something. God stoops o'er his head,
Satan looks up between his feet—both tug—
He's left, himself, i' the middle: the soul wakes

And grows. Prolong that battle through his life!
Never leave growing till the life to come!
Here, we've got callous to the Virgin's winks
That used to puzzle people wholesomely:
Men have outgrown the shame of being fools.
What are the laws of nature, not to bend
If the Church bid them? brother Newman asks.
Up with the Immaculate Conception, then—
On to the rack with faith!—is my advice!
Will not that hurry us upon our knees,
Knocking our breasts, "It can't be—yet it shall!
Who am I, the worm, to argue with my Pope?
Low things confound the high things!" and so forth.
That's better than acquitting God with grace
As some folks do. He's tried—no case is proved,
Philosophy is lenient—he may go!

You'll say—the old system's not so obsolete
But men believe still: ay, but who and where?
King Bomba's lazzaroni foster yet
The sacred flame, so Antonelli writes;
But even of these, what ragamuffin-saint
Believes God watches him continually,
As he believes in fire that it will burn,
Or rain that it will drench him? Break fire's law,
Sin against rain, although the penalty
Be just a singe or soaking? "No," he smiles;
"Those laws are laws that can enforce themselves."

The sum of all is—yes, my doubt is great,
My faith's still greater, then my faith's enough.
I have read much, thought much, experienced much,
Yet would die rather than avow my fear
The Naples' liquefaction may be false,
When set to happen by the palace-clock
According to the clouds or dinner-time.

I hear you recommend, I might at least
Eliminate, decrassify my faith
Since I adopt it; keeping what I must
And leaving what I can—such points as this.
I won't—that is, I can't throw one away.
Supposing there's no truth in what I hold
About the need of trial to man's faith,
Still, when you bid me purify the same,
To such a process I discern no end.
Clearing off one excrescence to see two,
There's ever a next in size, now grown as big,
That meets the knife: I cut and cut again!
First cut the Liquefaction, what comes last
But Fichte's clever cut at God himself?
Experimentalize on sacred things?
I trust nor hand nor eye nor heart nor brain
To stop betimes: they all get drunk alike.
The first step, I am master not to take.

You'd find the cutting-process to your taste
As much as leaving growths of lies unpruned,
Nor see more danger in it,—you retort.
Your taste's worth mine; but my taste proves more wise
When we consider that the steadfast hold
On the extreme end of the chain of faith
Gives all the advantage, makes the difference
With the rough purblind mass we seek to rule:
We are their lords, or they are free of us,
Just as we tighten or relax our hold.
So, other matters equal, we'll revert
To the first problem—which, if solved my way
And thrown into the balance, turns the scale—
How we may lead a comfortable life,
How suit our luggage to the cabin's size.

Of course you are remarking all this time
How narrowly and grossly I view life,
Respect the creature-comforts, care to rule
The masses, and regard complacently
"The cabin," in our old phrase. Well, I do.
I act for, talk for, live for this world now,
As this world calls for action, life and talk:
No prejudice to what next world may prove,
Whose new laws and requirements, my best pledge
To observe them, is that I observe these now,
Doing hereafter what I do meanwhile.
Let us concede (gratuitously though)
Next life relieves the soul of body, yields
Pure spiritual enjoyment: well, my friend,
Why lose this life i' the meantime, since its use
May be to make the next life more intense?

Do you know, I have often had a dream
(Work it up in your next month's article)
Of man's poor spirit in its progress, still
Losing true life for ever and a day
Through ever trying to be and ever being—
In the evolution of successive spheres—
Before its actual sphere and place of life,
Halfway into the next, which having reached,
It shoots with corresponding foolery
Halfway into the next still, on and off!
As when a traveller, bound from North to South,
Scouts fur in Russia: what's its use in France?
In France spurns flannel: where's its need in Spain?
In Spain drops cloth, too cumbrous for Algiers!
Linen goes next, and last the skin itself,
A superfluity at Timbuctoo.
When, through his journey, was the fool at ease?
I'm at ease now, friend; worldly in this world,

I take and like its way of life; I think
My brothers, who administer the means,
Live better for my comfort—that's good too;
And God, if he pronounce upon it all,
Approves my service, which is better still.
If he keep silence,—why, for you or me
Or that brute-beast pulled-up in to-day's "Times,"
What odds is't, save to ourselves, what life we lead?

   You meet me at this issue: you declare—
All special-pleading done with—truth is truth,
And justifies itself by undreamed ways.
You don't fear but it's better, if we doubt,
To say so, act up to our truth perceived
However feebly. Do then,—act away!
'Tis there I'm on the watch for you. How one acts
Is, both of us agree, our chief concern:
And how you'll act is what I fain would see
If, like the candid person you appear,
You dare to make the most of your life's scheme
As I of mine, live up to its full law
Since there's no higher law that counterchecks.
Put natural religion to the test
You've just demolished the revealed with—quick,
Down to the root of all that checks your will,
All prohibition to lie, kill and thieve,
Or even to be an atheistic priest!
Suppose a pricking to incontinence—
Philosophers deduce you chastity
Or shame, from just the fact that at the first
Whoso embraced a woman in the field,
Threw club down, and forewent his brains beside,
So, stood a ready victim in the reach
Of any brother savage, club in hand;
Hence saw the use of going out of sight

In wood or cave to prosecute his loves:
I read this in a French book t'other day.
Does law so analysed coerce you much?
Oh, men spin clouds of fuzz where matters end,
But you who reach where the first thread begins,
You'll soon cut that!—which means you can, but won't,
Through certain instincts, blind, unreasoned out,
You dare not set aside, you can't tell why,
But there they are, and so you let them rule.
Then, friend, you seem as much a slave as I,
A liar, conscious coward and hypocrite,
Without the good the slave expects to get,
Suppose he has a master after all!
You own your instincts? why, what else do I,
Who want, am made for, and must have a God
Ere I can be aught, do aught?—no mere name
Want, but the true thing with what proves its truth,
To wit, a relation from that thing to me,
Touching from head to foot—which touch I feel,
And with it take the rest, this life of ours!
I live my life here; yours you dare not live.

—Not as I state it, who (you please subjoin)
Disfigure such a life and call it names.
While, to your mind, remains another way
For simple men: knowledge and power have rights,
But ignorance and weakness have rights too.
There needs no crucial effort to find truth
If here or there or anywhere about:
We ought to turn each side, try hard and see,
And if we can't, be glad we've earned at least
The right, by one laborious proof the more,
To graze in peace earth's pleasant pasturage.
Men are not angels, neither are they brutes.
Something we may see, all we cannot see.

What need of lying? I say, I see all,
And swear to each detail the most minute
In what I think a Pan's face—you, mere cloud:
I swear I hear him speak and see him wink,
For fear, if once I drop the emphasis,
Mankind may doubt there's any cloud at all.
You take the simpler life—ready to see,
Willing to see (for no cloud's worth a face)—
And leaving quiet what no strength can move,
And which, who bids you move? who has the right?
I bid you; but you are God's sheep, not mine:
"*Pastor est tui Dominus.*" You find
In this the pleasant pasture of our life
Much you may eat without the least offence,
Much you don't eat because your maw objects,
Much you would eat but that your fellow-flock
Open great eyes at you and even butt,
And thereupon you like your mates so well
You cannot please yourself, offending them;
Though when they seem exorbitantly sheep,
You weigh your pleasure with their butts and bleats
And strike the balance. Sometimes certain fears
Restrain you, real checks since you find them so;
Sometimes you please yourself and nothing checks:
And thus you graze through life with not one lie,
And like it best.

        But do you, in truth's name?
If so, you beat—which means you are not I—
Who needs must make earth mine and feed my fill
Not simply unbutted at, unbickered with,
But motioned to the velvet of the sward
By those obsequious wethers' very selves.
Look at me, sir; my age is double yours:
At yours, I knew beforehand, so enjoyed,

What now I should be—as, permit the word,
I pretty well imagine your whole range
And stretch of tether twenty years to come.
We both have minds and bodies much alike.
In truth's name, don't you want my bishopric,
My daily bread, my influence and my state?
You're young. I'm old; you must be old one day;
Will you find then, as I do hour by hour,
Women their lovers kneel to, who cut curls
From your fat lap-dog's ear to grace a brooch—
Dukes, who petition just to kiss your ring—
With much beside you know or may conceive?
Suppose we die to-night: well, here am I,
Such were my gains, life bore this fruit to me,
While writing all the same my articles
On music, poetry, the fictile vase
Found at Albano, chess, Anacreon's Greek.
But you—the highest honour in your life,
The thing you'll crown yourself with, all your days,
Is—dining here and drinking this last glass
I pour you out in sign of amity
Before we part for ever. Of your power
And social influence, worldly worth in short,
Judge what's my estimation by the fact,
I do not condescend to enjoin, beseech,
Hint secrecy on one of all these words!
You're shrewd and know that should you publish one
The world would brand the lie—my enemies first,
Who'd sneer—"the bishop's an arch-hypocrite,
And knave perhaps, but not so frank a fool"
Whereas I should not dare for both my ears
Breathe one such syllable, smile one such smile,
Before the chaplain who reflects myself—
My shade's so much more potent than your flesh.
What's your reward, self-abnegating friend?

Stood you confessed of those exceptional
And privileged great natures that dwarf mine—
A zealot with a mad ideal in reach,
A poet just about to print his ode,
A statesman with a scheme to stop this war,
An artist whose religion is his art—
I should have nothing to object: such men
Carry the fire, all things grow warm to them,
Their drugget's worth my purple, they beat me.
But you,—you're just as little those as I—
You, Gigadibs, who, thirty years of age,
Write stately for Blackwood's Magazine,
Believe you see two points in Hamlet's soul
Unseized by the Germans yet—which view you'll
        print—
Meantime the best you have to show being still
That lively lightsome article we took
Almost for the true Dickens,—what's its name?
"The Slum and Cellar—or Whitechapel life
Limned after dark!" it made me laugh, I know,
And pleased a month and brought you in ten pounds.
—Success I recognize and compliment,
And therefore give you, if you choose, three words
(The card and pencil-scratch is quite enough)
Which whether here, in Dublin, or New York,
Will get you, prompt as at my eyebrow's wink,
Such terms as never you aspired to get
In all our own reviews and some not ours.
Go write your lively sketches! be the first
"Blougram, or The Eccentric Confidence"—
Or better simply say, "The Outward-bound."
Why, men as soon would throw it in my teeth
As copy and quote the infamy chalked broad
About me on the church-door opposite.
You will not wait for that experience though,

I fancy, howsoever you decide,
To discontinue—not detesting, not
Defaming, but at least—despising me!

Over his wine so smiled and talked his hour
Sylvester Blougram, styled *in partibus*
Episcopus, nec non—(the deuce knows what
It's changed to by our novel hierarchy)
With Gigadibs the literary man,
Who played with spoons, explored his plate's design,
And ranged the olive stones about its edge,
While the great bishop rolled him out a mind.
Long crumpled, till creased consciousness lay smooth.

For Blougram, he believed, say, half he spoke.
The other portion, as he shaped it thus
For argumentatory purposes,
He felt his foe was foolish to dispute.
Some arbitrary accidental thoughts
That crossed his mind, amusing because new,
He chose to represent as fixtures there,
Invariable convictions (such they seemed
Beside his interlocutor's loose cards
Flung daily down, and not the same way twice)
While certain hell-deep instincts, man's weak tongue
Is never bold to utter in their truth
Because styled hell-deep ('tis an old mistake
To place hell at the bottom of the earth),
He ignored these,—not having in readiness
Their nomenclature and philosophy:
He said true things, but called them by wrong names.
"On the whole," he thought, "I justify myself
On every point where cavillers like this
Oppugn my life: he tries one kind of fence,
I close, he's worsted, that's enough for him.
He's on the ground! if ground should break away

I take my stand on, there's a firmer yet
Beneath it, both of us may sink and reach.
His ground was over mine and broke the first:
So let him sit with me this many a year!"

He did not sit five minutes. Just a week
Sufficed his sudden healthy vehemence.
Something had struck him in the "Outward-bound"
Another way than Blougram's purpose was:
And having bought, not cabin-furniture
But settler's-implements (enough for three)
And started for Australia—there, I hope,
By this time he has tested his first plough,
And studied his last chapter of St. John.

One Word More

TO E. B. B.

Epilogue to *Men and Women*

There they are, my fifty men and women
Naming me the fifty poems finished!
Take them, Love, the book and me together:
Where the heart lies, let the brain lie also.

Rafael made a century of sonnets,
Made and wrote them in a certain volume
Dinted with the silver-pointed pencil
Else he only used to draw Madonnas:
These, the world might view—but one, the volume.
Who that one, you ask? Your heart instructs you.
Did she live and love it all her life-time?
Die, and let it drop beside her pillow

Where it lay in place of Rafael's glory,
Rafael's cheek so duteous and so loving—
Cheek, the world was wont to hail a painter's,
Rafael's cheek, her love had turned a poet's?

You and I would rather read that volume,
(Taken to his beating bosom by it)
Lean and list the bosom-beats of Rafael,
Would we not? than wonder at Madonnas—
Her, San Sisto names, and Her, Foligno,
Her, that visits Florence in a vision,
Her, that's left with lilies in the Louvre—
Seen by us and all the world in circle.

You and I will never read that volume.
Guido Reni, like his own eye's apple
Guarded long the treasure-book and loved it.
Guido Reni dying, all Bologna
Cried, and the world cried too, "Ours, the treasure!"
Suddenly, as rare things will, it vanished.

Dante once prepared to paint an angel:
Whom to please? You whisper "Beatrice."
While he mused and traced it and retraced it,
(Peradventure with a pen corroded
Still by drops of that hot ink he dipped for,
When, his left-hand i' the hair o' the wicked,
Back he held the brow and pricked its stigma,
Bit into the live man's flesh for parchment,
Loosed him, laughed to see the writing rankle,
Let the wretch go festering through Florence)—
Dante, who loved well because he hated,
Hated wickedness that hinders loving,
Dante standing, studying his angel,—
In there broke the folk of his Inferno.
Says he—"Certain people of importance"

(Such he gave his daily dreadful line to)
"Entered and would seize, forsooth, the poet."
Says the poet—"Then I stopped my painting."

You and I would rather see that angel,
Painted by the tenderness of Dante,
Would we not?—than read a fresh Inferno.

You and I will never see that picture,
While he mused on love and Beatrice,
While he softened o'er his outlined angel,
In they broke, those "people of importance:"
We and Bice bear the loss for ever.

What of Rafael's sonnets, Dante's picture?
This: no artist lives and loves, that longs not
Once, and only once, and for one only,
(Ah, the prize!) to find his love a language
Fit and fair and simple and sufficient—
Using nature that's an art to others,
Not, this one time, art that's turned his nature.
Ay, of all the artists living, loving,
None but would forego his proper dowry,—
Does he paint? he fain would write a poem,—
Does he write? he fain would paint a picture,
Put to proof art alien to the artist's,
Once, and only once, and for one only,
So to be the man and leave the artist,
Gain the man's joy, miss the artist's sorrow.

Wherefore? Heaven's gift takes earth's abatement!
He who smites the rock and spreads the water,
Bidding drink and live a crowd beneath him,
Even he, the minute makes immortal,
Proves, perchance, but mortal in the minute,
Desecrates, belike, the deed in doing.
While he smites, how can he but remember,

So he smote before, in such a peril,
When they stood and mocked—"Shall smiting help us?"
When they drank and sneered—"A stroke is easy!"
When they wiped their mouths and went their journey,
Throwing him for thanks—"But drought was pleasant."
Thus old memories mar the actual triumph;
Thus the doing savours of disrelish;
Thus achievement lacks a gracious somewhat;
O'er-importuned brows becloud the mandate,
Carelessness or consciousness—the gesture.
For he bears an ancient wrong about him,
Sees and knows again those phalanxed faces,
Hears, yet one time more, the 'customed prelude—
"How shouldst thou, of all men, smite, and save us?"
Guesses what is like to prove the sequel—
"Egypt's flesh-pots—nay, the drought was better."

Oh, the crowd must have emphatic warrant!
Theirs, the Sinai-forehead's cloven brilliance,
Right-arm's rod-sweep, tongue's imperial fiat.
Never dares the man put off the prophet.

Did he love one face from out the thousands,
(Were she Jethro's daughter, white and wifely,
Were she but the Aethiopian bondslave,)
He would envy yon dumb patient camel,
Keeping a reserve of scanty water
Meant to save his own life in the desert;
Ready in the desert to deliver
(Kneeling down to let his breast be opened)
Hoard and life together for his mistress.

I shall never, in the years remaining,
Paint you pictures, no, nor carve you statues,
Make you music that should all-express me;
So it seems: I stand on my attainment.

This of verse alone, one life allows me;
Verse and nothing else have I to give you.
Other heights in other lives, God willing:
All the gifts from all the heights, your own, Love!

Yet a semblance of resource avails us—
Shade so finely touched, love's sense must seize it.
Take these lines, look lovingly and nearly,
Lines I write the first time and the last time.
He who works in fresco, steals a hair-brush,
Curbs the liberal hand, subservient proudly,
Cramps his spirit, crowds its all in little,
Makes a strange art of an art familiar,
Fills his lady's missal-marge with flowerets.
He who blows thro' bronze, may breathe thro' silver,
Fitly serenade a slumbrous princess.
He who writes, may write for once as I do.

Love, you saw me gather men and women,
Live or dead or fashioned by my fancy,
Enter each and all, and use their service,
Speak from every mouth,—the speech, a poem.
Hardly shall I tell my joys and sorrows,
Hopes and fears, belief and disbelieving:
I am mine and yours—the rest be all men's,
Karshish, Cleon, Norbert and the fifty.
Let me speak this once in my true person,
Not as Lippo, Roland or Andrea,
Though the fruit of speech be just this sentence:
Pray you, look on these my men and women,
Take and keep my fifty poems finished;
Where my heart lies, let my brain lie also!
Poor the speech; be how I speak, for all things.

Not but that you know me! Lo, the moon's self!
Here in London, yonder late in Florence,

Still we find her face, the thrice-transfigured.
Curving on a sky imbrued with colour,
Drifted over Fiesole by twilight,
Came she, our new crescent of a hair's-breadth.
Full she flared it, lamping Samminiato,
Rounder 'twixt the cypresses and rounder,
Perfect till the nightingales applauded.
Now, a piece of her old self, impoverished,
Hard to greet, she traverses the houseroofs,
Hurries with unhandsome thrift of silver,
Goes dispiritedly, glad to finish.

What, there's nothing in the moon noteworthy?
Nay: for if that moon could love a mortal,
Use, to charm him (so to fit a fancy),
All her magic ('tis the old sweet mythos),
She would turn a new side to her mortal,
Side unseen of herdsman, huntsman, steersman—
Blank to Zoroaster on his terrace,
Blind to Galileo on his turret,
Dumb to Homer, dumb to Keats—him, even!
Think, the wonder of the moonstruck mortal—
When she turns round, comes again in heaven,
Opens out anew for worse or better!
Proves she like some portent of an iceberg
Swimming full upon the ship it founders,
Hungry with huge teeth of splintered crystals!
Proves she as the paved work of a sapphire
Seen by Moses when he climbed the mountain?
Moses, Aaron, Nadab and Abihu
Climbed and saw the very God, the Highest,
Stand upon the paved work of a sapphire.
Like the bodied heaven in his clearness
Shone the stone, the sapphire of that paved work,
When they ate and drank and saw God also!

What were seen? None knows, none ever shall know.
Only this is sure—the sight were other,
Not the moon's same side, born late in Florence,
Dying now impoverished here in London.
God be thanked, the meanest of his creatures
Boasts two soul-sides, one to face the world with,
One to show a woman when he loves her!

This I say of me, but think of you, Love!
This to you-yourself my moon of poets!
Ah, but that's the world's side, there's the wonder,
Thus they see you, praise you, think they know you!
Out of my own self, I dare to phrase it.
But the best is when I glide from out them,
Cross a step or two of dubious twilight,
Come out on the other side, the novel
Silent silver lights and darks undreamed of,
Where I hush and bless myself with silence.

Oh, their Rafael of the dear Madonnas,
Oh, their Dante of the dread Inferno,
Wrote one song—and in my brain I sing it,
Drew one angel—borne, see, on my bosom!

Emily Brontë

(1818–1848)

The night is darkening round me

The night is darkening round me,
The wild winds coldly blow;
But a tyrant spell has bound me
And I cannot, cannot go.

The giant trees are bending
Their bare boughs weighed with snow,
And the storm is fast descending
And yet I cannot go.

Clouds beyond clouds above me,
Wastes beyond wastes below;
But nothing drear can move me;
I will not, cannot go.

Plead for Me

O thy bright eyes must answer now,
When Reason, with a scornful brow,
Is mocking at my overthrow;
O thy sweet tongue must plead for me
And tell why I have chosen thee!

Stern Reason is to judgement come
Arrayed in all her forms of gloom;
Wilt thou my advocate be dumb?
No, radiant angel, speak and say
Why I did cast the world away;

Why I have persevered to shun
The common paths that others run;
And on a strange road journeyed on
Heedless alike of Wealth and Power—
Of Glory's wreath and Pleasure's flower.

These once indeed seemed Beings divine,
And they perchance heard vows of mine
And saw my offerings on their shrine—
But, careless gifts are seldom prized,
And mine were worthily despised;

So with a ready heart I swore
To seek their altar-stone no more,
And gave my spirit to adore
Thee, ever present, phantom thing—
My slave, my comrade, and my King!

A slave because I rule thee still;
Incline thee to my changeful will
And make thy influence good or ill—
A comrade, for by day and night
Thou art my intimate delight—

My Darling Pain that wounds and sears
And wrings a blessing out from tears
By deadening me to real cares;
And yet, a king—though prudence well
Have taught thy subject to rebel.

And am I wrong to worship where
Faith cannot doubt nor Hope despair

Since my own soul can grant my prayer?
Speak, God of Visions, plead for me
And tell why I have chosen thee!

Fall, leaves, fall

Fall, leaves, fall; die, flowers, away;
Lengthen night and shorten day;
Every leaf speaks bliss to me
Fluttering from the autumn tree.
I shall smile when wreaths of snow
Blossom where the rose should grow;
I shall sing when night's decay
Ushers in a drearier day.

Remembrance

[R. Alcona to J. Brenzaida]

Cold in the earth, and the deep snow piled above thee!
Far, far removed, cold in the dreary grave!
Have I forgot, my Only Love, to love thee,
Severed at last by Time's all-wearing wave?

Now, when alone, do my thoughts no longer hover
Over the mountains on Angora's shore;
Resting their wings where heath and fern-leaves cover
That noble heart for ever, ever more?

Cold in the earth, and fifteen wild Decembers
From those brown hills have melted into spring—

Faithful indeed is the spirit that remembers
After such years of change and suffering!

Sweet Love of youth, forgive if I forget thee
While the World's tide is bearing me along:
Sterner desires and darker hopes beset me,
Hopes which obscure but cannot do thee wrong.

No other Sun has lightened up my heaven;
No other Star has ever shone for me:
All my life's bliss from thy dear life was given—
All my life's bliss is in the grave with thee.

But when the days of golden dreams had perished
And even Despair was powerless to destroy,
Then did I learn how existence could be cherished,
Strengthened and fed without the aid of joy;

Then did I check the tears of useless passion,
Weaned my young soul from yearning after thine;
Sternly denied its burning wish to hasten
Down to that tomb already more than mine!

And even yet, I dare not let it languish,
Dare not indulge in Memory's rapturous pain;
Once drinking deep of that divinest anguish,
How could I seek the empty world again?

The Two Children

Heavy hangs the raindrop
From the burdened spray;
Heavy broods the damp mist
On uplands far away;

Heavy looms the dull sky,
Heavy rolls the sea—
And heavy beats the young heart
Beneath that lonely tree.

Never has a blue streak
Cleft the clouds since morn—
Never has his grim Fate
Smiled since he was born.

Frowning on the infant,
Shadowing childhood's joy,
Guardian angel knows not
That melancholy boy.

Day is passing swiftly
Its sad and sombre prime;
Youth is fast invading
Sterner manhood's time.

All the flowers are praying
For sun before they close,
And he prays too, unknowing,
That sunless human rose!

Blossoms, that the west wind
Has never wooed to blow,
Scentless are your petals,
Your dew as cold as snow.

Soul, where kindred kindness
No early promise woke,
Barren is your beauty
As weed upon the rock.

Wither, Brothers, wither,
You were vainly given—
Earth reserves no blessing
For the unblessed of Heaven!

Child of Delight! with sunbright hair,
And seablue, seadeep eyes;
Spirit of Bliss, what brings thee here,
Beneath these sullen skies?

Thou shouldst live in eternal spring,
Where endless day is never dim;
Why, seraph, has thy erring wing
Borne thee down to weep with him?

"Ah, not from heaven am I descended,
And I do not come to mingle tears;
But sweet is day, though with shadows blended;
And, though clouded, sweet are youthful years.

"I, the image of light and gladness,
Saw and pitied that mournful boy,
And I swore to take his gloomy sadness,
And give to him my beamy joy.

"Heavy and dark the night is closing;
Heavy and dark may its biding be:
Better for all from grief reposing,
And better for all who watch like me.

"Guardian angel, he lacks no longer;
Evil fortune he need not fear:
Fate is strong, but Love is stronger;
And more unsleeping than angel's care."

No coward soul is mine

No coward soul is mine
No trembler in the world's storm-troubled sphere:
I see Heaven's glories shine,
And Faith shines equal arming me from Fear.

O God within my breast,
Almighty ever-present Deity!
Life, that in me hast rest,
As I Undying Life, have power in Thee!

Vain are the thousand creeds
That move men's hearts, unutterably vain,
Worthless as withered weeds,
Or idlest froth amid the boundless main,

To waken doubt in one
Holding so fast by thy infinity,
So surely anchored on
The steadfast rock of Immortality.

With wide-embracing love
Thy spirit animates eternal years,
Pervades and broods above,
Changes, sustains, dissolves, creates and rears.

Though Earth and man were gone,
And suns and universes ceased to be,
And thou wert left alone,
Every Existence would exist in thee.

There is not room for Death
Nor atom that his might could render void:
Since thou art Being and Breath,
And what thou art may never be destroyed.

John Henry, Cardinal Newman

(1801–1890)

The Pillar of the Cloud

Lead, Kindly Light, amid the encircling gloom,
   Lead Thou me on!
The night is dark, and I am far from home—
   Lead Thou me on!
Keep Thou my feet; I do not ask to see
The distant scene,—one step enough for me.

I was not ever thus, nor pray'd that Thou
   Shouldst lead me on.
I loved to choose and see my path; but now
   Lead Thou me on!
I loved the garish day, and, spite of fears,
Pride ruled my will: remember not past years.

So long Thy power hath blest me, sure it still
   Will lead me on,
O'er moor and fen, o'er crag and torrent, till
   The night is gone;
And with the morn those angel faces smile
Which I have loved long since, and lost awhile.

FROM *The Dream of Gerontius*

FIFTH CHORUS OF ANGELS

Praise to the Holiest in the height,
    And in the depth be praise,
In all His words most wonderful;
    Most sure in all His ways!

O loving wisdom of our God!
    When all was sin and shame,
A second Adam to the fight
    And to the rescue came.

O wisest love! that flesh and blood,
    Which did in Adam fail,
Should strive afresh against the foe,
    Should strive and should prevail;

And that a higher gift than grace
    Should flesh and blood refine,
God's presence and His very Self,
    And Essence all-divine.

O generous love! that He who smote
    In man for man the foe,
The double agony in man
    For man should undergo;

And in the garden secretly,
    And on the cross on high,
Should teach His brethren, and inspire
    To suffer and to die.

Matthew Arnold

(1822–1888)

In Utrumque Paratus

If, in the silent mind of One all-pure,
    At first imagined lay
The sacred world; and by procession sure
From those still deeps, in form and colour drest,
Seasons alternating, and night and day,
The long-mused thought to north, south, east, and west.
    Took then its all-seen way;

O waking on a world which thus-wise springs!
    Whether it needs thee count
Betwixt thy waking and the birth of things
Ages or hours—O waking on life's stream!
By lonely pureness to the all-pure fount
(Only by this thou canst) the colour'd dream
    Of life remount!

Thin, thin the pleasant human noises grow,
    And faint the city gleams;
Rare the lone pastoral huts—marvel not thou!
The solemn peaks but to the stars are known,
But to the stars, and the cold lunar beams;
Alone the sun arises, and alone
    Spring the great streams.

But, if the wild unfather'd mass no birth
    In divine seats hath known;

In the blank, echoing solitude if Earth,
Rocking her obscure body to and fro,
Ceases not from all time to heave and groan,
Unfruitful oft, and at her happiest throe
    Forms, what she forms, alone;

O seeming sole to awake, thy sun-bathed head
    Piercing the solemn cloud
Round thy still dreaming brother-world outspread!
O man, whom Earth, thy long-vext mother, bare
Not without joy—so radiant, so endow'd
(Such happy issue crown'd her painful care)—
    Be not too proud!

Oh when most self-exalted most alone,
    Chief dreamer, own thy dream!
Thy brother-world stirs at thy feet unknown;
Who hath a monarch's hath no brother's part—
Yet doth thine inmost soul with yearning teem.
—Oh, what a spasm shakes the dreamer's heart!
    "I, too, but seem."

To Marguerite

Yes! in the sea of life enisled,
With echoing straits between us thrown,
Dotting the shoreless watery wild,
We mortal millions live *alone*.
The islands feel the enclasping flow,
And then their endless bounds they know.

But when the moon their hollows lights,
And they are swept by balms of spring,
And in their glens, on starry nights,

The nightingales divinely sing;
And lovely notes, from shore to shore,
Across the sounds and channels pour—

Oh! then a longing like despair
Is to their farthest caverns sent;
For surely once, they feel, we were
Parts of a single continent!
Now round us spreads the watery plain—
Oh might our marges meet again!

Who order'd, that their longing's fire
Should be, as soon as kindled, cool'd?
Who renders vain their deep desire?—
A God, a God their severance ruled!
And bade betwixt their shores to be
The unplumb'd, salt, estranging sea.

Dover Beach

The sea is calm to-night.
The tide is full, the moon lies fair
Upon the straits;—on the French coast, the light
Gleams, and is gone; the cliffs of England stand,
Glimmering and vast, out in the tranquil bay.
Come to the window, sweet is the night-air!
Only, from the lone line of spray
Where the sea meets the moon-blanch'd sand,
Listen! you hear the grating roar
Of pebbles which the waves draw back, and fling,
At their return, up the high strand,
Begin, and cease, and then again begin,
With tremulous cadence slow, and bring
The eternal note of sadness in.

Sophocles long ago
Heard it on the Ægæan, and it brought
Into his mind the turbid ebb and flow
Of human misery; we
Find also in the sound a thought,
Hearing it by this distant northern sea.

The Sea of Faith
Was once, too, at the full, and round earth's shore
Lay like the folds of a bright girdle furl'd.
But now I only hear
Its melancholy, long, withdrawing roar,
Retreating, to the breath
Of the night-wind down the vast edges drear
And naked shingles of the world.

Ah, love, let us be true
To one another! for the world, which seems
To lie before us like a land of dreams,
So various, so beautiful, so new,
Hath really neither joy, nor love, nor light,
Nor certitude, nor peace, nor help for pain;
And we are here as on a darkling plain
Swept with confused alarms of struggle and flight,
Where ignorant armies clash by night.

Growing Old

What is it to grow old?
Is it to lose the glory of the form,
The lustre of the eye?
Is it for beauty to forego her wreath?
—Yes, but not this alone.

Is it to feel our strength—
Not our bloom only, but our strength—decay?
Is it to feel each limb
Grow stiffer, every function less exact,
Each nerve more loosely strung?

Yes, this, and more; but not,
Ah, 'tis not what in youth we dream'd 'twould be!
'Tis not to have our life
Mellow'd and soften'd as with sunset-glow,
A golden day's decline.

'Tis not to see the world
As from a height, with rapt prophetic eyes,
And heart profoundly stirr'd;
And weep, and feel the fulness of the past,
The years that are no more.

It is to spend long days
And not once feel that we were ever young;
It is to add, immured
In the hot prison of the present, month
To month with weary pain.

It is to suffer this,
And feel but half, and feebly, what we feel.
Deep in our hidden heart
Festers the dull remembrance of a change,
But no emotion—none.

It is—last stage of all—
When we are frozen up within, and quite
The phantom of ourselves,
To hear the world applaud the hollow ghost
Which blamed the living man.

The Last Word

Creep into thy narrow bed,
Creep, and let no more be said!
Vain thy onset! all stands fast.
Thou thyself must break at last.

Let the long contention cease!
Geese are swans, and swans are geese.
Let them have it how they will!
Thou art tired; best be still.

They out-talked thee, hissed thee, tore thee?
Better men fared thus before thee;
Fired their ringing shot and pass'd,
Hotly charged—and broke at last.

Charge once more, then, and be dumb!
Let the victors, when they come,
When the forts of folly fall,
Find thy body by the wall!

The Scholar-Gipsy

Go, for they call you, shepherd, from the hill;
Go, shepherd, and untie the wattled cotes!
No longer leave thy wistful flock unfed,
Nor let thy bawling fellows rack their throats,
Nor the cropp'd herbage shoot another head.
But when the fields are still,

And the tired men and dogs all gone to rest,
    And only the white sheep are sometimes seen
    Cross and recross the strips of moon-blanch'd
        green,
Come, shepherd, and again begin the quest!

Here, where the reaper was at work of late—
    In this high field's dark corner, where he leaves
    His coat, his basket, and his earthen cruse,
And in the sun all morning binds the sheaves,
    Then here, at noon, comes back his stores to use—
      Here will I sit and wait,
While to my ear from uplands far away
    The bleating of the folded flocks is borne,
    With distant cries of reapers in the corn—
All the live murmur of a summer's day.

Screen'd in this nook o'er the high, half-reap'd field,
    And here till sun-down, shepherd! will I be.
    Through the thick corn the scarlet poppies peep
And round green roots and yellowing stalks I see
    Pale pink convolvulus in tendrils creep;
      And air-swept lindens yield
Their scent, and rustle down their perfumed showers
    Of bloom on the bent grass where I am laid,
    And bower me from the August sun with shade;
And the eye travels down to Oxford's towers.

And near me on the grass lies Glanvil's book—
    Come, let me read the oft-read tale again!
    The story of that Oxford scholar poor
Of pregnant parts and quick inventive brain,
    Who, tired of knocking at preferment's door,
      One summer-morn forsook
His friends, and went to learn the gipsy-lore,
    And roam'd the world with that wild brotherhood,

And came, as most men deem'd, to little good,
But came to Oxford and his friends no more.

But once, years after, in the country-lanes,
    Two scholars, whom at college erst he knew,
    Met him, and of his way of life enquired;
Whereat he answer'd, that the gipsy-crew,
    His mates, had arts to rule as they desired
        The workings of men's brains,
And they can bind them to what thoughts they will.
    "And I," he said, "the secret of their art,
    When fully learn'd, will to the world impart;
But it needs heaven-sent moments for this skill."

This said, he left them, and return'd no more.—
    But rumors hung about the country-side,
    That the lost Scholar long was seen to stray,
Seen by rare glimpses, pensive and tongue-tied,
    In hat of antique shape, and cloak of grey,
        The same the gipsies wore.
Shepherds had met him on the Hurst in spring;
    At some lone alehouse in the Berkshire moors,
    On the warm ingle-bench, the smock-frock'd boors
Had found him seated at their entering,

But, 'mid their drink and clatter, he would fly.
    And I myself seem half to know thy looks,
    And put the shepherds, wanderer! on thy trace;
And boys who in lone wheatfields scare the rooks
    I ask if thou hast pass'd their quiet place;
        Or in my boat I lie
Moor'd to the cool bank in the summer-heats,
    Mid wide grass meadows which the sunshine fills,
    And watch the warm green-muffled Cumner hills,
And wonder if thou haunt'st their shy retreats.

For most, I know, thou lov'st retired ground!
  Thee, at the ferry Oxford riders blithe,
    Returning home on summer-nights, have met
Crossing the stripling Thames at Bab-lock-hithe,
    Trailing in the cool stream thy fingers wet,
      As the punt's rope chops round;
And leaning backward in a pensive dream,
    And fostering in thy lap a heap of flowers
    Pluck'd in shy fields and distant Wychwood
        bowers,
And thine eyes resting on the moonlit stream.

And then they land, and thou art seen no more!—
  Maidens, who from the distant hamlets come
    To dance around the Fyfield elm in May,
Oft through the darkening fields have seen thee roam,
    Or cross a stile into the public way.
      Oft thou hast given them store
Of flowers—the frail-leaf'd, white anemony,
    Dark bluebells drench'd with dews of summer eves,
    And purple orchises with spotted leaves—
But none hath words she can report of thee.

And, above Godstow Bridge, when hay-time's here
  In June, and many a scythe in sunshine flames,
    Men who through those wide fields of breezy grass
Where black-wing'd swallows haunt the glittering
        Thames,
    To bathe in the abandon'd lasher pass,
      Have often pass'd thee near
Sitting upon the river bank o'ergrown;
    Mark'd thine outlandish garb, thy figure spare,
    Thy dark vague eyes, and soft abstracted air—
But, when they came from bathing, thou wast gone!

At some lone homestead in the Cumner hills,
  Where at her open door the housewife darns,

Thou hast been seen, or hanging on a gate
To watch the threshers in the mossy barns.
Children, who early range these slopes and late
For cresses from the rills,
Have known thee eyeing, all an April-day,
The springing pastures and the feeding kine;
And mark'd thee, when the stars come out and
shine,
Through the long dewy grass move slow away.

In autumn, on the skirts of Bagley Wood—
Where most the gipsies by the turf-edged way
Pitch their smoked tents, and every bush you see
With scarlet patches tagg'd and shreds of grey,
Above the forest-ground call'd Thessaly—
The blackbird, picking food,
Sees thee, nor stops his meal, nor fears at all:
So often has he known thee past him stray,
Rapt, twirling in thy hand a wither'd spray,
And waiting for the spark from heaven to fall.

And once, in winter, on the causeway chill
Where home through flooded fields foot-travellers go,
Have I not pass'd thee on the wooden bridge,
Wrapt in thy cloak and battling with the snow,
Thy face tow'rd Hinksey and its wintry ridge?
And thou hast climb'd the hill,
And gain'd the white brow of the Cumner range;
Turn'd once to watch, while thick the snowflakes
fall,
The line of festal light in Christ-Church hall—
Then sought thy straw in some sequester'd grange.

But what—I dream! Two hundred years are flown
Since first thy story ran through Oxford halls,
And the grave Glanvil did the tale inscribe

That thou wert wander'd from the studious walls
    To learn strange arts, and join a gipsy-tribe:
        And thou from earth art gone
Long since, and in some quiet churchyard laid—
    Some country-nook, where o'er thy unknown
        grave
    Tall grasses and white flowering nettles wave,
Under a dark, red-fruited yew-tree's shade.

—No, no, thou hast not felt the lapse of hours!
    For what wears out the life of mortal men?
        'Tis that from change to change their being rolls;
    'Tis that repeated shocks, again, again,
        Exhaust the energy of strongest souls,
            And numb the elastic powers.
Till having used our nerves with bliss and teen,
    And tired upon a thousand schemes our wit,
    To the just-pausing Genius we remit
Our worn-out life, and are—what we have been.

Thou hast not lived, why should'st thou perish, so?
    Thou hadst *one* aim, *one* business, *one* desire;
        Else wert thou long since number'd with the dead!
    Else hadst thou spent, like other men, thy fire!
        The generations of thy peers are fled,
            And we ourselves shall go;
But thou possessest an immortal lot,
    And we imagine thee exempt from age,
    And living as thou liv'st on Glanvil's page,
Because thou hadst—what we, alas! have not.

For early didst thou leave the world, with powers
    Fresh, undiverted to the world without,
        Firm to their mark, not spent on other things;
    Free from the sick fatigue, the languid doubt,

Which much to have tried, in much been baffled,
      brings.
    O life unlike to ours!
Who fluctuate idly without term or scope,
    Of whom each strives, nor knows for what he
      strives,
    And each half lives a hundred different lives;
Who wait like thee, but not, like thee, in hope.

Thou waitest for the spark from heaven! and we,
  Light half-believers of our casual creeds,
    Who never deeply felt, nor clearly will'd,
  Whose insight never has borne fruit in deeds,
    Whose vague resolves never have been fulfill'd;
      For whom each year we see
    Breeds new beginnings, disappointments new;
    Who hesitate and falter life away,
    And lose to-morrow the ground won to-day—
Ah! do not we, wanderer! await it too?

Yes, we await it!—but it still delays,
  And then we suffer! and amongst us one,
    Who most has suffer'd, takes dejectedly
His seat upon the intellectual throne;
  And all his store of sad experience he
      Lays bare of wretched days;
    Tells us his misery's birth and growth and signs,
    And how the dying spark of hope was fed,
    And how the breast was soothed, and how the head,
And all his hourly varied anodynes.

This for our wisest! and we others pine,
  And wish the long unhappy dream would end,
    And waive all claim to bliss, and try to bear;
  With close-lipp'd patience for our only friend,
    Sad patience, too near neighbour to despair—
      But none has hope like thine!

Thou through the fields and through the woods dost
    stray,
    Roaming the country-side, a truant boy,
    Nursing thy project in unclouded joy,
And every doubt long blown by time away.

O born in days when wits were fresh and clear,
    And life ran gaily as the sparkling Thames;
      Before this strange disease of modern life,
    With its sick hurry, its divided aims,
      Its heads o'ertax'd, its palsied hearts, was rife—
        Fly hence, our contact fear!
Still fly, plunge deeper in the bowering wood!
    Averse, as Dido did with gesture stern
    From her false friend's approach in Hades turn,
Wave us away, and keep thy solitude!

Still nursing the unconquerable hope,
    Still clutching the inviolable shade,
      With a free, onward impulse brushing through,
    By night, the silver'd branches of the glade—
      Far on the forest-skirts, where none pursue,
        On some mild pastoral slope
Emerge, and resting on the moonlit pales
    Freshen thy flowers as in former years
    With dew, or listen with enchanted ears,
From the dark dingles, to the nightingales!

But fly our paths, our feverish contact fly!
    For strong the infection of our mental strife,
      Which, though it gives no bliss, yet spoils for rest;
    And we should win thee from thy own fair life,
      Like us distracted, and like us unblest.
        Soon, soon thy cheer would die,
Thy hopes grow timorous, and unfix'd thy powers,
    And thy clear aims be cross and shifting made;

And then thy glad perennial youth would fade,
Fade, and grow old at last, and die like ours.

Then fly our greetings, fly our speech and smiles!
—As some grave Tyrian trader, from the sea,
Descried at sunrise an emerging prow
Lifting the cool-hair'd creepers stealthily,
The fringes of a southward-facing brow
Among the Ægean isles;
And saw the merry Grecian coaster come,
Freighted with amber grapes, and Chian wine,
Green, bursting figs, and tunnies steep'd in brine—
And knew the intruders on his ancient home,

The young light-hearted masters of the waves—
And snatch'd his rudder, and shook out more sail,
And day and night held on indignantly
O'er the blue Midland waters with the gale,
Betwixt the Syrtes and soft Sicily,
To where the Atlantic raves
Outside the western straits; and unbent sails
There, where down cloudy cliffs, through sheets of
foam,
Shy traffickers, the dark Iberians come;
And on the beach undid his corded bales.

Rugby Chapel

November, 1857

Coldly, sadly descends
The autumn-evening. The field
Strewn with its dank yellow drifts
Of wither'd leaves, and the elms,

Fade into dimness apace,
Silent;—hardly a shout
From a few boys late at their play!
The lights come out in the street,
In the school-room windows;—but cold,
Solemn, unlighted, austere,
Through the gathering darkness, arise
The chapel-walls, in whose bound
Thou, my father! art laid.

There thou dost lie, in the gloom
Of the autumn evening. But ah!
That word, *gloom*, to my mind
Brings thee back in the light
Of thy radiant vigour, again;
In the gloom of November we pass'd
Days not dark at thy side;
Seasons impair'd not the ray
Of thy buoyant cheerfulness clear.
Such thou wast! and I stand
In the autumn evening, and think
Of bygone autumns with thee.

Fifteen years have gone round
Since thou arosest to tread,
In the summer-morning, the road
Of death, at a call unforeseen,
Sudden. For fifteen years,
We who till then in thy shade
Rested as under the boughs
Of a mighty oak, have endured
Sunshine and rain as we might,
Bare, unshaded, alone,
Lacking the shelter of thee.

O strong soul, by what shore
Tarriest thou now? For that force,

Surely, has not been left vain!
Somewhere, surely, afar,
In the sounding labour-house vast
Of being, is practised that strength,
Zealous, beneficent, firm!

Yes, in some far-shining sphere,
Conscious or not of the past,
Still thou performest the word
Of the Spirit in whom thou dost live—
Prompt, unwearied, as here!
Still thou upraisest with zeal
The humble good from the ground,
Sternly repressest the bad!
Still, like a trumpet, dost rouse
Those who with half-open eyes
Tread the border-land dim
'Twixt vice and virtue; reviv'st,
Succourest!—this was thy work,
This was thy life upon earth.

What is the course of the life
Of mortal men on the earth?—
Most men eddy about
Here and there—eat and drink,
Chatter and love and hate,
Gather and squander, are raised
Aloft, are hurl'd in the dust,
Striving blindly, achieving
Nothing; and then they die—
Perish;—and no one asks
Who or what they have been,
More than he asks what waves,
In the moonlit solitudes mild
Of the midmost Ocean, have swell'd,
Foam'd for a moment, and gone.

And there are some, whom a thirst
Ardent, unquenchable, fires,
Not with the crowd to be spent,
Not without aim to go round
In an eddy of purposeless dust,
Effort unmeaning and vain.
Ah yes! some of us strive
Not without action to die
Fruitless, but something to snatch
From dull oblivion, nor all
Glut the devouring grave!
We, we have chosen our path—
Path to a clear-purposed goal,
Path of advance!—but it leads
A long, steep journey, through sunk
Gorges, o'er mountains in snow.
Cheerful, with friends, we set forth—
Then, on the height, comes the storm.
Thunder crashes from rock
To rock, the cataracts reply,
Lightnings dazzle our eyes.
Roaring torrents have breach'd
The track, the stream-bed descends
In the place where the wayfarer once
Planted his footstep—the spray
Boils o'er its borders! aloft
The unseen snow-beds dislodge
Their hanging ruin; alas,
Havoc is made in our train!
Friends, who set forth at our side,
We, we only are left!
With frowning foreheads, with lips
Sternly compress'd, we strain on,
Falter, are lost in the storm.
On—and at nightfall at last

Come to the end of our way,
To the lonely inn 'mid the rocks;
Where the gaunt and taciturn host
Stands on the threshold, the wind
Shaking his thin white hairs—
Holds his lantern to scan
Our storm-beat figures, and asks:
Whom in our party we bring?
Whom we have left in the snow?

Sadly we answer: We bring
Only ourselves! we lost
Sight of the rest in the storm.
Hardly ourselves we fought through,
Stripp'd, without friends, as we are.
Friends, companions, and train,
The avalanche swept from our side.

But thou would'st not *alone*
Be saved, my father! *alone*
Conquer and come to thy goal,
Leaving the rest in the wild.
We were weary, and we
Fearful, and we in our march
Fain to drop down and to die.
Still thou turnedst, and still
Beckonedst the trembler, and still
Gavest the weary thy hand.

If, in the paths of the world,
Stones might have wounded thy feet,
Toil or dejection have tried
Thy spirit, of that we saw
Nothing—to us thou wast still
Cheerful, and helpful, and firm!
Therefore to thee it was given

Many to save with thyself;
And, at the end of thy day,
O faithful shepherd! to come,
Bringing thy sheep in thy hand.

And through thee I believe
In the noble and great who are gone;
Pure souls honour'd and blest
By former ages, who else—
Such, so soulless, so poor,
Is the race of men whom I see—
Seem'd but a dream of the heart,
Seem'd but a cry of desire.
Yes! I believe that there lived
Others like thee in the past,
Not like the men of the crowd
Who all round me to-day
Bluster or cringe, and make life
Hideous, and arid, and vile;
But souls temper'd with fire,
Fervent, heroic, and good,
Helpers and friends of mankind.

Servants of God!—or sons
Shall I not call you? because
Not as servants ye knew
Your Father's innermost mind,
His, who unwillingly sees
One of his little ones lost—
Yours is the praise, if mankind
Hath not as yet in its march
Fainted, and fallen, and died!

See! In the rocks of the world
Marches the host of mankind,
A feeble, wavering line.

Where are they tending?—A God
Marshall'd them, gave them their goal.
Ah, but the way is so long!
Years they have been in the wild!
Sore thirst plagues them, the rocks,
Rising all round, overawe;
Factions divide them; their host
Threatens to break, to dissolve.
Ah, keep, keep them combined!
Else, of the myriads who fill
That army, not one shall arrive;
Sole they shall stray; in the rocks
Labour for ever in vain,
Die one by one in the waste.

Then, in such hour of need
Of your fainting, dispirited race,
Ye, like angels, appear,
Radiant with ardour divine!
Beacons of hope, ye appear!
Languor is not in your heart,
Weakness is not in your word,
Weariness not on your brow.
Ye alight in our van! at your voice,
Panic, despair, flee away.
Ye move through the ranks, recall
The stragglers, refresh the outworn,
Praise, re-inspire the brave!
Order, courage, return.
Eyes rekindling, and prayers,
Follow your steps as ye go.
Ye fill up the gaps in our files,
Strengthen the wavering line,
Stablish, continue our march,

On, to the bound of the waste,
On, to the City of God.

Stanzas from the Grande Chartreuse

Through Alpine meadows soft-suffused
With rain, where thick the crocus blows,
Past the dark forges long disused,
The mule-track from Saint Laurent goes.
The bridge is cross'd, and slow we ride,
Through forest, up the mountain-side.

The autumnal evening darkens round,
The wind is up, and drives the rain;
While, hark! far down, with strangled sound
Doth the Dead Guier's stream complain,
Where that wet smoke, among the woods,
Over his boiling cauldron broods.

Swift rush the spectral vapours white
Past limestone scars with ragged pines,
Showing—then blotting from our sight!—
Halt—through the cloud-drift something shines!
High in the valley, wet and drear,
The huts of Courrerie appear.

Strike leftward! cries our guide; and higher
Mounts up the stony forest-way.
At last the encircling trees retire;
Look! through the showery twilight grey
What pointed roofs are these advance?—
A palace of the Kings of France?

Approach, for what we seek is here!
Alight, and sparely sup, and wait
For rest in this outbuilding near;
Then cross the sward and reach that gate.
Knock; pass the wicket! Thou art come
To the Carthusians' world-famed home.

The silent courts, where night and day
Into their stone-carved basins cold
The splashing icy fountains play—
The humid corridors behold!
Where, ghostlike in the deepening night,
Cowl'd forms brush by in gleaming white.

The chapel, where no organ's peal
Invests the stern and naked prayer—
With penitential cries they kneel
And wrestle; rising then, with bare
And white uplifted faces stand,
Passing the Host from hand to hand;

Each takes, and then his visage wan
Is buried in his cowl once more.
The cells!—the suffering Son of Man
Upon the wall—the knee-worn floor—
And where they sleep, that wooden bed,
Which shall their coffin be, when dead!

The library, where tract and tome
Not to feed priestly pride are there,
To hymn the conquering march of Rome,
Nor yet to amuse, as ours are!
They paint of souls the inner strife,
Their drops of blood, their death in life.

The garden, overgrown—yet mild,
See, fragrant herbs are flowering there!

Strong children of the Alpine wild
Whose culture is the brethren's care;
Of human tasks their only one,
And cheerful works beneath the sun.

Those halls, too, destined to contain
Each its own pilgrim-host of old,
From England, Germany, or Spain—
All are before me! I behold
The House, the Brotherhood austere!
—And what am I, that I am here?

For rigorous teachers seized my youth,
And purged its faith, and trimm'd its fire,
Show'd me the high, white star of Truth,
There bade me gaze, and there aspire.
Even now their whispers pierce the gloom:
What dost thou in this living tomb?

Forgive me, masters of the mind!
At whose behest I long ago
So much unlearnt, so much resign'd—
I come not here to be your foe!
I seek these anchorites, not in ruth,
To curse and to deny your truth;

Not as their friend, or child, I speak!
But as, on some far northern strand,
Thinking of his own Gods, a Greek
In pity and mournful awe might stand
Before some fallen Runic stone—
For both were faiths, and both are gone.

Wandering between two worlds, one dead,
The other powerless to be born,
With nowhere yet to rest my head,
Like these, on earth I wait forlorn.

Their faith, my tears, the world deride—
I come to shed them at their side.
Oh, hide me in your gloom profound,
Ye solemn seats of holy pain!
Take me, cowl'd forms, and fence me round,
Till I possess my soul again;
Till free my thoughts before me roll,
Not chafed by hourly false control!

For the world cries your faith is now
But a dead time's exploded dream;
My melancholy, sciolists say,
Is a pass'd mode, an outworn theme—
As if the world had ever had
A faith, or sciolists been sad!

Ah, if it *be* pass'd, take away,
At least, the restlessness, the pain;
Be man henceforth no more a prey
To these out-dated stings again!
The nobleness of grief is gone—
Ah, leave us not the fret alone!

But—if you cannot give us ease
Last of the race of them who grieve
Here leave us to die out with these
Last of the people who believe!
Silent, while years engrave the brow;
Silent—the best are silent now.

Achilles ponders in his tent,
The kings of modern thought are dumb;
Silent they are, though not content,
And wait to see the future come.
They have the grief men had of yore,
But they contend and cry no more.

Our fathers water'd with their tears
This sea of time whereon we sail,
Their voices were in all men's ears
Who pass'd within their puissant hail.
Still the same ocean round us raves,
But we stand mute, and watch the waves.

For what avail'd it, all the noise
And outcry of the former men?—
Say, have their sons achieved more joys,
Say, is life lighter now than then?
The sufferers died, they left their pain—
The pangs which tortured them remain.

What helps it now, that Byron bore,
With haughty scorn which mock'd the smart,
Through Europe to the Ætolian shore
The pageant of his bleeding heart?
That thousands counted every groan,
And Europe made his woe her own?

What boots it, Shelley! that the breeze
Carried thy lovely wail away,
Musical through Italian trees
Which fringe thy soft blue Spezzian bay?
Inheritors of thy distress
Have restless hearts one throb the less?

Or are we easier, to have read,
O Obermann! the sad. stern page,
Which tells us how thou hidd'st thy head
From the fierce tempest of thine age
In the lone brakes of Fontainebleau,
Or chalets near the Alpine snow?

Ye slumber in your silent grave!—
The world, which for an idle day

Grace to your mood of sadness gave,
Long since hath flung her weeds away.
The eternal trifler breaks your spell;
But we—we learnt your lore too well!

Years hence, perhaps, may dawn an age,
More fortunate, alas! than we,
Which without hardness will be sage,
And gay without frivolity.
Sons of the world, oh, speed those years;
But, while we wait, allow our tears!

Allow them! We admire with awe
The exulting thunder of your race;
You give the universe your law,
You triumph over time and space!
Your pride of life, your tireless powers,
We laud them, but they are not ours.

We are like children rear'd in shade
Beneath some old-world abbey wall,
Forgotten in a forest-glade,
And secret from the eyes of all.
Deep, deep the greenwood round them waves,
Their abbey, and its close of graves!

But, where the road runs near the stream,
Oft through the trees they catch a glance
Of passing troops in the sun's beam—
Pennon, and plume, and flashing lance!
Forth to the world those soldiers fare,
To life, to cities, and to war!

And through the wood, another way,
Faint bugle-notes from far are borne,
Where hunters gather, staghounds bay,
Round some fair forest-lodge at morn.

Gay dames are there, in sylvan green;
Laughter and cries—those notes between!
The banners flashing through the trees
Make their blood dance and chain their eyes
That bugle-music on the breeze
Arrests them with a charm'd surprise.
Banner by turns and bugle woo:
Ye shy recluses, follow too!

O children, what do ye reply?—
"Action and pleasure, will ye roam
Through these secluded dells to cry
And call us?—but too late ye come!
Too late for us your call ye blow,
Whose bent was taken long ago.

"Long since we pace this shadow'd nave,
We watch those yellow tapers shine,
Emblems of hope over the grave,
In the high altar's depth divine;
The organ carries to our ear
Its accents of another sphere.

"Fenced early in this cloistral round
Of reverie, of shade, of prayer,
How should we grow in other ground?
How can we flower in foreign air?
—Pass, banners, pass, and bugles, cease;
And leave our desert to its peace!"

Obermann Once More

"Savez-vous quelque bien qui console du regret d'un monde?"
                                        —*Obermann*

Glion?—Ah, twenty years, it cuts
All meaning from a name!
White houses prank where once were huts.
Glion, but not the same!

And yet I know not! All unchanged
The turf, the pines, the sky!
The hills in their old order ranged;
The lake, with Chillon by!

And 'neath those chestnut-trees, where stiff
And stony mounts the way,
Their crackling husk-heaps burn, as if
I left them yesterday!

Across the valley, on that slope,
The huts of Avant shine!
Its pines, under their branches, ope
Ways for the pasturing kine.

Full-foaming milk-pails, Alpine fare,
Sweet heaps of fresh-cut grass,
Invite to rest the traveller there
Before he climb the pass—

The gentian-flower'd pass, its crown
With yellow spires aflame;
Whence drops the path to Allière down,
And walls where Byron came,

By their green river, who doth change
His birth-name just below;
Orchard, and croft, and full-stored grange
Nursed by his pastoral flow.

But stop!—to fetch back thoughts that stray
Beyond this gracious bound,
The cone of Jaman, pale and grey,
See, in the blue profound!

Ah, Jaman! delicately tall
Above his sun-warm'd firs—
What thoughts to me his rocks recall,
What memories he stirs!

And who but thou must be, in truth,
Obermann! with me here?
Thou master of my wandering youth,
But left this many a year!

Yes, I forget the world's work wrought,
Its warfare waged with pain;
An eremite with thee, in thought
Once more I slip my chain,

And to thy mountain-chalet come,
And lie beside its door,
And hear the wild bee's Alpine hum,
And thy sad, tranquil lore!

Again I feel its words inspire
Their mournful calm; serene,
Yet tinged with infinite desire
For all that *might* have been—

The harmony from which man swerved
Made his life's rule once more!

The universal order served,
Earth happier than before!

—While thus I mused, night gently ran
Down over hill and wood.
Then, still and sudden, Obermann
On the grass near me stood.

Those pensive features well I knew,
On my mind, years before,
Imaged so oft! imaged so true!
—A shepherd's garb he wore,

A mountain-flower was in his hand,
A book was in his breast.
Bent on my face, with gaze that scann'd
My soul, his eyes did rest.

"And is it thou," he cried, "so long
Held by the world which we
Loved not, who turnest from the throng
Back to thy youth and me?

"And from thy world, with heart opprest,
Choosest thou *now* to turn?—
Ah me! we anchorites read things best!
Clearest their course discern!

"Thou fled'st me when the ungenial earth,
Man's work-place, lay in gloom.
Return'st thou in her hour of birth,
Of hopes and hearts in bloom?

"Perceiv'st thou not the change of day?
Ah! Carry back thy ken,
What, some two thousand years! Survey
The world as it was then!

"Like ours it look'd in outward air.
Its head was clear and true,
Sumptuous its clothing, rich its fare,
No pause its action knew;

"Stout was its arm, each thew and bone
Seem'd puissant and alive—
But, ah! its heart, its heart was stone,
And so it could not thrive!

"On that hard Pagan world disgust
And secret loathing fell.
Deep weariness and sated lust
Made human life a hell.

"In his cool hall, with haggard eyes,
The Roman noble lay;
He drove abroad, in furious guise,
Along the Appian way.

"He made a feast, drank fierce and fast,
And crown'd his hair with flowers—
No easier nor no quicker pass'd
The impracticable hours.

"The brooding East with awe beheld
Her impious younger world.
The Roman tempest swell'd and swell'd,
And on her head was hurl'd.

"The East bow'd low before the blast
In patient, deep disdain;
She let the legions thunder past,
And plunged in thought again.

"So well she mused, a morning broke
Across her spirit grey;
A conquering, new-born joy awoke,
And fill'd her life with day.

" 'Poor world,' she cried, 'so deep accurst,
That runn'st from pole to pole
To seek a draught to slake thy thirst—
Go, seek it in thy soul!'

"She heard it, the victorious West,
In crown and sword array'd!
She felt the void which mined her breast,
She shiver'd and obey'd.

"She veil'd her eagles, snapp'd her sword,
And laid her sceptre down;
Her stately purple she abhorr'd,
And her imperial crown.

"She broke her flutes, she stopp'd her sports,
Her artists could not please;
She tore her books, she shut her courts,
She fled her palaces;

"Lust of the eye and pride of life
She left it all behind,
And hurried, torn with inward strife,
The wilderness to find.

"Tears wash'd the trouble from her face!
She changed into a child!
'Mid weeds and wrecks she stood—a place
Of ruin—but she smiled!

"Oh, had I lived in that great day,
How had its glory new
Fill'd earth and heaven, and caught away
My ravish'd spirit too!

"No thoughts that to the world belong
Had stood against the wave

Of love which set so deep and strong
From Christ's then open grave.

"No cloister-floor of humid stone
Had been too cold for me.
For me no Eastern desert lone
Had been too far to flee.

"No lonely life had pass'd too slow
When I could hourly scan
Upon his Cross, with head sunk low,
That nail'd, thorn-crowned Man!

"Could see the Mother with the Child
Whose tender winning arts
Have to his little arms beguiled
So many wounded hearts!

"And centuries came and ran their course,
And unspent all that time
Still, still went forth that Child's dear force,
And still was at its prime.

"Ay, ages long endured his span
Of life—'tis true received—
That gracious Child, that thorn-crown'd Man!
—He lived while we believed.

"While we believed, on earth he went,
And open stood his grave.
Men call'd from chamber, church, and tent;
And Christ was by to save.

"Now he is dead! Far hence he lies
In the lorn Syrian town;
And on his grave, with shining eyes,
The Syrian stars look down.

"In vain men still, with hoping new,
Regard his death-place dumb.
And say the stone is not yet to,
And wait for words to come.

"Ah, o'er that silent sacred land,
Of sun, and arid stone,
And crumbling wall, and sultry sand,
Sounds now one word alone!

"Unduped of fancy, henceforth man
Must labour!—must resign
His all too human creeds, and scan
Simply the way divine!

"But slow that tide of common thought,
Which bathed our life, retired;
Slow, slow the old world wore to nought,
And pulse by pulse expired.

"Its frame yet stood without a breach
When blood and warmth were fled;
And still it spake its wonted speech—
But every word was dead.

"And oh, we cried, that on this corse
Might fall a freshening storm!
Rive its dry bones, and with new force
A new-sprung world inform!

"—Down came the storm! O'er France it pass'd
In sheets of scathing fire;
All Europe felt that fiery blast,
And shook as it rush'd by her.

"Down came the storm! In ruins fell
The worn-out world we knew.
It pass'd, that elemental swell!
Again appear'd the blue;

"The sun shone in the new-wash'd sky,
And what from heaven saw he?
Blocks of the past, like icebergs high,
Float on a rolling sea!

"Upon them plies the race of man
All it before endeavour'd;
'Ye live,' I cried, 'ye work and plan,
And know not ye are sever'd!

" 'Poor fragments of a broken world
Whereon men pitch their tent!
Why were ye too to death not hurl'd
When your world's day was spent?

" 'That glow of central fire is done
Which with its fusing flame
Knit all your parts, and kept you one—
But ye, ye are the same!

" 'The past, its mask of union on,
Had ceased to live and thrive.
The past, its mask of union gone,
Say, is it more alive?

" 'Your creeds are dead, your rites are dead,
Your social order too!
Where tarries he, the Power who said:
See, I make all things new?

" 'The millions suffer still, and grieve,
And what can helpers heal
With old-world cures men half believe
For woes they wholly feel?

" 'And yet they have such need of joy!
And joy whose grounds are true;

And joy that should all hearts employ
As when the past was new!

"'Ah, not the emotion of that past,
Its common hope, were vain!
Some new such hope must dawn at last,
Or man must toss in pain.

"But now the old is out of date,
The new is not yet born,
And who can be *alone* elate,
While the world lies forlorn?"

"Then to the wilderness I fled.
There among Alpine snows
And pastoral huts I hid my head,
And sought and found repose.

"It was not yet the appointed hour.
Sad, patient, and resign'd,
I watch'd the crocus fade and flower,
I felt the sun and wind.

"The day I lived in was not mine,
Man gets no second day.
In dreams I saw the future shine—
But ah! I could not stay!

"Action I had not, followers, fame;
I pass'd obscure, alone.
The after-world forgets my name,
Nor do I wish it known.

"Composed to bear, I lived and died,
And knew my life was vain,
With fate I murmur not, nor chide,
At Sèvres by the Seine

"(If Paris that brief flight allow)
My humble tomb explore!
It bears: *Eternity, be thou
My refuge!* and no more.

"But thou, whom fellowship of mood
Did make from haunts of strife
Come to my mountain-solitude
And learn my frustrate life;

"O thou, who, ere thy flying span
Was past of cheerful youth,
Didst seek the solitary man
And love his cheerless truth—

"Despair not thou as I despair'd,
Nor be cold gloom thy prison!
Forward the gracious hours have fared,
And see! the sun is risen!

"He breaks the winter of the past;
A green, new earth appears.
Millions, whose life in ice lay fast,
Have thoughts, and smiles, and tears.

"What though there still need effort, strife?
Though much be still unwon?
Yet warm it mounts, the hour of life!
Death's frozen hour is done.'

"The world's great order dawns in sheen,
After long darkness rude,
Divinelier imaged, clearer seen,
With happier zeal pursued.

"With hope extinct and brow composed
I mark'd the present die;

Its term of life was nearly closed,
Yet it had more than I.

"But thou, though to the world's new hour
Thou come with aspect marr'd,
Shorn of the joy, the bloom, the power,
Which best beseem its bard—

"Though more than half thy years be past,
And spent thy youthful prime;
Though, round thy firmer manhood cast,
Hang weeds of our sad time

"Whereof thy youth felt all the spell,
And traversed all the shade—
Though late, though dimm'd, though weak, yet tell
Hope to a world new-made!

"Help it to reach that deep desire,
The want which rack'd our brain,
Consumed our heart with thirst like fire,
Immedicable pain;

"Which to the wilderness drove out
Our life, to Alpine snow,
And palsied all our deed with doubt,
And all our work with woe—

"What still of strength is left, employ,
That end to help attain:
One common wave of thought and joy
Lifting mankind again!"

The vision ended; I awoke
As out of sleep, and no
Voice moved;—only the torrent broke
The silence, far below.

Soft darkness on the turf did lie.
Solemn, o'er hut and wood,

In the yet star-sown nightly sky,
The peak of Jaman stood.

Still in my soul the voice I heard
Of Obermann!—away
I turned; by some vague impulse stirr'd,
Along the rocks of Naye

Past Sonchaud's piny flanks I gaze
And the blanch'd summit bare
Of Malatrait, to where in haze
The Valais opens fair,

And the domed Velan with his snows,
Behind the upcrowding hills,
Doth all the heavenly opening close
Which the Rhone's murmur fills;—

And glorious there, without a sound,
Across the glimmering lake,
High in the Valais-depth profound,
I saw the morning break.

Poor Matthias

Poor Matthias!—Found him lying
Fall'n beneath his perch and dying?
Found him stiff, you say, though warm—
All convulsed his little form?
Poor canary! many a year
Well he knew his mistress dear;
Now in vain you call his name,
Vainly raise his rigid frame,
Vainly warm him in your breast,
Vainly kiss his golden crest,

Smooth his ruffled plumage fine,
Touch his trembling beak with wine.
One more gasp—it is the end!
Dead and mute our tiny friend!
—Songster thou of many a year,
Now thy mistress brings thee here,
Says, it fits that I rehearse,
Tribute due to thee, a verse,
Meed for daily song of yore
Silent now for evermore.

Poor Matthias! Wouldst thou have
More than pity? claims't a stave?
—Friends more near us than a bird
We dismiss'd without a word.
Rover, with the good brown head,
Great Atossa, they are dead;
Dead, and neither prose nor rhyme
Tells the praises of their prime.
Thou didst know them old and grey,
Know them in their sad decay.
Thou hast seen Atossa sage
Sit for hours beside thy cage;
Thou wouldst chirp, thou foolish bird,
Flutter, chirp—she never stirr'd!
What were now these toys to her?
Down she sank amid her fur;
Eyed thee with a soul resign'd—
And thou deemedst cats were kind!
—Cruel, but composed and bland,
Dumb, inscrutable and grand,
So Tiberius might have sat,
Had Tiberius been a cat.

Rover died—Atossa too.
Less than they to us are you!

Nearer human were their powers,
Closer knit their life with ours.
Hands had stroked them, which are cold,
Now for years, in churchyard mould;
Comrades of our past were they,
Of that unreturning day.
Changed and aging, they and we
Dwelt, it seem'd, in sympathy.
Alway from their presence broke
Somewhat which remembrance woke
Of the loved, the lost, the young—
Yet they died, and died unsung.

Geist came next, our little friend;
Geist had verse to mourn his end.
Yes, but that enforcement strong
Which compell'd for Geist a song—
All that gay courageous cheer,
All that human pathos dear;
Soul-fed eyes with suffering worn,
Pain heroically borne,
Faithful love in depth divine—
Poor Matthias, were they thine?

Max and Kaiser we to-day
Greet upon the lawn at play;
Max a dachshound without blot—
Kaiser should be, but is not.
Max, with shining yellow coat,
Prinking ears and dewlap throat—
Kaiser, with his collie face,
Penitent for want of race.
—Which may be the first to die,
Vain to augur, they or I?
But, as age comes on, I know,
Poet's fire gets faint and low;

If so be that travel they
First the inevitable way,
Much I doubt if they shall have
Dirge from me to crown their grave.

    Yet, poor bird, thy tiny corse
Moves me, somehow, to remorse;
Something haunts my conscience, brings
Sad, compunctious visitings.
Other favourites, dwelling here,
Open lived to us, and near;
Well we knew when they were glad,
Plain we saw if they were sad,
Joy'd with them when they were gay,
Soothed them in their last decay;
Sympathy could feel and show
Both in weal of theirs and woe.

    Birds, companions more unknown,
Live beside us, but alone;
Finding not, do all they can,
Passage from their souls to man.
Kindness we bestow, and praise,
Laud their plumage, greet their lays;
Still, beneath their feather'd breast,
Stirs a history unexpress'd.
Wishes there, and feelings strong,
Incommunicably throng;
What they want, we cannot guess,
Fail to track their deep distress—
Dull look on when death is nigh,
Note no change, and let them die.
Poor Matthias! couldst thou speak,
What a tale of thy last week!
Every morning did we pay
Stupid salutations gay,

Suited well to health, but how
Mocking, how incongruous now!
Cake we offer'd, sugar, seed,
Never doubtful of thy need;
Praised, perhaps, thy courteous eye,
Praised thy golden livery.
Gravely thou the while, poor dear!
Sat'st upon thy perch to hear,
Fixing with a mute regard
Us, thy human keepers hard,
Troubling, with our chatter vain,
Ebb of life, and mortal pain—
Us, unable to divine
Our companion's dying sign,
Or o'erpass the severing sea
Set betwixt ourselves and thee,
Till the sand thy feathers smirch
Fallen dying off thy perch!

Was it, as the Grecian sings,
Birds were born the first of things,
Before the sun, before the wind,
Before the gods, before mankind,
Airy, ante-mundane throng—
Witness their unworldly song!
Proof they give, too, primal powers,
Of a prescience more than ours—
Teach us, while they come and go,
When to sail, and when to sow.
Cuckoo calling from the hill,
Swallow skimming by the mill,
Swallows trooping in the sedge,
Starlings swirling from the hedge,
Mark the seasons, map our year,
As they show and disappear.

But, with all this travail sage
Brought from that anterior age,
Goes an unreversed decree
Whereby strange are they and we;
Making want of theirs, and plan,
Indiscernible by man.

No, away with tales like these
Stol'n from Aristophanes!
Does it, if we miss your mind,
Prove us so remote in kind?
Birds! we but repeat on you
What amongst ourselves we do.
Somewhat more or somewhat less,
'Tis the same unskilfulness.
What you feel, escapes our ken—
Know we more our fellow men?
Human suffering at our side,
Ah, like yours is undescried!
Human longings, human fears,
Miss our eyes and miss our ears.
Little helping, wounding much,
Dull of heart, and hard of touch,
Brother man's despairing sign
Who may trust us to divine?
Who assure us, sundering powers
Stand not 'twixt his soul and ours?

Poor Matthias! See, thy end
What a lesson doth it lend!
For that lesson thou shalt have,
Dead canary bird, a stave!
Telling how, one stormy day,
Stress of gale and showers of spray
Drove my daughter small and me
Inland from the rocks and sea.

Driv'n inshore, we follow down
Ancient streets of Hastings town—
Slowly thread them—when behold,
French canary-merchant old
Shepherding his flock of gold
In a low dim-lighted pen
Scann'd of tramps and fishermen!
There a bird, high-coloured, fat,
Proud of port, though something squat—
Pursy, play'd-out Philistine—
Dazzled Nelly's youthful eyne.
But, far in, obscure, there stirr'd
On his perch a sprightlier bird,
Courteous-eyed, erect and slim;
And I whisper'd: "Fix on *him!*"
Home we brought him, young and fair,
Songs to trill in Surrey air.
Here Matthias sang his fill,
Saw the cedars of Pains Hill;
Here he pour'd his little soul,
Heard the murmur of the Mole.
Eight in number now the years
He hath pleased our eyes and ears;
Other favourites he hath known
Go, and now himself is gone.
—Fare thee well, companion dear!
Fare for ever well, nor fear,
Tiny though thou art, to stray
Down the uncompanion'd way!
We without thee, little friend,
Many years have not to spend;
What are left, will hardly be
Better than we spent with thee.

Walt Whitman

(1819–1892)

Whoever you are holding me now in hand

Whoever you are holding me now in hand,
Without one thing all will be useless,
I give you fair warning before you attempt me further,
I am not what you supposed, but far different.

Who is he that would become my follower?
Who would sign himself a candidate for my affections?

The way is suspicious, the result uncertain, perhaps de-
   structive,
You would have to give up all else, I alone would expect
   to be your sole and exclusive standard,
Your novitiate would even then be long and exhausting,
The whole past theory of your life and all conformity to
   the lives around you would have to be abandon'd,
Therefore release me now before troubling yourself any
   further, let go your hand from my shoulders,
Put me down and depart on your way.

Or else by stealth in some wood for trial,
Or back of a rock in the open air,
(For in any roof'd room of a house I emerge not, nor in
   company,
And in libraries I lie as one dumb, a gawk, or unborn,
   or dead,)
But just possibly with you on a high hill, first watching

lest any person for miles around approach unawares,

Or possibly with you sailing at sea, or on the beach of
the sea or some quiet island,

Here to put your lips upon mine I permit you,

With the comrade's long-dwelling kiss or the new hus-
band's kiss,

For I am the new husband and I am the comrade.

Or if you will, thrusting me beneath your clothing,

Where I may feel the throbs of your heart or rest upon
your hip,

Carry me when you go forth over land or sea;

For thus merely touching you is enough, is best,

And thus touching you would I silently sleep and be
carried eternally.

But these leaves conning you con at peril,

For these leaves and me you will not understand,

They will elude you at first and still more afterward, I
will certainly elude you,

Even while you should think you had unquestionably
caught me, behold!

Already you see I have escaped from you.

For it is not for what I have put into it that I have writ-
ten this book,

Nor is it by reading it you will acquire it,

Nor do those know me best who admire me and vaunt-
ingly praise me,

Nor will the candidates for my love (unless at most a
very few) prove victorious,

Nor will my poems do good only, they will do just as
much evil, perhaps more,

For all is useless without that which you may guess at
many times and not hit, that which I hinted at;

Therefore release me and depart on your way.

Respondez!

Respondez! Respondez!
(The war is completed—the price is paid—the title is
   settled beyond recall;)
Let every one answer! let those who sleep be waked! let
   none evade!
Must we still go on with our affectations and sneak-
   ing?
Let me bring this to a close—I pronounce openly for a
   new distribution of roles;
Let that which stood in front go behind! and let that
   which was behind advance to the front and speak;
Let murderers, bigots, fools, unclean persons, offer new
   propositions!
Let the old propositions be postponed!
Let faces and theories be turn'd inside out! let meanings
   be freely criminal, as well as results!
Let there be no suggestion above the suggestion of
   drudgery!
Let none be pointed toward his destination! (Say! do
   you know your destination?)
Let men and women be mock'd with bodies and mock'd
   with Souls!
Let the love that waits in them, wait! let it die, or pass
   still-born to other spheres!
Let the sympathy that waits in every man, wait! or let
   it also pass, a dwarf, to other spheres!
Let contradictions prevail! let one thing contradict an-
   other! and let one line of my poems contradict an-
   other!

Let the people sprawl with yearning, aimless hands! let their tongues be broken! let their eyes be discouraged! let none descend into their hearts with the fresh lusciousness of love!

(Stifled, O days! O lands! in every public and private corruption!

Smother'd in thievery, impotence, shamelessness, mountain-high;

Brazen effrontery, scheming, rolling like ocean's waves around and upon you, O my days! my lands!

For not even those thunderstorms, nor fiercest lightnings of the war, have purified the atmosphere;)

—Let the theory of America still be management, caste, comparison! (Say! what other theory would you?)

Let them that distrust birth and death still lead the rest! (Say! why shall they not lead you?)

Let the crust of hell be neared and trod on! let the days be darker than the nights! let slumber bring less slumber than waking time brings!

Let the world never appear to him or her for whom it was all made!

Let the heart of the young man still exile itself from the heart of the old man! and let the heart of the old man be exiled from that of the young man!

Let the sun and moon go! let scenery take the applause of the audience! let there be apathy under the stars!

Let freedom prove no man's inalienable right! every one who can tyrannize, let him tyrannize to his satisfaction!

Let none but infidels be countenanced!

Let the eminence of meanness, treachery, sarcasm, hate, greed, indecency, impotence, lust, be taken for granted above all! let writers, judges, governments, households, religions, philosophies, take such for granted above all!

Let the worst men beget children out of the worst women!

Let the priest still play at immortality!

Let death be inaugurated!

Let nothing remain but the ashes of teachers, artists, moralists, lawyers, and learn'd and polite persons!

Let him who is without my poems be assassinated!

Let the cow, the horse, the camel, the garden-bee—let the mud-fish, the lobster, the mussel, eel, the sting-ray, and the grunting pig-fish—let these, and the like of these, be put on a perfect equality with man and woman!

Let churches accommodate serpents, vermin, and the corpses of those who have died of the most filthy diseases!

Let marriage slip down among fools, and be for none but fools!

Let men among themselves talk and think forever obscenely of women! and let women among themselves talk and think obscenely of men!

Let us all, without missing one, be exposed in public, naked, monthly, at the peril of our lives! let our bodies be freely handled and examined by whoever chooses!

Let nothing but copies at second hand be permitted to exist upon the earth!

Let the earth desert God, nor let there ever henceforth be mention'd the name of God!

Let there be no God!

Let there be money, business, imports, exports, custom, authority, precedents, pallor, dyspepsia, smut, ignorance, unbelief!

Let judges and criminals be transposed! let the prison-keepers be put in prison! let those that were prisoners take the keys! (Say! why might they not just as well be transposed?)

Let the slaves be masters! let the masters become slaves!

Let the reformers descend from the stands where they are forever bawling! let an idiot or insane person appear on each of the stands!

Let the Asiatic, the African, the European, the American, and the Australian, go armed against the murderous stealthiness of each other! let them sleep armed! let none believe in good will!

Let there be no unfashionable wisdom! let such be scorn'd and derided off from the earth!

Let a floating cloud in the sky—let a wave of the sea—let growing mint, spinach, onions, tomatoes—let these be exhibited as shows, at a great price for admission!

Let all the men of These States stand aside for a few smouchers! let the few seize on what they choose! let the rest, gawk, giggle, starve, obey!

Let shadows be furnish'd with genitals! let substances be deprived of their genitals!

Let there be wealthy and immense cities—but still through any of them, not a single poet, savior, knower, lover!

Let the infidels of These States laugh all faith away!

If one man be found who has faith, let the rest set upon him!

Let them affright faith! let them destroy the power of breeding faith!

Let the she-harlots and the he-harlots be prudent! let them dance on, while seeming lasts! (O seeming! seeming! seeming!)

Let the preachers recite creeds! let them still teach only what they have been taught!

Let insanity still have charge of sanity!

Let books take the place of trees, animals, rivers, clouds!

Let the daub'd portraits of heroes supersede heroes!

Let the manhood of man never take steps after itself!

Let it take steps after eunuchs, and after consumptive and genteel persons!

Let the white person again tread the black person under his heel! (Say! which is trodden under heel, after all?)

Let the reflections of the things of the world be studied in mirrors! let the things themselves still continue unstudied!

Let a man seek pleasure everywhere except in himself!

Let a woman seek happiness everywhere except in herself!

(What real happiness have you had one single hour through your whole life?)

Let the limited years of life do nothing for the limitless years of death! (What do you suppose death will do, then?)

Out of the cradle endlessly rocking

Out of the cradle endlessly rocking,

Out of the mocking-bird's throat, the musical shuttle,

Out of the Ninth-month midnight,

Over the sterile sands and the fields beyond, where the child leaving his bed wander'd alone, bareheaded, barefoot,

Down from the shower'd halo,

Up from the mystic play of shadows twining and twisting as if they were alive,

Out from the patches of briers and blackberries,

From the memories of the bird that chanted to me,

From your memories sad brother, from the fitful risings
    and fallings I heard,
From under that yellow half-moon late-risen and swol-
    len as if with tears,
From those beginning notes of yearning and love there
    in the mist,
From the thousand responses of my heart never to
    cease,
From the myriad thence-arous'd words,
From the word stronger and more delicious than any,
From such as now they start the scene revisiting,
As a flock, twittering, rising, or overhead passing,
Borne hither, ere all eludes me, hurriedly,
A man, yet by these tears a little boy again,
Throwing myself on the sand, confronting the waves,
I, chanter of pains and joys, uniter of here and here-
    after,
Taking all hints to use them, but swiftly leaping beyond
    them,
A reminiscence sing.

Once Paumanok,
When the lilac-scent was in the air and Fifth-month
    grass was growing,
Up this seashore in some briers,
Two feather'd guests from Alabama, two together,
And their nest, and four light-green eggs spotted with
    brown,
And every day the he-bird to and fro near at hand,
And every day the she-bird crouch'd on her nest, silent,
    with bright eyes,
And every day I, a curious boy, never too close, never
    disturbing them,
Cautiously peering, absorbing, translating.

Shine! shine! shine!
Pour down your warmth, great sun!
While we bask, we two together,

Two together!
Winds blow south, or winds blow north,
Day come white, or night come black,
Home, or rivers and mountains from home,
Singing all time, minding no time,
While we two keep together.

Till of a sudden,
May-be kill'd, unknown to her mate,
One forenoon the she-bird crouch'd not on the nest,
Nor return'd that afternoon, nor the next,
Nor ever appear'd again.

And thenceforward all summer in the sound of the sea,
And at night under the full of the moon in calmer
    weather,
Over the hoarse surging of the sea,
Or flitting from brier to brier by day,
I saw, I heard at intervals the remaining one, the he-
    bird,
The solitary guest from Alabama.

Blow! blow! blow!
Blow up sea-winds along Paumanok's shore;
I wait and I wait till you blow my mate to me.

Yes, when the stars glisten'd,
All night long on the prong of a moss-scallop'd stake,
Down almost amid the slapping waves,
Sat the lone singer wonderful causing tears.

He call'd on his mate,
He pour'd forth the meanings which I of all men know.

Yes my brother I know,
The rest might not, but I have treasur'd every note,
For more than once dimly down to the beach gliding,
Silent, avoiding the moonbeams, blending myself with
    the shadows,
Recalling now the obscure shapes, the echoes, the
    sounds and sights after their sorts,
The white arms out in the breakers tirelessly tossing,
I, with bare feet, a child, the wind wafting my hair,
Listen'd long and long.

Listen'd to keep, to sing, now translating the notes,
Following you my brother.

Soothe! soothe! soothe!
Close on its wave soothes the wave behind,
And again another behind embracing and lapping,
    every one close,
But my love soothes not me, not me.

Low hangs the moon, it rose late,
It is lagging—O I think it is heavy with love, with love.

O madly the sea pushes upon the land,
With love, with love.

O night! do I not see my love fluttering out among the
    breakers?
What is that little black thing I see there in the white?

Loud! loud! loud!
Loud I call to you, my love!
High and clear I shoot my voice over the waves,
Surely you must know who is here, is here,
You must know who I am, my love.

Low-hanging moon!
What is that dusky spot in your brown yellow?

O it is the shape, the shape of my mate!
O moon do not keep her from me any longer.

Land! land! O land!
Whichever way I turn, O I think you could give me my
*   mate back again if you only would,*
For I am almost sure I see her dimly whichever way I
*   look.*

O rising stars!
Perhaps the one I want so much will rise, will rise with
*   some of you.*

O throat! O trembling throat!
Sound clearer through the atmosphere!
Pierce the woods, the earth,
Somewhere listening to catch you must be the one I
*   want.*

Shake out carols!
Solitary here, the night's carols!
Carols of lonesome love! death's carols!
Carols under that lagging, yellow, waning moon!
O under that moon where she droops almost down into
*   the sea!*
O reckless despairing carols.

But soft! sink low!
Soft! let me just murmur,
And do you wait a moment you husky-nois'd sea,
For somewhere I believe I heard my mate responding to
*   me,*
So faint, I must be still, be still to listen,
But not altogether still, for then she might not come
*   immediately to me.*

Hither my love!
Here I am! here!

With this just-sustain'd note I announce myself to you,
This gentle call is for you my love, for you.

Do not be decoy'd elsewhere,
That is the whistle of the wind, it is not my voice,
That is the fluttering, the fluttering of the spray,
Those are the shadows of leaves.

O darkness! O in vain!
O I am very sick and sorrowful.

O brown halo in the sky near the moon, drooping upon
　the sea!
O troubled reflection in the sea!
O throat! O throbbing heart!
And I singing uselessly, uselessly all the night.

O past! O happy life! O song of joy!
In the air, in the woods, over fields,
Loved! loved! loved! loved!
But my mate no more, no more with me!
We two together no more.

The aria sinking,
All else continuing, the stars shining,
The winds blowing, the notes of the birds continuous
　echoing,
With angry moans the fierce old mother incessantly
　moaning,
On the sands of Paumanok's shore gray and rustling,
The yellow half-moon enlarged, sagging down, droop-
　ing, the face of the sea almost touching,
The boy ecstatic, with his bare feet the waves, with his
　hair the atmosphere dallying,
The love in the heart long pent, now loose, now at last
　tumultuously bursting,

The aria's meaning, the ears, the soul, swiftly deposit-
     ing,
The strange tears down the cheeks coursing,
The colloquy there, the trio, each uttering,
The undertone, the savage old mother incessantly cry-
     ing,
To the boy's soul's questions sullenly timing, some
     drown'd secret hissing,
To the outsetting bard.

Demon or bird! (said the boy's soul,)
Is it indeed toward your mate you sing? or is it really
     to me?
For I, that was a child, my tongue's use sleeping, now
     I have heard you,
Now in a moment I know what I am for, I awake,
And already a thousand singers, a thousand songs,
     clearer, louder and more sorrowful than yours,
A thousand warbling echoes have started to life within
     me, never to die.

O you singer solitary, singing by yourself, projecting
     me,
O solitary me listening, never more shall I cease per-
     petuating you,
Never more shall I escape, never more the reverbera-
     tions,
Never more the cries of unsatisfied love be absent from
     me,
Never again leave me to be the peaceful child I was
     before what there in the night,
By the sea under the yellow and sagging moon,
The messenger there arous'd, the fire, the sweet hell
     within,
The unknown want, the destiny of me.

O give me the clew! (it lurks in the night here some-
where,)
O if I am to have so much, let me have more!

A word then, (for I will conquer it,)
The word final, superior to all,
Subtle, sent up—what is it?—I listen;
Are you whispering it, and have been all the time, you
sea waves?
Is that it from your liquid rims and wet sands?

Whereto answering, the sea,
Delaying not, hurrying not,
Whisper'd me through the night, and very plainly be-
fore daybreak,
Lisp'd to me the low and delicious word death,
And again death, death, death, death,
Hissing melodious, neither like the bird nor like my
arous'd child's heart,
But edging near as privately for me rustling at my feet,
Creeping thence steadily up to my ears and laving me
softly all over.
Death, death, death, death, death.

Which I do not forget,
But fuse the song of my dusky demon and brother,
That he sang to me in the moonlight on Paumanok's
gray beach,
With the thousand responsive songs at random,
My own songs awaked from that hour,
And with them the key, the word up from the waves,
The word of the sweetest song and and all songs,
That strong and delicious word which, creeping to my
feet,
(Or like some old crone rocking the cradle, swathed in
sweet garments, bending aside,)
The sea whisper'd me.

When I peruse the conquer'd fame

When I peruse the conquer'd fame of heroes and the
    victories of mighty generals, I do not envy the gen-
    erals,
Nor the President in his Presidency, nor the rich in his
    great house,
But when I hear of the brotherhood of lovers, how it
    was with them,
How together through life, through dangers, odium,
    unchanging, long and long,
Through youth and through middle and old age, how
    unfaltering, how affectionate and faithful they were,
Then I am pensive—I hastily walk away fill'd with the
    bitterest envy.

A sight in camp in the daybreak gray and dim

A sight in camp in the daybreak gray and dim,
As from my tent I emerge so early sleepless,
As slow I walk in the cool fresh air the path near by
    the hospital tent,
Three forms I see on stretchers lying, brought out there
    untended lying,
Over each the blanket spread, ample brownish woolen
    blanket,
Gray and heavy blanket, folding, covering all.

Curious I halt and silent stand,
Then with light fingers I from the face of the nearest
  the first just lift the blanket;
Who are you elderly man so gaunt and grim, with well-
  gray'd hair, and flesh all sunken about the eyes?
Who are you my dear comrade?

Then to the second I step—and who are you my child
  and darling?
Who are you sweet boy with cheeks yet blooming?

Then to the third—a face nor child nor old, very calm,
  as of beautiful yellow-white ivory;
Young man I think I know you—I think this face is the
  face of the Christ himself,
Dead and divine and brother of all, and here again he
  lies.

Dirge for Two Veterans

The last sunbeam
Lightly falls from the finish'd Sabbath,
On the pavement here, and there beyond it is looking,
  Down a new-made double grave.

Lo, the moon ascending,
Up from the east the silvery round moon,
Beautiful over the house-tops, ghastly, phantom moon,
  Immense and silent moon.

I see a sad procession,
And I hear the sound of coming full-key'd bugles,
All the channels of the city streets they're flooding,
  As with voices and with tears.

I hear the great drums pounding,
And the small drums steady whirring,
And every blow of the great convulsive drums,
	Strikes me through and through.

For the son is brought with the father,
(In the foremost ranks of the fierce assault they fell,
Two veterans son and father dropt together,
	And the double grave awaits them.)

Now nearer blow the bugles,
And the drums strike more convulsive,
And the daylight o'er the pavement quite has faded,
	And the strong dead-march enwraps me.

In the eastern sky up-buoying,
The sorrowful vast phantom moves illumin'd,
('Tis some mother's large transparent face,
	In heaven brighter growing.)

O strong dead-march you please me!
O moon immense with your silvery face you soothe me!
O my soldiers twain! O my veterans passing to burial!
	What I have I also give you.

The moon gives you light,
And the bugles and the drums give you music,
And my heart, O my soldiers, my veterans,
	My heart gives you love.

When lilacs last in the dooryard bloom'd

1

When lilacs last in the dooryard bloom'd,
And the great star early droop'd in the western sky in
	the night,

I mourn'd, and yet shall mourn with ever-returning
    spring.

Ever-returning spring, trinity sure to me you bring,
Lilac blooming perennial and drooping star in the west,
And thought of him I love.

2

O powerful western fallen star!
O shades of night—O moody, tearful night!
O great star disappear'd—O the black murk that hides
    the star!
O cruel hands that hold me powerless—O helpless soul
    of me!
O harsh surrounding cloud that will not free my soul.

3

In the dooryard fronting an old farm-house near the
    white-wash'd palings,
Stands the lilac-bush tall-growing with heart-shaped
    leaves of rich green,
With many a pointed blossom rising delicate, with the
    perfume strong I love,
With every leaf a miracle—and from this bush in the
    dooryard,
With delicate-color'd blossoms and heart-shaped leaves
    of rich green,
A sprig with its flower I break.

4

In the swamp in secluded recesses,
A shy and hidden bird is warbling a song.

Solitary the thrush,
The hermit withdrawn to himself, avoiding the settle-
    ments,
Sings by himself a song.

Song of the bleeding throat,
Death's outlet song of life, (for well dear brother I
    know,
If thou wast not granted to sing thou would'st surely
    die.)

5

Over the breast of the spring, the land, amid cities,
Amid lanes and through old woods, where lately the
    violets peep'd from the ground, spotting the gray
    debris,
Amid the grass in the fields each side of the lanes, pass-
    ing the endless grass,
Passing the yellow-spear'd wheat, every grain from its
    shroud in the dark-brown fields uprisen,
Passing the apple-tree blows of white and pink in the
    orchards,
Carrying a corpse to where it shall rest in the grave,
Night and day journeys a coffin.

6

Coffin that passes through lanes and streets,
Through day and night with the great cloud darkening
    the land,
With the pomp of the inloop'd flags with the cities
    draped in black,
With the show of the States themselves as of crape-
    veil'd women standing,

With processions long and winding and the flambeaus
   of the night,
With the countless torches lit, with the silent sea of
   faces and the unbared heads,
With the waiting depot, the arriving coffin, and the
   sombre faces,
With dirges through the night, with the thousand voices
   rising strong and solemn,
With all the mournful voices of the dirges pour'd
   around the coffin,
The dim-lit churches and the shuddering organs—
   where amid these you journey,
With the tolling tolling bells' perpetual clang,
Here, coffin that slowly passes,
I give you my sprig of lilac.

7

(Nor for you, for one alone,
Blossoms and branches green to coffins all I bring,
For fresh as the morning, thus would I chant a song
   for you O sane and sacred death.

All over bouquets of roses,
O death, I cover you over with roses and early lilies,
But mostly and now the lilac that blooms the first,
Copious I break, I break the sprigs from the bushes,
With loaded arms I come, pouring for you,
For you and the coffins all of you O death.)

8

O western orb sailing the heaven,
Now I know what you must have meant as a month
   since I walk'd,

As I walk'd in silence the transparent shadowy night,

As I saw you had something to tell as you bent to me
night after night,

As you droop'd from the sky low down as if to my side,
(while the other stars all look'd on,)

As we wander'd together the solemn night, (for some-
thing I know not what kept me from sleep,)

As the night advanced, and I saw on the rim of the west
how full you were of woe,

As I stood on the rising ground in the breeze in the cool
transparent night,

As I watch'd where you pass'd and was lost in the
netherward black of the night,

As my soul in its trouble dissatisfied sank, as where you
sad orb,

Concluded, dropt in the night, and was gone.

9

Sing on there in the swamp,

O singer bashful and tender, I hear your notes, I hear
your call,

I hear, I come presently, I understand you,

But a moment I linger, for the lustrous star has detain'd
me,

The star my departing comrade holds and detains me.

10

O how shall I warble myself for the dead one there I
loved?

And how shall I deck my song for the large sweet soul
that has gone?

And what shall my perfume be for the grave of him I
love?

Sea-winds blown from east and west,
Blown from the Eastern sea and blown from the West-
    ern sea, till there on the prairies meeting,
These and with these and the breath of my chant,
I'll perfume the grave of him I love.

11

O what shall I hang on the chamber walls?
And what shall the pictures be that I hang on the walls,
To adorn the burial-house of him I love?

Pictures of growing spring and farms and homes,
With the Fourth-month eve at sundown, and the gray
    smoke lucid and bright,
With floods of the yellow gold of the gorgeous, in-
    dolent, sinking sun, burning, expanding the air,
With the fresh sweet herbage under foot, and the pale
    green leaves of the trees prolific,
In the distance the flowing glaze, the breast of the river,
    with a wind-dapple here and there,
With ranging hills on the banks, with many a line
    against the sky, and shadows,
And the city at hand with dwellings so dense, and
    stacks of chimneys,
And all the scenes of life and the workshops, and the
    workmen homeward returning.

12

Lo, body and soul—this land,
My own Manhattan with spires, and the sparkling and
    hurrying tides, and the ships,
The varied and ample land, the South and the North
    in the light, Ohio's shores and flashing Missouri,

And ever the far-spreading prairies cover'd with grass
and corn.

Lo, the most excellent sun so calm and haughty,
The violet and purple morn with just-felt breezes,
The gentle soft-born measureless light,
The miracle spreading bathing all, the fulfill'd noon,
The coming eve delicious, the welcome night and the
stars,
Over my cities shining all, enveloping man and land.

13

Sing on, sing on you gray-brown bird,
Sing from the swamps, the recesses, pour your chant
from the bushes,
Limitless out of the dusk, out of the cedars and pines.

Sing on dearest brother, warble your reedy song,
Loud human song, with voice of uttermost woe.

O liquid and free and tender!
O wild and loose to my soul—O wondrous singer!
You only I hear—yet the star holds me, (but will soon
depart,)
Yet the lilac with mastering odor holds me.

14

Now while I sat in the day and look'd forth,
In the close of the day with its light and the fields of
spring, and the farmers preparing their crops,
In the large unconscious scenery of my land with its
lakes and forests,
In the heavenly aerial beauty, (after the perturb'd
winds and the storms,)

Under the arching heavens of the afternoon swift pass-
ing, and the voices of children and women,
The many-moving sea-tides, and I saw the ships how
they sail'd,
And the summer approaching with richness, and the
fields all busy with labor,
And the infinite separate houses, how they all went on,
each with its meals and minutia of daily usages,
And the streets how their throbbings throbb'd, and the
cities pent—lo, then and there,
Falling upon them all and among them all, enveloping
me with the rest,
Appear'd the cloud, appear'd the long black trail,
And I knew death, its thought, and the sacred knowl-
edge of death.

Then with the knowledge of death as walking one side
of me,
And the thought of death close-walking the other side
of me,
And I in the middle as with companions, and as holding
the hands of companions,
I fled forth to the hiding receiving night that talks not,
Down to the shores of the water, the path by the swamp
in the dimness,
To the solemn shadowy cedars and ghostly pines so still.

And the singer so shy to the rest receiv'd me,
The gray-brown bird I know receiv'd us comrades three,
And he sang the carol of death, and a verse for him I
love.

From deep secluded recesses,
From the fragrant cedars and the ghostly pines so still,
Came the carol of the bird.

And the charm of the carol rapt me,
As I held as if by their hands my comrades in the night,
And the voice of my spirit tallied the song of the bird.

Come lovely and soothing death,
Undulate round the world, serenely arriving, arriving,
In the day, in the night, to all, to each,
Sooner or later delicate death.

Prais'd be the fathomless universe,
For life and joy, and for objects and knowledge curious,
And for love, sweet love—but praise! praise! praise!
For the sure-enwinding arms of cool-enfolding death

Dark mother always gliding near with soft feet,
Have none chanted for thee a chant of fullest welcome?
Then I chant it for thee, I glorify thee above all,
I bring thee a song that when thou must indeed come,
    come unfalteringly.

Approach strong deliveress,
When it is so, when thou hast taken them I joyously
    sing the dead,
Lost in the loving floating ocean of thee,
Laved in the flood of thy bliss O death.

From me to thee glad serenades,
Dances for thee I propose saluting thee, adornments and
    feastings for thee,
And the sights of the open landscape and the high-
    spread sky are fitting,
And life and the fields, and the huge and thoughtful
    night.

The night in silence under many a star,
The ocean shore and the husky whispering wave whose
    voice I know,

*And the soul turning to thee O vast and well-veil'd
  death,*
And the body gratefully nestling close to thee.

Over the tree-tops I float thee a song,
*Over the rising and sinking waves, over the myriad
  fields and the prairies wide,*
*Over the dense-pack'd cities all and the teeming
  wharves and ways,*
I float this carol with joy, with joy to thee O death.

15

To the tally of my soul,
Loud and strong kept up the gray-brown bird,
With pure deliberate notes spreading filling the night.

Loud in the pines and cedars dim,
Clear in the freshness moist and the swamp-perfume,
And I with my comrades there in the night.

While my sight that was bound in my eyes unclosed,
As to long panoramas of visions.

And I saw askant the armies,
I saw as in noiseless dreams hundreds of battle-flags,
Borne through the smoke of the battles and pierc'd with
  missiles I saw them,
And carried hither and yon through the smoke, and torn
  and bloody,
And at last but a few shreds left on the staffs, (and all
  in silence,)
And the staffs all splinter'd and broken.

I saw battle-corpses, myriads of them,
And the white skeletons of young men, I saw them,

I saw the debris and debris of all the slain soldiers of
  the war,
But I saw they were not as was thought,
They themselves were fully at rest, they suffer'd not,
The living remain'd and suffer'd, the mother suffer'd,
And the wife and the child and the musing comrade
  suffer'd,
And the armies that remain'd suffer'd.

16

Passing the visions, passing the night,
Passing, unloosing the hold of my comrades' hands,
Passing the song of the hermit bird and the tallying
  song of my soul,
Victorious song, death's outlet song, yet varying ever-
  altering song,
As low and wailing, yet clear the notes, rising and fall-
  ing, flooding the night,
Sadly sinking and fainting, as warning and warning, and
  yet again bursting with joy,
Covering the earth and filling the spread of the heaven,
As that powerful psalm in the night I heard from re-
  cesses,
Passing, I leave thee lilac with heart-shaped leaves,
I leave thee there in the door-yard, blooming, returning
  with spring.

I cease from my song for thee,
From my gaze on thee in the west, fronting the west,
  communing with thee,
O comrade lustrous with silver face in the night.

Yet each to keep and all, retrievements out of the night,
The song, the wondrous chant of the grav-brown bird,

And the tallying chant, the echo arous'd in my soul,

With the lustrous and drooping star with the countenance full of woe,

With the holders holding my hand nearing the call of the bird,

Comrades mine and I in the midst, and their memory ever to keep, for the dead I loved so well,

For the sweetest, wisest soul of all my days and lands—and this for his dear sake,

Lilac and star and bird twined with the chant of my soul,

There in the fragrant pines and the cedars dusk and dim.

Faces

1

Sauntering the pavement or riding the country by-road, lo, such faces!

Faces of friendship, precision, caution, suavity, ideality,

The spiritual-prescient face, the always welcome common benevolent face,

The face of the singing of music, the grand faces of natural lawyers and judges broad at the back-top,

The faces of hunters and fishers bulged at the brows, the shaved blanch'd faces of orthodox citizens,

The pure, extravagant, yearning, questioning artist's face,

The ugly face of some beautiful soul, the handsome detested or despised face,

The sacred faces of infants, the illuminated face of the mother of many children,

The face of an amour, the face of veneration,
The face as of a dream, the face of an immobile rock,
The face withdrawn of its good and bad, a castrated
  face,
A wild hawk, his wings clipp'd by the clipper,
A stallion that yielded at last to the thongs and knife
  of the gelder.

Sauntering the pavement thus, or crossing the ceaseless
  ferry, faces and faces and faces,
I see them and complain not, and am content with all.

2

Do you suppose I could be content with all if I thought
  them their own finalè?

This now is too lamentable a face for a man,
Some abject louse asking leave to be, cringing for it,
Some milk-nosed maggot blessing what lets it wrig to its
  hole.

This face is a dog's snout sniffing for garbage,
Snakes nest in that mouth, I hear the sibilant threat.

This face is a haze more chill than the arctic sea,
Its sleepy and wabbling icebergs crunch as they go.

This is a face of bitter herbs, this an emetic, they need
  no label,
And more of the drug-shelf, laudanum, caoutchouc, or
  hog's-lard.

This face is an epilepsy, its wordless tongue gives out
  the unearthly cry,
Its veins down the neck distend, its eyes roll till they
  show nothing but their whites,

Its teeth grit, the palms of the hands are cut by the
 turn'd-in nails,
The man falls struggling and foaming to the ground,
 while he speculates well.

This face is bitten by vermin and worms,
And this is some murderer's knife with a half-pull'd
 scabbard.

This face owes to the sexton his dismalest fee,
An unceasing death-bell tolls there.

3

Features of my equals would you trick me with your
 creas'd and cadaverous march?
Well, you cannot trick me.

I see your rounded never-erased flow,
I see 'neath the rims of your haggard and mean dis-
 guises.

Splay and twist as you like, poke with the tangling fores
 of fishes or rats,
You'll be unmuzzled, you certainly will.

I saw the face of the most smear'd and slobbering idiot
 they had at the asylum,
And I knew for my consolation what they knew not,
I knew of the agents that emptied and broke my
 brother,
The same wait to clear the rubbish from the fallen
 tenement,
And I shall look again in a score or two of ages,
And I shall meet the real landlord perfect and unharm'd,
 every inch as good as myself.

4

The Lord advances, and yet advances,
Always the shadow in front, always the reach'd hand
bringing up the laggards.

Out of this face emerge banners and horses—O superb!
I see what is coming,
I see the high pioneer-caps, see staves of runners clear-
ing the way,
I hear the victorious drums.

This face is a life-boat,
This is the face commanding and bearded, it asks no
odds of the rest,
This face is flavor'd fruit ready for eating,
This face of a healthy honest boy is the programme of
all good.

These faces bear testimony slumbering or awake,
They show their descent from the Master himself.

Of the word I have spoken I except not one—red,
white, black, are all deific,
In each house is the ovum, it comes forth after a thou-
sand years.

Spots or cracks at the windows do not disturb me,
Tall and sufficient stand behind and make signs to me,
I read the promise and patiently wait.

This is a full-grown lily's face,
She speaks to the limber-hipp'd man near the garden
pickets,
Come here she blushingly cries, *Come nigh to me lim-
ber-hipp'd man,*

Stand at my side till I lean as high as I can upon you,
Fill me with albescent honey, bend down to me,
Rub to me with your chafing beard, rub to my breast
*   and shoulders.*

5

The old face of the mother of many children,
Whist! I am fully content.

Lull'd and late is the smoke of the First-day morning,
It hangs low over the rows of trees by the fences,
It hangs thin by the sassafras and wild-cherry and cat-
    brier under them.

I saw the rich ladies in full dress at the soiree,
I heard what the singers were singing so long,
Heard who sprang in crimson youth from the white
    froth and the water-blue.

Behold a woman!
She looks out from her quaker cap, her face is clearer
    and more beautiful than the sky.

She sits in an armchair under the shaded porch of the
    farmhouse,
The sun just shines on her old white head.

Her ample gown is of cream-hued linen,
Her grandsons raised the flax, and her grand-daughters
    spin it with the distaff and the wheel.

The melodious character of the earth,
The finish beyond which philosophy cannot go and does
    not wish to go,
The justified mother of men.

To a Locomotive in Winter

Thee for my recitative,
Thee in the driving storm even as now, the snow, the
    winter-day declining,
Thee in thy panoply, thy measur'd dual throbbing and
    thy beat convulsive,
Thy black cylindric body, golden brass and silvery steel,
Thy ponderous side-bars, parallel and connecting rods,
    gyrating, shuttling at thy sides,
Thy metrical, now swelling pant and roar, now taper-
    ing in the distance,
Thy great protruding head-light fix'd in front,
Thy long, pale, floating vapor-pennants, tinged with
    delicate purple,
The dense and murky clouds out-belching from thy
    smoke-stack,
Thy knitted frame, thy springs and valves, the trem-
    ulous twinkle of thy wheels,
Thy train of cars behind, obedient, merrily following,
Through gale or calm, now swift, now slack, yet steadily
    careering;
Type of the modern—emblem of motion and power—
    pulse of the continent,
For once come serve the Muse and merge in verse, even
    as here I see thee,
With storm and buffeting gusts of wind and falling
    snow,
By day thy warning ringing bell to sound its notes,
By night thy silent signal lamps to swing.

Fierce-throated beauty!

Roll through my chant with all thy lawless music, thy
　　swinging lamps at night,

Thy madly-whistled laughter, echoing, rumbling like an
　　earthquake, rousing all,

Law of thyself complete, thine own track firmly holding,

(No sweetness debonair of tearful harp or glib piano
　　thine,)

Thy trills of shrieks by rocks and hills return'd,

Launch'd o'er the prairies wide, across the lakes,

To the free skies unpent and glad and strong.

Passage to India

1

Singing my days,

Singing the great achievements of the present,

Singing the strong light works of engineers,

Our modern wonders, (the antique ponderous Seven
　　outvied,)

In the Old World the east the Suez canal,

The New by its mighty railroad spann'd,

The seas inlaid with eloquent gentle wires;

Yet first to sound, and ever sound, the cry with thee O
　　soul,

The Past! the Past! the Past!

The Past—the dark unfathom'd retrospect!

The teeming gulf—the sleepers and the shadows!

The past—the infinite greatness of the past!

For what is the present after all but a growth out of the
　　past?

(As a projectile form'd, impell'd, passing a certain line,
   still keeps on,
So the present, utterly form'd, impell'd by the past.)

2

Passage O soul to India!
Eclaircise the myths Asiatic, the primitive fables.

Not you alone proud truths of the world,
Nor you alone ye facts of modern science,
But myths and fables of eld, Asia's, Africa's fables,
The far-darting beams of the spirit, the unloos'd dreams,
The deep diving bibles and legends,
The daring plots of the poets, the elder religions;
O you temples fairer than lilies pour'd over by the ris-
   ing sun!
O you fables spurning the known, eluding the hold of
   the known, mounting to heaven!
You lofty and dazzling towers, pinnacled, red as roses,
   burnish'd with gold!
Towers of fables immortal fashion'd from mortal
   dreams!
You too I welcome and fully the same as the rest!
You too with joy I sing.

Passage to India!
Lo, soul, seest thou not God's purpose from the first?
The earth to be spann'd, connected by network,
The races, neighbors, to marry and be given in marriage,
The oceans to be cross'd, the distant brought near,
The lands to be welded together.

A worship new I sing,
You captains, voyagers, explorers, yours,

You engineers, you architects, machinists, yours,
You, not for trade or transportation only,
But in God's name, and for thy sake O soul.

3

Passage to India!
Lo soul for thee of tableaus twain.
I see in one the Suez canal initiated, open'd,
I see the procession of steamships, the Empress Eu-
genie's leading the van,
I mark from on deck the strange landscape, the pure
sky, the level sand in the distance,
I pass swiftly the picturesque groups, the workmen
gather'd,
The gigantic dredging machines.

In one again, different, (yet thine, all thine, O soul, the
same,)
I see over my own continent the Pacific railroad sur-
mounting every barrier,
I see continual trains of cars winding along the Platte
carrying freight and passengers,
I hear the locomotives rushing and roaring, and the
shrill steam-whistle,
I hear the echoes reverberate through the grandest
scenery in the world,
I cross the Laramie plains, I note the rocks in grotesque
shapes, the buttes,
I see the plentiful larkspur and wild onions, the barren,
colorless, sage-deserts,
I see in glimpses afar or towering immediately above
me the great mountains, I see the Wind river and
the Wahsatch mountains,

I see the Monument mountain and the Eagle's Nest, I
    pass the Promontory, I ascend the Nevadas,
I scan the noble Elk mountain and wind around its
    base,
I see the Humboldt range, I thread the valley and cross
    the river,
I see the clear waters of lake Tahoe, I see forests of
    majestic pines,
Or crossing the great desert, the alkaline plains, I be-
    hold enchanting mirages of waters and meadows,
Marking through these and after all, in duplicate slen-
    der lines,
Bridging the three or four thousand miles of land travel,
Tying the Eastern to the Western sea,
The road between Europe and Asia.

(Ah Genoese thy dream! thy dream!
Centuries after thou art laid in thy grave,
The shore thou foundest verifies thy dream.)

4

Passage to India!
Struggles of many a captain, tales of many a sailor dead,
Over my mood stealing and spreading they come,
Like clouds and cloudlets in the unreach'd sky.

Along all history, down the slopes,
As a rivulet running, sinking now, and now again to the
    surface rising,
A ceaseless thought, a varied train—lo, soul, to thee,
    thy sight, they rise,
The plans, the voyages again, the expeditions;
Again Vasco de Gama sails forth,
Again the knowledge gain'd, the mariner's compass,

Lands found and nations born, thou born America,
For purpose vast, man's long probation fill'd,
Thou rondure of the world at last accomplish'd.

5

O vast Rondure, swimming in space,
Cover'd all over with visible power and beauty,
Alternate light and day and the teeming spiritual darkness,
Unspeakable high processions of sun and moon and countless stars above,
Below, the manifold grass and waters, animals, mountains, trees,
With inscrutable purpose, some hidden prophetic intention,
Now first it seems my thought begins to span thee.

Down from the gardens of Asia descending radiating,
Adam and Eve appear, then their myriad progeny after them,
Wandering, yearning, curious, with restless explorations,
With questionings, baffled, formless, feverish, with never-happy hearts,
With that sad incessant refrain, *Wherefore unsatisfied soul?* and *Whither O mocking life?*

Ah who shall soothe these feverish children?
Who justify these restless explorations?
Who speak the secret of impassive earth?
Who bind it to us? what is this separate Nature so unnatural?
What is this earth to our affections? (unloving earth, without a throb to answer ours,
Cold earth, the place of graves.)

Yet soul be sure the first intent remains, and shall be
carried out,
Perhaps even now the time has arrived.

After the seas are all cross'd, (as they seem already
cross'd,)
After the great captains and engineers have accom-
plish'd their work,
After the noble inventors, after the scientists, the chem-
ist, the geologist, ethnologist,
Finally shall come the poet worthy that name,
The true son of God shall come singing his songs.

Then not your deeds only O voyagers, O scientists and
inventors, shall be justified,
All these hearts as of fretted children shall be sooth'd,
All affection shall be fully responded to, the secret shall
be told,
All these separations and gaps shall be taken up and
hook'd and link'd together,
The whole earth, this cold, impassive, voiceless earth,
shall be completely justified,
Trinitas divine shall be gloriously accomplish'd and
compacted by the true son of God, the poet,
(He shall indeed pass the straits and conquer the moun-
tains,
He shall double the cape of Good Hope to some pur-
pose,)
Nature and Man shall be disjoin'd and diffused no more,
The true son of God shall absolutely fuse them.

6

Year at whose wide-flung door I sing!
Year of the purpose accomplish'd!
Year of the marriage of continents, climates and oceans!

(No mere doge of Venice now wedding the Adriatic,)
I see O year in you the vast terraqueous globe given
and giving all,
Europe to Asia, Africa join'd, and they to the New
World,
The lands, geographies, dancing before you, holding a
festival garland,
As brides and bridegrooms hand in hand.

Passage to India!
Cooling airs from Caucasus, far, soothing cradle of
man,
The river Euphrates flowing, the past lit up again.

Lo soul, the retrospect brought forward,
The old, most populous, wealthiest of earth's lands,
The streams of the Indus and the Ganges and their
many affluents,
(I my shores of America walking to-day behold, resum-
ing all,)
The tale of Alexander on his warlike marches suddenly
dying,
On one side China and on the other side Persia and
Arabia,
To the south the great seas and the bay of Bengal,
The flowing literatures, tremendous epics, religions,
castes,
Old occult Brahma interminably far back, the tender
and junior Buddha,
Central and southern empires and all their belongings,
possessors,
The wars of Tamerlane, the reign of Aurungzebe,
The traders, rulers, explorers, Moslems, Venetians, By-
zantium, the Arabs, Portuguese,
The first travelers famous yet, Marco Polo, Batouta the
Moor,

Doubts to be solv'd, the map incognita, blanks to be fill'd,
The foot of man unstay'd, the hands never at rest,
Thyself O soul that will not brook a challenge.

The mediæval navigators rise before me,
The world of 1492, with its awaken'd enterprise,
Something swelling in humanity now like the sap of the earth in spring,
The sunset splendor of chivalry declining.

And who art thou sad shade?
Gigantic, visionary, thyself a visionary,
With majestic limbs and pious beaming eyes,
Spreading around with every look of thine a golden world,
Enhuing it with gorgeous hues.

As the chief histrion,
Down to the footlights walks in some great scena,
Dominating the rest I see the Admiral himself,
(History's type of courage, action, faith,)
Behold him sail from Palos leading his little fleet,
His voyage behold, his return, his great fame,
His misfortunes, calumniators, behold him a prisoner, chain'd,
Behold his dejection, poverty, death.

(Curious in time I stand, noting the efforts of heroes,
Is the deferment long? bitter the slander, poverty, death?
Lies the seed unreck'd for centuries in the ground? lo, to God's due occasion,
Uprising in the night, it sprouts, blooms,
And fills the earth with use and beauty.)

7

Passage indeed O soul to primal thought,
Not lands and seas alone, thy own clear freshness,
The young maturity of brood and bloom,
To realms of budding bibles.

O soul, repressless, I with thee and thou with me,
Thy circumnavigation of the world begin,
Of man, the voyage of his mind's return,
To reason's early paradise,
Back, back to wisdom's birth, to innocent intuitions,
Again with fair creation.

8

O we can wait no longer,
We too take ship O soul,
Joyous we too launch out on trackless seas,
Fearless for unknown shores on waves of ecstasy to sail,
Amid the wafting winds, (thou pressing me to thee, I
    thee to me, O soul,)
Caroling free, singing our song of God,
Chanting our chant of pleasant exploration.

With laugh and many a kiss,
(Let others deprecate, let others weep for sin, remorse,
    humiliation,)
O soul thou pleasest me, I thee.

Ah more than any priest O soul we too believe in God,
But with the mystery of God we dare not dally.

O soul thou pleasest me, I thee,
Sailing these seas or on the hills, or waking in the night,

Thoughts, silent thoughts, of Time and Space and
    Death, like waters flowing,
Bear me indeed as through the regions infinite,
Whose air I breathe, whose ripples hear, lave me all
    over,
Bathe me O God in thee, mounting to thee,
I and my soul to range in range of thee.

O Thou transcendent,
Nameless, the fibre and the breath,
Light of the light, shedding forth universes, thou centre
    of them,
Thou mightier centre of the true, the good, the loving,
Thou moral, spiritual fountain—affection's source—
    thou reservoir,
(O pensive soul of me—O thirst unsatisfied—waitest
    not there?
Waitest not haply for us somewhere there the Comrade
    perfect?)
Thou pulse—thou motive of the stars, suns, systems,
That, circling, move in order, safe, harmonious,
Athwart the shapeless vastnesses of space,
How should I think, how breathe a single breath, how
    speak, if, out of myself,
I could not launch, to those, superior universes?

Swiftly I shrivel at the thought of God,
At Nature and its wonders, Time and Space and Death,
But that I, turning, call to thee O soul, thou actual Me,
And lo, thou gently masterest the orbs,
Thou matest Time, smilest content at Death,
And fillest, swellest full the vastnesses of Space.

Greater than stars or suns,
Bounding O soul thou journeyest forth;
What love than thine and ours could wider amplify?

What aspirations, wishes, outvie thine and ours O soul?
What dreams of the ideal? what plans of purity, perfection, strength,
What cheerful willingness for others' sake to give up all?
For others' sake to suffer all?

Reckoning ahead O soul, when thou, the time achiev'd,
The seas all cross'd, weather'd the capes, the voyage done,
Surrounded, copest, frontest God, yieldest, the aim attain'd,
As fill'd with friendship, love complete, the Elder Brother found,
The Younger melts in fondness in his arms.

9

Passage to more than India!
Are thy wings plumed indeed for such far flights?
O soul, voyagest thou indeed on voyages like those?
Disportest thou on waters such as those?
Soundest below the Sanscrit and the Vedas?
Then have thy bent unleash'd.

Passage to you, your shores, ye aged fierce enigmas!
Passage to you, to mastership of you, ye strangling problems!
You, strew'd with the wrecks of skeletons, that, living, never reach'd you.

Passage to more than India!
O secret of the earth and sky!
Of you O waters of the sea! O winding creeks and rivers!
Of you O woods and fields! of you strong mountains of my land!
Of you O prairies! of you gray rocks!

O morning red! O clouds! O rain and snows!
O day and night, passage to you!

O sun and moon and all you stars, Sirius and Jupiter!
Passage to you!

Passage, immediate passage! the blood burns in my
    veins!
Away O soul! hoist instantly the anchor!
Cut the hawsers—haul out—shake out every sail!
Have we not stood here like trees in the ground long
    enough?
Have we not grovel'd here long enough, eating and
    drinking like mere brutes?
Have we not darken'd and dazed ourselves with books
    long enough?

Sail forth—steer for the deep waters only,
Reckless O soul, exploring, I with thee, and thou with
    me,
For we are bound where mariner has not yet dared to
    go,
And we will risk the ship, ourselves and all.

O my brave soul!
O farther farther sail!
O daring joy, but safe! are they not all the seas of God?
O farther, farther, farther sail!

The Last Invocation

At the last, tenderly,
From the walls of the powerful fortress'd house,
From the clasp of the knitted locks, from the keep of
    the well-closed doors,
Let me be wafted.

Let me glide noiselessly forth;
With the key of softness unlock the locks—with a whis-
  per,
Set ope the doors O soul.

Tenderly—be not impatient,
(Strong is your hold O mortal flesh,
Strong is your hold O love.)

Herman Melville

(1819–1891)

The Portent

Hanging from the beam,
  Slowly swaying (such the law),
Gaunt the shadow on your green,
  Shenandoah!
The cut in on the crown
(Lo, John Brown),
And the stabs shall heal no more.

Hidden in the cap
  Is the anguish none can draw;
So your future veils its face,
  Shenandoah!
But the streaming beard is shown
(Weird John Brown),
The meteor of the war.

In the Prison Pen

Listless he eyes the palisades
  And sentries in the glare;
'Tis barren as a pelican-beach—
  But his world is ended there.

Nothing to do; and vacant hands
   Bring on the idiot-pain;
He tries to think—to recollect,
   But the blur is on his brain.

Around him swarm the plaining ghosts
   Like those on Virgil's shore—
A wilderness of faces dim,
   And pale ones gashed and hoar.

A smiting sun. No shed, no tree;
   He totters to his lair—
A den that sick hands dug in earth
   Ere famine wasted there,

Or, dropping in his place, he swoons,
   Walled in by throngs that press,
Till forth from the throngs they bear him dead—
   Dead in his meagreness.

In the Pauper's Turnip-Field

Crow, in pulpit lone and tall
Of yon charred hemlock, grimly dead,
Why on me in preachment call—
Me, by nearer preachment led
Here in homily of my hoe.
The hoe, the hoe,
My heavy hoe
That earthward bows me to foreshow
A mattock heavier than the hoe.

A Dirge for McPherson

KILLED IN FRONT OF ATLANTA

(*July 1864*)

Arms reversed and banners craped—
    Muffled drums;
Snowy horses sable-draped—
    McPherson comes.

      But, tell us, shall we know him more,
      Lost-Mountain and lone Kenesaw?

Brave the sword upon the pall—
    A gleam in gloom;
So a bright name lighteth all
    McPherson's doom.

Bear him through the chapel-door—
    Let priest in stole
Pace before the warrior
    Who led. Bell—toll!

Lay him down within the nave,
    The Lesson read—
Man is noble, man is brave,
    But man's—a weed.

Take him up again and wend
    Graveward, nor weep:
There's a trumpet that shall rend
    This Soldier's sleep.

Pass the ropes the coffin round,
   And let descend;
Prayer and volley—let it sound
   McPherson's end.

> *True fame is his, for life is o'er—*
> *Sarpedon of the mighty war.*

The Martyr

INDICATIVE OF THE PASSION OF THE PEOPLE ON THE 15TH DAY OF APRIL, 1865

Good Friday was the day
   Of the prodigy and crime,
When they killed him in his pity,
   When they killed him in his prime
Of clemency and calm—
     When with yearning he was filled
     To redeem the evil-willed,
And, though conqueror, be kind;
   But they killed him in his kindness,
   In their madness and their blindness,
And they killed him from behind.

     There is sobbing of the strong,
        And a pall upon the land;
     But the People in their weeping
        Bare the iron hand:
     Beware the People weeping
        When they bare the iron hand.

He lieth in his blood—
   The father in his face;

They have killed him, the Forgiver—
   The Avenger takes his place,
The Avenger wisely stern,
     Who in righteousness shall do
     What the heavens call him to,
And the parricides remand;
   For they killed him in his kindness,
   In their madness and their blindness,
And his blood is on their hand.

     There is sobbing of the strong,
       And a pall upon the land;
     But the People in their weeping
       Bare the iron hand:
     Beware the People weeping
       When they bare the iron hand.

A Requiem for Soldiers
Lost in Ocean Transports

When, after storms that woodlands rue,
   To valleys comes atoning dawn,
The robins blithe their orchard-sports renew;
   And meadow-larks, no more withdrawn,
Carolling fly in the languid blue;
The while, from many a hid recess,
Alert to partake the blessedness,
The pouring mites their airy dance pursue.
   So, after ocean's ghastly gales,
When laughing light of hoyden morning breaks,
     Every finny hider wakes—
   From vaults profound swims up with glittering
     scales;

Through the delightsome sea he sails,
With shoals of shining tiny things
Frolic on every wave that flings
    Against the prow its showery spray;
All creatures joying in the morn,
Save them forever from joyance torn,
    Whose bark was lost where now the dolphins play;
Save them that by the fabled shore,
    Down the pale stream are washed away,
Far to the reef of bones are borne;
    And never revisits them the light,
Nor sight of long-sought land and pilot more;
    Nor heed they now the lone bird's flight
Round the lone spar where mid-sea surges pour.

FROM *Bridegroom Dick*

Where's Commander All-a-Tanto?
Where's Orlop Bob singing up from below?
Where's Rhyming Ned? has he spun his last canto?
Where's Jewsharp Jim? Where's Rigadoon Joe?
Ah, for the music over and done,
The band all dismissed save the droned trombone!
Where's Glen o' the gun-room, who loved Hot-Scotch—
Glen, prompt and cool in a perilous watch?
Where's flaxen-haired Phil? a grey lieutenant?
Or rubicund, flying a dignified pennant?
But where sleeps his brother?—the cruise it was o'er,
But ah, for death's grip that welcomed him ashore!
Where's Sid, the cadet, so frank in his brag,
Whose toast was audacious—*"Here's Sid, and Sid's
    flag!"*
Like holiday craft that have sunk unknown,

May a lark of a lad go lonely down?
Who takes the census under the sea?
Can others like old ensigns be,
Bunting I hoisted to flutter at the gaff—
Rags in end that once were flags
Gallant streaming from the staff?
Such scurvy doom could the chances deal
To Top-Gallant Harry and Jack Genteel?
Lo, Genteel Jack in hurricane weather,
Shagged like a bear, like a red lion roaring;
But O, so fine in his chapeau and feather,
In port to the ladies never once *jawing*;
All bland *politesse*, how urbane was he—
"Oui, mademoiselle"—*"Ma chère amie!"*

'Twas Jack got up the ball at Naples,
Gay in the old *Ohio* glorious;
His hair was curled by the berth-deck barber,
Never you'd deemed him a cub of rude Boreas;
In tight little pumps, with the grand dames in rout,
A-flinging his shapely foot all about;
His watch-chain with love's jewelled tokens abounding,
Curls ambrosial shaking out odours,
Waltzing along the batteries, astounding
The gunner glum and the grim-visaged loaders.

Wife, where be all these blades, I wonder,
Pennoned fine fellows, so strong, so gay?
Never their colours with a dip dived under;
Have they hauled them down in a lack-lustre day,
Or beached their boats in the Far, Far Away?
Hither and thither, blown wide asunder,
Where's this fleet, I wonder and wonder.
Slipt their cables, rattled their adieu
(Whereaway pointing? to what rendezvous?),
Out of sight, out of mind, like the crack *Constitution,*

And many a keel time never shall renew—
Bon Homme Dick o' the buff Revolution,
The *Black Cockade* and the staunch *True-Blue.*

Doff hats to Decatur! But where is his blazon?
Must merited fame endure time's wrong—
Glory's ripe grape wizen up to a raisin?
Yes! For Nature teems, and the years are strong,
And who can keep the tally o' the names that fleet
  along?

But his frigate, wife, his bride? Would blacksmiths
  brown
Into smithereens smite the solid old renown?

Riveting the bolts in the ironclad's shell,
Hark to the hammers with a *rat-tat-tat;*
"Handier a *Derby* than a laced cocked hat!
The *Monitor* was ugly, but she served us right well,
Better than the *Cumberland,* a beauty and the belle."

Better than the Cumberland!—Heart alive in me!
That battlemented hull, Tantallon o' the sea,
Kicked in, as at Boston the taxed chests o' tea!
Aye, spurned by the *ram,* once a tall, shapely craft,
But lopped by the *Rebs* to an iron-beaked raft—
A blacksmith's unicorn in armour *cap-à-pie.*

Under the water-line a *ram's* blow is dealt:
And foul fall the knuckles that strike below the belt.
Nor brave the inventions that serve to replace
The openness of valour while dismantling the grace.

Aloof from all this and the never-ending game,
Tantamount to teetering, plot and counterplot;
Impenetrable armour—all-perforating shot;
Aloof, bless God, ride the warships of old,

A grand fleet moored in the roadstead of fame;
Not submarine sneaks with *them* are enrolled;
Their long shadows dwarf us, their flags are as flame.

Don't fidget so, wife; an old man's passion
Amounts to no more than this smoke that I puff;
There, there, now, buss me in good old fashion;
A died-down candle will flicker in the snuff.

But one last thing let your old babbler say,
What Decatur's coxswain said who was long ago
　hearsed,
"Take in your flying-kites, for there comes a lubber's
　day
When gallant things will go, and the three-deckers
　first."

My pipe is smoked out, and the grog runs slack;
But bowse away, wife, at your blessed Bohea;
This empty can here must needs solace me—
Nay, sweetheart, nay; I take that back;
Dick drinks from your eyes and he finds no lack!

(*Lines 346–438*)

The Maldive Shark

About the Shark, phlegmatical one,
Pale sot of the Maldive sea,
The sleek little pilot-fish, azure and slim,
How alert in attendance be.
From his saw-pit of mouth, from his charnel of maw
They have nothing of harm to dread,
But liquidly glide on his ghastly flank
Or before his Gorgonian head;

Or lurk in the port of serrated teeth
In white triple tiers of glittering gates,
And there find a haven when peril's abroad,
An asylum in jaws of the Fates!
They are friends; and friendly they guide him to prey,
Yet never partake of the treat—
Eyes and brains to the dotard lethargic and dull,
Pale ravener of horrible meat.

To Ned

Where is the world we roved, Ned Bunn?
   Hollows thereof lay rich in shade
By voyagers old inviolate thrown
   Ere Paul Pry cruised with Pelf and Trade.
To us old lads some thoughts come home
Who roamed a world young lads no more shall roam.

Nor less the satiate year impends
   When, wearying of routine-resorts,
The pleasure-hunter shall break loose,
   Ned, for our Pantheistic ports:—
Marquesas and glenned isles that be
Authentic Edens in a Pagan sea.

The charm of scenes untried shall lure,
   And, Ned, a legend urge the flight—
The Typee-truants under stars
   Unknown to Shakespeare's *Midsummer-Night;*
And man, if lost to Saturn's Age,
Yet feeling life no Syrian pilgrimage.

But, tell, shall he, the tourist, find
   Our isles the same in violet-glow

Enamouring us what years and years—
   Ah, Ned, what years and years ago!
Well, Adam advances, smart in pace,
But scarce by violets that advance you trace.

But we, in anchor-watches calm,
   The Indian Psyche's languor won,
And, musing, breathed primeval balm
   From Edens ere yet overrun;
Marvelling mild if mortal twice,
Here and hereafter, touch a Paradise.

The Berg

A DREAM

I saw a ship of martial build
(Her standards set, her brave apparel on)
Directed as by madness mere
Against a stolid iceberg steer,
Nor budge it, though the infatuate ship went down.
The impact made huge ice-cubes fall
Sullen, in tons that crashed the deck;
But that one avalanche was all—
No other movement save the foundering wreck.

Along the spurs of ridges pale,
Not any slenderest shaft and frail,
A prism over glass-green gorges lone,
Toppled; nor lace of traceries fine,
Nor pendant drops in grot or mine
Were jarred, when the stunned ship went down.
Nor sole the gulls in cloud that wheeled
Circling one snow-flanked peak afar,

But nearer fowl the floes that skimmed
And crystal beaches, felt no jar.
No thrill transmitted stirred the lock
Of jack-straw needle-ice at base;
Towers undermined by waves—the block
Atilt impending—kept their place.
Seals, dozing sleek on sliddery ledges
Slipt never, when by loftier edges
Through very inertia overthrown,
The impetuous ship in bafflement went down.

Hard Berg (methought), so cold, so vast,
With mortal damps self-overcast;
Exhaling still thy dankish breath—
Adrift dissolving, bound for death;
Though lumpish thou, a lumbering one—
A lumbering lubbard, loitering slow,
Impingers rue thee and go down,
Sounding thy precipice below,
Nor stir the slimy slug that sprawls
Along thy dead indifference of walls.

After the Pleasure Party

LINES TRACED UNDER AN IMAGE OF AMOR THREATENING

Fear me, virgin whosoever
Taking pride from love exempt,
Fear me, slighted. Never, never
Brave me, nor my fury tempt:
Downy wings, but wroth they beat
Tempest even in reason's seat.

Behind the house the upland falls
With many an odorous tree—
White marbles gleaming through green halls,
Terrace by terrace, down and down,
And meets the starlit Mediterranean Sea.

'Tis Paradise. In such an hour
Some pangs that rend might take release.
Nor less perturbed who keeps this bower
Of balm, nor finds balsamic peace?
From whom the passionate words in vent
After long revery's discontent?

Tired of the homeless deep,
Look how their flight yon hurrying billows urge,
Hitherward but to reap
Passive repulse from the iron-bound verge!
Insensate, can they never know
'Tis mad to wreck the impulsion so?

An art of memory is, they tell:
But to forget! forget the glade
Wherein Fate sprung Love's ambuscade,
To flout pale years of cloistral life
And flush me in this sensuous strife.
'Tis Vesta struck with Sappho's smart.
No fable her delirious leap:
With more of cause in desperate heart,
Myself could take it—but to sleep!

Now first I fell, what all may ween,
That soon or late, if faded e'en,
One's sex asserts itself. Desire,
The dear desire through love to sway,
Is like the Geysers that aspire—
Through cold obstruction win their fervid way.

But baffled here—to take disdain,
To feel rule's instinct, yet not reign;
To dote, to come to this drear shame—
Hence the winged blaze that sweeps my soul
Like prairie fires that spurn control,
Where withering weeds incense the flame.

And kept I long heaven's watch for this,
Contemning love, for this, even this?
O terrace chill in Northern air,
O reaching ranging tube I placed
Against yon skies, and fable chased
Till, fool, I hailed for sister there
Starred Cassiopea in Golden Chair.
In dream I throned me, nor I saw
In cell the idiot crowned with straw.

And yet, ah yet scarce ill I reigned,
Through self-illusion self-sustained,
When now—enlightened, undeceived—
What gain I barrenly bereaved!
Than this can be yet lower decline—
Envy and spleen, can these be mine?

The pleasant girl demure that trod
Beside our wheels that climbed the way,
And bore along a blossoming rod
That looked the sceptre of May-Day—
On her—to fire this petty hell,
His softened glance how moistly fell!
The cheat! on briars her buds were strung;
And wiles peeped forth from mien how meek
The innocent bare-foot! young, so young!
To girls, strong man's a novice weak.
To tell such beads! And more remain,
Sad rosary of belittling pain.

When after lunch and sallies gay,
Like the Decameron folk we lay
In sylvan groups; and I—let be!
O, dreams he, can he dream that one
Because not roseate feels no sun?
The plain lone bramble thrills with Spring
As much as vines that grapes shall bring.

Me now fair studies charm no more.
Shall great thoughts writ, or high themes sung
Damask wan cheeks—unlock his arm
About some radiant ninny flung?
How glad with all my starry lore,
I'd buy the veriest wanton's rose
Would but my bee therein repose.

Could I remake me! or set free
This sexless bound in sex, then plunge
Deeper than Sappho, in a lunge
Piercing Pan's paramount mystery!
For, Nature, in no shallow surge
Against thee either sex may urge,
Why hast thou made us but in halves—
Co-relatives? This makes us slaves.
If these co-relatives never meet
Self-hood itself seems incomplete.
And such the dicing of blind fate
Few matching halves here meet and mate.
What Cosmic jest or Anarch blunder
The human integral clove asunder
And shied the fractions through life's gate?

Ye stars that long your votary knew
Rapt in her vigil, see me here!
Whither is gone the spell ye threw
When rose before me Cassiopea?

Usurped on by love's stronger reign—
But lo, your very selves do wane:
Light breaks—truth breaks! Silvered no more,
But chilled by dawn that brings the gale
Shivers yon bramble above the vale,
And disillusion opens all the shore.

One knows not if Urania yet
The pleasure-party may forget;
Or whether she lived down the strain
Of turbulent heart and rebel brain;
For Amor so resents a slight,
And her's had been, such haught disdain,
He long may wreak his boyish spite,
And boy-like, little reck the pain.

One knows not, no. But late in Rome
(For queens discrowned a congruous home)
Entering Albani's porch she stood
Fixed by an antique pagan stone
Colossal carved. No anchorite seer,
Not Thomas à Kempis, monk austere,
Religious more are in their tone;
Yet far, how far from Christian heart
That form august of heathen Art.
Swayed by its influence, long she stood,
Till surged emotion seething down,
She rallied and this mood she won:

Languid in frame for me,
To-day by Mary's convent shrine,
Touched by her picture's moving plea
In that poor nerveless hour of mine,
I mused—A wanderer still must grieve.
Half I resolved to kneel and believe,
Believe and submit, the veil take on.

But thee, armed Virgin! less benign,
Thee now I invoke, thou mightier one.
Helmeted woman—if such term
Befit thee, far from strife
Of that which makes the sexual feud
And clogs the aspirant life—
O self-reliant, strong and free,
Thou in whom power and peace unite,
Transcender! raise me up to thee,
Raise me and arm me!

          Fond appeal.
For never passion peace shall bring,
Nor Art inanimate for long
Inspire. Nothing may help or heal
While Amor incensed remembers wrong.
Vindictive, not himself he'll spare;
For scope to give his vengeance play
Himself he'll blaspheme and betray.

Then for Urania, virgins everywhere,
O pray! Example take too, and have care.

The Ravaged Villa

In shards the sylvan vases lie,
   Their links of dance undone,
And brambles wither by thy brim,
   Choked fountain of the sun!
The spider in the laurel spins,
   The weed exiles the flower:
And, flung to kiln, Apollo's bust
   Makes lime for Mammon's tower.

Monody

To have known him, to have loved him
    After loneness long;
And then to be estranged in life,
    And neither in the wrong;
And now for death to set his seal—
    Ease me, a little ease, my song!

By wintry hills his hermit-mound
    The sheeted snow-drifts drape,
And houseless there the snow-bird flits
    Beneath the fir-trees' crape:
Glazed now with ice the cloistral vine
    That hid the shyest grape.

Fragments of a Lost Gnostic Poem of the Twelfth Century

.   .   .

Found a family, build a state,
The pledged event is still the same:
Matter in end will never abate
His ancient brutal claim.

.   .   .

Indolence is heaven's ally here,
And energy the child of hell:
The Good Man pouring from his pitcher clear,
But brims the poisoned well.

Billy in the Darbies

FROM *Billy Budd*

Good of the Chaplain to enter Lone Bay
And down on his marrow-bones here and pray
For the likes just o' me, Billy Budd.—But look:
Through the port comes the moon-shine astray!
It tips the guard's cutlass and silvers this nook;
But 'twill die in the dawning of Billy's last day.
A jewel-block they'll make of me to-morrow,
Pendant pearl from the yard-arm-end
Like the ear-drop I gave to Bristol Molly—
O, 'tis me, not the sentence they'll suspend.
Ay, Ay, all is up; and I must up too
Early in the morning, aloft from alow.
On an empty stomach, now, never it would do.
They'll give me a nibble—bit o' biscuit ere I go.
Sure, a messmate will reach me the last parting cup;
But, turning heads away from the hoist and the belay,
Heaven knows who will have the running of me up!
No pipe to those halyards—but aren't it all sham?
A blur's in my eyes; it is dreaming that I am.
A hatchet to my panzer? all adrift to go?
The drum roll to grog, and Billy never know?
But the Dansker he has promised to stand by the plank;
So I'll shake a friendly hand ere I sink.
But—no! It is dead then I'll be, come to think.—
I remember Taff the Welshman when he sank.
And his cheek it was like the budding pink.
But me they'll lash me in hammock, drop me deep.

Fathoms down, fathoms down, how I'll dream fast
   asleep.
I feel it stealing now. Sentry, are you there?
Just ease these darbies at the wrist,
And roll me over fair.
I am sleepy, and the oozy weeds about me twist.

Sidney Lanier

(1842–1881)

Resurrection

Sometimes, in morning sunlights by the river,
  Where in the early fall long grasses wave,
Light winds from over the moorland sink and shiver
  And sigh as if just blown across a grave.

And then I pause and listen to this sighing,
  And look with strange eyes on the well-known stream,
And hear wild birth-cries uttered by the dying,
  And know men waking who appear to dream.

Then from the water-lilies there uprises
  The vast still face of all the life I know,
Changed now, and full of wonders and surprises,
  With fire in eyes that once were glazed with snow.

Smooth are the brows old Pain had erewhile wrinkled,
  And peace and strength about the calm lips dwell.
Clean of the ashes that repentance sprinkled,
  The meek head poises like a flower-bell.

All ancient scars of wanton wars have vanished;
  And what blue bruises grappling Sense had left,
And sad remains of redder stains, are banished,
  And the dim blotch of heart-committed theft.

Oh! vast still vision of transfigured features,
  Unvisited by secret crimes and dooms,

Remain, remain above yon water-creatures,
 Stand, shine above yon water-lily blooms.

For eighteen centuries ripple down the river,
 And windy times the stalks of empires wave;
Let the winds come from the moor and sigh and shiver
 Fain, fain am I, o CHRIST, to pass the gravel

FROM *Hymns of the Marshes*

SUNRISE

In my sleep I was fain of their fellowship, fain
 Of the live-oak, the marsh, and the main.
The little green leaves would not let me alone in my
           sleep;
Up-breathed from the marshes, a message of range and
           of sweep,
Interwoven with waftures of wild sea-liberties, drifting,
 Came through the lapped leaves sifting, sifting,
   Came to the gates of sleep.
Then my thoughts, in the dark of the dungeon-keep
Of the Castle of Captives hid in the City of Sleep,
Upstarted, by twos and by threes assembling:
 The gates of sleep fell a-trembling
Like as the lips of a lady that forth falter *yes*,
     Shaken with happiness:
   The gates of sleep stood wide.

I have waked, I have come, my beloved! I might not
           abide:
I have come ere the dawn, O beloved, my live-oaks, to
           hide
   In your gospelling glooms,—to be

As a lover in heaven, the marsh my marsh and the sea
        my sea.

Tell me, sweet burly-bark'd, man-bodied Tree
That mine arms in the dark are embracing, dost know
From what fount are these tears at thy feet which flow?
They rise not from reason, but deeper inconsequent
        deeps.
      Reason's not one that weeps.
    What logic of greeting lies
Betwixt dear over-beautiful trees and the rain of the
        eyes?

O cunning green leaves, little masters! like as ye gloss
All the dull-tissued dark with your luminous darks that
        emboss
The vague blackness of night into pattern and plan,
        So,
   (But would I could know, but would I could know,)
With your question embroid'ring the dark of the ques-
        tion of man,—
So, with your silences purfling this silence of man
While his cry to the dead for some knowledge is under
        the ban,
       Under the ban,—
    So, ye have wrought me
Designs on the night of our knowledge,—yea, ye have
        taught me,
        So,
   That haply we know somewhat more than we know.

      Ye lispers, whisperers, singers in storms,
      Ye consciences murmuring faiths under forms,
      Ye ministers meet for each passion that grieves,
      Friendly, sisterly, sweetheart leaves,
Oh, rain me down from your darks that contain me

Wisdoms ye winnow from winds that pain me,—
Sift down tremors of sweet-within-sweet
That advise me of more than they bring,—repeat
Me the woods-smell that swiftly but now brought **breath**
From the heaven-side bank of the river of death,—
   Teach me the terms of silence,—preach me
   The passion of patience,—sift me,—impeach me,—
      And there, oh there
As ye hang with your myriad palms upturned in the **air,**
      Pray me a myriad prayer.

     My gossip, the owl,—is it thou
That out of the leaves of the low-hanging bough,
   As I pass to the beach, art stirred?
   Dumb woods, have ye uttered a bird?

      .   .   .

Reverend Marsh, low-couched along the sea,
  Old chemist, rapt in alchyemy,
   Distilling silence,—lo,
That which our father-age had died to know—
  The menstruum that dissolves all matter—thou
Hast found it: for this silence, filling now
The globèd charity of receiving space,
This solves us all: man, matter, doubt, disgrace,
Death, love, sin, sanity,
Must in yon silence, clear solution lie.
Too clear! That crystal nothing who'll peruse?
The blackest night could bring us brighter news.
Yet precious qualities of silence haunt
Round these vast margins, ministrant.
Oh, if thy soul's at latter gasp for space,
With trying to breathe no bigger than thy race
Just to be fellow'd, when that thou hast found
No man with room, or grace enough of bound

To entertain that New thou tell'st, thou art,—
'Tis here, 'tis here, thou canst unhand thy heart
And breathe it free, and breathe it free,
By rangy marsh, in lone sea-liberty.

The tide's at full: the marsh with flooded streams
Glimmers, a limpid labyrinth of dreams.
Each winding creek in grave entrancement lies
A rhapsody of morning-stars. The skies
Shine scant with one forked galaxy,—
The marsh brags ten: looped on his breast they lie.

Oh, what if a sound should be made!
Oh, what if a bound should be laid
To this bow-and-string tension of beauty and silence
        a-spring,—
To the bend of beauty the bow, or the hold of silence
        the string!
I fear me, I fear me yon dome of diaphanous gleam
Will break as a bubble o'er-blown in a dream,—
Yon dome of too-tenuous tissues of space and of night,
Over-weighted with stars, over-freighted with light,
Over-sated with beauty and silence, will seem
    But a bubble that broke in a dream,
If a bound of degree to this grace be laid,
      Or a sound or a motion made.

But no: it is made: list! somewhere,—mystery, where?
        In the leaves? in the air?
In my heart? is a motion made:
'Tis a motion of dawn, like a flicker of shade on shade.
In the leaves 'tis palpable: low multitudinous stirring
Upwinds through the woods; the little ones, softly con-
        ferring,
Have settled my lord's to be looked for; so; they are
        still;

But the air and my heart and the earth are a-thrill,—
And look where the wild duck sails round the bend of
       the river,—
  And look where a passionate shiver
  Expectant is bending the blades
Of the marsh-grass in serial shimmers and shades,—
And invisible wings, fast fleeing, fast fleeting,
       Are beating
The dark overhead as my heart beats,—and steady and
       free
Is the ebb-tide flowing from marsh to sea—
    (Run home, little streams,
    With your lapfulls of stars and dreams),—
And a sailor unseen is hoisting a-peak,
For list, down the inshore curve of the creek
    How merrily flutters the sail,—
And lo, in the East! Will the East unveil?
The East is unveiled, the East hath confessed
A flush: 'tis dead; 'tis alive: 'tis dead, ere the West
Was aware of it: nay, 'tis abiding, 'tis unwithdrawn:
    Have a care, sweet Heaven! 'Tis Dawn.

Now a dream of a flame through that dream of a flush
      is up rolled:
  To the zenith ascending, a dome of undazzling gold
Is builded, in shape as a bee-hive, from out of the sea:
The hive is of gold undazzling, but oh, the Bee,
  The star-fed Bee, the build-fire Bee,
  Of dazzling gold is the great Sun-Bee
That shall flash from the hive-hole over the sea.

    Yet now the dew-drop, now the morning gray,
    Shall live their little lucid sober day
    Ere with the sun their souls exhale away.
Now in each pettiest personal sphere of dew
The summ'd morn shines complete as in the blue

Big dew-drop of all heaven: with these lit shrines
O'er-silvered to the farthest sea-confines,
The sacramental marsh one pious plain
Of worship lies. Peace to the ante-reign
Of Mary Morning, blissful mother mild,
Minded of nought but peace, and of a child.

Not slower than Majesty moves, for a mean and a
        measure
Of motion,—not faster than dateless Olympian leisure
Might pace with unblown ample garments from
        pleasure to pleasure,—
The wave-serrate sea-rim sinks unjarring, unreeling,
    Forever revealing, revealing, revealing,
Edgewise, bladewise, halfwise, wholewise,—'tis done!
        Good-morrow, lord Sun!
With several voice, with ascription one,
The woods and the marsh and the sea and my soul
Unto thee, whence the glittering stream of all morrows
        doth roll,
Cry good and past-good and most heavenly morrow,
        lord Sun.

O Artisan born in the purple,—Workman Heat,—
Parter of passionate atoms that travail to meet
And be mixed in the death-cold oneness,—innermost
        Guest
At the marriage of elements,—fellow of publicans,—
        blest
King in the blouse of flame, that loiterest o'er
The idle skies yet laborest fast evermore—
Thou, in the fine forge-thunder, thou, in the beat
Of the heart of a man, thou Motive,—Laborer Heat:
Yea, Artist, thou, of whose art yon sea's all news,
With his inshore greens and manifold mid-sea blues,

Pearl-glint, shell-tint, ancientest perfectest hues
Ever shaming the maidens,—lily and rose
Confess thee, and each mild flame that glows
In the clarified virginal bosoms of stones that shine,
   It is thine, it is thine:

Thou chemist of storms, whether driving the winds
   a-swirl
Or a-flicker the subtiler essences polar that whirl
In the magnet earth,—yea, thou with a storm for a
   heart,
Rent with debate, many-spotted with question, part
From part oft sundered, yet ever a globèd light,
Yet ever the artist, ever more large and bright
Than the eye of a man may avail of:—manifold One,
I must pass from thy face, I must pass from the face of
   the Sun:
Old Want is awake and agog, every wrinkle a-frown;
The worker must pass to his work in the terrible town:
But I fear not, nay, and I fear not the thing to be done;
  I am strong with the strength of my lord the Sun:
How dark, how dark soever the race that must needs be
   run,
   I am lit with the Sun.

Oh, never the mast-high run of the seas
   Of traffic shall hide thee,
Never the hell-colored smoke of the factories
   Hide thee,
Never the reek of the time's fen-politics
   Hide thee,
And ever my heart through the night shall with
   knowledge abide thee,
And ever by day shall my spirit, as one that hath tried
   thee,

Labor, at leisure, in art,—till yonder beside thee
My soul shall float, friend Sun,
The day being done.

The Revenge of Hamish

It was three slim does and a ten-tined buck in the
bracken lay;
And all of a sudden the sinister smell of a man,
Awaft on a wind-shift, wavered and ran
Down the hill-side and sifted along through the bracken
and passed that way.

Then Nan got a-tremble at nostril; she was the daintiest
doe;
In the print of her velvet flank on the velvet fern
She reared, and rounded her ears in turn.
Then the buck leapt up, and his head as a king's to a
crown did go

Full high in the breeze, and he stood as if Death had
the form of a deer;
And the two slim does long lazily stretching arose,
For their day-dream slowlier came to a close,
Till they woke and were still, breath-bound with wait-
ing and wonder and fear.

Then Alan the huntsman sprang over the hillock, the
hounds shot by,
The does and the ten-tined buck made a marvellous
bound,
The hounds swept after with never a sound,
But Alan loud winded his horn in sign that the quarry
was nigh.

For at dawn of that day proud Maclean of Lochbuy to
    the hunt had waxed wild,
    And he cursed at old Alan till Alan fared off with the
        hounds
    For to drive him the deer to the lower glen-grounds:
"I will kill a red deer," quoth Maclean, "in the sight of
    the wife and the child."

So gayly he paced with the wife and the child to his
    chosen stand;
    But he hurried tall Hamish the henchman ahead: "Go
        turn,"—
    Cried Maclean—"if the deer seek to cross to the burn,
Do thou turn them to me: nor fail, lest thy back be red
    as thy hand."

Now hard-fortuned Hamish, half blown of his breath
    with the height of the hill,
    Was white in the face when the ten-tined buck and
        the does
    Drew leaping to burn-ward; huskily rose
His shouts, and his nether lip twitched, and his legs
    were o'er-weak for his will.

So the deer darted lightly by Hamish and bounded
    away to the burn.
    But Maclean never bating his watch tarried waiting
    below.
    Still Hamish hung heavy with fear for to go
All the space of an hour; then he went, and his face
    was greenish and stern,

And his eye sat back in the socket, and shrunken the
    eyeballs shone,
    As withdrawn from a vision of deeds it were shame to
    see.

"Now, now, grim henchman, what is't with thee?"
Brake Maclean, and his wrath rose red as a beacon the
 wind hath upblown.

"Three does and a ten-tined buck made out," spoke
 Hamish, full mild,
  "And I ran for to turn, but my breath it was blown,
  and they passed;
  I was weak, for ye called ere I broke me my fast."
Cried Maclean: "Now a ten-tined buck in the sight of
 the wife and the child

I had killed if the gluttonous kern had not wrought me
 a snail's own wrong!"
  Then he sounded, and down came kinsmen and
  clansmen all:
  "Ten blows, for ten tine, on his back let fall,
And reckon no stroke if the blood follow not at the bite
 of thong!"

So Hamish made bare, and took him his strokes; at the
 last he smiled.
  "Now I'll to the burn," quoth Maclean, "for it still
  may be,
  If a slimmer-paunched henchman will hurry with me,
I shall kill me the ten-tined buck for a gift to the wife
 and the child!"

Then the clansmen departed, by this path and that; and
 over the hill
  Sped Maclean with an outward wrath for an inward
  shame;
  And that place of the lashing full quiet became;
And the wife and the child stood sad; and bloody-
 backed Hamish sat still.

But look! red Hamish has risen; quick about and about
 turns he.

"There is none betwixt me and the crag-top!" he
    screams under breath.
    Then, livid as Lazarus lately from death,
He snatches the child from the mother, and clambers
    the crag toward the sea.

Now the mother drops breath; she is dumb, and her
    heart goes dead for a space,
    Till the motherhood, mistress of death, shrieks,
    shrieks through the glen,
    And that place of the lashing is live with men,
And Maclean, and the gillie that told him, dash up in
    a desperate race.

Not a breath's time for asking; an eye-glance reveals all
    the tale untold.
    They follow mad Hamish afar up the crag toward the
    sea,
    And the lady cries: "Clansmen, run for a fee!—
Yon castle and lands to the two first hands that shall
    hook him and hold

Fast Hamish back from the brink!"—and ever she flies
    up the steep,
    And the clansmen pant, and they sweat, and they
    jostle and strain.
    But, mother, 'tis vain; but, father, 'tis vain;
Stern Hamish stands bold on the brink, and dangles the
    child o'er the deep.

Now a faintness falls on the men that run, and they all
    stand still.
    And the wife prays Hamish as if he were God, on her
    knees,
    Crying: "Hamish! O Hamish! but please, but please
For to spare him!" and Hamish still dangles the child,
    with a wavering will.

On a sudden he turns; with a sea-hawk scream, and a
    gibe, and a song,
  Cries: "So; I will spare ye the child if, in sight of ye
    all,
  Ten blows on Maclean's bare back shall fall,
And ye reckon no stroke if the blood follow not at the
    bite of the thong!"

Then Maclean he set hardly his tooth to his lip that his
    tooth was red,
  Breathed short for a space, said: "Nay, but it never
    shall be!
  Let me hurl off the damnable hound in the sea!"
But the wife: "Can Hamish go fish us the child from
    the sea, if dead?

Say yea!—Let them lash *me*, Hamish?"—"Nay"—
  "Husband, the lashing will heal;
  But, oh, who will heal me the bonny sweet bairn in
    his grave?
  Could ye cure me my heart with the death of a
    knave?
Quick! Love! I will bare thee—so—kneel!" Then
    Maclean 'gan slowly to kneel

With never a word, till presently downward he jerked to
    the earth.
  Then the henchman—he that smote Hamish—would
    tremble and lag;
  "Strike, hard!" quoth Hamish, full stern, from the
    crag;
Then he struck him, and "One!" sang Hamish, and
    danced with the child in his mirth.

And no man spake beside Hamish; he counted each
    stroke with a song.

When the last stroke fell, then he moved him a pace
    down the height,
  And he held forth the child in the heartaching sight
Of the mother, and looked all pitiful grave, as repenting
    a wrong.

And there as the motherly arms stretched out with the
    thanks-giving prayer—
  And there as the mother crept up with a fearful swift
    pace,
  Till her finger nigh felt of the bairnie's face—
In a flash fierce Hamish turned round and lifted the
    child in the air,

And sprang with the child in his arms from the horrible
    height in the sea,
  Shrill screeching, "Revenge!" in the wind-rush; and
    pallid Maclean,
  Age-feeble with anger and impotent pain,
Crawled up on the crag, and lay flat, and locked hold of
    dead roots of a tree—

And gazed hungrily o'er, and the blood from his back
    drip-dripped in the brine,
  And a sea-hawk flung down a skeleton fish as he flew,
  And the mother stared white on the waste of blue,
And the wind drove a cloud to seaward, and the sun
    began to shine.

A Ballad of Trees and the Master

    Into the woods my Master went,
    Clean forspent, forspent.
    Into the woods my Master came,

Forspent with love and shame.
But the olives they were not blind to Him,
The little gray leaves were kind to Him:
The thorn-tree had a mind to Him
When into the woods He came.

Out of the woods my Master went,
And He was well content.
Out of the woods my Master came,
Content with death and shame.
When Death and Shame would woo Him last,
From under the trees they drew Him last:
'Twas on a tree they slew Him—last
When out of the woods He came.

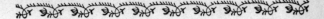

Charles L. Dodgson
(Lewis Carroll)

(1832–1898)

The Hunting of the Snark

FIT THE FIRST

The Landing

"Just the place for a Snark!" the Bellman cried,
    As he landed his crew with care;
Supporting each man on the top of the tide
    By a finger entwined in his hair.

"Just the place for a Snark! I have said it twice:
    That alone should encourage the crew.
Just the place for a Snark! I have said it thrice:
    What I tell you three times is true."

The crew was complete: it included a Boots—
    A marker of Bonnets and Hoods—
A Barrister, brought to arrange their disputes—
    And a Broker, to value their goods.

A Billiard-marker, whose skill was immense,
    Might perhaps have won more than his share—
But a Banker, engaged at enormous expense,
    Had the whole of their cash in his care.

There was also a Beaver, that paced on the deck,
    Or would sit making lace in the bow:

And had often (the Bellman said) saved them from
  wreck,
  Though none of the sailors knew how.

There was one who was famed for the number of things
  He forgot when he entered the ship:
His umbrella, his watch, all his jewels and rings,
  And the clothes he had bought for the trip.

He had forty-two boxes, all carefully packed,
  With his name painted clearly on each:
But, since he omitted to mention the fact,
  They were all left behind on the beach.

The loss of his clothes hardly mattered, because
  He had seven coats on when he came,
With three pair of boots—but the worst of it was,
  He had wholly forgotten his name.

He would answer to "Hi!" or to any loud cry,
  Such as "Fry me!" or "Fritter my wig!"
To "What-you-may-call-um!" or "What-was-his-name!"
  But especially "Thing-um-a-jig!"

While, for those who preferred a more forcible word,
  He had different names from these:
His intimate friends called him "Candle-ends,"
  And his enemies "Toasted-cheese."

"His form is ungainly—his intellect small—"
  (So the Bellman would often remark)
"But his courage is perfect! And that, after all,
  Is the thing that one needs with a Snark."

He would joke with hyænas, returning their stare
  With an impudent wag of the head:
And he once went a walk, paw-in-paw, with a bear,
  "Just to keep up its spirits," he said.

He came as a Baker: but owned, when too late—
    And it drove the poor Bellman half-mad—
He could only bake Bride-cake—for which, I may state,
    No materials were to be had.

The last of the crew needs especial remark,
    Though he looked an incredible dunce:
He had just one idea—but, that one being "Snark,"
    The good Bellman engaged him at once.

He came as a Butcher: but gravely declared,
    When the ship had been sailing a week,
He could only kill Beavers. The Bellman looked scared,
    And was almost too frightened to speak:

But at length he explained, in a tremulous tone,
    There was only one Beaver on board;
And that was a tame one he had of his own,
    Whose death would be deeply deplored.

The Beaver, who happened to hear the remark,
    Protested, with tears in its eyes,
That not even the rapture of hunting the Snark
    Could atone for that dismal surprise!

It strongly advised that the Butcher should be
    Conveyed in a separate ship:
But the Bellman declared that would never agree
    With the plans he had made for the trip:

Navigation was always a difficult art,
    Though with only one ship and one bell:
And he feared he must really decline, for his part,
    Undertaking another as well.

The Beaver's best course was, no doubt, to procure
    A second-hand dagger-proof coat—

So the Baker advised it—and next, to insure
   Its life in some Office of note:

This the Banker suggested, and offered for hire
   (On moderate terms), or for sale,
Two excellent Policies, one Against Fire,
   And one Against Damage From Hail.

Yet still, ever after that sorrowful day,
   Whenever the Butcher was by,
The Beaver kept looking the opposite way,
   And appeared unaccountably shy.

FIT THE SECOND

The Bellman's Speech

The Bellman himself they all praised to the skies—
   Such a carriage, such ease and such grace!
Such solemnity, too! One could see he was wise,
   The moment one looked in his face!

He had bought a large map representing the sea,
   Without the least vestige of land:
And the crew were much pleased when they found it
     to be
   A map they could all understand.

"What's the good of Mercator's North Poles and Equa-
     tors,
   Tropics, Zones, and Meridian Lines?"
So the Bellman would cry: and the crew would reply
   "They are merely conventional signs!

"Other maps are such shapes, with their islands and
     capes!
   But we've got our brave Captain to thank"

(So the crew would protest) "that he's bought *us* the
    best—
  A perfect and absolute blank!"

This was charming, no doubt: but they shortly found
    out
  That the Captain they trusted so well
Had only one notion for crossing the ocean,
  And that was to tingle his bell.

He was thoughtful and grave—but the orders he gave
  Were enough to bewilder a crew.
When he cried "Steer to starboard, but keep her head
    larboard!"
  What on earth was the helmsman to do?

Then the bowsprit got mixed with the rudder sometimes:
  A thing, as the Bellman remarked,
That frequently happens in tropical climes,
  When a vessel is, so to speak, "snarked."

But the principal failing occurred in the sailing,
  And the Bellman, perplexed and distressed,
Said he *had* hoped, at least, when the wind blew due
    East,
  That the ship would *not* travel due West!

But the danger was past—they had landed at last,
  With their boxes, portmanteaus, and bags:
Yet at first sight the crew were not pleased with the
    view,
  Which consisted of chasms and crags.

The Bellman perceived that their spirits were low,
  And repeated in musical tone
Some jokes he had kept for a season of woe—
  But the crew would do nothing but groan.

He served out some grog with a liberal hand,
    And bade them sit down on the beach:
And they could not but own that their Captain looked
      grand,
    As he stood and delivered his speech.

"Friends, Romans, and countrymen, lend me your ears!"
    (They were all of them fond of quotations:
So they drank to his health, and they gave him three
      cheers,
    While he served out additional rations).

"We have sailed many months, we have sailed many
      weeks,
    (Four weeks to the month you may mark),
But never as yet ('tis your Captain who speaks)
    Have we caught the least glimpse of a Snark!

"We have sailed many weeks, we have sailed many days,
    (Seven days to the week I allow),
But a Snark, on the which we might lovingly gaze,
    We have never beheld till now!

"Come, listen, my men, while I tell you again
    The five unmistakable marks
By which you may know, wheresoever you go,
    The warranted genuine Snarks.

"Let us take them in order. The first is the taste,
    Which is meagre and hollow, but crisp:
Like a coat that is rather too tight in the waist,
    With a flavour of Will-o'-the-Wisp.

"Its habit of getting up late you'll agree
    That it carries too far, when I say
That it frequently breakfasts at five-o'clock tea,
    And dines on the following day.

"The third is its slowness in taking a jest.
   Should you happen to venture on one,
It will sigh like a thing that is deeply distressed:
   And it always looks grave at a pun.

"The fourth is its fondness for bathing-machines,
   Which it constantly carries about,
And believes that they add to the beauty of scenes—
   A sentiment open to doubt.

"The fifth is ambition. It next will be right
   To describe each particular batch:
Distinguishing those that have feathers, and bite,
   From those that have whiskers, and scratch.

"For, although common Snarks do no manner of harm,
   Yet I feel it my duty to say
Some are Boojums—" The Bellman broke off in alarm,
   For the Baker had fainted away.

FIT THE THIRD

The Baker's Tale

They roused him with muffins—they roused him with
   ice—
   They roused him with mustard and cress—
They roused him with jam and judicious advice—
   They set him conundrums to guess.

When at length he sat up and was able to speak,
   His sad story he offered to tell;
And the Bellman cried "Silence! Not even a shriek!"
   And excitedly tingled his bell.

There was silence supreme! Not a shriek, not a scream,
   Scarcely even a howl or a groan,

As the man they called "Ho!" told his story of woe
  In an antediluvian tone.

"My father and mother were honest, though poor—"
  "Skip all that!" cried the Bellman in haste.
"If it once becomes dark, there's no chance of a Snark—
  We have hardly a minute to waste!"

"I skip forty years," said the Baker, in tears,
  "And proceed without further remark
To the day when you took me aboard of your ship
  To help you in hunting the Snark.

"A dear uncle of mine (after whom I was named)
  Remarked, when I bade him farewell—"
"Oh, skip your dear uncle!" the Bellman exclaimed,
  As he angrily tingled his bell.

"He remarked to me then," said that mildest of men,
  " 'If your Snark be a Snark, that is right:
Fetch it home by all means—you may serve it with
    greens,
  And it's handy for striking a light.

" 'You may seek it with thimbles—and seek it with care,
  You may hunt it with forks and hope;
You may threaten its life with a railway-share;
  You may charm it with smiles and soap—' "

("That's exactly the method," the Bellman bold
  In a hasty parenthesis cried,
"That's exactly the way I have always been told
  That the capture of Snarks should be tried!")

" 'But oh, beamish nephew, beware of the day,
  If your Snark be a Boojum! For then
You will softly and suddenly vanish away,
  And never be met with again!'

"It is this, it is this that oppresses my soul,
　　When I think of my uncle's last words:
And my heart is like nothing so much as a bowl
　　Brimming over with quivering curds!

"It is this, it is this—" "We have had that before!"
　　The Bellman indignantly said.
And the Baker replied "Let me say it once more.
　　It is this, it is this that I dread!

"I engage with the Snark—every night after dark—
　　In a dreamy delirious fight:
I serve it with greens in those shadowy scenes,
　　And I use it for striking a light:

"But if ever I meet with a Boojum, that day,
　　In a moment (of this I am sure),
I shall softly and suddenly vanish away—
　　And the notion I cannot endure!"

FIT THE FOURTH

The Hunting

The Bellman looked uffish, and wrinkled his brow.
　　"If only you'd spoken before!
It's excessively awkward to mention it now,
　　With the Snark, so to speak, at the door!

"We should all of us grieve, as you well may believe
　　If you never were met with again—
But surely, my man, when the voyage began,
　　You might have suggested it then?

"It's excessively awkward to mention it now—
　　As I think I've already remarked."
And the man they called "Hi!" replied, with a sigh,
　　"I informed you the day we embarked.

"You may charge me with murder—or want of sense--
    (We are all of us weak at times):
But the slightest approach to a false pretence
    Was never among my crimes!

"I said it in Hebrew—I said it in Dutch—
    I said it in German and Greek:
But I wholly forgot (and it vexes me much)
    That English is what you speak!"

" 'Tis a pitiful tale," said the Bellman, whose face
    Had grown longer at every word:
"But, now that you've stated the whole of your case,
    More debate would be simply absurd.

"The rest of my speech" (he exclaimed to his men)
    "You shall hear when I've leisure to speak it.
But the Snark is at hand, let me tell you again!
    'Tis your glorious duty to seek it!

"To seek it with thimbles, to seek it with care;
    To pursue it with forks and hope;
To threaten its life with a railway-share;
    To charm it with smiles and soap!

"For the Snark's a peculiar creature, that won't
    Be caught in a commonplace way.
Do all that you know, and try all that you don't:
    Not a chance must be wasted to-day!

"For England expects—I forbear to proceed:
    'Tis a maxim tremendous, but trite:
And you'd best be unpacking the things that you need
    To rig yourselves out for the fight."

Then the Banker endorsed a blank cheque (which he
    crossed),
    And changed his loose silver for notes.

The Baker with care combed his whiskers and hair.
  And shook the dust out of his coats.

The Boots and the Broker were sharpening a spade—
  Each working the grindstone in turn:
But the Beaver went on making lace, and displayed
  No interest in the concern:

Though the Barrister tried to appeal to its pride,
  And vainly proceeded to cite
A number of cases, in which making laces
  Had been proved an infringement of right.

The maker of Bonnets ferociously planned
  A novel arrangement of bows:
While the Billiard-marker with quivering hand
  Was chalking the tip of his nose.

But the Butcher turned nervous, and dressed himself
      fine,
  With yellow kid gloves and a ruff—
Said he felt it exactly like going to dine,
  Which the Bellman declared was all "stuff."

"Introduce me, now there's a good fellow," he said,
  "If we happen to meet it together!"
And the Bellman, sagaciously nodding his head,
  Said "That must depend on the weather."

The Beaver went simply galumphing about,
  At seeing the Butcher so shy:
And even the Baker, though stupid and stout,
  Made an effort to wink with one eye.

"Be a man!" cried the Bellman in wrath, as he heard
  The Butcher beginning to sob.
"Should we meet with Jubjub, that desperate bird,
  We shall need all our strength for the job!"

FIT THE FIFTH

The Beaver's Lesson

They sought it with thimbles, they sought it with care;
   They pursued it with forks and hope;
They threatened its life with a railway-share;
   They charmed it with smiles and soap.

Then the Butcher contrived an ingenious plan
   For making a separate sally;
And had fixed on a spot unfrequented by man,
   A dismal and desolate valley.

But the very same plan to the Beaver occurred:
   It had chosen the very same place:
Yet neither betrayed, by a sign or a word,
   The disgust that appeared in his face.

Each thought he was thinking of nothing but "Snark"
   And the glorious work of the day;
And each tried to pretend that he did not remark
   That the other was going that way.

But the valley grew narrow and narrower still,
   And the evening got darker and colder,
Till (merely from nervousness, not from good will)
   They marched along shoulder to shoulder.

Then a scream, shrill and high, rent the shuddering sky,
   And they knew that some danger was near:
The Beaver turned pale to the tip of its tail,
   And even the Butcher felt queer.

He thought of his childhood, left far far behind—
   That blissful and innocent state—

The sound so exactly recalled to his mind
    A pencil that squeaks on a slate!

" 'Tis the voice of the Jubjub!" he suddenly cried.
    (This man, that they used to call "Dunce.")
"As the Bellman would tell you," he added with pride,
    "I have uttered that sentiment once.

" 'Tis the note of the Jubjub! Keep count, I entreat.
    You will find I have told it you twice.
'Tis the song of the Jubjub! The proof is complete.
    If only I've stated it thrice."

The Beaver had counted with scrupulous care,
    Attending to every word:
But it fairly lost heart, and outgrabe in despair,
    When the third repetition occurred.

It felt that, in spite of all possible pains,
    It had somehow contrived to lose count,
And the only thing now was to rack its poor brains
    By reckoning up the amount.

"Two added to one—if that could but be done,"
    It said, "with one's fingers and thumbs!"
Recollecting with tears how, in earlier years,
    It had taken no pains with its sums.

"The thing can be done," said the Butcher, "I think
    The things must be done, I am sure.
The thing shall be done! Bring me paper and ink,
    The best there is time to procure."

The Beaver brought paper, portfolio, pens,
    And ink in unfailing supplies:
While strange creepy creatures came out of their dens,
    And watched them with wondering eyes.

So engrossed was the Butcher, he heeded them not
    As he wrote with a pen in each hand,
And explained all the while in a popular style
    Which the Beaver could well understand.

"Taking Three as the subject to reason about—
    A convenient number to state—
We add Seven, and Ten, and then multiply out
    By One Thousand diminished by Eight.

"The result we proceed to divide, as you see,
    By Nine Hundred and Ninety and Two:
Then subtract Seventeen, and the answer must be
    Exactly and perfectly true.

"The method employed I would gladly explain,
    While I have it so clear in my head,
If I had but the time and you had but the brain—
    But much yet remains to be said.

"In one moment I've seen what has hitherto been
    Enveloped in absolute mystery,
And without extra charge I will give you at large
    A Lesson in Natural History."

In his genial way he proceeded to say
    (Forgetting all laws of propriety,
And that giving instruction, without introduction,
    Would have caused quite a thrill in Society),

"As to temper the Jubjub's a desperate bird,
    Since it lives in perpetual passion:
Its taste in costume is entirely absurd—
    It is ages ahead of the fashion:

"But it knows any friend it has met once before:
    It never will look at a bribe:

And in charity-meetings it stands at the door,
  And collects—though it does not subscribe.

"Its flavour when cooked is more exquisite far
  Than mutton, or oysters, or eggs:
(Some think it keeps best in an ivory jar,
  And some, in mahogany kegs:)

"You boil it in sawdust: you salt it in glue:
  You condense it with locusts and tape:
Still keeping one principal object in view—
  To preserve its symmetrical shape."

The Butcher would gladly have talked till next day,
  But he felt that the Lesson must end,
And he wept with delight in attempting to say
  He considered the Beaver his friend.

While the Beaver confessed, with affectionate looks
  More eloquent even than tears,
It had learned in ten minutes far more than all books
  Would have taught it in seventy years.

They returned hand-in-hand, and the Bellman, un-
    manned
  (For a moment) with noble emotion,
Said "This amply repays all the wearisome days
  We have spent on the billowy ocean!"

Such friends, as the Beaver and Butcher became,
  Have seldom if ever been known;
In winter or summer, 'twas always the same—
  You could never meet either alone.

And when quarrels arose—as one frequently finds
  Quarrels will, spite of every endeavour—
The song of the Jubjub recurred to their minds,
  And cemented their friendship for ever!

FIT THE SIXTH

The Barrister's Dream

They sought it with thimbles, they sought it with care;
  They pursued it with forks and hope;
They threatened its life with a railway-share;
  They charmed it with smiles and soap.

But the Barrister, weary of proving in vain
  That the Beaver's lace-making was wrong,
Fell asleep, and in dreams saw the creature quite plain
  That his fancy had dwelt on so long.

He dreamed that he stood in a shadowy Court,
  Where the Snark, with a glass in its eye,
Dressed in gown, bands, and wig, was defending a pig
  On the charge of deserting its sty.

The Witnesses proved, without error or flaw,
  That the sty was deserted when found:
And the Judge kept explaining the state of the law
  In a soft under-current of sound.

The indictment had never been clearly expressed,
  And it seemed that the Snark had begun,
And had spoken three hours, before any one guessed
  What the pig was supposed to have done.

The Jury had each formed a different view
  (Long before the indictment was read),
And they all spoke at once, so that none of them knew
  One word that the others had said.

"You must know—" said the Judge: but the Snark exclaimed "Fudge!
  That statute is obsolete quite!

Let me tell you, my friends, the whole question depends
 On an ancient manorial right.

"In the matter of Treason the pig would appear
 To have aided, but scarcely abetted:
While the charge of Insolvency fails, it is clear,
 If you grant the plea 'never indebted.'

"The fact of Desertion I will not dispute:
 But its guilt, as I trust, is removed
(So far as relates to the costs of this suit)
 By the Alibi which has been proved.

"My poor client's fate now depends on your votes."
 Here the speaker sat down in his place,
And directed the Judge to refer to his notes
 And briefly to sum up the case.

But the Judge said he never had summed up before;
 So the Snark undertook it instead,
And summed it so well that it came to far more
 Than the Witnesses ever had said!

When the verdict was called for, the Jury declined,
 As the word was so puzzling to spell;
But they ventured to hope that the Snark wouldn't mind
 Undertaking that duty as well.

So the Snark found the verdict, although, as it owned,
 It was spent with the toils of the day:
When it said the word "GUILTY!" the Jury all groaned,
 And some of them fainted away.

Then the Snark pronounced sentence, the Judge being
  quite
 Too nervous to utter a word:
When it rose to its feet, there was silence like night,
 And the fall of a pin might be heard.

"Transportation for life" was the sentence it gave,
  "And *then* to be fined forty pound."
The Jury all cheered, though the Judge said he feared
  That the phrase was not legally sound.

But their wild exultation was suddenly checked
  When the jailer informed them, with tears,
Such a sentence would have not the slightest effect,
  As the pig had been dead for some years.

The Judge left the Court, looking deeply disgusted:
  But the Snark, though a little aghast,
As the lawyer to whom the defence was intrusted,
  Went bellowing on to the last.

Thus the Barrister dreamed, while the bellowing seemed
  To grow every moment more clear:
Till he woke to the knell of a furious bell,
  Which the Bellman rang close at his ear.

FIT THE SEVENTH

The Banker's Fate

They sought it with thimbles, they sought it with care;
  They pursued it with forks and hope;
They threatened its life with a railway-share;
  They charmed it with smiles and soap.

And the Banker, inspired with a courage so new
  It was matter for general remark,
Rushed madly ahead and was lost to their view
  In his zeal to discover the Snark.

But while he was seeking with thimbles and care,
  A Bandersnatch swiftly drew nigh
And grabbed at the Banker, who shrieked in despair,
  For he knew it was useless to fly.

He offered large discount—he offered a cheque
    (Drawn "to bearer") for seven-pounds-ten:
But the Bandersnatch merely extended its neck
    And grabbed at the Banker again.

Without rest or pause—while those frumious jaws
    Went savagely snapping around—
He skipped and he hopped, and he floundered and
        flopped,
    Till fainting he fell to the ground.

The Bandersnatch fled as the others appeared
    Led on by that fear-stricken yell:
And the Bellman remarked "It is just as I feared!"
    And solemnly tolled on his bell.

He was black in the face, and they scarcely could trace
    The least likeness to what he had been:
While so great was his fright that his waistcoat turned
        white—
    A wonderful thing to be seen!

To the horror of all who were present that day,
    He uprose in full evening dress,
And with senseless grimaces endeavoured to say
    What his tongue could no longer express.

Down he sank in a chair—ran his hands through his
        hair—
    And chanted in mimsiest tones
Words whose utter inanity proved his insanity,
    While he rattled a couple of bones.

"Leave him here to his fate—it is getting so late!"
    The Bellman exclaimed in a fright.
"We have lost half the day. Any further delay,
    And we sha'n't catch a Snark before night!"

FIT THE EIGHTH

The Vanishing

They sought it with thimbles, they sought it with care;
  They pursued it with forks and hope;
They threatened its life with a railway-share;
  They charmed it with smiles and soap.

They shuddered to think that the chase might fail,
  And the Beaver, excited at last,
Went bounding along on the tip of its tail,
  For the daylight was nearly past.

"There is Thingumbob shouting!" the Bellman said.
  "He is shouting like mad, only hark!
He is waving his hands, he is wagging his head,
  He has certainly found a Snark!"

They gazed in delight, while the Butcher exclaimed
  "He was always a desperate wag!"
They beheld him—their Baker—their hero unnamed—
  On the top of a neighbouring crag,

Erect and sublime, for one moment of time,
  In the next, that wild figure they saw
(As if stung by a spasm) plunge into a chasm,
  While they waited and listened in awe.

"It's a Snark!" was the sound that first came to their ears,
  And seemed almost too good to be true.
Then followed a torrent of laughter and cheers:
  Then the ominous words "It's a Boo—"

Then, silence. Some fancied they heard in the air
  A weary and wandering sigh

That sounded like "—jum!" but the others declare
   It was only a breeze that went by.

They hunted till darkness came on, but they found
   Not a button, or feather, or mark,
By which they could tell that they stood on the ground
   Where the Baker had met with the Snark.

In the midst of the word he was trying to say,
   In the midst of his laughter and glee,
He had softly and suddenly vanished away—
   For the Snark *was* a Boojum, you see.

Dante Gabriel Rossetti

(1828–1882)

Jenny

"Vengeance of Jenny's case! Fie on her! Never
name her, child!"—*Mrs. Quickly*

Lazy laughing languid Jenny,
Fond of a kiss and fond of a guinea,
Whose head upon my knee to-night
Rests for a while, as if grown light
With all our dances and the sound
To which the wild tunes spun you round:
Fair Jenny mine, the thoughtless queen
Of kisses which the blush between
Could hardly make much daintier;
Whose eyes are as blue skies, whose hair
Is countless gold incomparable:
Fresh flower, scarce touched with signs that tell
Of Love's exuberant hotbed:—Nay,
Poor flower left torn since yesterday
Until to-morrow leave you bare;
Poor handful of bright spring-water
Flung in the whirlpool's shrieking face;
Poor shameful Jenny, full of grace
Thus with your head upon my knee;—
Whose person or whose purse may be
The lodestar of your reverie?

This room of yours, my Jenny, looks
A change from mine so full of books,

Whose serried ranks hold fast, forsooth,
So many captive hours of youth,—
The hours they thieve from day and night
To make one's cherished work come right,
And leave it wrong for all their theft,
Even as to-night my work was left:
Until I vowed that since my brain
And eyes of dancing seemed so fain,
My feet should have some dancing too:—
And thus it was I met with you.
Well, I suppose 'twas hard to part,
For here I am. And now, sweetheart,
You seem too tired to get to bed.

It was a careless life I led
When rooms like this were scarce so strange
Not long ago. What breeds the change,—
The many aims or the few years?
Because to-night it all appears
Something I do not know again.

The cloud's not danced out of my brain,—
The cloud that made it turn and swim
While hour by hour the books grew dim.
Why, Jenny, as I watch you there,—
For all your wealth of loosened hair,
Your silk ungirdled and unlac'd
And warm sweets open to the waist,
All golden in the lamplight's gleam,—
You know not what a book you seem,
Half-read by lightning in a dream!
How should you know, my Jenny? Nay,
And I should be ashamed to say:—
Poor beauty, so well worth a kiss!
But while my thought runs on like this

With wasteful whims more than enough,
I wonder what you're thinking of.

    If of myself you think at all,
What is the thought?—conjectural
On sorry matters best unsolved?—
Or inly is each grace revolved
To fit me with a lure?—or (sad
To think!) perhaps you're merely glad
That I'm not drunk or ruffianly
And let you rest upon my knee.

    For sometimes, were the truth confess'd,
You're thankful for a little rest,—
Glad from the crush to rest within,
From the heart-sickness and the din
Where envy's voice at virtue's pitch
Mocks you because your gown is rich;
And from the pale girl's dumb rebuke,
Whose ill-clad grace and toil-worn look
Proclaim the strength that keeps her weak,
And other nights than yours bespeak;
And from the wise unchildish elf,
To schoolmate lesser than himself
Pointing you out, what thing you are:—
Yes, from the daily jeer and jar,
From shame and shame's outbraving too,
Is rest not sometimes sweet to you?—
But most from the hatefulness of man
Who spares not to end what he began,
Whose acts are ill and his speech ill,
Who, having used you at his will,
Thrusts you aside, as when I dine
I serve the dishes and the wine.

Well, handsome Jenny mine, sit up:
I've filled our glasses, let us sup,
And do not let me think of you,
Lest shame of yours suffice for two.
What, still so tired? Well, well then, keep
Your head there, so you do not sleep;
But that the weariness may pass
And leave you merry, take this glass.
Ah! lazy lily hand, more bless'd
If ne'er in rings it had been dress'd
Nor ever by a glove conceal'd!

Behold the lilies of the field,
They toil not neither do they spin;
(So doth the ancient text begin,—
Not of such rest as one of these
Can share.) Another rest and ease.
Along each summer-sated path
From its new lord the garden hath,
Than that whose spring in blessings ran
Which praised the bounteous husbandman,
Ere yet, in days of hankering breath,
The lilies sickened unto death.

What, Jenny, are your lilies dead?
Aye, and the snow-white leaves are spread
Like winter on the garden-bed.
But you had roses left in May,—
They were not gone too. Jenny, nay,
But must your roses die, and those
Their purfled buds that should unclose?
Even so; the leaves are curled apart,
Still red as from the broken heart,
And here's the naked stem of thorns.

Nay, nay, mere words. Here nothing warns
As yet of winter. Sickness here
Or want alone could waken fear,—
Nothing but passion wrings a tear.
Except when there may rise unsought
Haply at times a passing thought
Of the old days which seem to be
Much older than any history
That is written in any book;
When she would lie in fields and look
Along the ground through the blown grass,
And wonder where the city was,
Far out of sight, whose broil and bale
They told her then for a child's tale.

Jenny, you know the city now,
A child can tell the tale there, how
Some things which are not yet enroll'd
In market-lists are bought and sold
Even till the early Sunday light,
When Saturday night is market-night
Everywhere, be it dry or wet,
And market-night in the Haymarket.
Our learned London children know,
Poor Jenny, all your pride and woe;
Have seen your lifted silken skirt
Advertise dainties through the dirt;
Have seen your coach-wheels splash rebuke
On virtue; and have learned your look
When, wealth and health slipped past, you stare
Along the streets alone, and there,
Round the long park, across the bridge,
The cold lamps at the pavement's edge
Wind on together and apart,
A fiery serpent for your heart.

Let the thoughts pass, an empty cloud!
Suppose I were to think aloud,—
What if to her all this were said?
Why, as a volume seldom read
Being opened half-way shuts again,
So might the pages of her brain
Be parted at such words, and thence
Close back upon the dusty sense.
For is there hue or shape defin'd
In Jenny's desecrated mind,
Where all contagious currents meet,
A Lethe of the middle street?
Nay, it reflects not any face,
Nor sound is in its sluggish pace,
But as they coil those eddies clot,
And night and day remembers not.

Why, Jenny, you're asleep at last!—
Asleep, poor Jenny, hard and fast,—
So young and soft and tired; so fair,
With chin thus nestled in your hair,
Mouth quiet, eyelids almost blue
As if some sky of dreams shone through!

Just as another woman sleeps!
Enough to throw one's thoughts in heaps
Of doubt and horror,—what to say
Or think,—this awful secret sway,
The potter's power over the clay!
Of the same lump (it has been said)
For honour and dishonour made,
Two sister vessels. Here is one.

My cousin Nell is fond of fun,
And fond of dress, and change, and praise,
So mere a woman in her ways:

And if her sweet eyes rich in youth
Are like her lips that tell the truth,
My cousin Nell is fond of love.
And she's the girl I'm proudest of.
Who does not prize her, guard her well?
The love of change, in cousin Nell,
Shall find the best and hold it dear:
The unconquered mirth turn quieter
Not through her own, through others' woe:
The conscious pride of beauty glow
Beside another's pride in her,
One little part of all they share.
For Love himself shall ripen these
In a kind of soil to just increase
Through years of fertilizing peace.

Of the same lump (as it is said)
For honour and dishonour made,
Two sister vessels. Here is one.

It makes a goblin of the sun.

So pure,—so fall'n! How dare to think
Of the first common kindred link?
Yet, Jenny, till the world shall burn
It seems that all things take their turn;
And who shall say but this fair tree
May need, in changes that may be,
Your children's children's charity?
Scorned then, no doubt, as you are scorn'd!
Shall no man hold his pride forewarn'd
Till in the end, the Day of Days,
At Judgement, one of his own race,
As frail and lost as you, shall rise,—
His daughter, with his mother's eyes?

How Jenny's clock ticks on the shelf!
Might not the dial scorn itself
That has such hours to register?
Yet as to me, even so to her
Are golden sun and silver moon,
In daily largesse of earth's boon,
Counted for life-coins to one tune.
And if, as blindfold fates are toss'd,
Through some one man this life be lost,
Shall soul not somehow pay for soul?

Fair shines the gilded aureole
In which our highest painters place
Some living woman's simple face.
And the stilled features thus descried
As Jenny's long throat droops aside,—
The shadows where the cheeks are thin,
And pure wide curve from ear to chin,—
With Raffael's, Leonardo's hand
To show them to men's souls, might stand,
Whole ages long, the whole world through,
For preachings of what God can do.
What has man done here? How atone,
Great God, for this which man has done?
And for the body and soul which by
Man's pitiless doom must now comply
With lifelong hell, what lullaby
Of sweet forgetful second birth
Remains? All dark. No sign on earth
What measure of God's rest endows
The many mansions of his house.

If but a woman's heart might see
Such erring heart unerringly
For once! But that can never be.

Like a rose shut in a book
In which pure women may not look,
For its base pages claim control
To crush the flower within the soul;
Where through each dead rose-leaf that clings,
Pale as transparent psyche-wings,
To the vile text, are traced such things
As might make lady's cheek indeed
More than a living rose to read;
So nought save foolish foulness may
Watch with hard eyes the sure decay;
And so the life-blood of this rose,
Puddled with shameful knowledge, flows
Through leaves no chaste hand may unclose:
Yet still it keeps such faded show
Of when 'twas gathered long ago,
That the crushed petals' lovely grain,
The sweetness of the sanguine stain,
Seen of a woman's eyes, must make
Her pitiful heart, so prone to ache,
Love roses better for its sake:—
Only that this can never be:—
Even so unto her sex is she.

Yet, Jenny, looking long at you,
The woman almost fades from view.
A cipher of man's changeless sum
Of lust, past, present, and to come,
Is left. A riddle that one shrinks
To challenge from the scornful sphinx.

Like a toad within a stone
Seated while Time crumbles on;
Which sits there since the earth was curs'd
For Man's transgression at the first;
Which, living through all centuries,

Not once has seen the sun arise;
Whose life, to its cold circle charmed,
The earth's whole summers have not warmed;
Which always—whitherso the stone
Be flung—sits there, deaf, blind, alone;—
Aye, and shall not be driven out
Till that which shuts him round about
Break at the very Master's stroke,
And the dust thereof vanish as smoke,
And the seed of Man vanish as dust:—
Even so within this world is Lust.

Come, come, what use in thoughts like this?
Poor little Jenny, good to kiss,—
You'd not believe by what strange roads
Thought travels, when your beauty goads
A man to-night to think of toads!
Jenny, wake up. . . . Why, there's the dawn!

And there's an early waggon drawn
To market, and some sheep that jog
Bleating before a barking dog;
And the old streets come peering through
Another night that London knew;
And all as ghostlike as the lamps.

So on the wings of day decamps
My last night's frolic. Glooms begin
To shiver off as lights creep in
Past the gauze curtains half drawn-to,
And the lamp's doubled shade grows blue,—
Your lamp, my Jenny, kept alight,
Like a wise virgin's, all one night!
And in the alcove coolly spread
Glimmers with dawn your empty bed;
And yonder your fair face I see

Reflected lying on my knee,
Where teems with first foreshadowings
Your pier-glass scrawled with diamond rings:
And on your bosom all night worn
Yesterday's rose now droops forlorn,
But dies not yet this summer morn.

And now without, as if some word
Had called upon them that they heard,
The London sparrows far and nigh
Clamour together suddenly;
And Jenny's cage-bird grown awake
Here in their song his part must take,
Because here too the day doth break.

And somehow in myself the dawn
Among stirred clouds and veils withdrawn
Strikes greyly on her. Let her sleep.
But will it wake her if I heap
These cushions thus beneath her head
Where my knee was? No,—there's your bed,
My Jenny, while you dream. And there
I lay among your golden hair
Perhaps the subject of your dreams,
These golden coins.
                        For still one deems
That Jenny's flattering sleep confers
New magic on the magic purse,—
Grim web, how clogged with shrivelled flies!
Between the threads fine fumes arise
And shape their pictures in the brain.
There roll no streets in glare and rain,
Nor flagrant man-swine whets his tusk;
But delicately sighs in musk
The homage of the dim boudoir;
Or like a palpitating star

Thrilled into song, the opera-night
Breathes faint in the quick pulse of light;
Or at the carriage-window shine
Rich wares for choice; or, free to dine,
Whirls through its hour of health (divine
For her) the concourse of the Park.
And though in the discounted dark
Her functions there and here are one,
Beneath the lamps and in the sun
There reigns at least the acknowledged belle
Apparelled beyond parallel.
Ah Jenny, yes, we know your dreams.

For even the Paphian Venus seems,
A goddess o'er the realms of love,
When silver-shrined in shadowy grove:
Aye, or let offerings nicely placed
But hide Priapus to the waist,
And whoso looks on him shall see
An eligible deity.

Why, Jenny, waking here alone
May help you to remember one,
Though all the memory's long outworn
Of many a double-pillowed morn.
I think I see you when you wake,
And rub your eyes for me, and shake
My gold, in rising, from your hair,
A Danaë for a moment there.

Jenny, my love rang true! for still
Love at first sight is vague, until
That tinkling makes him audible.

And must I mock you to the last,
Ashamed of my own shame,—aghast
Because some thoughts not born amiss

Rose at a poor fair face like this?
Well, of such thoughts so much I know:
In my life, as in hers, they show,
By a far gleam which I may near,
A dark path I can strive to clear.

Only one kiss. Good-bye, my dear.

The Blessed Damozel

The blessed damozel leaned out
   From the gold bar of Heaven;
Her eyes were deeper than the depth
   Of waters stilled at even;
She had three lilies in her hand,
   And the stars in her hair were seven.

Her robe, ungirt from clasp to hem,
   No wrought flowers did adorn,
But a white rose of Mary's gift,
   For service meetly worn;
Her hair that lay along her back
   Was yellow, like ripe corn.

Herseemed she scarce had been a day
   One of God's choristers;
The wonder was not yet quite gone
   From that still look of hers;
Albeit, to them she left, her day
   Had counted as ten years.

(To one, it is ten years of years.
   . . . Yet now, and in this place,
Surely she leaned o'er me—her hair

Fell all about my face. . . .
Nothing: the autumn fall of leaves.
    The whole year sets apace.)

It was the rampart of God's house
    That she was standing on;
By God built over the sheer depth
    The which is Space begun;
So high, that looking downward thence
    She scarce could see the sun.

It lies in Heaven, across the flood
    Of ether, as a bridge.
Beneath, the tides of day and night
    With flame and darkness ridge
The void, as low as where this earth
    Spins like a fretful midge.

Around her, lovers, newly met
    'Mid deathless love's acclaims,
Spoke evermore among themselves
    Their heart-remembered names;
And the souls mounting up to God
    Went by her like thin flames.

And still she bowed herself and stooped
    Out of the circling charm;
Until her bosom must have made
    The bar she leaned on warm,
And the lilies lay as if asleep
    Along her bended arm.

From the fixed place of Heaven she saw
    Time like a pulse shake fierce
Through all the worlds. Her gaze still strove
    Within the gulf to pierce
Its path; and now she spoke as when
    The stars sang in their spheres.

The sun was gone now; the curled moon
    Was like a little feather
Fluttering far down the gulf; and now
    She spoke through the still weather.
Her voice was like the voice the stars
    Had when they sang together.

(Ah sweet! Even now, in that bird's song,
    Strove not her accents there,
Fain to be hearkened? When those bells
    Possessed the mid-day air,
Strove not her steps to reach my side
    Down all the echoing stair?)

"I wish that he were come to me,
    For he will come," she said.
"Have I not prayed in Heaven?—on earth,
    Lord, Lord, has he not pray'd?
Are not two prayers a perfect strength?
    And shall I feel afraid?

"When round his head the aureole clings,
    And he is clothed in white,
I'll take his hand and go with him
    To the deep wells of light;
As unto a stream we will step down,
    And bathe there in God's sight.

"We two will stand beside that shrine,
    Occult, withheld, untrod,
Whose lamps are stirred continually
    With prayer sent up to God;
And see our old prayers, granted, melt
    Each like a little cloud.

"We two will lie i' the shadow of
    That living mystic tree

Within whose secret growth the Dove
   Is sometimes felt to be,
While every leaf that His plumes touch
   Saith His Name audibly.

"And I myself will teach to him,
   I myself, lying so,
The songs I sing here; which his voice
   Shall pause in, hushed and slow,
And find some knowledge at each pause,
   Or some new thing to know."

(Alas! we two, we two, thou say'st!
   Yea, one wast thou with me
That once of old. But shall God lift
   To endless unity
The soul whose likeness with thy soul
   Was but its love for thee?)

"We two," she said, "will seek the groves
   Where the lady Mary is,
With her five handmaidens, whose names
   Are five sweet symphonies,
Cecily, Gertrude, Magdalen,
   Margaret and Rosalys.

"Circlewise sit they, with bound locks
   And foreheads garlanded;
Into the fine cloth white like flame
   Weaving the golden thread,
To fashion the birth-robes for them
   Who are just born, being dead.

"He shall fear, haply, and be dumb:
   Then will I lay my cheek
To his, and tell about our love,
   Not once abashed or weak:

And the dear Mother will approve
   My pride, and let me speak.

"Herself shall bring us, hand in hand,
   To Him round whom all souls
Kneel, the clear-ranged unnumbered heads
   Bowed with their aureoles:
And angels meeting us shall sing
   To their citherns and citoles.

"There will I ask of Christ the Lord
   This much for him and me:—
Only to live as once on earth
   With Love,—only to be,
As then awhile, for ever now
   Together, I and he."

She gazed and listened and then said,
   Less sad of speech than mild,—
"All this is when he comes." She ceased.
   The light thrilled towards her, fill'd
With angels in strong level flight.
   Her eyes prayed, and she smil'd.

(I saw her smile.) But soon their path
   Was vague in distant spheres:
And then she cast her arms along
   The golden barriers,
And laid her face between her hands,
   And wept. (I heard her tears.)

FROM *The House of Life*

SILENT NOON

Your hands lie open in the long fresh grass,—
  The finger-points look through like rosy blooms:
  Your eyes smile peace. The pasture gleams and
    glooms
'Neath billowing skies that scatter and amass.
All round our nest, far as the eye can pass,
  Are golden kingcup-fields with silver edge
  Where the cow-parsley skirts the hawthorn-hedge.
'Tis visible silence, still as the hour-glass.

Deep in the sun-searched growths the dragon-fly
Hangs like a blue-thread loosened from the sky:—
  So this wing'd hour is dropt to us from above.
Oh! clasp we to our hearts, for deathless dower,
This close-companioned inarticulate hour
  When two-fold silence was the song of love.

WILLOWWOOD

I sat with Love upon a woodside well,
  Leaning across the water, I and he;
  Nor ever did he speak nor looked at me,
But touched his lute wherein was audible
The certain secret thing he had to tell:
  Only our mirrored eyes met silently
  In the low wave; and that sound came to be
The passionate voice I knew; and my tears fell.

And at their fall, his eyes beneath grew hers;
And with his foot and with his wing-feathers
   He swept the spring that watered my heart's drouth.
Then the dark ripples spread to waving hair,
And as I stooped, her own lips rising there
   Bubbled with brimming kisses at my mouth.

WITHOUT HER

What of her glass without her? The blank gray
   There where the pool is blind of the moon's face.
   Her dress without her? The tossed empty space
Of cloud-rack whence the moon has passed away.
Her paths without her? Day's appointed sway
   Usurped by desolate night. Her pillowed place
   Without her? Tears, ah me! for love's good grace,
And cold forgetfulness of night or day.

What of the heart without her? Nay, poor heart,
   Of thee what word remains ere speech be still?
   A wayfarer by barren ways and chill,
Steep ways and weary, without her thou art,
Where the long cloud, the long wood's counterpart,
   Sheds doubled darkness up the labouring hill.

BARREN SPRING

Once more the changed year's turning wheel returns:
   And as a girl sails balanced in the wind,
   And now before and now again behind
Stoops as it swoops, with cheek that laughs and burns,—
So Spring comes merry towards me here, but earns
   No answering smile from me, whose life is twin'd
   With the dead boughs that winter still must bind,
And whom to-day the Spring no more concerns.

Behold, this crocus is a withering flame;
  This snowdrop, snow; this apple-blossom's part
  To breed the fruit that breeds the serpent's art.
Nay, for these Spring-flowers, turn thy face from them,
Nor stay till on the year's last lily-stem
  The white cup shrivels round the golden heart.

A SUPERSCRIPTION

Look in my face; my name is Might-have-been;
  I am also called No-more, Too-late, Farewell;
  Unto thine ear I hold the dead-sea-shell
Cast up thy Life's foam-fretted feet between;
Unto thine eyes the glass where that is seen
  Which had Life's form and Love's, but by my spell
  Is now a shaken shadow intolerable,
Of ultimate things unuttered the frail screen.

Mark me, how still I am! But should there dart
  One moment through thy soul the soft surprise
  Of that winged Peace which lulls the breath of
    sighs,—
Then shalt thou see me smile, and turn apart
Thy visage to mine ambush at thy heart
  Sleepless with cold commemorative eyes.

The Woodspurge

The wind flapped loose, the wind was still,
Shaken out dead from tree and hill:
I had walked on at the wind's will,—
I sat now, for the wind was still.

Between my knees my forehead was,—
My lips, drawn in, said not Alas!
My hair was over in the grass,
My naked ears heard the day pass.

My eyes, wide open, had the run
Of some ten weeds to fix upon;
Among those few, out of the sun,
The woodspurge flowered, three cups in one.

From perfect grief there need not be
Wisdom or even memory:
One thing then learnt remains to me,—
The woodspurge has a cup of three.

Lilith

FOR A PICTURE

Of Adam's first wife, Lilith, it is told
  (The witch he loved before the gift of Eve,)
That, ere the snake's, her sweet tongue could deceive
And her enchanted hair was the first gold.
And still she sits, young while the earth is old,
  And, subtly of herself contemplative,
  Draws men to watch the bright net she can weave,
Till heart and body and life are in its hold.

The rose and poppy are her flowers; for where
  Is he not found, O Lilith, whom shed scent
And soft-shed kisses and soft sleep shall snare?
  Lo! as that youth's eyes burned at thine, so went
  Thy spell through him, and left his straight neck bent,
And round his heart one strangling golden hair.

The Orchard-Pit

Piled deep below the screening apple-branch
   They lie with bitter apples in their hands:
And some are only ancient bones that blanch,
And some had ships that last year's wind did launch,
   And some were yesterday the lords of lands.

In the soft dell, among the apple-trees,
   High up above the hidden pit she stands,
And there for ever sings, who gave to these,
That lie below, her magic hour of ease,
   And those her apples holden in their hands.

This in my dreams is shown me; and her hair
   Crosses my lips and draws my burning breath;
Her song spreads golden wings upon the air,
Life's eyes are gleaming from her forehead fair,
   And from her breasts the ravishing eyes of Death.

Men say to me that sleep hath many dreams,
   Yet I knew never but this dream alone:
There, from a dried-up channel, once the stream's,
The glen slopes up; even such in sleep it seems
   As to my waking sight the place well known.

.   .   .   .

My love I call her, and she loves me well:
   But I love her as in the maelstrom's cup
The whirled stone loves the leaf inseparable
That clings to it round all the circling swell,
   And that the same last eddy swallows up.

Christina Rossetti

(1830–1894)

The Convent Threshold

There's blood between us, love, my love,
There's father's blood, there's brother's blood;
And blood's a bar I cannot pass:
I choose the stairs that mount above,
Stair after golden skyward stair,
To city and to sea of glass.
My lily feet are soiled with mud,
With scarlet mud which tells a tale
Of hope that was, of guilt that was,
Of love that shall not yet avail;
Alas, my heart, if I could bare
My heart, this self-same stain is there:
I seek the sea of glass and fire
To wash the spot, to burn the snare;
Lo, stairs are meant to lift us higher:
Mount with me, mount the kindled stair.

Your eyes look earthward, mine look up.
I see the far-off city grand,
Beyond the hills a watered land,
Beyond the gulf a gleaming strand
Of mansions where the righteous sup;
Who sleep at ease among their trees,
Or wake to sing a cadenced hymn
With Cherubim and Seraphim;

They bore the Cross, they drained the cup,
Racked, roasted, crushed, wrenched limb from limb,
They the offscouring of the world:
The heaven of starry heavens unfurled,
The sun before their face is dim.

You looking earthward, what see you?
Milk-white, wine-flushed among the vines,
Up and down leaping, to and fro,
Most glad, most full, made strong with wines,
Blooming as peaches pearled with dew,
Their golden windy hair afloat,
Love-music warbling in their throat,
Young men and women come and go.

You linger, yet the time is short:
Flee for your life, gird up your strength
To flee: the shadows stretched at length
Show that day wanes, that night draws nigh;
Flee to the mountain, tarry not.
Is this a time for smile and sigh,
For songs among the secret trees
Where sudden bluebirds nest and sport?
The time is short and yet you stay:
To-day, while it is called to-day,
Kneel, wrestle, knock, do violence, pray:
To-day is short, to-morrow nigh:
Why will you die? why will you die?

You sinned with me a pleasant sin:
Repent with me, for I repent.
Woe's me the lore I must unlearn!
Woe's me that easy way we went,
So rugged when I would return!
How long until my sleep begin,
How long shall stretch these nights and days?

Surely, clean Angels cry, she prays;
She laves her soul with tedious tears:
How long must stretch these years and years?

I turn from you my cheeks and eyes,
My hair which you shall see no more,—
Alas for joy that went before,
For joy that dies, for love that dies.
Only my lips still turn to you,
My livid lips that cry, Repent!
O weary life, O weary Lent,
O weary time whose stars are few!

How should I rest in Paradise,
Or sit on steps of Heaven alone?
If Saints and Angels spoke of love
Should I not answer from my throne?
Have pity upon me, ye my friends,
For I have heard the sound thereof:
Should I not turn with yearning eyes,
Turn earthwards with a pitiful pang?
O save me from a pang in Heaven!
By all the gifts we took and gave,
Repent, repent, and be forgiven:
This life is long, but yet it ends;
Repent and purge your soul and save:
No gladder song the morning stars
Upon their birthday morning sang
Than Angels sing when one repents.

I tell you what I dreamed last night:
A spirit with transfigured face
Fire-footed clomb an infinite space.
I heard his hundred pinions clang,
Heaven-bells rejoicing rang and rang,

Heaven-air was thrilled with subtle scents,
Worlds spun upon their rushing cars:
He mounted shrieking: "Give me light!"
Still light was poured on him, more light;
Angels, Archangels he outstripped,
Exultant in exceeding might,
And trod the skirts of Cherubim.
Still "Give me light," he shrieked; and dipped
His thirsty face, and drank a sea,
Athirst with thirst it could not slake.
I saw him, drunk with knowledge, take
From arching brows the aureole crown,—
His locks writhed like a cloven snake,—
He left his throne to grovel down
And lick the dust of Seraphs' feet:
For what is knowledge duly weighed?
Knowledge is strong, but love is sweet;
Yea, all the progress he had made
Was but to learn that all is small
Save love, for love is all in all.

I tell you what I dreamed last night:
It was not dark, it was not light,
Cold dews had drenched my plenteous hair
Through clay; you came to seek me there.
And "Do you dream of me?" you said.
My heart was dust that used to leap
To you; I answered half asleep:
"My pillow is damp, my sheets are red,
There's a leaden tester to my bed:
Find you a warmer playfellow,
A warmer pillow for your head,
A kinder love to love than mine."
You wrung your hands; while I like lead

Crushed downwards through the sodden earth:
You smote your hands but not in mirth,
And reeled but were not drunk with wine.

For all night long I dreamed of you:
I woke and prayed against my will,
Then slept to dream of you again.
At length I rose and knelt and prayed:
I cannot write the words I said,
My words were slow, my tears were few;
But through the dark my silence spoke
Like thunder. When this morning broke,
My face was pinched, my hair was gray,
And frozen blood was on the sill
Where stifling in my struggle I lay.

If now you saw me you would say:
Where is the face I used to love?
And I would answer: Gone before;
It tarries veiled in Paradise.
When once the morning star shall rise,
When earth with shadow flees away
And we stand safe within the door,
Then you shall lift the veil thereof.
Look up, rise up: for far above
Our palms are grown, our place is set;
There we shall meet as once we met,
And love with old familiar love.

Dream-Love

Young Love lies sleeping
    In May-time of the year,
Among the lilies,

Lapped in the tender light:
White lambs come grazing,
    White doves come building there;
And round about him
    The May-bushes are white.

Soft moss the pillow
    For O, a softer cheek;
Broad leaves cast shadow
    Upon the heavy eyes:
There winds and waters
    Grow lulled and scarcely speak;
There twilight lingers
    The longest in the skies.

Young Love lies dreaming;
    But who shall tell the dream?
A perfect sunlight
    On rustling forest tips;
Or perfect moonlight
    Upon a rippling stream;
Or perfect silence,
    Or song of cherished lips.

Burn odors round him
    To fill the drowsy air;
Weave silent dances
    Around him to and fro;
For O, in waking,
    The sights are not so fair,
And song and silence
    Are not like these below.

Young Love lies dreaming
    Till summer days are gone,—
Dreaming and drowsing
    Away to perfect sleep:

He sees the beauty
   Sun hath not looked upon,
And tastes the fountain
   Unutterably deep.

Him perfect music
   Doth hush unto his rest,
And through the pauses
   The perfect silence calms:
O, poor the voices
   Of earth from east to west,
And poor earth's stillness
   Between her stately palms.

Young Love lies drowsing
   Away to poppied death;
Cool shadows deepen
   Across the sleeping face:
So fails the summer
   With warm, delicious breath;
And what hath autumn
   To give us in its place?

Draw close the curtains
   Of branched evergreen;
Change cannot touch them
   With fading fingers sere:
Here the first violets
   Perhaps will bud unseen,
And a dove, maybe,
   Return to nestle here.

A Life's Parallels

Never on this side of the grave again,
    On this side of the river,
On this side of the garner of the grain,
    Never,—

Ever while time flows on and on and on,
    That narrow noiseless river,
Ever while corn bows heavy-headed, wan,
    Ever,—

Never despairing, often fainting, rueing,
    But looking back, ah never!
Faint yet pursuing, faint yet still pursuing
    Ever.

Luscious and Sorrowful

Beautiful, tender, wasting away for sorrow;
Thus to-day; and how shall it be with thee tomorrow?
    Beautiful, tender—what else?
        A hope tells.

Beautiful, tender, keeping the jubilee
In the land of home together, past death and sea;
    No more change or death, no more
        Salt sea-shore.

Spring Quiet

Gone were but the Winter,
   Come were but the Spring,
I would go to a covert
   Where the birds sing;

Where in the white-thorn
   Singeth a thrush,
And a robin sings
   In the holly-bush

Full of fresh scents
   Are the budding boughs,
Arching high over
   A cool green house:

Full of sweet scents,
   And whispering air
Which sayeth softly:
   "We spread no snare;

"Here dwell in safety,
   Here dwell alone,
With a clear stream
   And a mossy stone.

"Here the sun shineth
   Most shadily;
Here is heard an echo
   Of the far sea,
Though far off it be."

Echo

Come to me in the silence of the night;
　　Come in the speaking silence of a dream;
Come with soft rounded cheeks and eyes as bright
　　As sunlight on a stream;
　　　　Come back in tears,
O memory, hope, love of finished years.

O dream how sweet, too sweet, too bitter sweet,
　　Whose wakening should have been in Paradise,
Where souls brimfull of love abide and meet;
　　Where thirsty longing eyes
　　　　Watch the slow door
That opening, letting in, lets out no more.

Yet come to me in dreams, that I may live
　　My very life again though cold in death:
Come back to me in dreams, that I may give
　　Pulse for pulse, breath for breath:
　　　　Speak low, lean low,
As long ago, my love, how long ago!

Good Friday

Am I a stone, and not a sheep,
　　That I can stand, O Christ, beneath Thy cross,
　　To number drop by drop Thy Blood's slow loss,
And yet not weep?

Not so those women loved
　　Who with exceeding grief lamented Thee;
　　Not so fallen Peter weeping bitterly;
Not so the thief was moved;

Not so the Sun and Moon
　　Which hid their faces in a starless sky,
　　A horror of great darkness at broad noon—
I, only I.

Yet give not o'er,
　　But seek Thy sheep, true Shepherd of the flock;
　　Greater than Moses, turn and look once more
And smite a rock.

Sleep at Sea

Sound the deep waters:—
　　Who shall sound that deep?—
Too short the plummet,
　　And the watchmen sleep.
Some dream of effort
　　Up a toilsome steep;
Some dream of pasture grounds
　　For harmless sheep.

White shapes flit to and fro
　　From mast to mast;
They feel the distant tempest
　　That nears them fast:
Great rocks are straight ahead,
　　Great shoals not past;
They shout to one another
　　Upon the blast.

O, soft the streams drop music
   Between the hills,
And musical the birds' nests
   Beside those rills
The nests are types of home
   Love-hidden from ills,
The nests are types of spirits
   Love-music fills.

So dream the sleepers,
   Each man in his place;
The lightning shows the smile
   Upon each face:
The ship is driving, driving,
   It drives apace:
And sleepers smile, and spirits
   Bewail their case.

The lightning glares and reddens
   Across the skies;
It seems but sunset
   To those sleeping eyes.
When did the sun go down
   On such a wise?
From such a sunset
   When shall day arise?

"Wake," call the spirits:
   But to heedless ears;
They have forgotten sorrows
   And hopes and fears;
They have forgotten perils
   And smiles and tears;
Their dream has held them long
   Long years and years.

"Wake," call the spirits again:
　　But it would take
A louder summons
　　To bid them awake.
Some dream of pleasure
　　For another's sake;
Some dream, forgetful
　　Of a lifelong ache.

One by one slowly,
　　Ah, how sad and slow!
Wailing and praying
　　The spirits rise and go:
Clear stainless spirits
　　White, as white as snow;
Pale spirits, wailing
　　For an overthrow.

One by one flitting,
　　Like a mournful bird
Whose song is tired at last
　　For not mate heard.
The loving voice is silent,
　　The useless word;
One by one flitting,
　　Sick with hope deferred.

Driving and driving,
　　The ship drives amain:
While swift from mast to mast
　　Shapes flit again,
Flit silent as the silence
　　Where men lie slain;
Their shadow cast upon the sails
　　Is like a stain.

No voice to call the sleepers,
   No hand to raise:
They sleep to death in dreaming
   Of length of days.
Vanity of vanities,
   The Preacher says:
Vanity is the end
   Of all their ways.

Eve

"While I sit at the door,
Sick to gaze within,
Mine eye weepeth sore
For sorrow and sin:
As a tree my sin stands
To darken all lands;
Death is the fruit it bore.

"How have Eden bowers grown
Without Adams to bend them!
How have Eden flowers blown,
Squandering their sweet breath,
Without me to tend them!
The Tree of Life was ours,
Tree twelvefold-fruited,
Most lofty tree that flowers,
Most deeply rooted:
I chose the Tree of Death.

"Hadst thou but said me nay,
Adam, my brother,
I might have pined away;

I, but none other:
God might have let thee stay
Safe in our garden
By putting me away
Beyond all pardon.

"I, Eve, sad mother
Of all who must live,
I, not another,
Plucked bitterest fruit to give
My friend, husband, lover.
O wanton eyes run over!
Who but I should grieve?—
Cain hath slain his brother:
Of all who must die mother,
Miserable Eve!"

Thus she sat weeping,
Thus Eve, our mother,
Where one lay sleeping
Slain by his brother.
Greatest and least
Each piteous beast
To hear her voice
Forgot his joys
And set aside his feast.

The mouse paused in his walk
And dropped his wheaten stalk;
Grave cattle wagged their heads
In rumination;
The eagle gave a cry
From his cloud station;
Larks on thyme beds
Forbore to mount or sing;
Bees drooped upon the wing;

The raven perched on high
Forgot his ration;
The conies in their rock,
A feeble nation,
Quaked sympathetical;
The mocking-bird left off to mock;
Huge camels knelt as if
In deprecation;
The kind hart's tears were falling;
Chattered the wistful stork;
Dove-voices with a dying fall
Cooed desolation,
Answering grief by grief.

Only the serpent in the dust,
Wriggling and crawling,
Grinned an evil grin, and thrust
His tongue out with its fork.

Amor Mundi

"Oh, where are you going with your lovelocks flowing,
    On the west wind blowing along this valley track?"
"The downhill path is easy, come with me an' it please
        ye,
    We shall escape the uphill by never turning back."

So they two went together in glowing August weather,
    The honey-breathing heather lay to their left and
        right;
And dear she was to doat on, her swift feet seemed to
        float on
    The air like soft twin pigeons too sportive to alight.

"Oh, what is that in heaven where grey cloudflakes are
   seven,
   Where blackest clouds hang riven just at the rainy
   skirt?"
"Oh, that's a meteor sent us, a message dumb, por-
   tentous,
   An undecipher'd solemn signal of help or hurt."

"Oh, what is that glides quickly where velvet flowers
   grow thickly,
   Their scent comes rich and sickly?" "A scaled and
   hooded worm."
"Oh, what's that in the hollow, so pale I quake to fol-
   low?"
   "Oh, that's a thin dead body which waits the eternal
   term."

"Turn again, O my sweetest,—turn again, false and
   fleetest:
   This beaten way thou beatest I fear is hell's own
   track."
"Nay, too steep for hill-mounting; nay, too late for cost
   counting:
   This downhill path is easy, but there's no turning
   back."

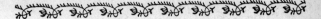

Emily Dickinson

(1830–1886)

The soul selects her own society

The soul selects her own society,
Then shuts the door;
On her divine majority
Obtrude no more.

Unmoved, she notes the chariot's pausing
At her low gate;
Unmoved, an emperor is kneeling
Upon her mat.

I've known her from an ample nation
Choose one;
Then close the valves of her attention
Like stone.

There's a certain slant of light

There's a certain slant of light,
On winter afternoons,
That oppresses, like the weight
Of cathedral tunes.

Heavenly hurt it gives us;
We can find no scar,

But internal difference
Where the meanings are.

None may teach it anything,
'Tis the seal, despair,—
An imperial affliction
Sent us of the air.

When it comes, the landscape listens,
Shadows hold their breath;
When it goes, 'tis like the distance
On the look of death.

Four trees upon a solitary acre

Four trees upon a solitary acre
Without design
Or order or apparent action
Maintain.

The sun upon a morning meets them,
The wind;
No nearer neighbor have they
But God.

The acre gives them place,
They, him, attention of passer-by—
Of shadow, or of squirrel, haply,
Or boy.

What deed is theirs unto the general nature,
What plan
They severally promote or hinder,
Unknown.

Farther in summer than the birds

Farther in summer than the birds,
Pathetic from the grass,
A minor nation celebrates
Its unobtrusive mass.

No ordinance is seen,
So gradual the grace,
A pensive custom it becomes,
Enlarging loneliness.

Antiquest felt at noon
When August, burning low,
Calls forth this spectral canticle,
Repose to typify.

Remit as yet no grace,
No furrow on the glow,
Yet a druidic difference
Enhances nature now.

I'll tell you how the sun rose

I'll tell you how the sun rose,—
A ribbon at a time.
The steeples swam in amethyst,
The news like squirrels ran.

The hills untied their bonnets,
The bobolinks begun.

Then I said softly to myself,
"That must have been the sun!"

•   •   •

But how he set, I know not.
There seemed a purple stile
Which little yellow boys and girls
Were climbing all the while

Till when they reached the other side,
A dominie in gray
Put gently up the evening bars,
And led the flock away.

The auctioneer of parting

The auctioneer of parting,
His "Going, going, gone,"
Shouts even from the crucifix
And brings his hammer down.

He only sells the wilderness.
The prices of despair
Range from a single human heart
To two—not any more.

A clock stopped—not the mantel's

A clock stopped—not the mantel's;
    Geneva's farthest skill
Can't put the puppet bowing
    That just now dangled still.

An awe came on the trinket!
   The figures hunched with pain,
Then quivered out of decimals
   Into degreeless noon.

It will not stir for doctors,
   This pendulum of snow;
The shopman importunes it,
   While cool, concernless No

Nods from the gilded pointers,
   Nods from the seconds slim,
Decades of arrogance between
   The dial life and him.

He scanned it, staggered, dropped the loop

He scanned it, staggered, dropped the loop
To past or period,
Caught helpless at a sense as if
His mind were going blind;

Groped up to see if God was there,
Groped backward at himself,
Caressed a trigger absently
And wandered out of life.

Rearrange a wife's affection

Rearrange a wife's affection?
When they dislocate my brain,
Amputate my freckled bosom,
Make me bearded like a man!

Blush, my spirit, in thy fastness,
Blush, my unacknowledged clay,
Seven years of troth have taught thee
More than wifehood ever may!

Love that never leaped its socket,
Trust entrenched in narrow pain,
Constancy through fire awarded,
Anguish bare of anodyne,

Burden borne so far triumphant
None suspect me of the crown,
For I wear the thorns till sunset,
Then my diadem put on.

Big my secret, but it's bandaged,
It will never get away
Till the day its weary keeper
Leads it through the grave to thee.

A faded boy in sallow clothes

A faded boy in sallow clothes
Who drove a lonesome cow
To pastures of oblivion—
A statesman's embryo.

The boys that whistled are extinct,
The cows that fed and thanked,
Remanded to a ballad's barn
Or clover's retrospect.

I taste a liquor never brewed

I taste a liquor never brewed,
From tankards scooped in pearl;
Not all the vats upon the Rhine
Yield such an alcohol!

Inebriate of air am I,
And debauchee of dew,
Reeling, through endless summer days,
From inns of molten blue.

When landlords turn the drunken bee
Out of the foxglove's door,
When butterflies renounce their drams,
I shall but drink the more!

Till seraphs swing their snowy hats,
And saints to windows run,
To see the little tippler
Leaning against the sun!

Because I could not stop for Death

Because I could not stop for Death,
He kindly stopped for me;
The carriage held but just ourselves
And Immortality.

We slowly drove, he knew no haste,
And I had put away

My labor, and my leisure too,
For his civility.

We passed the school where children played
Their lessons scarcely done;
We passed the fields of gazing grain,
We passed the setting sun.

We paused before a house that seemed
A swelling of the ground;
The roof was scarcely visible,
The cornice but a mound.

Since then 'tis centuries; but each
Feels shorter than the day
I first surmised the horses' heads
Were toward eternity.

We do not play on graves

We do not play on graves
Because there isn't room;
Besides, it isn't even,
It slants, and people come

And put a flower on it,
And hang their faces so,
We're fearing that their hearts will drop
And crush our pretty play.

And so we move as far
As enemies away,
Just looking round to see how far
It is, occasionally.

This dirty little heart

This dirty little heart
Is freely mine—
I won it with a bun—
A freckled shrine,

But eligibly fair
To him who sees
The visage of the soul
And not the knees.

Bloom is result

Bloom is result. To meet a flower
And casually glance
Would cause one scarcely to suspect
The minor circumstance

Assisting in the bright affair
So intricately done,
Then offered as a butterfly
To the meridian.

To pack the bud, oppose the worm,
Obtain its right of dew,
Adjust the heat, elude the wind,
Escape the prowling bee,

Great nature not to disappoint
Awaiting her that day—
To be a flower is profound
Responsibility!

How the waters closed above him

How the waters closed above him
We shall never know;
How he stretched his anguish to us,
That is covered too.

Spreads the pond her base of lilies
Bold above the boy
Whose unclaimèd hat and jacket
Sum the history.

The last night that she lived

The last night that she lived,
It was a common night,
Except the dying; this to us
Made nature different.

We noticed smallest things,—
Things overlooked before,
By this great light upon our minds
Italicized, as 'twere.

That others could exist
While she must finish quite,
A jealousy for her arose
So nearly infinite.

We waited while she passed;
It was a narrow time,

Too jostled were our souls to speak,
At length the notice came.

She mentioned, and forgot;
Then lightly as a reed
Bent to the water, shivered scarce,
Consented, and was dead.

And we, we placed the hair,
And drew the head erect;
And then an awful leisure was,
Our faith to regulate.

How many times these low feet staggered

How many times these low feet staggered,
Only the soldered mouth can tell;
Try! can you stir the awful rivet?
Try! can you lift the hasps of steel?

Stroke the cool forehead, hot so often,
Lift, if you can, the listless hair;
Handle the adamantine fingers
Never a thimble more shall wear.

Buzz the dull flies on the chamber window;
Brave shines the sun through the freckled pane;
Fearless the cobweb swings from the ceiling—
Indolent housewife, in daisies lain!

Ample make this bed

Ample make this bed.
Make this bed with awe;
In it wait till judgment break
Excellent and fair.

Be its mattress straight,
Be its pillow round;
Let no sunrise' yellow noise
Interrupt this ground.

The sky is low, the clouds are mean

The sky is low, the clouds are mean,
A traveling flake of snow
Across a barn or through a rut
Debates if it will go.

A narrow wind complains all day
How some one treated him;
Nature, like us, is sometimes caught
Without her diadem.

I started early, took my dog

I started early, took my dog,
And visited the sea;
The mermaids in the basement
Came out to look at me,

And frigates in the upper floor
Extended hempen hands,
Presuming me to be a mouse
Aground, upon the sands.

But no man moved me till the tide
Went past my simple shoe,
And past my apron and my belt,
And past my bodice too,

And made as he would eat me up
As wholly as a dew
Upon a dandelion's sleeve—
And then I started too.

And he—he followed close behind;
I felt his silver heel
Upon my ankle,—then my shoes
Would overflow with pearl.

Until we met the solid town,
No man he seemed to know;
And bowing with a mighty look
At me, the sea withdrew.

I've seen a dying eye

I've seen a dying eye
Run round and round a room
In search of something, as it seemed,
Then cloudier become;
And then, obscure with fog,
And then be soldered down,
Without disclosing what it be,
'Twere blessed to have seen.

I cannot live with you

I cannot live with you,
It would be life,
And life is over there
Behind the shelf

The sexton keeps the key to,
Putting up
Our life, his porcelain,
Like a cup

Discarded of the housewife,
Quaint or broken;
A newer Sèvres pleases,
Old ones crack.

I could not die with you,
For one must wait
To shut the other's gaze down,—
You could not.

And I, could I stand by
And see you freeze,
Without my right of frost,
Death's privilege?

Nor could I rise with you,
Because your face
Would put out Jesus',
That new grace

Glow plain and foreign
On my homesick eye,

Except that you, than he
Shone closer by.

They'd judge us—how?
For you served Heaven, you know,
Or sought to;
I could not,

Because you saturated sight,
And I had no more eyes
For sordid excellence
As Paradise.

And were you lost, I would be,
Though my name
Rang loudest
On the heavenly fame.

And were you saved,
And I condemned to be
Where you were not,
That self were hell to me.

So we must keep apart,
You there, I here,
With just the door ajar
That oceans are,
And prayer,
And that pale sustenance,
Despair!

The waters chased him as he fled

The waters chased him as he fled,
Not daring look behind;
A billow whispered in his ear,

"Come home with me, my friend!
My parlor is of shriven glass,
My pantry has a fish
For every palate in the year."
To this revolting bliss
The object floating at his side
Made no distinct reply.

I have never seen volcanoes

I have never seen volcanoes,
But when travelers tell
How those old phlegmatic mountains,
Usually so still,

Bear within appalling ordnance,
Fire and smoke and gun,
Taking villages for breakfast,
And appalling men,

If the stillness is volcanic
In the human face
When upon a pain Titanic
Features keep their place;

If at length the smouldering anguish
Will not overcome,
And the palpitating vineyard
In the dust be thrown;

If some loving antiquary
On Resumption morn
Will not cry with joy, "Pompeii!"
To the hills return!

I felt a funeral in my brain

I felt a funeral in my brain,
  And mourners, to and fro,
Kept treading, treading, till it seemed
  That sense was breaking through.

And when they all were seated,
  A service like a drum
Kept beating, beating, till I thought
  My mind was going numb.

And then I heard them lift a box,
  And creak across my soul
With those same boots of lead, again.
  Then space began to toll

As all the heavens were a bell,
  And Being but an ear,
And I and silence some strange race,
  Wrecked, solitary, here.

A narrow fellow in the grass

A narrow fellow in the grass
Occasionally rides;
You may have met him,—did you not?
His notice sudden is.

The grass divides as with a comb,
A spotted shaft is seen;

And then it closes at your feet
And opens further on.

He likes a boggy acre,
A floor to cool for corn.
Yet when a child, and barefoot,
I more than once, at morn,

Have passed, I thought, a whip-lash
Unbraiding in the sun,—
When, stooping to secure it,
It wrinkled, and was gone.

Several of nature's people
I know, and they know me;
I feel for them a transport
Of cordiality;

But never met this fellow,
Attended or alone,
Without a tighter breathing,
And zero at the bone.

A route of evanescence

A route of evanescence
With a revolving wheel;
A resonance of emerald,
A rush of cochineal;
And every blossom on the bush
Adjusts its tumbled head,—
The mail from Tunis, probably,
An easy morning's ride.

To hear an oriole sing

To hear an oriole sing
May be a common thing,
Or only a divine.

It is not of the bird
Who sings the same, unheard,
As unto crowd.

The fashion of the ear
Attireth that it hear
In dun or fair.

So whether it be rune,
Or whether it be none,
Is of within;

The "tune is in the tree,"
The sceptic showeth me;
"No, sir! In thee!"

Our journey had advanced

Our journey had advanced;
Our feet were almost come
To that odd fork in Being's road,
Eternity by term.

Our pace took sudden awe,
Our feet reluctant led.

412 EMILY DICKINSON

Before were cities, but between,
The forest of the dead.

Retreat was out of hope,—
Behind, a sealed route,
Eternity's white flag before,
And God at every gate.

As imperceptibly as grief

As imperceptibly as grief
The summer lapsed away,—
Too imperceptible, at last,
To seem like perfidy.

A quietness distilled,
As twilight long begun,
Or Nature, spending with herself
Sequestered afternoon.

The dust drew earlier in,
The morning foreign shone,—
A courteous, yet harrowing grace,
As guest who would be gone.

And thus, without a wing,
Or service of a keel,
Our summer made her light escape
Into the beautiful.

The bustle in a house

The bustle in a house
The morning after death
Is solemnest of industries
Enacted upon earth,—

The sweeping up the heart,
And putting love away
We shall not want to use again
Until eternity.

"Heavenly Father," take to thee

"Heavenly Father," take to thee
The supreme iniquity,
Fashioned by thy candid hand
In a moment contraband.
Though to trust us seem to us
More respectful—"we are dust."
We apologize to Thee
For Thine own Duplicity.

William Morris

(1834–1896)

FROM *Love Is Enough*

Love is enough: though the World be a-waning
And the woods have no voice but the voice of complain-
    ing,
  Though the sky be too dark for dim eyes to discover
The gold-cups and daisies fair blooming thereunder,
Though the hills be held shadows, and the sea a dark
    wonder,
  And this day draw a veil over all deeds passed over,
Yet their hands shall not tremble, their feet shall not
    falter;
The void shall not weary, the fear shall not alter
  These lips and these eyes of the loved and the lover.

Love is enough: it grew up without heeding
  In the days when ye knew not its name nor its meas-
    ure,
  And its leaflets untrodden by the light feet of pleasure
Had no boast of the blossom, no sign of the seeding,
  As the morning and evening passed over its treasure.

And what do ye say then?—That Spring long departed
  Has brought forth no child to the softness and
    showers;

—That we slept and we dreamed through the Sum-
    mer of flowers;
We dreamed of the Winter, and waking dead-hearted
    Found Winter upon us and waste of dull hours.

Nay, Spring was o'er-happy and knew not the reason,
    And Summer dreamed sadly, for she thought all was
        ended
    In her fulness of wealth that might not be amended;
But this is the harvest and the garnering season,
    And the leaf and the blossom in the ripe fruit are
        blended.

It sprang without sowing, it grew without heeding,
    Ye knew not its name and ye knew not its measure,
    Ye noted it not mid your hope and your pleasure;
There was pain in its blossom, despair in its seeding,
    But daylong your bosom now nurseth its treasure.

Love is enough: cherish life that abideth,
    Lest ye die ere ye know him, and curse and misname
        him;
For who knows in what ruin of all hope he hideth,
    On what wings of the terror of darkness he rideth?
    And what is the joy of man's life that ye blame him
        For his bliss grown a sword, and his rest grown a
        fire?

Ye who tremble for death, or the death of desire,
    Pass about the cold winter-tide garden and ponder
On the rose in his glory amidst of June's fire,
    On the languor of noontide that gathered the thunder,
    On the morn and its freshness, the eve and its won-
        der:

Ye may wake it no more—shall Spring come to
   awaken?

Live on, for Love liveth, and earth shall be shaken
   By the wind of his wings on the triumphing morning,
When the dead, and their deeds that die not shall
      awaken,
      And the world's tale shall sound in your trumpet of
         warning,
      And the sun smite the banner called Scorn of the
         Scorning,
         And dead pain ye shall trample, dead fruitless de-
            sire,
         As ye wend to pluck out the new world from the
            fire.

A Garden by the Sea

I know a little garden-close,
Set thick with lily and red rose,
Where I would wander if I might
From dewy morn to dewy night,
And have one with me wandering.

And though within it no birds sing,
And though no pillared house is there,
And though the apple-boughs are bare
Of fruit and blossom, would to God
Her feet upon the green grass trod,
And I beheld them as before.

There comes a murmur from the shore,
And in the close two fair streams are,
Drawn from the purple hills afar,

Drawn down unto the restless sea:
Dark hills whose heath-bloom feeds no bee,
Dark shore no ship has ever seen,
Tormented by the billows green
Whose murmur comes unceasingly
Unto the place for which I cry.

For which I cry both day and night,
For which I let slip all delight,
Whereby I grow both deaf and blind,
Careless to win, unskilled to find,
And quick to lose what all men seek.

Yet tottering as I am and weak,
Still have I left a little breath
To seek within the jaws of death
An entrance to that happy place,
To seek the unforgotten face,
Once seen, once kissed, once reft from me
Anigh the murmuring of the sea.

The Haystack in the Floods

Had she come all the way for this,
To part at last without a kiss?
Yea, had she borne the dirt and rain
That her own eyes might see him slain
Beside the haystack in the floods?

Along the dripping leafless woods,
The stirrup touching either shoe,
She rode astride as troopers do;
With kirtle kilted to her knee,
To which the mud splash'd wretchedly;

And the wet dripp'd from every tree
Upon her head and heavy hair,
And on her eyelids broad and fair;
The tears and rain ran down her face.
By fits and starts they rode apace,
And very often was his place
Far off from her; he had to ride
Ahead, to see what might betide
When the roads cross'd; and sometimes, when
There rose a murmuring from his men,
Had to turn back with promises;
Ah me! she had but little ease;
And often for pure doubt and dread
She sobb'd, made giddy in the head
By the swift riding; while, for cold,
Her slender fingers scarce could hold
The wet reins; yea, and scarcely, too,
She felt the foot within her shoe
Against the stirrup: all for this,
To part at last without a kiss
Beside the haystack in the floods.

For when they near'd that old soak'd hay,
They saw across the only way
That Judas, Godmar, and the three
Red running lions dismally
Grinn'd from his pennon, under which,
In one straight line along the ditch,
They counted thirty heads.

              So then,
While Robert turn'd round to his men,
She saw at once the wretched end,
And, stooping down, tried hard to rend
Her coif the wrong way from her head,

And hid her eyes; while Robert said:
"Nay, love, 'tis scarcely two to one,
At Poictiers where we made them run
So fast—why, sweet my love, good cheer,
The Gascon frontier is so near,
Nought after this."

           But, "O," she said,
"My God! my God! I have to tread
The long way back without you; then
The court at Paris; those six men;
The gratings of the Chatelet;
The swift Seine on some rainy day
Like this, and people standing by,
And laughing, while my weak hands try
To recollect how strong men swim.
All this, or else a life with him,
For which I should be damned at last,
Would God that this next hour were past!"

He answer'd not, but cried his cry,
"St. George for Marny!" cheerily;
And laid his hand upon her rein.
Alas! no man of all his train
Gave back that cheery cry again;
And, while for rage his thumb beat fast
Upon his sword-hilt, some one cast
About his neck a kerchief long,
And bound him.

           Then they went along
To Godmar; who said: "Now, Jehane,
Your lover's life is on the wane
So fast, that, if this very hour
You yield not as my paramour,

He will not see the rain leave off—
Nay, keep your tongue from gibe and scoff,
Sir Robert, or I slay you now."

She laid her hand upon her brow,
Then gazed upon the palm, as though
She thought her forehead bled, and—"No!"
She said, and turn'd her head away,
As there were nothing else to say,
And everything were settled: red
Grew Godmar's face from chin to head:
"Jehane, on yonder hill there stands
My castle, guarding well my lands:
What hinders me from taking you,
And doing that I list to do
To your fair wilful body, while
Your knight lies dead?"

                A wicked smile
Wrinkled her face, her lips grew thin,
A long way out she thrust her chin:
"You know that I should strangle you
While you were sleeping; or bite through
Your throat, by God's help—ah!" she said,
"Lord Jesus, pity your poor maid!
For in such wise they hem me in,
I cannot choose but sin and sin,
Whatever happens: yet I think
They could not make me eat or drink,
And so should I just reach my rest."
"Nay, if you do not my behest,
O Jehane! though I love you well,"
Said Godmar, "would I fail to tell
All that I know?" "Foul lies," she said.
"Eh? lies my Jehane? by God's head,
At Paris folks would deem them true!

Do you know, Jehane, they cry for you:
'Jehane the brown! Jehane the brown!
Give us Jehane to burn or drown!'—
Eh—gag me Robert!—sweet my friend,
This were indeed a piteous end
For those long fingers, and long feet,
And long neck, and smooth shoulders sweet:
An end that few men would forget
That saw it—So, an hour yet:
Consider, Jehane, which to take
Of life or death!"

    So, scarce awake,
Dismounting, did she leave that place,
And totter some yards: with her face
Turn'd upward to the sky she lay,
Her head on a wet heap of hay,
And fell asleep: and while she slept
And did not dream, the minutes crept
Round to the twelve again; but she,
Being waked at last, sigh'd quietly,
And strangely childlike came, and said:
"I will not." Straightway Godmar's head,
As though it hung on strong wires, turn'd
Most sharply round, and his face burn'd.

For Robert—both his eyes were dry,
He could not weep, but gloomily
He seem'd to watch the rain; yea, too,
His lips were firm; he tried once more
To touch her lips; she reach'd out, sore
And vain desire so tortured them,
The poor grey lips, and now the hem
Of his sleeve brush'd them.

    With a start
Up Godmar rose, thrust them apart;

From Robert's throat he loosed the bands
Of silk and mail; with empty hands
Held out, she stood and gazed, and saw,
The long bright blade without a flaw
Glide out from Godmar's sheath, his hand
In Robert's hair; she saw him bend
Back Robert's head; she saw him send
The thin steel down; the blow told well,
Right backward the knight Robert fell,
And moan'd as dogs do, being half dead,
Unwitting, as I deem: so then
Godmar turn'd grinning to his men,
Who ran, some five or six, and beat
His head to pieces at their feet.

Then Godmar turn'd again and said:
"So, Jehane, the first fitte is read!
Take note, my lady, that your way
Lies backward to the Chatelet!"
She shook her head and gazed awhile
At her cold hands with a rueful smile,
As though this thing had made her mad.

This was the parting that they had
Beside the haystack in the floods.

For the Bed at Kelmscott

The wind's on the wold
And the night is a-cold,
And Thames runs chill
Twixt mead and hill,
But kind and dear

Is the old house here,
And my heart is warm
Midst winter's harm.
Rest, then and rest,
And think of the best
Twixt summer and spring
When all birds sing
In the town of the tree,
And ye lie in me
And scarce dare move
Lest earth and its love
Should fade away
Ere the full of the day.

I am old and have seen
Many things that have been,
Both grief and peace,
And wane and increase.
No tale I tell
Of ill or well,
But this I say,
Night treadeth on day,
And for worst and best
Right good is rest.

FROM *The Story of Sigurd the Volsung*

SIGURD RIDETH TO THE GLITTERING HEATH

Again on the morrow morning doth Sigurd the Volsung
    ride,
And Regin, the Master of Masters, is faring by his side,
And they leave the dwelling of kings and ride the sum-
    mer land,

Until at the eve of the day the hills are on either hand:

Then they wend up higher and higher, and over the heaths they fare

Till the moon shines broad on the midnight, and they sleep 'neath the heavens bare;

And they waken and look behind them, and lo, the dawning of day

And the little land of the Helper and its valleys far away;

But the mountains rise before them, a wall exceeding great.

Then spake the Master of Masters: "We have come to the garth and the gate:

There is youth and rest behind thee and many a thing to do,

There is many a fond desire, and each day born anew;

And the land of the Volsungs to conquer, and many a people's praise:

And for me there is rest it may be, and the peaceful end of days.

We have come to the garth and the gate; to the hall-door now shall we win,

Shall we go to look on the high-seat and see what sitteth therein?"

"Yea, and what else?" said Sigurd, "was thy tale but mockeries,

And have I been drifted hither on a wind of empty lies?"

"It was sooth, it was sooth," said Regin, "and more might I have told

Had I heart and space to remember the deeds of the days of old."

And he hung down his head as he spake it, and was silent a little space;

And when it was lifted again there was fear in the
   Dwarf-king's face.
And he said: "Thou knowest my thought, and wise-
   hearted art thou grown:
It were well if thine eyes were blinder, and we each
   were faring alone,
And I with my eld and my wisdom, and thou with thy
   youth and thy might;
Yet whiles I dream I have wrought thee, a beam of the
   morning bright,
A fatherless motherless glory, to work out my desire;
Then high my hope ariseth, and my heart is all afire
For the world I behold from afar, and the day that yet
   shall be;
Then I wake and all things I remember and a youth
   from the Kings I see—
—The child of the Wood-abider, the seed of a con-
   quered King,
The sword that the Gods have fashioned, the fate that
   men shall sing:—
Ah might the world run backward to the days of the
   Dwarfs of old,
When I hewed out the pillars of crystal, and smoothed
   the walls of gold!"

Nought answered the Son of Sigmund; nay he heard
   him nought at all,
Save as though the wind were speaking in the bights of
   the mountain-hall:
But he leapt aback of Greyfell, and the glorious sun rose
   up,
And the heavens glowed above him like the bowl of
   Baldur's cup,
And a golden man was he waxen; as the heart of the
   sun he seemed

While over the feet of the mountains like blood the new
    light streamed;
Then Sigurd cried to Greyfell and swift for the pass he
    rode,
And Regin followed after as a man bowed down by a
    load.

Day-long they fared through the mountains, and that
    highway's fashioner
Forsooth was a fearful craftsman, and his hands the
    waters were,
And the heaped-up ice was his mattock, and the fire-
    blast was his man,
And never a whit he heeded though his walls were
    waste and wan,
And the guest-halls of that wayside great heaps of the
    ashes spent.
But, each as a man alone, through the sun-bright day
    they went,
And they rode till the moon rose upward, and the stars
    were small and fair,
Then they slept on the long-slaked ashes beneath the
    heavens bare;
And the cold dawn came and they wakened, and the
    King of the Dwarf-kind seemed
As a thing of that wan land fashioned; but Sigurd
    glowed and gleamed
Amid the shadowless twilight by Greyfell's cloudy
    flank,
As a little space they abided while the latest star-world
    shrank;
On the backward road looked Regin and heard how
    Sigurd drew
The girths of Greyfell's saddle, and the voice of his
    sword he knew,

And he feared to look on the Volsung, as thus he fell to
    speak:

"I have seen the Dwarf-folk mighty, I have seen the
    God-folk weak;
And now, though our might be minished, yet have we
    gifts to give.
When men desire and conquer, most sweet is their life
    to live;
When men are young and lovely there is many a thing
    to do,
And sweet is their fond desire and the dawn that springs
    anew."

"This gift," said the Son of Sigurd, "the Norns shall give
    me yet,
And no blossoms slain by the sunshine while the leaves
    with dew are wet."

Then Regin turned and beheld him: "Thou shalt deem
    it hard and strange,
When the hand hath encompassed it all, and yet thy life
    must change.
Ah, long were the lives of men-folk, if betwixt the Gods
    and them
Were mighty warders watching mid the earth's and
    heaven's hem!
Is there any man so mighty he would cast his gift
    away,—
The heart's desire accomplished, and life so long a day,
That the dawn should be forgotten ere the even was
    begun?"

Then Sigurd laughed and answered: "Fare forth, O
    glorious sun;
Bright end from bright beginning, and the mid-way
    good to tell,

And death, and deeds accomplished, and all remem-
bered well!

Shall the day go past and leave us, and we be left with
night,

To tread the endless circle, and strive in vain to smite?

But thou—wilt thou still look backward? thou sayst I
know thy thought:

Thou hast whetted the sword for the slaying, it shall
turn aside for nought.

Fear not! with the Gold and the wisdom thou shalt deem
thee God alone,

And mayst do and undo at pleasure, nor be bound by
right nor wrong:

And then, if no God I be waxen, I shall be the weak
with the strong."

And his war-gear clanged and tinkled as he leapt to the
saddle-stead:

And the sun rose up at their backs and the grey world
changed to red,

And away to the west went Sigurd by the glory
wreathed about,

But little and black was Regin as a fire that dieth out.

Day-long they rode the mountains by the crags exceed-
ing old,

And the ash that the first of the Dwarf-kind found dull
and quenched and cold.

Then the moon in the mid-sky swam, and the stars were
fair and pale,

And beneath the naked heaven they slept in an ash-grey
dale;

And again at the dawn-dusk's ending they stood upon
their feet,

And Sigurd donned his war-gear nor his eyes would
Regin meet.

A clear streak widened in heaven low down above the
    earth;
And above it lay the cloud-flecks, and the sun, anigh its
    birth,
Unseen, their hosts was staining with the very hue of
    blood,
And ruddy by Greyfell's shoulder the Son of Sigmund
    stood.

Then spake the Master of Masters: "What is thine hope
    this morn
That thou dightest thee, O Sigurd, to ride this world
    forlorn?"

"What needeth hope," said Sigurd, "when the heart of
    the Volsungs turns
To the light of the Glittering Heath, and the house
    where the Waster burns?
I shall slay the Foe of the Gods, as thou badst me a
    while agone,
And then with the Gold and its wisdom shalt thou be
    left alone."

"O Child," said the King of the Dwarf-kind, "when the
    day at last comes round
For the dread and the Dusk of the Gods, and the kin of
    the Wolf is unbound,
When the sword shall hew the fire, and the wildfire
    beateth thy shield,
Shalt thou praise the wages of hope and the Gods that
    pitched the field?"

"O Foe of the Gods," said Sigurd, "wouldst thou hide
    the evil thing,
And the curse that is greater than thou, lest death end
    thy labouring,

Lest the night should come upon thee amidst thy toil for
    nought?
It is me, it is me that thou fearest, if indeed I know thy
    thought;
Yea me, who would utterly light the face of all good and
    ill,
If not with the fruitful beams that the summer shall ful-
    fill,
Then at least with the world a-blazing, and the glare of
    the grinded sword."

And he sprang aloft to the saddle as he spake the latest
    word,
And the Wrath sang loud in the sheath as it ne'er had
    sung before,
And the cloudy flecks were scattered like flames on the
    heaven's floor,
And all was kindled at once, and that trench of the
    mountains grey
Was filled with the living light as the low sun lit the way:
But Regin turned from the glory with blinded eyes and
    dazed,
And lo, on the cloudy war-steed how another light there
    blazed,
And a great voice came from amidst it:
                        "O Regin, in good sooth,
I have hearkened not nor heeded the words of thy fear
    and thy ruth:
Thou hast told thy tale and thy longing, and thereto I
    hearkened well:—
Let it lead thee up to heaven, let it lead thee down to
    hell,
The deed shall be done tomorrow: thou shalt have that
    measureless Gold,

And devour the garnered wisdom that blessed thy realm
    of old,
That hath lain unspent and begrudged in the very heart
    of hate:
With the blood and the might of thy brother thine
    hunger shalt thou sate;
And this deed shall be mine and thine; but take heed for
    what followeth then!
Let each do after his kind! I shall do the deeds of men;
I shall harvest the field of their sowing, in the bed of
    their strewing shall sleep;
To them shall I give my life-days, to the Gods my glory
    to keep.
But thou with the wealth and the wisdom that the best
    of the Gods might praise,
If thou shalt indeed excel them and become the hope of
    the days,
Then me in turn hast thou conquered, and I shall be in
    turn
Thy fashioned brand of the battle through good and evil
    to burn,
Or the flame that sleeps in thy stithy for the gathered
    winds to blow,
When thou listest to do and undo and thine uttermost
    cunning to show.
But indeed I wot full surely that thou shalt follow thy
    kind;
And for all that cometh after, the Norns shall loose and
    bind."

Then his bridle-reins rang sweetly, and the warding-
    walls of death,
And Regin drew up to him, and the Wrath sang loud
    in the sheath,

And forth from the trench in the mountains by the west-
    ward way they ride;
And little and black goes Regin by the golden Volsung's
    side;
But no more his head is drooping, for he seeth the Elf-
    king's Gold;
The garnered might and the wisdom e'en now his eyes
    behold.

So up and up they journeyed, and ever as they went
About the cold-slaked forges, o'er many a cloud-swept
    bent,
Betwixt the walls of blackness, by shores of the fishless
    meres,
And the fathomless desert waters, did Regin cast his
    fears,
And wrap him in desire; and all alone he seemed
As a God to his heirship wending, and forgotten and
    undreamed
Was all the tale of Sigurd, and the folk he had toiled
    among,
And the Volsungs, Odin's children, and the men-folk fair
    and young.

So on they ride to the westward, and huge were the
    mountains grown
And the floor of the heaven was mingled with that toss-
    ing world of stone:
And they rode till the noon was forgotten and the sun
    was waxen low,
And they tarried not, though he perished, and the world
    grew dark below.
Then they rode a mighty desert, a glimmering place and
    wide,
And into a narrow pass high-walled on either side

By the blackness of the mountains, and barred aback and
    in face
By the empty night of the shadow; a windless silent
    place:
But the white moon shone o'erhead mid the small sharp
    stars and pale,
And each as a man alone they rode on the highway of
    bale.

So ever they wended upward, and the midnight hour
    was o'er,
And the stars grew pale and paler, and failed from the
    heaven's floor,
And the moon was a long while dead, but where was the
    promise of day?
No change came over the darkness, no streak of the
    dawning grey;
No sound of the wind's uprising adown the night there
    ran:
It was blind as the Gaping Gulf ere the first of the
    worlds began.

Then athwart and athwart rode Sigurd and sought the
    walls of the pass,
But found no wall before him; and the road rang hard as
    brass
Beneath the hoofs of Greyfell, as up and up he trod:
—Was it the daylight of Hell, or the night of the door-
    way of God?

But lo, at the last a glimmer, and a light from the west
    there came,
And another and another, like the points of far-off
    flame;
And they grew and brightened and gathered; and
    whiles together they ran

Like the moonwake over the waters; and whiles they
    were scant and wan,
Some greater and some lesser, like the boats of fishers
    laid
About the sea of midnight; and a dusky dawn they
    made,
A faint and glimmering twilight: So Sigurd strains his
    eyes,
And he sees how a land deserted all round about him
    lies
More changeless than mid-ocean, as fruitless as its floor:
Then the heart leaps up within him, for he knows that
    his journey is o'er,
And there he draweth bridle on the first of the Glitter-
    ing Heath:
And the Wrath is waken merry and sings in the golden
    sheath
As he leaps adown from Greyfell, and stands upon his
    feet,
And wends his ways through the twilight the Foe of the
    Gods to meet.

(From Book II)

FROM *The Hollow Land*

SONG

Christ keep the Hollow Land
    Through the sweet springtide,
When the apple-blossoms bless
    The lowly bent hill side.

Christ keep the Hollow Land
    All the summer-tide;

Still we cannot understand
    Where the waters glide:

Only dimly seeing them
    Coldly slipping through
Many green-lipped cavern mouths
    Where the hills are blue.

Algernon Charles Swinburne

(1837–1909)

FROM *Atalanta in Calydon*

[*Invocations*]

CHIEF HUNTSMAN. Maiden, and mistress of the months
    and stars
Now folded in the flowerless fields of heaven,
Goddess whom all gods love with threefold heart,
Being treble in thy divided deity,
A light for dead men and dark hours, a foot
Swift on the hills as morning, and a hand
To all things fierce and fleet that roar and range
Mortal, with gentler shafts than snow or sleep;
Hear now and help and lift no violent hand,
But favourable and fair as thine eye's beam
Hidden and shown in heaven; for I all night
Amid the king's hounds and the hunting men
Have wrought and worshipped toward thee; nor shall
    man
See goodlier hounds or deadlier edge of spears;
But for the end, that lies unreached at yet
Between the hands and on the knees of gods.
O fair-faced sun killing the stars and dews
And dreams and desolation of the night!
Rise up, shine, stretch thine hand out, with thy bow
Touch the most dimmest height of trembling heaven,
And burn and break the dark about thy ways,
Shot through and through with arrows; let thine hair

Lighten as flame above that flameless shell
Which was the moon, and thine eyes fill the world
And thy lips kindle with swift beams; let earth
Laugh, and the long sea fiery from thy feet
Through all the roar and ripple of streaming springs
And foam in reddening flakes and flying flowers
Shaken from hands and blown from lips of nymphs
Whose hair or breast divides the wandering wave
With salt close tresses cleaving lock to lock,
All gold, or shuddering and unfurrowed snow;
And all the winds about thee with their wings,
And fountain-heads of all the watered world;
Each horn of Acheloüs, and the green
Euenus, wedded with the straitening sea.
For in fair time thou comest; come also thou,
Twin-born with him, and virgin, Artemis,
And give our spears their spoil, the wild boar's hide,
Sent in thine anger against us for sin done
And bloodless altars without wine or fire.
Him now consume thou; for thy sacrifice
With sanguine-shining steam divides the dawn,
And one, the maiden rose of all thy maids,
Arcadian Atalanta, snowy-souled,
Fair as the snow and footed as the wind,
From Ladon and well-wooded Mænalus
Over the firm hills and the fleeting sea
Hast thou drawn hither, and many an armèd king,
Heroes, the crown of men, like gods in fight.
Moreover out of all the Ætolian land,
From the full-flowered Lelantian pasturage
To what of fruitful field the son of Zeus
Won from the roaring river and labouring sea
When the wild god shrank in his horn and fled
And foamed and lessened through his wrathful fords,
Leaving clear lands that steamed with sudden sun,

These virgins with the lightening of the day
Bring thee fresh wreaths and their own sweeter hair,
Luxurious locks and flower-like mixed with flowers,
Clean offering, and chaste hymns; but me the time
Divides from these things; whom do thou not less
Help and give honour, and to mine hounds good speed,
And edge to spears, and luck to each man's hand.

CHORUS. When the hounds of spring are on winter's
        traces,
    The mother of months in meadow or plain
Fills the shadows and windy places
    With lisp of leaves and ripple of rain;
And the brown bright nightingale amorous
Is half assuaged for Itylus,
For the Thracian ships and the foreign faces,
    The tongueless vigil, and all the pain.

Come with bows bent and with emptying of quivers,
    Maiden most perfect, lady of light,
With a noise of winds and many rivers,
    With a clamour of waters, and with might;
Bind on thy sandals, O thou most fleet,
Over the splendour and speed of thy feet;
For the faint east quickens, the wan west shivers,
    Round the feet of the day and the feet of the night.

Where shall we find her, how shall we sing to her,
    Fold our hands round her knees, and cling?
O that man's heart were as fire and could spring to her,
    Fire, or the strength of the streams that spring!
For the stars and the winds are unto her
As raiment, as songs of the harp-player;
For the risen stars and the fallen cling to her,
    And the southwest-wind and the west-wind sing.

For winter's rains and ruins are over,
  And all the season of snows and sins;
The days dividing lover and lover,
  The light that loses, the night that wins;
And time remembered is grief forgotten,
And frosts are slain and flowers begotten,
And in green underwood and cover
  Blossom by blossom the spring begins.

The full streams feed on flower of rushes,
  Ripe grasses trammel a travelling foot,
The faint fresh flame of the young year flushes
  From leaf to flower and flower to fruit;
And fruit and leaf are as gold and fire,
And the oat is heard above the lyre,
And the hoofèd heel of a satyr crushes
  The chestnut-husk at the chestnut-root.

And Pan by noon and Bacchus by night,
  Fleeter of foot than the fleet-foot kid,
Follows with dancing and fills with delight
  The Mænad and the Bassarid;
And soft as lips that laugh and hide
The laughing leaves of the trees divide,
And screen from seeing and leave in sight
  The god pursuing, the maiden hid.

The ivy falls with the Bacchanal's hair
  Over her eyebrows hiding her eyes;
The wild vine slipping down leaves bare
  Her bright breast shortening into sighs;
The wild vine slips with the weight of its leaves,
But the berried ivy catches and cleaves
To the limbs that glitter, the feet that scare
  The wolf that follows, the fawn that flies.

(Lines 1–120)

A Leave-Taking

Let us go hence, my songs; she will not hear.
Let us go hence together without fear;
Keep silence now, for singing-time is over,
And over all things and all things dear.
She loves not you nor me as all we love her.
Yea, though we sang as angels in her ear,
　　　She would not hear.

Let us rise up and part; she will not know.
Let us go seaward as the great winds go,
Full of blown sand and foam; what help is here?
There is no help, for all these things are so,
And all the world is bitter as a tear.
And how these things are, though ye strove to show,
　　　She would not know.

Let us go home and hence; she will not weep,
We gave love many dreams and days to keep,
Flowers without scent, and fruits that would not grow,
Saying, "If thou wilt, thrust in thy sickle and reap."
All is reaped now; no grass is left to mow;
And we that sowed, though all we fell on sleep,
　　　She would not weep.

Let us go hence and rest; she will not love.
She shall not hear us if we sing hereof,
Nor see love's ways, how sore they are and steep.
Come hence, let be, lie still; it is enough.
Love is a barren sea, bitter and deep;
And though she saw all heaven in flower above,
　　　She would not love.

Let us give up, go down; she will not care.
Though all the stars made gold of all the air,
And the sea moving saw before it move
One moon-flower making all the foam-flowers fair;
Though all those waves went over us, and drove
Deep down the stifling lips and drowning hair,
        She would not care.

Let us go hence, go hence; she will not see.
Sing all once more together: surely she,
She too, remembering days and words that were,
Will turn a little toward us, sighing; but we,
We are hence, we are gone, as though we had not been
            there.
Nay, and though all men seeing had pity on me,
        She would not see.

Hymn to Proserpine

(AFTER THE PROCLAMATION IN ROME
OF THE CHRISTIAN FAITH)

Vicisti, Galilæe

I have lived long enough, having seen one thing, that
    love hath an end;
Goddess and maiden and queen, be near me now and
    befriend.
Thou art more than the day or the morrow, the seasons
    that laugh or that weep;
For these give joy and sorrow; but thou, Proserpina,
    sleep.
Sweet is the treading of wine, and sweet the feet of the
    dove;

But a goodlier gift is thine than foam of the grapes or
love.

Yea, is not even Apollo, with hair and harpstring of
gold,

A bitter God to follow, a beautiful God to behold?

I am sick of singing; the bays burn deep and chafe: I
am fain

To rest a little from praise and grievous pleasure and
pain.

For the Gods we know not of, who give us our daily
breath,

We know they are cruel as love or life, and lovely as
death.

O Gods dethroned and deceased, cast forth, wiped out
in a day!

From your wrath is the world released, redeemed from
your chains, men say.

New Gods are crowned in the city; their flowers have
broken your rods;

They are merciful, clothed with pity, the young com-
passionate Gods.

But for me their new device is barren, the days are bare;

Things long past over suffice, and men forgotten that
were,

Time and the Gods are at strife; ye dwell in the midst
thereof,

Draining a little life from the barren breasts of love.

I say to you, cease, take rest; yea, I say to you all, be
at peace,

Till the bitter milk of her breast and the barren bosom
shall cease.

Wilt thou yet take all, Galilean? but these thou shalt not
take,

The laurel, the palms and the pæan, the breasts of the
nymphs in the brake;

Breasts more soft than a dove's, that tremble with tenderer breath;

And all the wings of the Loves, and all the joy before death;

All the feet of the hours that sound as a single lyre,

Dropped and deep in the flowers, with strings that flicker like fire.

More than these wilt thou give, things fairer than all these things?

Nay, for a little we live, and life hath mutable wings.

A little while and we die; shall life not thrive as it may?

For no man under the sky lives twice, outliving his day.

And grief is a grievous thing, and a man hath enough of his tears:

Why should he labour, and bring fresh grief to blacken his years?

Thou hast conquered, O pale Galilean; the world has grown grey from thy breath;

We have drunken of things Lethean, and fed on the fullness of death.

Laurel is green for a season, and love is sweet for a day;

But love grows bitter with treason, and laurel outlives not May.

Sleep, shall we sleep after all? for the world is not sweet in the end;

For the old faiths loosen and fall, the new years ruin and rend.

Fate is a sea without shore, and the soul is a rock that abides;

But her ears are vexed with the roar and her face with the foam of the tides.

O lips that the live blood faints in, the leavings of racks and rods!

O ghastly glories of saints, dead limbs of gibbeted Gods!

Though all men abase them before you in spirit, and all
  knees bend,

I kneel not neither adore you, but standing, look to the
  end.

All delicate days and pleasant, all spirits and sorrows are
  cast

Far out with the foam of the present that sweeps to the
  surf of the past:

Where beyond the extreme sea-wall, and between the
  remote sea-gates,

Waste water washes, and tall ships founder, and deep
  death waits:

Where, mighty with deepening sides, clad about with
  the seas as with wings,

And impelled of invisible tides, and fulfilled of unspeak-
  able things,

White-eyed and poisonous-finned, shark-toothed and
  serpentine-curled,

Rolls, under the whitening wind of the future, the wave
  of the world.

The depths stand naked in sunder behind it, the storms
  flee away;

In the hollow before it the thunder is taken and snared
  as a prey;

In its sides is the north-wind bound; and its salt is of
  all men's tears;

With light of ruin, and sound of changes, and pulse of
  years:

With travail of day after day, and with trouble of hour
  upon hour;

And bitter as blood is the spray; and the crests are as
  fangs that devour:

And its vapour and storm of its steam as the sighing of
  spirits to be;

And its noise as the noise in a dream; and its depth as
the roots of the sea:

And the height of its heads as the height of the utmost
stars of the air:

And the ends of the earth at the might thereof tremble,
and time is made bare.

Will ye bridle the deep sea with reins, will ye chasten
the high sea with rods?

Will ye take her to chain her with chains, who is older
than all ye Gods?

All ye as a wind shall go by, as a fire shall ye pass and
be past;

Ye are Gods, and behold, ye shall die, and the waves be
upon you at last.

In the darkness of time, in the deeps of the years, in the
changes of things,

Ye shall sleep as a slain man sleeps, and the world shall
forget you for kings.

Though the feet of thine high priests tread where thy
lords and our forefathers trod,

Though these that were Gods are dead, and thou being
dead art a God,

Though before thee the throned Cytherean be fallen,
and hidden her head,

Yet thy kingdom shall pass, Galilean, thy dead shall go
down to thee dead.

Of the maiden thy mother men sing as a goddess with
grace clad around;

Thou art throned where another was king; where an-
other was queen she is crowned.

Yea, once we had sight of another: but now she is
queen, say these.

Not as thine, not as thine was our mother, a blossom of
flowering seas,

Clothed round with the world's desire as with raiment,
and fair as the foam,

And fleeter than kindled fire, and a goddess, and mother
of Rome.

For thine came pale and a maiden, and sister to sorrow;
but ours,

Her deep hair heavily laden with odour and colour of
flowers,

White rose of the rose-white water, a silver splendour,
a flame,

Bent down unto us that besought her, and earth grew
sweet with her name.

For thine came weeping, a slave among slaves, and re-
jected; but she

Came flushed from the full-flushed wave, and imperial,
her foot on the sea.

And the wonderful waters knew her, the winds and the
viewless ways,

And the roses grew rosier, and bluer the sea-blue stream
of the bays.

Ye are fallen, our lords, by what token? we wist that ye
should not fall.

Ye were all so fair that are broken; and one more fair
than ye all.

But I turn to her still, having seen she shall surely abide
in the end;

Goddess and maiden and queen, be near me now and
befriend.

O daughter of earth, of my mother, her crown and blos-
som of birth,

I am also, I also, thy brother; I go as I came unto earth.

In the night where thine eyes are as moons are in
heaven, the night where thou art,

Where the silence is more than all tunes, where sleep
overflows from the heart,

Where the poppies are sweet as the rose in our world,
and the red rose is white,

And the wind falls faint as it blows with the fume of the
flowers of the night,

And the murmur of spirits that sleep in the shadow of
Gods from afar

Grows dim in thine ears and deep as the deep dim soul
of a star,

In the sweet low light of thy face, under heavens untrod
by the sun,

Let my soul with their souls find place, and forget what
is done and undone.

Thou art more than the Gods who number the days of
our temporal breath;

For these give labour and slumber; but thou, Pro-
serpina, death.

Therefore now at thy feet I abide for a season in silence.
I know

I shall die as my fathers died, and sleep as they sleep;
even so.

For the glass of the years is brittle wherein we gaze for
a span;

A little soul for a little bears up this corpse which is
man.

So long I endure, no longer; and laugh not again,
neither weep.

For there is no God found stronger than death; and
death is a sleep.

Erotion

Sweet for a little even to fear, and sweet
O love, to lay down fear at love's fair feet;
Shall not some fiery memory of his breath
Lie sweet on lips that touch the lips of death?
You leave me not; yet, if thou wilt, be free;
Love me no more, but love my love of thee,
Love where thou wilt, and live thy life; and I,
One thing I can, and one love cannot—die.
Pass from me; yet thine arms, thine eyes, thine hair,
Feed my desire and deaden my despair.
Yet once more ere time change us, ere my cheek
Whiten, ere hope be dumb or sorrow speak,
Yet once more ere thou hate me, one full kiss;
Keep other hours for others, save me this.
Yea, and I will not (if it please thee) weep,
Lest thou be sad; I will but sigh, and sleep.
Sweet, does death hurt? thou canst not do me wrong:
I shall not lack thee, as I loved thee, long.
Hast thou not given me above all that live
Joy, and a little sorrow shalt not give?
What even though fairer fingers of strange girls
Pass nestling through thy beautiful boy's curls
As mine did, or those curled lithe lips of thine
Meet theirs as these, all theirs come after mine;
And though I were not, though I be not, best,
I have loved and love thee more than all the rest.
O love, O lover, loose or hold me fast,
I had thee first, whoever had thee last;
Fairer or not, what need I know, what care?
To thy fair bud my blossom once seemed fair.

Why am I fair at all before thee, why
At all desired? seeing thou art fair, not I.
I shall be glad of thee, O fairest head,
Alive, alone, without thee, with thee, dead:
I shall remember while the light lives yet,
And in the night-time I shall not forget.
Though (as thou wilt) thou leave me ere life leave,
I will not, for thy love I will not grieve;
Not as they use who love not more than I,
Who love not as I love thee though I die;
And though thy lips, once mine, be oftener prest
To many another brow and balmier breast,
And sweeter arms, or sweeter to thy mind,
Lull thee or lure, more fond thou wilt not find.

Stage Love

When the game began between them for a jest,
He played king and she played queen to match the best;
Laughter soft as tears, and tears that turned to laughter,
These were things she sought for years and sorrowed
    after.

Pleasure with dry lips, and pain that walks by night;
All the sting and all the stain of long delight;
These were things she knew not of, that knew not of
    her,
When she played at half a love with half a lover.

Time was chorus, gave them cues to laugh or cry;
They would kill, befool, amuse him, let him die;
Set him webs to weave to-day and break to-morrow,
Till he died for good in play, and rose in sorrow.

What the years mean; how time dies and is not slain;
How love grows and laughs and cries and wanes again;
These were things she came to know, and take their
    measure,
When the play was played out so for one man's pleasure.

A Dialogue

I

Death, if thou wilt, fain would I plead with thee:
Canst thou not spare, of all our hopes have built,
One shelter where our spirits fain would be,
    Death, if thou wilt?

No dome with suns and dews impearled and gilt,
Imperial: but some roof of wildwood tree,
Too mean for sceptre's heft or swordblade's hilt.

Some low sweet roof where love might live, set free
From change and fear and dreams of grief or guilt;
Canst thou not leave life even thus much to see,
    Death, if thou wilt?

II

Man, what art thou to speak and plead with me?
What knowest thou of my workings, where and how
What things I fashion? Nay, behold and see,
    Man, what art thou?

Thy fruits of life, and blossoms of thy bough,
What are they but my seedlings? Earth and sea
Bear nought but when I breathe on it must bow.

Bow thou too down before me: though thou be
Great, all the pride shall fade from off thy brow,
When Time and strong Oblivion ask of thee,
    Man, what art thou?

III

Death, if thou be or be not, as was said,
Immortal; if thou make us nought, or we
Survive: thy power is made but of our dread,
    Death, if thou be.

Thy might is made out of our fear of thee:
Who fears thee not, hath plucked from off thine head
The crown of cloud that darkens earth and sea.

Earth, sea, and sky, as rain or vapour shed,
Shall vanish; all the shows of them shall flee:
Then shall we know full surely, quick or dead,
    Death, if thou be.

In Memory of Walter Savage Landor

Back to the flower-town, side by side,
    The bright months bring,
New-born, the bridegroom and the bride,
    Freedom and spring.

The sweet land laughs from sea to sea,
    Filled full of sun;
All things come back to her, being free;
    All things but one.

In many a tender wheaten plot
    Flowers that were dead

Live, and old suns revive; but not
    That holier head.

By this white wandering waste of sea,
    Far north, I hear
One face shall never turn to me
    As once this year:

Shall never smile and turn and rest
    On mine as there,
Nor one most sacred hand be prest
    Upon my hair.

I came as one whose thoughts half linger,
    Half run before;
The youngest to the oldest singer
    That England bore.

I found him whom I shall not find
    Till all grief end,
In holiest age our mightiest mind,
    Father and friend.

But thou, if any thing endure,
    If hope there be,
O spirit that man's life left pure,
    Man's death set free,

Not with disdain of days that were
    Look earthward now;
Let dreams revive the reverend hair,
    The imperial brow;

Come back in sleep, for in the life
    Where thou art not
We find none like thee. Time and strife
    And the world's lot

Move thee no more; but love at least
   And reverent heart,
May move thee, royal and released,
   Soul, as thou art.

And thou, his Florence, to thy trust
   Receive and keep,
Keep safe his dedicated dust,
   His sacred sleep.

So shall thy lovers, come from far,
   Mix with thy name
As morning-star with evening-star
   His faultless fame.

The Garden of Proserpine

Here, where the world is quiet;
   Here, where all trouble seems
Dead winds' and spent waves' riot
   In doubtful dreams of dreams;
I watch the green field growing
For reaping folk and sowing,
For harvest-time and mowing,
   A sleepy world of streams.

I am tired of tears and laughter,
   And men that laugh and weep;
Of what may come hereafter
   For men that sow to reap:
I am weary of days and hours,
Blown buds of barren flowers,
Desires and dreams and powers
   And everything but sleep.

Here life has death for neighbour,
   And far from eye or ear
Wan waves and wet winds labour,
   Weak ships and spirits steer;
They drive adrift, and whither
They wot not who make thither;
But no such winds blow hither,
   And no such things grow here.

No growth of moor or coppice,
   No heather-flower or vine,
But bloomless buds of poppies,
   Green grapes of Proserpine,
Pale beds of blowing rushes
Where no leaf blooms or blushes
Save this whereout she crushes
   For dead men deadly wine.

Pale, without name or number,
   In fruitless fields of corn,
They bow themselves and slumber
   All night till light is born;
And like a soul belated,
In hell and heaven unmated,
By cloud and mist abated
   Comes out of darkness morn.

Though one were strong as seven,
   He too with death shall dwell,
Nor wake with wings in heaven,
   Nor weep for pains in hell;
Though one were fair as roses,
His beauty clouds and closes;
And well though love reposes,
   In the end it is not well.

Pale, beyond porch and portal,
    Crowned with calm leaves, she stands
Who gathers all things mortal
    With cold immortal hands;
Her languid lips are sweeter
Than love's who fears to greet her
To men that mix and meet her
    From many times and lands.

She waits for each and other,
    She waits for all men born;
Forgets the earth her mother,
    The life of fruits and corn;
And spring and seed and swallow
Take wing for her and follow
Where summer song rings hollow
    And flowers are put to scorn.

There go the loves that wither,
    The old loves with wearier wings;
And all dead years draw thither,
    And all disastrous things;
Dead dreams of days forsaken,
Blind buds that snows have shaken,
Wild leaves that winds have taken
    Red strays of ruined springs.

We are not sure of sorrow,
    And joy was never sure;
To-day will die to-morrow;
    Time stoops to no man's lure;
And love, grown faint and fretful,
With lips but half regretful
Sighs, and with eyes forgetful
    Weeps that no loves endure.

From too much love of living,
  From hope and fear set free,
We thank with brief thanksgiving
  Whatever gods may be
That no life lives for ever;
That dead men rise up never;
That even the weariest river
  Winds somewhere safe to sea.

Then star nor sun shall waken,
  Nor any change of light:
Nor sound of waters shaken,
  Nor any sound or sight:
Nor wintry leaves nor vernal,
Nor days nor things diurnal;
Only the sleep eternal
  In an eternal night.

Sapphics

All the night sleep came not upon my eyelids,
Shed not dew, nor shook nor unclosed a feather,
Yet with lips shut close and with eyes of iron
  Stood and beheld me.

Then to me so lying awake a vision
Came without sleep over the seas and touched me,
Softly touched mine eyelids and lips; and I too,
  Full of the vision,

Saw the white implacable Aphrodite,
Saw the hair unbound and the feet unsandalled
Shine as fire of sunset on western waters;
  Saw the reluctant

Feet, the straining plumes of the doves that drew her,
Looking always, looking with necks reverted,
Back to Lesbos, back to the hills whereunder
   Shone Mitylene;

Heard the flying feet of the Loves behind her
Make a sudden thunder upon the waters,
As the thunder flung from the strong unclosing
   Wings of a great wind.

So the goddess fled from her place, with awful
Sound of feet and thunder of wings around her;
While behind a clamour of singing women
   Severed the twilight.

Ah the singing, ah the delight, the passion!
All the Loves wept, listening; sick with anguish,
Stood the crowned nine Muses about Apollo;
   Fear was upon them,

While the tenth sang wonderful things they knew not.
Ah the tenth, the Lesbian! the nine were silent,
None endured the sound of her song for weeping;
   Laurel by laurel,

Faded all their crowns; but about her forehead,
Round her woven tresses and ashen temples
White as dead snow, paler than grass in summer,
   Ravaged with kisses,

Shone a light of fire as a crown for ever.
Yea, almost the implacable Aphrodite
Paused, and almost wept; such a song was that song.
   Yea, by her name too

Called her, saying, "Turn to me, O my Sappho";
Yet she turned her face from the Loves, she saw not

Tears for laughter darken immortal eyelids,
   Heard not about her

Fearful fitful wings of the doves departing,
Saw not how the bosom of Aphrodite
Shook with weeping, saw not her shaken raiment,
   Saw not her hands wrung;

Saw the Lesbians kissing across their smitten
Lutes with lips more sweet than the sound of lute-
    strings,
Mouth to mouth and hand upon hand, her chosen,
   Fairer than all men;

Only saw the beautiful lips and fingers,
Full of songs and kisses and little whispers,
Full of music; only beheld among them
   Soar, as a bird soars

Newly fledged, her visible song, a marvel,
Made of perfect sound and exceeding passion,
Sweetly shapen, terrible, full of thunders,
   Clothed with the wind's wings.

Then rejoiced she, laughing with love, and scattered
Roses, awful roses of holy blossom;
Then the Loves thronged sadly with hidden faces
   Round Aphrodite,

Then the Muses, stricken at heart, were silent;
Yea, the gods waxed pale; such a song was that song.
All reluctant, all with a fresh repulsion,
   Fled from before her.

All withdrew long since, and the land was barren,
Full of fruitless women and music only.
Now perchance, when winds are assuaged at sunset,
   Lulled at the dewfall,

By the grey sea-side, unassuaged, unheard of,
Unbeloved, unseen in the ebb of twilight,
Ghosts of outcast women return lamenting,
    Purged not in Lethe,

Clothed about with flame and with tears, and singing
Songs that move the heart of the shaken heaven,
Songs that break the heart of the earth with pity,
    Hearing, to hear them.

Super Flumina Babylonis

By the waters of Babylon we sat down and wept,
    Remembering thee,
That for ages of agony hast endured and slept,
    And wouldst not see.

By the waters of Babylon we stood up and sang,
    Considering thee,
That a blast of deliverance in the darkness rang,
    To set thee free.

And with trumpets and thunderings and with morning
        song
    Came up the light;
And thy spirit uplifted thee to forget thy wrong
    As day doth night.

And thy sons were dejected not any more, as then
    When thou wast shamed;
When thy lovers went heavily without heart, as men
    Whose life was maimed.

In the desolate distances, with a great desire
    For thy love's sake,

With our hearts going back to thee, they were filled with
    fire,
    Were nigh to break.

It was said to us: "Verily ye are great of heart,
    But ye shall bend;
Ye are bondsmen and bondswomen, to be scourged and
    smart,
    To toil and tend."

And with harrows men harrowed us, and subdued with
    spears,
    And crushed with shame;
And the summer and winter was, and the length of
    years,
    And no change came.

By the rivers of Italy, by the sacred streams,
    By town, by tower,
There was feasting with revelling, there was sleep with
    dreams,
    Until thine hour.

And they slept and they rioted on their rose-hung beds,
    With mouths on flame,
And with love-locks vine-chapleted, and with rose-
    crowned heads
    And robes of shame.

And they knew not their forefathers, nor the hills and
    streams
    And words of power,
Nor the gods that were good to them, but with songs
    and dreams
    Filled up their hour.

By the rivers of Italy, by the dry streams' beds,
    When thy time came,

There was casting of crowns from them, from their
    young men's heads,
    The crowns of shame.

By the horn of Eridanus, by the Tiber mouth,
    As the day rose,
They arose up and girded them to the north and south,
    By seas, by snows.

As a water in January the frost confines,
    Thy kings bound thee;
As a water in April is, in the new-blown vines,
    Thy sons made free.

And thy lovers that looked for thee, and that mourned
    from far,
    For thy sake dead,
We rejoiced in the light of thee, in the signal star
    Above thine head.

In thy grief had we followed thee, in thy passion loved,
    Loved in thy loss;
In thy shame we stood fast to thee, with thy pangs were
    moved,
    Clung to thy cross.

By the hillside of Calvary we beheld thy blood,
    Thy bloodred tears,
As a mother's in bitterness, an unebbing flood,
    Years upon years.

And the north was Gethsemane, without leaf or bloom,
    A garden sealed;
And the south was Aceldama, for a sanguine fume
    Hid all the field.

By the stone of the sepulchre we returned to weep,
    From far, from prison;

And the guards by it keeping it we beheld asleep,
    But thou wast risen.

And an angel's similitude by the unsealed grave,
    And by the stone:
And the voice was angelical, to whose words God gave
    Strength like his own.

"Lo, the graveclothes of Italy that are folded up
    In the grave's gloom!
And the guards as men wrought upon with a charmèd
      cup,
    By the open tomb.

"And her body most beautiful, and her shining head,
    These are not here;
For your mother, for Italy, is not surely dead:
    Have ye no fear.

"As of old time she spake to you, and you hardly heard,
    Hardly took heed,
So now also she saith to you, yet another word,
    Who is risen indeed.

"By my saying she saith to you, in your ears she saith,
    Who hear these things,
Put no trust in men's royalties, nor in great men's breath,
    Nor words of kings.

"For the life of them vanishes and is no more seen,
    Nor no more known;
Nor shall any remember him if a crown hath been,
    Or where a throne.

"Unto each man his handiwork, unto each his crown,
    The just Fate gives;
Whoso takes the world's life on him and his own lays
      down,
    He, dying so, lives.

"Whoso bears the whole heaviness of the wronged
    world's weight
        And puts it by,
It is well with him suffering, though he face man's fate;
        How should he die?

"Seeing death has no part in him any more, no power
        Upon his head;
He has bought his eternity with a little hour,
        And is not dead.

"For an hour, if ye look for him, he is no more found,
        For one hour's space;
Then lift ye up your eyes to him and behold him
        crowned,
        A deathless face.

"On the mountains of memory, by the world's well-
        springs,
        In all men's eyes,
Where the light of the life of him is on all past things,
        Death only dies.

"Not the light that was quenched for us, nor the deeds
        that were,
        Nor the ancient days,
Nor the sorrows not sorrowful, nor the face most fair
        Of perfect praise."

So the angel of Italy's resurrection said,
        So yet he saith;
So the son of her suffering, that from breasts nigh dead
        Drew life, not death.

That the pavement of Golgotha should be white as
        snow,

Not red but white;
That the waters of Babylon should no longer flow,
And men see light.

A Ballad of François Villon

PRINCE OF ALL BALLAD-MAKERS

Bird of the bitter bright grey golden morn
   Scarce risen upon the dusk of dolorous years,
First of us all and sweetest singer born
   Whose far shrill note the world of new men hears
   Cleave the cold shuddering shade as twilight clears;
When song new-born put off the old world's attire
And felt its tune on her changed lips expire,
   Writ foremost on the roll of them that came
Fresh girt for service of the latter lyre,
   Villon, our sad bad glad mad brother's name!

Alas the joy, the sorrow, and the scorn,
   That clothed thy life with hopes and sins and fears,
And gave thee stones for bread and tares for corn
   And plume-plucked gaol-birds for thy starveling peers
   Till death clipt close their flight with shameful shears;
Till shifts came short and loves were hard to hire,
When lilt of song nor twitch of twangling wire
   Could buy thee bread or kisses; when light fame
Spurned like a ball and haled through brake and briar,
   Villon, our sad bad glad mad brother's name!

Poor splendid wings so frayed and soiled and torn!
   Poor kind wild eyes so dashed with light quick tears!
Poor perfect voice, most blithe when most forlorn,
   That rings athwart the sea whence no man steers

Like joy-bells crossed with death-bells in our ears!
What far delight has cooled the fierce desire
That like some ravenous bird was strong to tire
   On that frail flesh and soul consumed with flame,
But left more sweet than roses to respire,
   Villon, our sad bad glad mad brother's name?

ENVOI

Prince of sweet songs made out of tears and fire,
A harlot was thy nurse, a God thy sire;
   Shame soiled thy song, and song assoiled thy shame.
But from thy feet now death has washed the mire,
Love reads our first at head of all our quire,
   Villon, our sad bad glad mad brother's name.

The Interpreters

Days dawn on us that make amends for many
     Sometimes,
When heaven and earth seem sweeter even than any
     Man's rhymes.

Light had not all been quenched in France, or quelled
     In Greece,
Had Homer sung not, or had Hugo held
     His peace.

Had Sappho's self not left her word thus long
     For token,
The sea round Lesbos yet in waves of song
     Had spoken.

And yet these days of subtler air and finer
     Delight,

When lovelier looks the darkness, and diviner
    The light—

The gift they give of all these golden hours,
    Whose urn
Pours forth reverberate rays or shadowing showers
    In turn—

Clouds, beams, and winds that make the live day's track
    Seem living—
What were they did no spirit give them back
    Thanksgiving?

Dead air, dead fire, dead shapes and shadows, telling
    Time nought;
Man gives them sense and soul by song, and dwelling
    In thought.

In human thought their being endures, their power
    Abides:
Else were their life a thing that each light hour
    Derides.

The years live, work, sigh, smile, and die, with all
    They cherish;
The soul endures, though dreams that fed it fall
    And perish.

In human thought have all things habitation;
    Our days
Laugh, lower, and lighten past, and find no station
    That stays.

But thought and faith are mightier things than time
    Can wrong,
Made splendid once with speech, or made sublime
    By song.

Remembrance, though the tide of change that rolls
    Wax hoary,
Gives earth and heaven, for song's sake and the soul's,
    Their glory.

FROM *By the North Sea*

A land that is lonelier than ruin;
    A sea that is stranger than death:
Far fields that a rose never blew in,
    Wan waste where the winds lack breath;
Waste endless and boundless and flowerless
    But of marsh-blossoms fruitless as free:
Where earth lies exhausted, as powerless
      To strive with the sea.

Far flickers the flight of the swallows,
    Far flutters the weft of the grass
Spun dense over desolate hollows
    More pale than the clouds as they pass:
Thick woven as the weft of a witch is
    Round the heart of a thrall that hath sinned,
Whose youth and the wrecks of its riches
      Are waifs on the wind.

The pastures are herdless and sheepless,
    No pasture or shelter for herds:
The wind is relentless and sleepless
    And restless and songless the birds;
Their cries from afar fall breathless,
    Their wings are as lightnings that flee;
For the land has two lords that are deathless:
      Death's self, and the sea.

These twain, as a king with his fellow,
   Hold converse of desolate speech:
And her waters are haggard and yellow
   And crass with the scurf of the beach:
And his garments are gray as the hoary
   Wan sky where the day lies dim;
And his power is to her, and his glory,
    As hers unto him.

In the pride of his power she rejoices,
   In her glory he glows and is glad:
In her darkness the sound of his voice is,
   With his breath she dilates, and is mad:
"If thou slay me, O death, and outlive me,
   Yet thy love hath fulfilled me of thee."
"Shall I give thee not back if thou give me,
    O sister, O sea?"

And year upon year dawns living,
   And age upon age drops dead:
And his hand is not weary of giving,
   And the thirst of her heart is not fed:
And the hunger that moans in her passion,
   And the rage in her hunger that roars,
As a wolf's that the winter lays lash on,
    Still calls and implores.

Her walls have no granite for girder,
   No fortalice fronting her stands;
But reefs the bloodguiltiest of murder
   Are less than the banks of her sands:
These number their slain by the thousand;
   For the ship hath no surety to be,
When the bank is abreast of her bows and
    Aflush with the sea.

No surety to stand, and no shelter
 To dawn out of darkness but one,
Out of waters that hurtle and welter,
 No succor to dawn with the sun
But a rest from the wind as it passes,
 Where, hardly redeemed from the waves,
Lie thick as the blades of the grasses
  The dead in their graves.

A multitude noteless of numbers,
 As wild weeds cast on an heap:
And sounder than sleep are their slumbers,
 And softer than song is their sleep;
And sweeter than all things, and stranger
 The sense, if perchance it may be,
That the wind is divested of danger
  And scatheless the sea.

That the roar of the banks they breasted
 Is hurtless as bellowing of herds,
And the strength of his wings that invested
 The wind, as the strength of a bird's:
As the sea-mew's might or the swallow's
 That cry to him back if he cries,
As over the graves and their hollows
  Days darken and rise.

As the souls of the dead men disburdened
 And clean of the sins that they sinned,
With a lovelier than man's life guerdoned,
 And delight as a wave's in the wind,
And delight as the wind's in the billow,
 Birds pass, and deride with their glee
The flesh that has dust for its pillow
  As wrecks have the sea.

When the ways of the sun wax dimmer,
   Wings flash through the dusk like beams;
As the clouds in the lit sky glimmer,
   The bird in the graveyard gleams;
As the cloud at its wing's edge whitens
   When the clarions of sunrise are heard,
The graves that the bird's note brightens
   Grow bright for the bird.

As the waves of the numberless waters
   That the wind cannot number who guides
Are the sons of the shore and the daughters
   Here lulled by the chime of the tides:
And here in the press of them standing
   We know not if these or if we
Live truliest, or anchored to landing,
   Or drifted to sea.

In the valley he named of decision,
   No denser were multitudes met
When the soul of the seer in her vision
   Saw nations for doom of them set;
Saw darkness in dawn, and the splendour
   Of judgment, the sword and the rod:
But the doom here of death is more tender,
   And gentler the god.

And gentler the wind from the dreary
   Sea-banks by the waves overlapped,
Being weary, speaks peace to the weary,
   From slopes that the tide-stream hath sapped;
And sweeter than all that we call so
   The seal of their slumber shall be
Till the graves that embosom them also
   Be sapped of the sea.

                                       (Part I)

Grand Chorus of Birds

FROM ARISTOPHANES

Attempted in English after the original meter

Come on then, ye dwellers by nature in darkness, and
like to the leaves' generations,
That are little of might, that are moulded of mire, un-
enduring and shadowlike nations,
Poor plumeless ephemerals, comfortless mortals, as vi-
sions of creatures fast fleeing,
Lift up your mind unto us that are deathless, and date-
less the date of our being:
Us, children of heaven, us, ageless for aye, us, all of
whose thoughts are eternal;
That ye may from henceforth, having heard of us all
things aright as to matters supernal,
Of the being of birds and beginning of gods, and of
streams, and the dark beyond reaching,
Truthfully knowing aright, in my name bid Prodicus
pack with his preaching.

It was Chaos and Night at the first, and the blackness
of darkness, and hell's broad border,
Earth was not, nor air, neither heaven; when in depths
of the womb of the dark without order
First thing first-born of the black-plumed Night was a
wind-egg hatched in her bosom,
Whence timely with seasons revolving again sweet Love
burst out as a blossom,
Gold wings glittering forth of his back, like whirlwinds
gustily turning.

He, after his wedlock with Chaos, whose wings are of darkness, in hell broad-burning,

For his nestlings begat him the race of us first, and up-raised us to light new-lighted.

And before this was not the race of the gods, until all things by Love were united;

And of kind united with kind in communion of nature the sky and the sea are

Brought forth, and the earth, and the race of the gods everlasting and blest. So that we are

Far away the most ancient of all things blest. And that we are of Love's generation

There are manifest manifold signs. We have wings, and with us have the Loves habitation;

And manifold fair young folk that forswore love once, ere the bloom of them ended,

Have the men that pursued and desired them subdued, by the help of us only befriended,

With such baits as a quail, a flamingo, a goose, or a cock's comb staring and splendid.

All best good things that befall men come from us birds, as is plain to all reason:

For first we proclaim and make known to them spring, and the winter and autumn in season;

Bid sow, when the crane starts clanging for Afric, in shrill-voiced emigrant number,

And calls to the pilot to hang up his rudder again for the season, and slumber;

And then weave cloak for Orestes the thief, lest he strip men of theirs if it freezes.

And again thereafter the kite reappearing announces a change in the breezes,

And that here is the season for shearing your sheep of their spring wool. Then does the swallow

Give you notice to sell your greatcoat, and provide
   something light for the heat that's to follow.

Thus are we as Ammon or Delphi unto you, Dodona,
   nay, Phoebus Apollo.

For, as first ye come all to get auguries of birds, even
   such is in all things your carriage,

Be the matter a matter of trade, or of earning your
   bread, or of any one's marriage.

And all things ye lay to the charge of a bird that belong
   to discerning prediction:

Winged fame is a bird, as you reckon: you sneeze, and
   the sign's as a bird for conviction:

All tokens are "birds" with you—sounds too, and lack-
   eys, and donkeys. Then must it not follow

That we ARE to you all as the manifest godhead that
   speaks in prophetic Apollo?

James Thomson ("B.V.")

(1834–1882)

FROM *The City of Dreadful Night*

The City is of Night; perchance of Death,
  But certainly of Night; for never there
Can come the lucid morning's fragrant breath
  After the dewy dawning's cold grey air;
The moon and stars may shine with scorn or pity;
The sun has never visited that city,
  For it dissolveth in the daylight fair.

Dissolveth like a dream of night away;
  Though present in distempered gloom of thought
And deadly weariness of heart all day.
  But when a dream night after night is brought
Throughout a week, and such weeks few or many
Recur each year for several years, can any
  Discern that dream from real life in aught?

For life is but a dream whose shapes return,
  Some frequently, some seldom, some by night
And some by day, some night and day: we learn,
  The while all change and many vanish quite,
In their recurrence with recurrent changes
A certain seeming order; where this ranges
  We count things real; such is memory's might.

A river girds the city west and south,
  The main north channel of a broad lagoon,

Regurging with the salt tides from the mouth;
  Waste marshes shine and glister to the moon
For leagues, then moorland black, then stony ridges;
Great piers and causeways, many noble bridges,
  Connect the town and islet suburbs strewn.

Upon an easy slope it lies at large,
  And scarcely overlaps the long curved crest
Which swells out two leagues from the river marge.
  A trackless wilderness rolls north and west,
Savannahs, savage woods, enormous mountains,
Bleak uplands, black ravines with torrent fountains;
  And eastward rolls the shipless sea's unrest.

The city is not ruinous, although
  Great ruins of an unremembered past,
With others of a few short years ago
  More sad, are found within its precincts vast.
The street-lamps always burn; but scarce a casement
In house or palace front from roof to basement
  Doth glow or gleam athwart the mirk air cast.

The street-lamps burn amidst the baleful glooms,
  Amidst the soundless solitudes immense
Of rangèd mansions dark and still as tombs.
  The silence which benumbs or strains the sense
Fulfils with awe the soul's despair unweeping;
Myriads of habitants are ever sleeping,
  Or dead, or fled from nameless pestilence!

Yet as in some necropolis you find
  Perchance one mourner to a thousand dead,
So there; worn faces that look deaf and blind
  Like tragic masks of stone. With weary tread,
Each wrapt in his own doom, they wander, wander,
Or sit foredone and desolately ponder
  Through sleepless hours with heavy drooping head.

Mature men chiefly, few in age or youth,
   A woman rarely, now and then a child:
A child! If here the heart turns sick with ruth
   To see a little one from birth defiled,
Or lame or blind, as preordained to languish
Through youthless life, think how it bleeds with anguish
   To meet one erring in that homeless wild.

They often murmur to themselves, they speak
   To one another seldom, for their woe
Broods maddening inwardly and scorns to wreak
   Itself abroad; and if at whiles it grow
To frenzy which must rave, none heeds the clamour,
Unless there waits some victim of like glamour,
   To rave in turn, who lends attentive show.

The City is of Night, but not of Sleep:
   There sweet sleep is not for the weary brain;
The pitiless hours like years and ages creep,
   A night seems termless hell. This dreadful strain
Of thought and consciousness which never ceases,
Or which some moments' stupor but increases,
   This, worse than woe, makes wretches there insane.

They leave all hope behind who enter there:
   One certitude while sane they cannot leave,
One anodyne for torture and despair;
   The certitude of Death, which no reprieve
Can put off long; and which, divinely tender,
But waits the outstretched hand to promptly render
   That draught whose slumber nothing can bereave.

                     (Part I)

As I came through the desert thus it was,
As I came through the desert: All was black,
In heaven no single star, on earth no track;

A brooding hush without a stir or note,
The air so thick it clotted in my throat;
And thus for hours; then some enormous things
Swooped past with savage cries and clanking wings:
> But I strode on austere;
> No hope could have no fear.

As I came through the desert thus it was,
As I came through the desert: Eyes of fire
Glared at me throbbing with a starved desire;
The hoarse and heavy and carnivorous breath
Was hot upon me from deep jaws of death;
Sharp claws, swift talons, fleshless fingers cold
Plucked at me from the bushes, tried to hold:
> But I strode on austere;
> No hope could have no fear.

As I came through the desert thus it was,
As I came through the desert: Lo you, there,
That hillock burning with a brazen glare;
Those myriad dusky flames with points a-glow
Which writhed and hissed and darted to and fro;
A Sabbath of the Serpents, heaped pell-mell
For Devil's roll-call and some *fête* of Hell:
> Yet I strode on austere;
> No hope could have no fear.

As I came through the desert thus it was,
As I came through the desert: Meteors ran
And crossed their javelins on the black sky-span;
The zenith opened to a gulf of flame,
The dreadful thunderbolts jarred earth's fixed frame;
The ground all heaved in waves of fire that surged
And weltered round me sole there unsubmerged:
> Yet I strode on austere;
> No hope could have no fear.

As I came through the desert thus it was,
As I came through the desert: Air once more,
And I was close upon a wild sea-shore;
Enormous cliffs arose on either hand,
The deep tide thundered up a league-broad strand;
White foambelts seethed there, wan spray swept and
          flew;
The sky broke, moon and stars and clouds and blue:
       And I strode on austere;
        No hope could have no fear.

As I came through the desert thus it was,
As I came through the desert: On the left
The sun arose and crowned a broad crag-cleft;
There stopped and burned out black, except a rim,
A bleeding eyeless socket, red and dim;
Whereon the moon fell suddenly south-west,
And stood above the right-hand cliffs at rest:
       Still I strode on austere
        No hope could have no fear.

As I came through the desert thus it was,
As I came through the desert: From the right
A shape came slowly with a ruddy light;
A woman with a red lamp in her hand,
Bareheaded and barefooted on that strand;
O desolation moving with such grace!
O anguish with such beauty in thy face!
       I fell as on my bier,
        Hope travailed with such fear.

As I came through the desert thus it was,
As I came through the desert: I was twain,
Two selves distinct that cannot join again;
One stood apart and knew but could not stir,
And watched the other stark in swoon and her;

And she came on, and never turned aside,
Between such sun and moon and roaring tide:
    And as she came more near
    My soul grew mad with fear.

As I came through the desert thus it was,
As I came through the desert: Hell is mild
And piteous matched with that accursèd wild;
A large black sign was on her breast that bowed,
A broad black band ran down her snow-white shroud;
That lamp she held was her own burning heart,
Whose blood-drops trickled step by step apart:
    The mystery was clear;
    Mad rage had swallowed fear.

As I came through the desert thus it was,
As I came through the desert: By the sea
She knelt and bent above that senseless me;
Those lamp-drops fell upon my white brow there,
She tried to cleanse them with her tears and hair;
She murmured words of pity, love, and woe,
She heeded not the level rushing flow:
    And mad with rage and fear,
    I stood stonebound so near.

As I came through the desert thus it was,
As I came through the desert: When the tide
Swept up to her there kneeling by my side,
She clasped that corpse-like me, and they were borne
Away, and this vile me was left forlorn;
I know the whole sea cannot quench that heart,
Or cleanse that brow, or wash those two apart:
    They love; their doom is drear,
    Yet they nor hope nor fear;
    But I, what do I here?

(Part IV, lines 7–106)

Coventry Patmore

(1823–1896)

A Farewell

With all my will, but much against my heart,
We two now part.
My Very Dear,
Our solace is, the sad road lies so clear.
It needs no art,
With faint, averted feet
And many a tear,
In our opposed paths to persevere.
Go thou to East, I West.
We will not say
There's any hope, it is so far away.
But, O, my Best,
When the one darling of our widowhead,
The nursling Grief,
Is dead,
And no dews blur our eyes
To see the peach-bloom come in evening skies,
Perchance we may,
Where now this night is day,
And even through faith of still averted feet,
Making full circle of our banishment,
Amazed meet;
The bitter journey to the bourne so sweet
Seasoning the termless feast of our content
With tears of recognition never dry.

To the Unknown Eros

What rumour'd heavens are these
Which not a poet sings,
O, Unknown Eros? What this breeze
Of sudden wings
Speeding at far returns of time from interstellar space
To fan my very face,
And gone as fleet,
Through delicatest ether feathering soft their solitary
      beat,
With ne'er a light plume dropp'd, nor any trace
To speak of whence they came, or whither they depart?
And why this palpitating heart,
This blind and unrelated joy,
This meaningless desire,
That moves me like the Child
Who in the flushing darkness troubled lies,
Inventing lonely prophecies,
Which even to his Mother mild
He dares not tell;
To which himself is infidel;
His heart not less on fire
With dreams impossible as wildest Arab Tale,
(So thinks the boy,)
With dreams that turn him red and pale,
Yet less impossible and wild
Than those which bashful Love, in his own way and
      hour,
Shall duly bring to flower?
O, Unknown Eros, sire of awful bliss,
What portent and what Delphic word,

Such as in form of snake forebodes the bird,
Is this?
In me life's even flood
What eddies thus?
What in its ruddy orbit lifts the blood,
Like a perturbed moon of Uranus,
Reaching to some great world in ungauged darkness
    hid;
And whence
This rapture of the sense
Which, by thy whisper bid,
Reveres with obscure rite and sacramental sign
A bond I know not of nor dimly can divine;
This subject loyalty which longs
For chains and thongs
Woven of gossamer and adamant,
To bind me to my unguess'd want,
And so to lie,
Between those quivering plumes that thro' fine ether
    pant,
For hopeless, sweet eternity?
What God unhonour'd hitherto in songs,
Or which, that now
Forgettest the disguise
That Gods must wear who visit human eyes,
Art Thou?
Thou art not Amor; or, if so, yon pyre,
That waits the willing victim, flames with vestal fire;
Nor mooned Queen of maids; or, if thou'rt she,
Ah, then, from Thee
Let Bride and Bridegroom learn what kisses be!
In what veil'd hymn
Or mystic dance
Would he that were thy Priest advance
Thine earthly praise, thy glory limn?

Say, should the feet that feel thy thought
In double-center'd circuit run,
In that compulsive focus, Nought,
In this a furnace like the sun;
And might some note of thy renown
And high behest
Thus in enigma be expressed:
"There lies the crown
Which all thy longing cures.
Refuse it, Mortal, that it may be yours!
It is a Spirit, though it seems red gold;
And such may no man, but by shunning, hold.
Refuse it, till refusing be despair;
And thou shalt feel the phantom in thy hair."

Legem Tuam Dilexi

The "Infinite," Word horrible! at feud
With life, and the braced mood
Of power and joy and love;
Forbidden, by wise heathen ev'n, to be
Spoken of Deity,
Whose Name, on popular altars, was "The Unknown,"
Because, or ere It was reveal'd as One
Confined in Three,
The people fear'd that it might prove
Infinity,
The blazon which the devils desired to gain;
And God, for their confusion, laugh'd consent;
Yet did so far relent,
That they might seek relief, and not in vain,
In dashing of themselves against the shores of pain,
Nor bides alone in hell

The bond-disdaining spirit boiling to rebel.
But for compulsion of strong grace,
The pebble in the road
Would straight explode,
And fill the ghastly boundlessness of space.
The furious power,
To soft growth twice constrain'd in leaf and flower,
Protests, and longs to flash its faint self far
Beyond the dimmest star.
The same
Seditious flame,
Beat backward with reduplicated might,
Struggles alive within its stricter term,
And is the worm.
And the just Man does on himself affirm
God's limits, and is conscious of delight,
Freedom and right;
And so His Semblance is, Who, every hour,
By day and night,
Buildeth new bulwarks 'gainst the Infinite.
For, ah, who can express
How full of bonds and simpleness
Is God,
How narrow is He,
And how the wide, waste field of possibility
Is only trod
Straight to His homestead in the human heart,
And all His art
Is as the babe's that wins his Mother to repeat
Her little song so sweet!
What is the chief news of the Night?
Lo, iron and salt, heat, weight and light
In every star that drifts on the great breeze!
And these
Mean Man,

Darling of God, Whose thoughts but live and move
Round him; Who woos his will
To wedlock with His own, and does distil
To that drop's span
The attar of all rose-fields of all love!
Therefore the soul select assumes the stress
Of bonds unbid, which God's own style express
Better than well,
And aye hath, cloister'd, borne,
To the Clown's scorn,
The fetters of the threefold golden chain:
Narrowing to nothing all his worldly gain;
(Howbeit in vain;
For to have nought
Is to have all things without care or thought!)
Surrendering, abject, to his equal's rule,
As though he were a fool,
The free wings of the will;
(More vainly still;
For none knows rightly what 'tis to be free
But only he
Who, vow'd against all choice, and fill'd with awe
Of the oftimes dumb or clouded Oracle,
Does wiser than to spell,
In his own suit, the least word of the Law!)
And, lastly, bartering life's dear bliss for pain;
But evermore in vain;
For joy (rejoice ye Few that tasted have!)
Is Love's obedience
Against the genial laws of natural sense,
Whose wide, self-dissipating wave,
Prison'd in artful dykes,
Trembling returns and strikes
Thence to its source again,
In backward billows fleet,

Crest crossing crest ecstatic as they greet,
Thrilling each vein,
Exploring every chasm and cove
Of the full heart with floods of honied love,
And every principal street
And obscure alley and lane
Of the intricate brain
With brimming rivers of light and breezes sweet
Of the primordial heat;
Till, unto view of me and thee,
Lost the intense life be,
Or ludicrously display'd, by force
Of distance; as a soaring eagle, or a horse
On far-off hillside shewn,
May seem a gust-driv'n rag or a dead stone.
Nor by such bonds alone—
But more I leave to say,
Fitly revering the Wild Ass's bray,
Also his hoof,
Of which, go where you will, the marks remain
Where the religious walls have hid the bright reproof.

To the Body

Creation's and Creator's crowning good;
Wall of infinitude·
Foundation of the sky,
In Heaven forecast
And long'd for from eternity,
Though laid the last;
Reverberating dome,
Of music cunningly built home
Against the void and indolent disgrace

Of unresponsive space;
Little, sequester'd pleasure-house
For God and for His Spouse;
Elaborately, yea, past conceiving, fair,
Since, from the graced decorum of the hair,
Ev'n to the tingling, sweet
Soles of the simple, earth-confiding feet,
And from the inmost heart
Outwards unto the thin
Silk curtains of the skin,
Every least part
Astonish'd hears
And sweet replies to some like region of the spheres;
Form'd for a dignity prophets but darkly name,
Lest shameless men cry "Shame!"
So rich with wealth conceal'd
That Heaven and Hell fight chiefly for this field;
Clinging to everything that pleases thee
With indefectible fidelity;
Alas, so true
To all thy friendships that no grace
Thee from thy sin can wholly disembrace;
Which thus 'bides with thee as the Jebusite,
That, maugre all God's promises could do,
The chosen People never conquer'd quite,
Who therefore lived with them,
And that by formal truce and as of right,
In metropolitan Jerusalem.
For which false fealty
Thou needs must, for a season, lie
In the grave's arms, foul and unshriven,
Albeit, in Heaven,
Thy crimson-throbbing Glow
Into its old abode aye pants to go,
And does with envy see

Enoch, Elijah, and the Lady, she
Who left the lilies in her body's lieu.
O, if the pleasures I have known in thee
But my poor faith's poor first-fruits be,
What quintessential, keen, ethereal bliss
Then shall be his
Who has thy birth-time's consecrating dew
For death's sweet chrism retain'd,
Quick, tender, virginal, and unprofaned!

George Meredith

(1828–1909)

Melampus

With love exceeding a simple love of the things
    That glide in grasses and rubble of woody wreck;
Or change their perch on a beat of quivering wings
    From branch to branch, only restful to pipe and peck;
Or, bristled, curl at a touch their snouts in a ball;
    Or cast their web between bramble and thorny hook;
The good physician Melampus, loving them all,
    Among them walked, as a scholar who reads a book.

For him the woods were a home and gave him the key
    Of knowledge, thirst for their treasures in herbs and
        flowers.
The secrets held by the creatures nearer than we
    To earth he sought, and the link of their life with
        ours:
And where alike we are, unlike where, and the veined
    Division, veined parallel, of a blood that flows
In them, in us, from the source by man unattained
    Save marks he well what the mystical woods disclose.

And this he deemed might be boon of love to a breast
    Embracing tenderly each little motive shape,
The prone, the flitting, who seek their food whither best
    Their wits direct, whither best from their foes escape:
For closer drawn to our mother's natural milk,
    As babes they learn where her motherly help is great:

489

They know the juice for the honey, juice for the silk,
　　And need they medical antidotes find them straight.

Of earth and sun they are wise, they nourish their
　　　broods,
　　Weave, build, hive, burrow and battle, take joy and
　　　pain
Like swimmers varying billows: never in woods
　　Runs white insanity fleeing itself: all sane
The woods revolve: as the tree its shadowing limns
　　To some resemblance in motion, the rooted life
Restrains disorder: you hear the primitive hymns
　　Of earth in woods issue wild of the web of strife.

Now sleeping once on a day of marvellous fire
　　A brood of snakes he had cherished in grave regret
That death his people had dealt their dam and their
　　　sire,
　　Through savage dread of them, crept to his neck, and
　　　set
Their tongues to lick him: the swift affectionate tongue
　　Of each ran licking the slumberer: then his ears
A forked red tongue tickled shrewdly: sudden upsprung,
　　He heard a voice piping: Ay, for he has no fears!

A bird said that, in the notes of birds, and the speech
　　Of men, it seemed: and another renewed: He moves
To learn and not to pursue, he gathers to teach;
　　He feeds his young as do we, and as we love loves.
No fears have I of a man who goes with his head
　　To earth, chance looking aloft at us, kind of hand:
I feel to him as to earth of whom we are fed;
　　I pipe him much for his good could he understand.

Melampus touched at his ears, laid finger on wrist:
　　He was not dreaming, he sensibly felt and heard.

Above, through leaves, where the tree-twigs thick inter-
    twist,
  He spied the birds and the bill of the speaking bird.
His cushion mosses in shades of various green,
    The lumped, the antlered, he pressed, while the
    sunny snake
Slipped under: draughts he had drunk of clear Hippo-
    crene,
  It seemed, and sat with a gift of the Gods awake.

Divinely thrilled was the man, exultingly full,
  As quick well-waters that come of the heart of earth,
Ere yet they dart in a brook are one bubble-pool
  To light and sound, wedding both at the leap of birth.
The soul of light vivid shone, a stream within stream;
  The soul of sound from a musical shell outflew;
Where others hear but a hum and see but a beam,
  The tongue and eye of the fountain of life he knew.

He knew the Hours: they were round him, laden with
    seed
  Of hours bestrewn upon vapor, and one by one
They winged as ripened in fruit the burden decreed
  For each to scatter; they flushed like the buds in sun,
Bequeathing seed to successive similar rings,
  Their sisters, bearers to men of what men have
    earned:
He knew them, talked with the yet unreddened; the
    stings,
  The sweets, they warmed at their bosoms divined, dis-
    cerned.

Not unsolicited, sought by diligent feet,
  By riddling fingers expanded, oft watched in growth
With brooding deep as the noon-ray's quickening wheat,

Ere touch'd the pendulous flower of the plants of
    sloth,
The plants of rigidness, answered question and squeeze,
    Revealing wherefore it bloomed uninviting, bent,
Yet making harmony breathe of life and disease,
    The deeper chord of a wonderful instrument.

So passed he luminous-eyed for earth and the fates
    We arm to bruise or caress us: his ears were charged
With tones of love in a whirl of voluble hates,
    With music wrought of distraction his ear enlarged.
Celestial-shining, though mortal, singer, though mute,
    He drew the Master of harmonies, voiced or stilled,
To seek him; heard at the silent medicine-root
    A song, beheld in fulfilment the unfulfilled.

Him Phœbus, lending to darkness colour and form
    Of light's excess, many lessons and counsels gave;
Showed Wisdom lord of the human intricate swarm,
    And whence prophetic it looks on the hives that rave,
And how acquired, of the zeal of love to acquire,
    And where it stands, in the centre of life a sphere;
And Measure, mood of the lyre, the rapturous lyre,
    He said was Wisdom, and struck him the notes to
        hear.

Sweet, sweet: 't was glory of vision, honey, the breeze
    In heat, the run of the river on root and stone,
All senses joined, as the sister Pierides
    Are one, uplifting their chorus, the Nine, his own.
In stately order, evolved of sound into sight,
    From sight to sound intershifting, the man descried
The growths of earth, his adored, like day out of night,
    Ascend in song, seeing nature and song allied.

And there vitality, there, there solely in song,
    Resides, where earth and her uses to men, their needs,

Their forceful cravings, the theme are: there is it strong,
  The Master said: and the studious eye that reads
(Yea, even as earth to the crown of Gods on the mount)
  In links divine with the lyrical tongue is bound.
Pursue thy craft: it is music drawn of a fount
  To spring perennial; well-spring is common ground.

Melampus dwelt among men: physician and sage,
  He served them, loving them, healing them; sick or
    maimed
Or them that frenzied in some delirious rage
  Outran the measure, his juice of the woods reclaimed.
He played on men, as his master, Phœbus, on strings
  Melodious: as the God did he drive and check,
Through love exceeding a simple love of the things
  That glide in grasses and rubble of woody wreck.

Lucifer in Starlight

On a starred night Prince Lucifer uprose.
Tired of his dark dominion swung the fiend
Above the rolling ball in cloud part screened,
Where sinners hugged their spectre of repose.
Poor prey to his hot fit of pride were those.
And now upon his western wing he leaned,
Now his huge bulk o'er Afric's sands careened,
Now the black planet shadowed Arctic snows.
Soaring through wider zones that pricked his scars
With memory of the old revolt from Awe,
He reached a middle height, and at the stars,
Which are the brain of heaven, he looked, and sank.
Around the ancient track marched, rank on rank,
The army of unalterable law.

FROM *Modern Love*

THE PROMISE IN DISTURBANCE

By this he knew she wept with waking eyes:
That, at his hand's light quiver by her head,
The strange low sobs that shook their common bed,
Were called into her with a sharp surprise,
And strangled mute, like little gaping snakes,
Dreadfully venomous to him. She lay
Stone-still, and the long darkness flowed away
With muffled pulses. Then, as midnight makes
Her giant heart of Memory and Tears
Drink the pale drug of silence, and so beat
Sleep's heavy measure, they from head to feet
Were moveless, looking through their dead black years,
By vain regret scrawled over the blank wall.
Like sculptured effigies they might be seen
Upon their marriage-tomb, the sword between;
Each wishing for the sword that severs all.

(i)

But where began the change; and what's my crime?
The wretch condemned, who has not been arraigned,
Chafes at his sentence. Shall I, unsustained,
Drag on Love's nerveless body thro' all time?
I must have slept, since now I wake. Prepare,
You lovers, to know Love a thing of moods:
Not like hard life, of laws. In Love's deep woods,
I dreamt of loyal Life:—the offence is there!
Love's jealous woods about the sun are curled;

At least, the sun far brighter there did beam.—
My crime is, that the puppet of a dream,
I plotted to be worthy of the world.
Oh, had I with my darling helped to mince
The facts of life, you still had seen me go
With hindward feather and with forward toe,
Her much-adored delightful Fairy Prince!

(x)

Here Jack and Tom are paired with Moll and Meg.
Curved open to the river-reach is seen
A country merry-making on the green.
Fair space for signal shakings of the leg.
That little screwy fiddler from his booth,
Whence flows one nut-brown stream, commands the
joints
Of all who caper here at various points.
I have known rustic revels in my youth:
The May-fly pleasures of a mind at ease.
An early goddess was a country lass:
A charmed Amphion-oak she tripped the grass.
What life was that I lived? The life of these?
Heaven keep them happy! Nature they seem near
They must, I think, be wiser than I am;
They have the secret of the bull and lamb.
'Tis true that when we trace its source, 'tis beer.

(xviii)

What are we first? First, animals; and next
Intelligences at a leap; on whom
Pale lies the distant shadow of the tomb,
And all that draweth on the tomb for text.
Into which state comes Love, the crowning sun:

Beneath whose light the shadow loses form.
We are the lords of life, and life is warm.
Intelligence and instinct now are one.
But nature says: "My children most they seem
When they least know me: therefore I decree
That they shall suffer." Swift doth young Love flee,
And we stand wakened, shivering from our dream.
Then if we study Nature we are wise.
Thus do the few who live but with the day:
The scientific animals are they.—
Lady, this is my sonnet to your eyes.

                              (xxx)

Mark where the pressing wind shoots javelin-like
Its skeleton shadow on the broad-backed wave!
Here is a fitting spot to dig Love's grave;
Here where the ponderous breakers plunge and strike,
And dart their hissing tongues high up the sand:
In hearing of the ocean, and in sight
Of those ribbed wind-streaks running into white.
If I the death of Love had deeply planned,
I never could have made it half so sure,
As by the unblest kisses which upbraid
The full-waked sense; or failing that, degrade!
'Tis morning: but no morning can restore
What we have forfeited. I see no sin:
The wrong is mixed. In tragic life, God wot,
No villain need be! Passions spin the plot:
We are betrayed by what is false within.

                              (xliii)

   It is the season of the sweet wild rose,
   My Lady's emblem in the heart of me!

So golden-crownèd shines she gloriously
And with that softest dream of blood she glows:
Mild as an evening heaven round Hesper bright!
I pluck the flower, and smell it, and revive
The time when in her eyes I stood alive.
I seem to look upon it out of Night.
Here's Madam, stepping hastily. Her whims
Bid her demand the flower, which I let drop.
As I proceed, I feel her sharply stop,
And crush it under heel with trembling limbs.
She joins me in a cat-like way, and talks
Of company, and even condescends
To utter laughing scandal of old friends.
These are the summer days, and these our walks.

                                        (*xlv*)

Thus piteously Love closed what he begat:
The union of this ever-diverse pair!
These two were rapid falcons in a snare,
Condemned to do the flitting of the bat.
Lovers beneath the singing sky of May,
They wandered once; clear as the dew on flowers:
But they fed not on the advancing hours:
Their hearts held cravings for the buried day.
Then each applied to each that fatal knife,
Deep questioning, which probes to endless dole.
Ah, what a dusty answer gets the soul
When hot for certainties in this our life!—
In tragic hints here see what evermore
Moves dark as yonder midnight ocean's force,
Thundering like ramping hosts of warrior horse,
To throw that faint thin line upon the shore!

                                        (*l*)

Gerard Manley Hopkins

(1844–1889)

The Wreck of the Deutschland

*To the happy memory of five Franciscan Nuns, exiles by
the Falk Laws, drowned between midnight and morning of
Dec. 7th, 1875*

I

Thou mastering me
  God! giver of breath and bread;
 World's strand, sway of the sea;
  Lord of living and dead;
Thou hast bound bones and veins in me, fastened me
    flesh,
And after it almost unmade, what with dread,
  Thy doing: and dost thou touch me afresh?
Over again I feel thy finger and find thee.

 I did say yes
  O at lightning and lashed rod;
 Thou heardst me truer than tongue confess
  Thy terror, O Christ, O God;
Thou knowest the walls, altar and hour and night:
The swoon of a heart that the sweep and the hurl of
    thee trod
  Hard down with a horror of height:
And the midriff astrain with leaning of, laced with fire
  of stress.

498

      The frown of his face
    Before me, the hurtle of hell
Behind, where, where was a, where was a place?
    I whirled out wings that spell
And fled with a fling of the heart to the heart of the
      Host.
My heart, but you were dovewinged, I can tell,
    Carrier-witted, I am bold to boast,
To flash from the flame to the flame then, tower from
      the grace to the grace.

      I am soft sift
    In an hourglass—at the wall
Fast, but mined with a motion, a drift,
    And it crowds and it combs to the fall;
I steady as a water in a well, to a poise, to a pane,
But roped with, always, all the way down from the
      tall
Fells or flanks of the voel, a vein
Of the gospel proffer, a pressure, a principle, Christ's
      gift.

      I kiss my hand
    To the stars, lovely-asunder
Starlight, wafting him out of it; and
    Glow, glory in thunder;
Kiss my hand to the dappled-with-damson west:
Since, tho' he is under the world's splendour and won-
      der,
His mystery must be instressed, stressed;
For I greet him the days I meet him, and bless when I
      understand.

      Not out of his bliss
    Springs the stress felt
Nor first from heaven (and few know this)

Swings the stroke dealt—
Stroke and a stress that stars and storms deliver,
That guilt is hushed by, hearts are flushed by and
    melt—
But it rides time like riding a river
(And here the faithful waver, the faithless fable and
    miss).

It dates from day
Of his going in Galilee;
Warm-laid grave of a womb-life grey;
Manger, maiden's knee;
The dense and the driven Passion, and frightful
    sweat;
Thence the discharge of it, there its swelling to be,
Though felt before, though in high flood yet—
What none would have known of it, only the heart,
    being hard at bay,

Is out with it! Oh,
We lash with the best or worst
Word last! How a lush-kept plush-capped sloe
Will, mouthed to flesh-burst,
Gush!—flush the man, the being with it, sour or
    sweet,
Brim, in a flash, full!—Hither then, last or first,
To hero of Calvary, Christ's feet—
Never ask if meaning it, wanting it, warned of it—men
    go.

Be adored among men,
God, three-numberèd form;
Wring thy rebel, dogged in den,
Man's malice, with wrecking and storm.
Beyond saying sweet, past telling of tongue,

Thou art lightning and love, I found it, a winter and
        warm;
  Father and fondler of heart thou hast wrung:
Hast thy dark descending and most art merciful then.

      With an anvil-ding
    And with fire in him forge thy will
  Or rather, rather then, stealing as Spring
    Through him, melt him but master him still:
Whether at once, as once at a crash Paul,
Or as Austin, a lingering-out swéet skill,
  Make mercy in all of us, out of us all
Mastery, but be adored, but be adored King.

II

    "Some find me a sword; some
    The flange and the rail; flame,
  Fang, or flood" goes Death on drum,
    And storms bugle his fame.
But wé dream we are rooted in earth—Dust!
Flesh falls within sight of us, we, though our flower
    the same,
  Wave with the meadow, forget that there must
The sour scythe cringe, and the blear share come.

    On Saturday sailed from Bremen,
    American-outward-bound,
  Take settler and seamen, tell men with women,
    Two hundred souls in the round—
O Father, not under thy feathers nor ever as guessing
The goal was a shoal, of a fourth the doom to be
    drowned;
  Yet did the dark side of the bay of thy blessing
Not vault them, the millions of rounds of thy mercy not
    reeve even them in?

Into the snows she sweeps,
  Hurling the haven behind,
The Deutschland, on Sunday; and so the sky keeps,
  For the infinite air is unkind,
And the sea flint-flake, black-backed in the regular
    blow,
Sitting Eastnortheast, in cursed quarter, the wind;
  Wiry and white-fiery and whirlwind-swivellèd snow
Spins to the widow-making unchilding unfathering
    deeps.

  She drove in the dark to leeward,
    She struck—not a reef or a rock
But the combs of a smother of sand: night drew her
    Dead to the Kentish Knock;
And she beat the bank down with her bows and the
    ride of her keel:
The breakers rolled on her beam with ruinous shock;
  And canvas and compass, the whorl and the wheel
Idle for ever to waft her or wind her with, these she
    endured.

  Hope had grown grey hairs,
    Hope had mourning on,
Trenched with tears, carved with cares,
    Hope was twelve hours gone;
And frightful a nightfall folded rueful a day
Nor rescue, only rocket and lightship, shone,
  And lives at last were washing away:
To the shrouds they took,—they shook in the hurling
    and horrible airs.

  One stirred from the rigging to save
    The wild woman-kind below,
With a rope's end round the man, handy and
    brave—

He was pitched to his death at a blow,
For all his dreadnought breast and braids of thew:
They could tell him for hours, dandled the to and fro
Through the cobbled foam-fleece, what could he do
With the burl of the fountains of air, buck and the flood
of the wave?

They fought with God's cold—
And they could not and fell to the deck
(Crushed them) or water (and drowned them) or
rolled
With the sea-romp over the wreck.
Night roared, with the heart-break hearing a heart-
broke rabble,
The woman's wailing, the crying of child without
check—
Till a lioness arose breasting the babble,
A prophetess towered in the tumult, a virginal tongue
told.

Ah, touched in your bower of bone
Are you! turned for an exquisite smart,
Have you! make words break from me here all
alone,
Do you!—mother of being in me, heart.
O unteachably after evil, but uttering truth,
Why, tears! is it? tears; such a melting, a madrigal
start!
Never-eldering revel and river of youth,
What can it be, this glee? the good you have there of
your own?

Sister, a sister calling
A master, her master and mine!—
And the inboard seas run swirling and hawling;
The rash smart sloggering brine

Blinds her; but she that weather sees one thing, one;
Has one fetch in her: she rears herself to divine
    Ears, and the call of the tall nun
To the men in the tops and the tackle rode over the
    storm's brawling.

    She was first of a five and came
    Of a coifèd sisterhood.
   (O Deutschland, double a desperate name!
    O world wide of its good!
But Gertrude, lily, and Luther, are two of a town,
Christ's lily and beast of the waste wood:
    From life's dawn it is drawn down,
Abel is Cain's brother and breasts they have sucked the
    same.)

    Loathed for a love men knew in them,
    Banned by the land of their birth,
  Rhine refused them. Thames would ruin them;
    Surf, snow, river and earth
Gnashed: but thou art above, thou Orion of light;
Thy unchancelling poising palms were weighing the
    worth,
    Thou martyr-master: in thy sight
Storm flakes were scroll-leaved flowers, lily showers—
    sweet heaven was astrew in them.

    Five! the finding and sake
    And cipher of suffering Christ.
    Mark, the mark is of man's make
    And the word of it Sacrificed.
But he scores it in scarlet himself on his own be-
    spoken,
Before-time-taken, dearest prizèd and priced—
    Stigma, signal, cinquefoil token
For lettering of the lamb's fleece, ruddying of the rose-
    flake.

Joy fall to thee, father Francis,
Drawn to the Life that died;
With the gnarls of the nails in thee, niche of the
lance, his
Lovescape crucified
And seal of his seraph-arrival! and these thy daugh-
ters
And five-livèd and leavèd favour and pride,
Are sisterly sealed in wild waters,
To bathe in his fall-gold mercies, to breathe in his all-
fire glances.

Away in the loveable west,
On a pastoral forehead of Wales,
I was under a roof here, I was at rest,
And they the prey of the gales;
She to the black-about air, to the breaker, the thickly
Falling flakes, to the throng that catches and quails
Was calling 'O Christ, Christ, come quickly':
The cross to her she calls Christ to her, christens her
wild-worst Best.

The majesty! what did she mean?
Breathe, arch and original Breath.
Is it love in her of the being as her lover had been?
Breathe, body of lovely Death.
They were else-minded then, altogether, the men
Woke thee with a *we are perishing* in the weather of
Gennesareth.
Or is it that she cried for the crown then,
The keener to come at the comfort for feeling the com-
bating keen?

For how to the heart's cheering
The down-dugged ground-hugged grey
Hovers off, the jay-blue heavens appearing

Of pied and peeled May!
Blue-beating and hoary-glow height; or night, still
    higher,
With belled fire and the moth-soft Milky Way,
    What by your measure is the heaven of desire,
The treasure never eyesight got, nor was ever guessed
    what for the hearing?

        No, but it was not these.
        The jading and jar of the cart,
    Time's tasking, it is fathers that asking for ease
        Of the sodden-with-its-sorrowing heart,
    Not danger, electrical horror; then further it finds
    The appealing of the Passion is tenderer in prayer
        apart:
    Other, I gather, in measure her mind's
Burden, in wind's burly and beat of endragonèd seas.

        But how shall I . . . make me room there:
        Reach me a . . . Fancy, come faster—
    Strike you the sight of it? look at it loom there,
        Thing that she . . . there then! the Master,
    Ipse, the only one, Christ, King, Head:
    He was to cure the extremity where he had cast her;
        Do, deal, lord it with living and dead;
Let him ride, her pride, in his triumph, despatch and
    have done with his doom there.

        Ah! there was a heart right
        There was single eye!
    Read the unshapeable shock night
        And knew the who and the why;
    Wording it how but by him that present and past,
    Heaven and earth are word of, worded by?—
        The Simon Peter of a soul! to the blast
Tarpeian-fast, but a blown beacon of light.

Jesu, heart's light,
Jesu, maid's son,
What was the feast followed the night
Thou hadst glory of this nun?—
Feast of the one woman without stain.
For so conceivèd, so to conceive thee is done;
But here was heart-throe, birth of a brain,
Word, that heard and kept thee and uttered thee out-
right.

Well, she has thee for the pain, for the
Patience; but pity of the rest of them!
Heart, go and bleed at a bitterer vein for the
Comfortless unconfessed of them—
No not uncomforted: lovely-felicitous Providence
Finger of a tender of, O of a feathery delicacy, the
breast of the
Maiden could obey so, be a bell to, ring of it, and
Startle the poor sheep back! is the shipwrack then a
harvest, does tempest carry the grain for
thee?

I admire thee, master of the tides,
Of the Yore-flood, of the year's fall;
The recurb and the recovery of the gulf's sides,
The girth of it and the wharf of it and the wall;
Stanching, quenching ocean of a motionable mind;
Ground of being, and granite of it: past all
Grasp God, throned behind
Death with a sovereignty that heeds but hides, bodes
but abides;

With a mercy that outrides
The all of water, an ark
For the listener; for the lingerer with a love glides
Lower than death and the dark;

A vein for the visiting of the past-prayer, pent in
    prison,
The-last-breath penitent spirits—the uttermost mark
    Our passion-plungèd giant risen,
The Christ of the Father compassionate, fetched in the
    storm of his strides.

    Now burn, new born to the world,
    Doubled-naturèd name,
  The heaven-flung, heart-fleshed, maiden-furled
    Miracle-in-Mary-of-flame,
Mid-numbered He in three of the thunder-throne!
Not a dooms-day dazzle in his coming nor dark as he
    came;
  Kind, but royally reclaiming his own;
A released shower, let flash to the shire, not a lightning
    of fire hard-hurled.

    Dame, at our door
    Drowned, and among our shoals,
  Remember us in the roads, the heaven-haven of the
    Reward:
  Our King back, oh, upon English souls!
Let him easter in us, be a dayspring to the dimness
    of us, be a crimson-cresseted east,
More brightening her, rare-dear Britain, as his reign
    rolls,
  Pride, rose, prince, hero of us, high-priest,
Our hearts' charity's hearth's fire, our thoughts' chiv-
    alry's throng's Lord.

The Windhover

TO CHRIST OUR LORD

I caught this morning morning's minion, king-
    dom of daylight's dauphin, dapple-dawn-drawn
      Falcon, in his riding
  Of the rolling level underneath him steady air, and
    striding
High there, how he rung upon the rein of a wimpling
    wing
In his ecstasy! then off, off forth on swing,
  As a skate's heel sweeps smooth on a bow-bend: the
    hurl and gliding
  Rebuffed the big wind. My heart in hiding
Stirred for a bird,—the achieve of, the mastery of the
    thing!

Brute beauty and valour and act, oh, air, pride, plume,
    here
  Buckle! AND the fire that breaks from thee then, a
    billion
Times told lovelier, more dangerous, O my chevalier!

  No wonder of it: shéer plód makes plough down
    sillion
Shine, and blue-bleak embers, ah my dear,
  Fall, gall themselves, and gash gold-vermilion.

Duns Scotus's Oxford

Towery city and branchy between towers;
Cuckoo-echoing, bell-swarmèd, lark-charmèd, rook-
    racked, river-rounded;
The dapple-eared lily below thee; that country and town
    did
Once encounter in, here coped and poisèd powers;

Thou hast a base and brickish skirt there, sours
That neighbour-nature thy grey beauty is grounded
Best in; graceless growth, thou hast confounded
Rural rural keeping—folk, flocks, and flowers.

Yet ah! this air I gather and I release
He lived on; these weeds and waters, these walls are
    what
He haunted who of all men most sways my spirits to
    peace;

Of realty the rarest-veinèd unraveller; a not
Rivalled insight, be rival Italy or Greece;
Who fired France for Mary without spot.

The Candle Indoors

Some candle clear burns somewhere I come by.
I muse at how its being puts blissful back
With yellowy moisture mild night's blear-all black,
Or to-fro tender trambeams truckle at the eye.
By that window what task what fingers ply,

I plod wondering, a-wanting, just for lack
Of answer the eagerer a-wanting Jessy or Jack
There God to aggrándise, God to glorify.—

Come you indoors, come home; your fading fire
Mend first and vital candle in close heart's vault:
You there are master, do your own desire;
What hinders? Are you beam-blind, yet to a fault
In a neighbour deft-handed? are you that liar
And, cast by conscience out, spendsavour salt?

Spring and Fall

TO A YOUNG CHILD

Márgarét, are you gríeving
Over Goldengrove unleaving?
Leáves, líke the things of man, you
With your fresh thoughts care for, can you?
Áh! ás the heart grows older
It will come to such sights colder
By and by, nor spare a sigh
Though worlds of wanwood leafmeal lie;
And yet you wíll weep and know why.
Now no matter, child, the name:
Sórrow's spríngs áre the same.
Nor mouth had, no nor mind, expressed
What heart heard of, ghost guessed:
It ís the blight man was born for,
It is Margaret you mourn for.

Carrion Comfort

Not, I'll not, carrion comfort, Despair, not feast on thee;
Not untwist—slack they may be—these last strands of
    man
In me ór, most weary, cry *I can no more.* I can;
Can something, hope, wish day come, not choose not
    to be.
But ah, but O thou terrible, why wouldst thou rude on
    me
Thy wring-world right foot rock? lay a lionlimb against
    me? scan
With darksome devouring eyes my bruisèd bones? and
    fan,
O in turns of tempest, me heaped there; me frantic to
    avoid thee and flee?

  Why? That my chaff might fly; my grain lie, sheer and
    clear.
Nay in all that toil, that coil, since (seems) I kissed the
    rod,
Hand rather, my heart lo! lapped strength, stole joy,
    would laugh, chéer.
Cheer whom though? the hero whose heaven-handling
    flung me, fóot tród
Me? or me that fought him? O which one? is it each
    one? That night, that year
Of now done darkness I wretch lay wrestling with (my
    God!) my God.

No worst, there is none

No worst, there is none. Pitched past pitch of grief,
More pangs will, schooled at forepangs, wilder wring.
Comforter, where, where is your comforting?
Mary, mother of us, where is your relief?
My cries heave, herds-long; huddle in a main, a chief
Woe, world-sorrow; on an age-old anvil wince and
    sing—
Then lull, then leave off. Fury had shrieked "No ling-
ering! Let me be fell: force I must be brief."

   O the mind, mind has mountains; cliffs of fall
Frightful, sheer, no-man-fathomed. Hold them cheap
May who ne'er hung there. Nor does long our small
Durance deal with that steep or deep. Here! creep,
Wretch, under a comfort serves in a whirlwind: all
Life death does end and each day dies with sleep.

I wake and feel the fell of dark

I wake and feel the fell of dark, not day.
What hours, O what black hoürs we have spent
This night! what sights you, heart, saw; ways you went!
And more must, in yet longer light's delay.
   With witness I speak this. But where I say
Hours I mean years, mean life. And my lament
Is cries countless, cries like dead letters sent
To dearest him that lives alas! away.

I am gall, I am heartburn. God's most deep decree
Bitter would have me taste: my taste was me;
Bones built in me, flesh filled, blood brimmed the curse.
 Selfyeast of spirit a dull dough sours. I see
The lost are like this, and their scourge to be
As I am mine, their sweating selves; but worse.

The Summer Malison

Maidens shall weep at merry morn,
And hedges break and lose the kine,
And field-flowers make the fields forlorn,
And noonday have a shallow shine,
And barley turn to weed and wild,
And seven ears crown the lodged corn,
And mother have no milk for child,
    And father be overworn.

And John shall lie, where winds are dead,
And hate the ill-visaged cursing tars,
And James shall hate his faded red,
Grown wicked in the wicked wars.
No rains shall fresh the flats of sea,
Nor close the clayfields' sharded sores,
And every heart think loathingly
    Its dearest changed to bores.

That Nature is a Heraclitean Fire and of the Comfort of the Resurrection

Cloud-Puffball, torn tufts, tossed pillows | flaunt forth,
　　then chevy on an air-
built thoroughfare: heaven-roysterers, in gay-gangs |
　　they throng; they glitter in marches.
Down roughcast, down dazzling whitewash, | wherever
　　an elm arches,
Shivelights and shadowtackle in long | lashes lace, lance,
　　and pair.
Delightfully the bright wind boisterous | ropes, wrestles,
　　beats earth bare
Of yestertempest's creases; | in pool and rut peel parches
Squandering ooze to squeezed | dough, crust, dust;
　　stanches, starches
Squadroned masks and manmarks | treadmire toil there
Footfretted in it. Million-fuelèd, | nature's bonfire burns
　　on.
But quench her bonniest, dearest | to her, her clearest-
　　selvèd spark
Man, how fast his firedint, | his mark on mind, is gone!
Both are in an unfathomable, all is in an enormous dark
Drowned. O pity and indig | nation! Manshape, that
　　shone
Sheer off, disseveral, a star, | death blots black out; nor
　　mark
　　　　　　Is any of him at all so stark
But vastness blurs and time | beats level. Enough! the
　　Resurrection,
A heart's-clarion! Away grief's gasping, | joyless days,
　　dejection.

Across my foundering deck shone

A beacon, an eternal beam. | Flesh fade, and mortal
trash

Fall to the residuary worm; | world's wildfire, leave but
ash:

In a flash, at a trumpet crash,

I am all at once what Christ is, | since he was what I am,
and

This Jack, joke, poor potsherd, | patch, matchwood, im-
mortal diamond,

Is immortal diamond.

Robert Bridges

(1844–1930)

London Snow

When men were all asleep the snow came flying,
In large white flakes falling on the city brown,
Stealthily and perpetually settling and loosely lying,
   Hushing the latest traffic of the drowsy town;
Deadening, muffling, stifling its murmurs failing;
Lazily and incessantly floating down and down:
   Silently sifting and veiling road, roof and railing;
Hiding difference, making unevenness even,
Into angles and crevices softly drifting and sailing.
   All night it fell, and when full inches seven
It lay in the depth of its uncompacted lightness,
The clouds blew off from a high and frosty heaven;
   And all woke earlier for the unaccustomed brightness
Of the winter dawning, the strange unheavenly glare:
The eye marvelled—marvelled at the dazzling white-
     ness;
   The ear hearkened to the stillness of the solemn air;
No sound of wheel rumbling nor of foot falling,
And the busy morning cries came thin and spare.
   Then boys I heard, as they went to school, calling,
They gathered up the crystal manna to freeze
Their tongues with tasting, their hands with snowball-
     ing;
   Or rioted in a drift, plunging up to the knees;
Or peering up from under the white-mossed wonder,

"O look at the trees!" they cried, "O look at the trees!"
    With lessened load a few carts creak and blunder,
Following along the white deserted way,
A country company long dispersed asunder:
    When now already the sun, in pale display
Standing by Paul's high dome, spread forth below
His sparkling beams, and awoke the stir of the day.

    For now doors open, and war is waged with the snow;
And trains of sombre men, past tale of number,
Tread long brown paths, as towards their toil they go:
    But even for them awhile no cares encumber
Their minds diverted; the daily word is unspoken,
The daily thoughts of labour and sorrow slumber
At the sight of the beauty that greets them, for the
    charm they have broken.

The Philosopher to His Mistress

Because thou canst not see,
Because thou canst not know
The black and hopeless woe
That hath encompassed me:
Because, should I confess
The thought of my despair,
My words would wound thee less
Than swords can hurt the air:

Because with thee I seem
As one invited near
To taste the fairy cheer
Of spirits in a dream;
Of whom he knoweth nought
Save that they vie to make

All motion, voice and thought
A pleasure for his sake:

Therefore more sweet and strange
Has been the mystery
Of thy long love to me,
That doth not quit, nor change,
Nor tax my solemn heart,
That kisseth in a gloom,
Knowing not who thou art
That givest, nor to whom.

Therefore the tender touch
Is more; more dear the smile:
And thy light words beguile
My wisdom overmuch:
And O with swiftness fly
The fancies of my song
To happy worlds, where I
Still in thy love belong.

The evening darkens over

The evening darkens over
After a day so bright
The windcapt waves discover
That wild will be the night.
There's sound of distant thunder.

The latest sea-birds hover
Along the cliff's sheer height;
As in the memory wander
Last flutterings of delight,
White wings lost on the white.

There's not a ship in sight;
And as the sun goes under
Thick clouds conspire to cover
The moon that should rise yonder.
Thou art alone, fond lover.

My delight and thy delight

My delight and thy delight
Walking, like two angels white,
In the gardens of the night:

My desire and thy desire
Twining to a tongue of fire,
Leaping live, and laughing higher;
Thro' the everlasting strife
In the mystery of life.

Love, from whom the world begun,
Hath the secret of the sun.

Love can tell, and love alone,
Whence the million stars were strewn,
Why each atom knows its own,
How, in spite of woe and death,
Gay is life, and sweet is breath:

This he taught us, this we knew,
Happy in his science true,
Hand in hand as we stood
Neath the shadows of the wood,
Heart to heart as we lay
In the dawning of the day.

November

The lonely season in lonely lands, when fled
Are half the birds, and mists lie low, and the sun
Is rarely seen, nor strayeth far from his bed;
The short days pass unwelcomed one by one.

Out by the ricks the mantled engine stands
Crestfallen, deserted,—for now all hands
Are told to the plough,—and ere it is dawn appear
The teams following and crossing far and near,
As hour by hour they broaden the brown bands
Of the striped fields; and behind them firk and prance
The heavy rooks, and daws grey-pated dance:
As awhile, surmounting a crest, in sharp outline
(A miniature of toil, a gem's design,)
They are pictured, horses and men, or now near by
Above the lane they shout lifting the share,
By the trim hedgerow bloom'd with purple air;
Where, under the thorns, dead leaves in huddle lie
Packed by the gales of Autumn, and in and out
The small wrens glide
With a happy note of cheer,
And yellow amorets flutter above and about,
Gay, familiar in fear.

And now, if the night shall be cold, across the sky
Linnets and twites, in small flocks helter-skelter,
All the afternoon to the gardens fly,
From the thistle-pastures hurrying to gain the shelter
Of American rhododendron or cherry-laurel:

And here and there, near chilly setting of sun,
In an isolated tree a congregation
Of starlings chatter and chide,
Thickset as summer leaves, in garrulous quarrel:
Suddenly they hush as one,—
The tree top springs,—
And off, with a whirr of wings,
They fly by the score
To the holly-thicket, and there with myriads more
Dispute for the roosts; and from the unseen nation
A babel of tongues, like running water unceasing,
Makes live the wood, the flocking cries increasing,
Wangling discordantly, incessantly,
While falls the night on them self-occupied;
The long dark night, that lengthens slow,
Deepening with Winter to starve grass and tree,
And soon bury in snow
The Earth, that, sleeping 'neath her frozen stole,
Shall dream a dream crept from the sunless pole
Of how her end shall be.

Eros

Why hast thou nothing in thy face?
Thou idol of the human race,
Thou tyrant of the human heart,
The flower of lovely youth that art;
Yea, and that standest in thy youth
An image of eternal Truth,
With thy exuberant flesh so fair,
That only Pheidias might compare,
Ere from his chaste marmoreal form
Time had decayed the colours warm;

Like to his gods in thy proud dress,
Thy starry sheen of nakedness.

Surely thy body is thy mind,
For in thy face is nought to find,
Only thy soft unchristen'd smile,
That shadows neither love nor guile,
But shameless will and power immense,
In secret sensuous innocence.

O king of joy, what is thy thought?
I dream thou knowest it is nought,
And wouldst in darkness come, but thou
Makest the light where'er thou go.
Ah yet no victim of thy grace,
None who e'er long'd for thy embrace,
Hath cared to look upon thy face.

Johannes Milton, Senex

Scazons

Since I believe in God the Father Almighty,
Man's Maker and Judge, Overruler of Fortune,
'Twere strange should I praise anything and refuse Him
    praise,
Should love the creature forgetting the Crēator,
Nor unto Himᵛin suff'ring and sorrow turn me:
Nay how coud I withdraw fromᵛHis embracing?

But since that I have seen not, and cannot know Him,
Nor in my earthly temple apprehend rightly
His wisdom and the heav'nly purpose eternal;
Therefore will I be bound to no studied system

Nor argument, nor with delusion enslave me,
Nor seek to pleáse Him in any foolish invention,
Which my spirit within me, that loveth beauty
And hateth evil, hath reprov'd as unworthy:

But I cherish my freedom in loving service,
Gratefully adoring for delight beyond asking
Or thinking, and in hours of anguish and darkness
Confiding always on ᵛHis excellent greatness.

Noel: Christmas Eve, 1913

Pax hominibus bonae voluntatis

A frosty Christmas Eve
   when the stars were shining
Fared I forth alone
   where westward falls the hill,
And from many a village
   in the water'd valley
Distant music reach'd me
   peals of bells aringing:
The constellated sounds
   ran sprinkling on earth's floor
As the dark vault above
   with stars was spangled o'er.

Then sped my thoughts to keep
   that first Christmas of all
When the shepherds watching
   by the folds ere the dawn
Heard music in the fields
   and marveling could not tell
Whether it were angels
   or the bright stars singing.

Now blessed be the tow'rs
  that crown England so fair
That stand up strong in prayer
  unto God for our souls:
Blessed be their founders
  (said I) an' our country folk
Who are ringing for Christ
  in the belfries to-night
With arms lifted to clutch
  the rattling ropes that race
Into the dark above
  and the mad romping din.

But to me heard afar
  it was starry music
Angels' song, comforting
  as the comfort of Christ
When he spake tenderly
  to his sorrowful flock:
The old words came to me
  by the riches of time
Mellow'd and transfigured
  as I stood on the hill
Heark'ning in the aspect
  of th'eternal silence.

Thomas Hardy

(1840–1928)

The Souls of the Slain

The thick lids of Night closed upon me
    Alone at the Bill
    Of the Isle by the Race—
Many-caverned, bald, wrinkled of face—
And with darkness and silence the spirit was on me
    To brood and be still.

No wind fanned the flats of the ocean,
    Or promontory sides,
    Or the ooze by the strand,
    Or the bent-bearded slope of the land,
Whose base took its rest amid everlong motion
    Of criss-crossing tides.

Soon from out of the Southward seemed nearing
    A whirr, as of wings
    Waved by mighty-vanned flies,
Or by night-moths of measureless size,
And in softness and smoothness well-nigh beyond hear-
      ing
    Of corporal things.

And they bore to the bluff, and alighted—
    A dim-discerned train
    Of sprites without mould,
Frameless souls none might touch or might hold—

On the ledge by the turreted lantern, far-sighted
   By men of the main.

And I heard them say "Home!" and I knew them
  For souls of the felled
  On the earth's nether bord
Under Capricorn, whither they'd warred,
And I neared in my awe, and gave heedfulness to them
  With breathings inheld.

Then, it seemed, there approached from the North-
    ward
  A senior soul-flame
  Of the like filmy hue:
And he met them and spake: "Is it you,
O my men?" Said they, "Aye! We bear homeward and
    hearthward
  To feast on our fame!"

"I've flown there before you," he said then:
  "Your households are well;
  But—your kin linger less
On your glory and war-mightiness
Than on dearer things." "—Dearer?" cried these from
    the dead then,
  "Of what do they tell?"

"Some mothers muse sadly, and murmur
  Your doings as boys—
  Recall the quaint ways
Of your babyhood's innocent days.
Some pray that, ere dying, your faith had grown firmer,
  And higher your joys.

"A father broods: 'Would I had set him
  To some humble trade,
  And so slacked his high fire,

And his passionate martial desire;
And told him no stories to woo him and whet him
    To this dire crusade!' "

"And, General, how hold out our sweethearts,
    Sworn loyal as doves?"
        —"Many mourn; many think
    It is not unattractive to prink
Them in sables for heroes. Some fickle and fleet hearts
    Have found them new loves."

"And our wives?" quoth another resignedly,
    "Dwell they on our deeds?"
        —"Deeds of home; that live yet
    Fresh as new—deeds of fondness or fret;
Ancient words that were kindly expressed or unkindly,
    These, these have their heeds."

—"Alas! then it seems that our glory
    Weighs less in their thought
    Than our old homely acts,
    And the long-ago commonplace facts
Of our lives—held by us as scarce part of our story,
    And rated as nought!"

Then bitterly some: "Was it wise now
    To raise such a tomb-door
    For such knowledge? Away!"
But the rest: "Fame we prized till to-day;
Yet that hearts keep us green for old kindness we prize
        now
    A thousand times more!"

Thus speaking, the trooped apparitions
    Began to disband
    And resolve them in two:
Those whose record was lovely and true

Bore to northward for home: those of bitter traditions
    Again left the land,

And, towering to seaward in legions,
    They paused at a spot
    Overbending the Race—
That engulphing, ghast, sinister place—
Whither headlong they plunged, to the fathomless
    regions
    Of myriads forgot.

And the spirits of those who were homing
    Passed on, rushingly,
    Like the Pentecost Wind:
And the whirr of their wayfaring thinned
And surceased on the sky, and but left in the gloaming
    Sea-mutterings and me.

The Lacking Sense

Scene.—A sad-coloured landscape. Waddon Vale

"O Time, whence comes the Mother's moody look amid
    her labours,
As of one who all unwittingly has wounded where she
    loves?
Why weaves she not her world-webs to according
    lutes and tabors,
With nevermore this too remorseful air upon her face,
    As of angel fallen from grace?"

—"Her look is but her story: construe not its symbols
    keenly:
In her wonderworks yea surely has she wounded
    where she loves.

The sense of ills misdealt for blisses blanks the mien
most queenly,
    Self-smitings kill self-joys; and everywhere beneath
the sun
        Such deeds her hands have done."

—"And how explains thy Ancient Mind her crimes upon
her creatures,
    These fallings from her fair beginnings, woundings
where she loves,
Into her would-be perfect motions, modes, effects, and
features
    Admitting cramps, black humours, wan decay, and
baleful blights,
        Distress into delights?"

—"Ah! knowest thou not her secret yet, her vainly veiled
deficience,
    Whence it comes that all unwittingly she wounds the
lives she loves?
That sightless are those orbs of hers?—which bar to her
omniscience
    Brings those fearful unfulfilments, that red ravage
through her zones
        Whereat all creation groans.

"She whispers it in each pathetic strenuous slow en-
deavor,
    When in mothering she unwittingly sets wounds on
what she loves;
Yet her primal doom pursues her, faultful, fatal is she
ever;
    Though so deft and nigh to vision is her facile finger-
touch
        That the seers marvel much.

"Deal, then, her groping skill no scorn, no note of male-
diction;
Not long on thee will press the hand that hurts the
lives it loves;
And while she plods dead-reckoning on, in darkness of
affliction,
Assist her where thy creaturely dependence can or
may,
For thou art of her clay."

Wessex Heights

There are some heights in Wessex, shaped as if by a
kindly hand
For thinking, dreaming, dying on, and at crises when I
stand,
Say, on Ingpen Beacon eastward, or on Wylls-Neck
westwardly,
I seem where I was before my birth, and after death
may be.

In the lowlands I have no comrade, not even the lone
man's friend—
Her who suffereth long and is kind; accepts what he is
too weak to mend:
Down there they are dubious and askance; there nobody
thinks as I,
But mind-chains do not clank where one's next neigh-
bour is the sky.

In the towns I am tracked by phantoms having weird
detective ways—

Shadows of beings who fellowed with myself of earlier
   days:
They hang about at places, and they say harsh heavy
   things—
Men with a wintry sneer, and women with tart disparag-
   ings.

Down there I seem to be false to myself, my simple self
   that was,
And is not now, and I see him watching, wondering
   what crass cause
Can have merged him into such a strange continuator as
   this,
Who yet has something in common with himself, my
   chrysalis.

I cannot go to the great grey Plain; there's a figure
   against the moon,
Nobody sees it but I, and it makes my breast beat out of
   tune;
I cannot go to the tall-spired town, being barred by the
   forms now passed
For everybody but me, in whose long vision they stand
   there fast.

There's a ghost at Yell'ham Bottom chiding loud at the
   fall of the night,
There's a ghost in Froom-side Vale, thin lipped and
   vague, in a shroud of white,
There is one in the railway train whenever I do not want
   it near,
I see its profile against the pane, saying what I would
   not hear.

As for one rare fair woman, I am now but a thought of
   hers,

I enter her mind and another thought succeeds me that
    she prefers;
Yet my love for her in its fulness she herself even did
    not know;
Well, time cures hearts of tenderness, and now I can
    let her go.

So I am found on Ingpen Beacon, or on Wylls-Neck to
    the west,
Or else on homely Bulbarrow, or little Pilsdon Crest,
Where men have never cared to haunt, nor women have
    walked with me,
And ghosts then keep their distance; and I know some
    liberty.

Channel Firing

That night your great guns, unawares,
Shook all our coffins as we lay,
And broke the chancel window-squares,
We thought it was the Judgment-day

And sat upright. While drearisome
Arose the howl of wakened hounds:
The mouse let fall the altar-crumb,
The worms drew back into the mounds,

The glebe cow drooled. Till God called, "No;
It's gunnery practice out at sea
Just as before you went below;
The world is as it used to be:

"All nations striving strong to make
Red war yet redder. Mad as hatters

They do no more for Christés sake
Than you who are helpless in such matters.

"That this is not the judgment-hour
For some of them's a blessed thing,
For if it were they'd have to scour
Hell's floor for so much threatening. . .

"Ha, ha. It will be warmer when
I blow the trumpet (if indeed
I ever do; for you are men,
And rest eternal sorely need)."

So down we lay again. "I wonder,
Will the world ever saner be,"
Said one, "than when He sent us under
In our indifferent century!"

And many a skeleton shook his head.
"Instead of preaching forty year,"
My neighbour Parson Thirdly said,
"I wish I had stuck to pipes and beer."

Again the guns disturbed the hour,
Roaring their readiness to avenge,
As far inland as Stourton Tower,
And Camelot, and starlit Stonehenge.

The Walk

You did not walk with me
Of late to the hill-top tree
    By the gated ways
    As in earlier days;
    You were weak and lame,

So you never came,
And I went alone, and I did not mind,
Not thinking of you as left behind.

I walked up there to-day
Just in the former way;
Surveyed around
The familiar ground
By myself again:
What difference, then?
Only that underlying sense
Of the look of a room on returning thence.

I found her out there

I found her out there
On a slope few see,
That falls westwardly
To the salt-edged air,
Where the ocean breaks
On the purple strand,
And the hurricane shakes
The solid land.

I brought her here,
And have laid her to rest
In a noiseless nest
No sea beats near.
She will never be stirred
In her loamy cell
By the waves long heard
And loved so well.

So she does not sleep
By those haunted heights

The Atlantic smites
And the blind gales sweep,
Whence she often would gaze
At Dundagel's famed head,
While the dipping blaze
Dyed her face fire-red;

And would sigh at the tale
Of sunk Lyonnesse,
As a wind-tugged tress
Flapped her cheek like a flail;
Or listen at whiles
With a thought-bound brow
To the murmuring miles
She is far from now.

Yet her shade, maybe,
Will creep underground
Till it catch the sound
Of that western sea
As it swells and sobs
Where she once domiciled,
And joy in its throbs
With the heart of a child.

The Voice

Woman much missed, how you call to me, call to me,
Saying that now you are not as you were
When you had changed from the one who was all to me,
But as at first, when our day was fair.

Can it be you that I hear? Let me view you, then,
Standing as when I drew near to the town

Where you would wait for me: yes, as I knew you then,
Even to the original air-blue gown!

Or is it only the breeze, in its listlessness
Travelling across the wet mead to me here,
You being ever dissolved to wan wistlessness,
Heard no more again far or near?

    Thus I; faltering forward,
    Leaves around me falling,
Wind oozing thin through the thorn from norward,
    And the woman calling.

After a Journey

Hereto I come to view a voiceless ghost;
    Whither, O whither will its whim now draw me?
Up the cliff, down, till I'm lonely, lost,
    And the unseen waters' ejaculations awe me.
Where you will next be there's no knowing,
    Facing round about me everywhere,
        With your nut-coloured hair,
And gray eyes, and rose-flush coming and going.

Yes: I have re-entered your olden haunts at last;
    Through the years, through the dead scenes I have
        tracked you;
What have you now found to say of our past—
    Scanned across the dark space wherein I have lacked
        you?
Summer gave us sweets, but autumn wrought division?
    Things were not lastly as firstly well
        With us twain, you tell?
But all's closed now, despite Time's derision.

I see what you are doing: you are leading me on
  To the spots we knew when we haunted here to-
      gether,
The waterfall, above which the mist-bow shone
  At the then fair hour in the then fair weather,
And the cave just under, with a voice still so hollow
  That it seems to call out to me from forty years ago,
      When you were all aglow,
And not the thin ghost that I now frailly follow!

Ignorant of what there is flitting here to see,
  The waked birds preen and the seals flop lazily,
Soon you will have, Dear, to vanish from me,
  For the stars close their shutters and the dawn
      whitens hazily.
Trust me, I mind not, though Life lours,
  The bringing me here; nay, bring me here again!
      I am just the same as when
Our days were a joy, and our paths through flowers.

The Phantom Horsewoman

Queer are the ways of a man I know:
      He comes and stands
      In a careworn craze,
      And looks at the sands
      And the seaward haze
      With moveless hands
      And face and gaze,
      Then turns to go . . .
And what does he see when he gazes so?

They say he sees as an instant thing
      More clear than to-day,

A sweet soft scene
That once was in play
By that briny green;
Yes, notes alway
Warm, real, and keen,
What his back years bring—
A phantom of his own figuring.

Of this vision of his they might say more:
Not only there
Does he see this sight,
But everywhere
In his brain—day, night,
As if on the air
It were drawn rose bright—
Yea, far from that shore
Does he carry this vision of heretofore:

A ghost-girl-rider. And though, toil-tried,
He withers daily,
Time touches her not,
But she still rides gaily
In his rapt thought
On that shagged and shaly
Atlantic spot,
And as when first eyed
Draws rein and sings to the swing of the tide.

First Sight of Her and After

A day is drawing to its fall
I had not dreamed to see;
The first of many to enthrall

My spirit, will it be?
Or is this eve the end of all
Such new delight for me?

I journey home: the pattern grows
Of moonshades on the way:
"Soon the first quarter, I suppose,"
Sky-glancing travellers say;
I realize that it, for those,
Has been a common day.

The Five Students

The sparrow dips in his wheel-rut bath,
The sun grows passionate-eyed,
And boils the dew to smoke by the paddock-path;
As strenuously we stride,—
Five of us; dark He, fair He, dark She, fair She, I,
All beating by.

The air is shaken, the high-road hot,
Shadowless swoons the day,
The greens are sobered and cattle at rest; but not
We on our urgent way,—
Four of us; fair She, dark She, fair He, I, are there,
But one—elsewhere.

Autumn moulds the hard fruit mellow,
And forward still we press
Through moors, briar-meshed plantations, clay-pits
yellow,
As in the spring hours—yes,
Three of us; fair He, fair She, I, as heretofore,
But—fallen one more.

The leaf drops: earthworms draw it in
    At night-time noiselessly,
The fingers of birch and beech are skeleton-thin,
    And yet on the beat are we,—
Two of us; fair She, I. But no more left to go
    The track we know.

Icicles tag the church-aisle leads,
    The flag-rope gibbers hoarse,
The home-bound foot-folk wrap their snow-flaked
    heads,
    Yet I still stalk the course—
One of us. . . . Dark and fair He, dark and fair She,
    gone
    The rest—anon.

Who's in the next room?

"Who's in the next room?—who?
    I seemed to see
Somebody in the dawning passing through,
    Unknown to me."
"Nay: you saw nought. He passed invisibly."

"Who's in the next room?—who?
    I seem to hear
Somebody muttering firm in a language new
    That chills the ear."
"No: you catch not his tongue who has entered there."

"Who's in the next room?—who?
    I seem to feel
His breath like a clammy draught, as if it drew
    From the Polar Wheel."
"No: none who breathes at all does the door conceal."

"Who's in the next room?—who?
A figure wan
With a message to one in there of something due?
Shall I know him anon?"
"Yea he; and he brought such; and you'll know him
anon."

Afterwards

When the Present has latched its postern behind my
tremulous stay,
And the May month flaps its glad green leaves like
wings,
Delicate-filmed as new-spun silk, will the neighbours
say,
"He was a man who used to notice such things"?

If it be in the dusk when, like an eyelid's soundless
blink,
The dewfall-hawk comes crossing the shades to alight
Upon the wind-warped upland thorn, a gazer may think,
"To him this must have been a familiar sight."

If I pass during some nocturnal blackness, mothy and
warm,
When the hedgehog travels furtively over the lawn,
One may say, "He strove that such innocent creatures
should come to no harm,
But he could do little for them; and now he is gone."

If, when hearing that I have been stilled at last, they
stand at the door,
Watching the full-starred heavens that winter sees,

Will this thought rise on those who will meet my face
  no more,
  "He was one who had an eye for such mysteries"?

And will any say when my bell of quittance is heard in
  the gloom,
  And a crossing breeze cuts a pause in its outrollings,
Till they rise again, as they were a new bell's boom,
  "He hears it not now, but used to notice such things"?

Charles M. Doughty

(1843–1926)

FROM *The Dawn in Britain*

[*Bladyn's Song of Cloten*]

Took Bladyn then his crowth, anew, and toucht
The warbeling strings; and weaved them, with his
    hands.
He chants, of valiant Cloten, prince of Kent.
To see his royal kin, in Gaul's mainland,
And visit foreign nations, Cloten sailed,
With warlike navy. But the prince's keel,
Whose pilot, in thick mist, had lost his course,
Was parted from the rest. Howbe, was this
Suspect, of treachery; in that king of Kent,
His son, for grievous guilt, had judged to death.
    Driving, at misadventure, they were met,
Of Frisic yawls, full of fierce weaponed wights;
And whose long weather-boards shingled with shields!
With these, that pirates were, they fight, for life;
Few, against many. And he, young valorous prince,
Hurt of a grapnel, which was hurled, inboard;
Being now his most men slain, was taken, uneath;
By might of many inthronging champions
    And when those all, in the king's ship, had spoiled;
They Cloten, did, on thwart row-bank, compel,
To drag an oar. But, displeased, the sea-gods
Loosed a main-tempest, on those pirate keels;

544

So that o'er-beat, the rugged risen waves,
Their boards. Nor labouring they, at sea, all night,
Might win to any haven. When gainst day, was;
They, fallen mongst breakers, split on some sharp
    skerries:
And every pirate soul drenched on their boards.
But Cloten, from the row-lock, who washt forth
Was, with his oar, whereto those bound him; rides,
It embraced, all that day, the windy surges,
(And he yet lives, by favour of some god!)
And the next night. Nigh noon, of second morrow,
Last cast the Cantion prince was, where, mongst rocks,
(That tempest ceased,) more gently runs the tide.
    Young Cloten seemed, all swollen, some cold white
    corse,
Which ebbing waves, on that shole sand, depose.
There warms him summer's sun; and turns, with pain,
A flickering life, unto his deadly flesh.
Like worm, he creeps, then, on the steepy strand;
His cords sith frets, and severs, on sharp rocks;
So finds, where fallen, together, two cliff-craigs
Make a sea-cave. There, gathered much salt moss,
Now in that hold, lies Cloten warm and sleeps:
That day outsleeps; and yet the long night sleeps;
Till murmuring, at his feet, mongst pebble stones,
The rising tide affrays him, in the gloom.
But pitying, gods; to whom young Cloten prays,
Bade Sleep, anew, his heavy eyelids close.
He slumbers, till a new sun climbs in heaven.
    Prince of the noble youth of warlike Kent,
He dreams, he walks, yet, in his father's court;
And sees there maiden, like to goddess bright,
Daughter of kings; for she, with gold, is crowned.
Him thought, he followed her, then, with long grief;
Because, how swift soe'er he moved his feet,

He might not her attain, through all the world!
He wakes, of all things, bare, and sighs; but joys,
That he is free, alwere on forlorn coast.
So went forth view, what this were for a shore:
And if, therein, that human kindness were.

Before the dawning ray, was Esla risen.
She, with sweet birds, hath sung her early lays,
To Sena's god; and beet his temple-fires.
By steepy headlands, thence, lo, she dismounts!
Like to a falcon gentle; so is light,
Or like sleep-walker, who none peril sees,
Adown the high-ribbed rocks, her virgin tread.
Would, after tempest, Esla, yet a child,
For a sweet incense, gather amber-stone,
And whelky shells; and play the strand along.

Esla is priestess, of the moon, in Sena;
And daughter to a king of Gaul's mainland.
Her garments, long, up-gathered, of white lawn;
Now, on this shore, sweet maiden, she paced down:
So skips, from stone, on her white feet, to stone;
And run salt waves, those gracious steps to kiss.
And, oft, in her disport, she, virgin, stoops,
On the white sand, to take up carnalines,
Or shells, like rosebuds, hid in coral moss.

Then, half-adawed, she stands, like hind, at gaze;
And looketh her about! She weens, she heard,
As moan; or the wind was, mongst fallen crags?
And for that sudden fear, she would have fled.
Like startled roe, yet listens! To her ears,
Then comes of plaint and song, as mingled voice;
Yet nothing like to her weird sisters' voice;
Though quake her tender joints, she nigher draws:
And spies some quick thing, like herself, in cave;
Save that, seems, this hath face of some sea-moss,

O'ergrown; and middle girt of tangle, hath;
For, in the sun, the prince had cast his cloth.
And, from a child, hath Esla seen no man.

    Whilst marvelling yet, she shrinks, as fowl, from
        hawk;
Lifts Cloten suppliant hands, as to a goddess!
For, such, he deems her, of this unknown coast.
He, of grace, her prays, she tell him, where he is?
Makes answer Esla; "This is island Sena":
Whereat he dreads the more; and, by the gods,
Bewray him not, conjures! whether she nymph
Were, of these shores; or, else, her nourisheth bread.
Which brings forth foster-bosom of earth's ground.
And saith, how hath he twice died, in these days:
Once, in salt-waves; once, by his enemies.

    And, piteous, promised Esla. She, sweet child,
Abhors her insane sisters' murderous mood.
Nor this, as they, one wrinkled, hideous;
But fairest wight, which she hath seen, on ground:
Such as, records her thought, her father was!
Wherefore, she kissed him; and did melt their hearts.

    The prince, then cheerfully beholding Esla,
Her heavenly aspect, knew to be the same,
Which him revealed was, in his long night vision.
Yet deems he her, surely, of some celestial seed.
Him Esla warns, keep close; lest startled mews,
With shrieks, and the wild terns, bewray his life;
To her weird sisters, peeping from the cliffs.

    Like as sand-piper runs, at the salt brinks;
So dancing she, on her white nimble feet,
To gather, hies, as the weird sisters wont,
Some wild meat. Cometh then, soon, again, sweet Esla:
And, to him, brings, her lapfull, of sea-eggs,
Salads and samphires of the windy cliffs:

And now mote she return, lest she were missed.
But she, at even, will come unto this place,
With weed and meat. A little thing, then asked
Cloten, which came into his sudden thought:
(He óf some, here, cast timber, would knit float;
And night-time, scape from Sena, and this sea-death;)
Where might he any willow-withies find?

    From him, by sharp wild crags, she lightly upclimbs.
And seemed, on those steep cliffs, some hovering bird,
That mounts! To sacred pool, is Esla went,
Round-grown of sallows, by their temple-path.
There, with sharp flint, she severs golden rods,
So, running, hurls her bundles, from the rocks.
Then certain her weird sisters chanced to pass;
Turning, towards noon, from Sena's sacred hearth.
They, seeing her do so, gan Esla call!
But she, a divine madness feigned anon;
Taught of some god, which her, to-day, bestraught,
Leaps mongst rough crags. As guileful lapwing lures,
Feet of crude fowler, from her fledgelings' nest;
So them she leads, so them misleads; as danced
She merry round, (whose murderous meaning is;
Seize on her tender limbs, and rend, and cast
Them, to sea's running waves, from these dread brinks!)
They hoary women, past now age and spent,
By cranks and windles, from those perilous rocks;
Aye crying, like to one wildered, were those wands,
Whence she a lattice to her bower would frame;
But that aye turn to serpents, in her hands;
Wherefore, for are they worms! she flings them forth,
Which eat the bramble-buds and whortle-berries!

    Nor fears death Esla: she would die, to save,
Whom her soul loves. Have outstripped her light feet,
Their cold lean joints. And now this passion past,
There fell a blindness, on them, from the gods.

Wakes Esla, all day, so she impatient is,
To keep his life, which hid under these brinks.
When erst, from heaven, the molten stars look forth;
After the sunny rays, she ready is;
Nor fears, where, like to walls, downhangs the cliff,
Descend; and seemed, by day, none footing was.
She hastes, for marked she mount the tide, beneath.

She goeth down, by sharp scaurs, such force hath
    love;
And lightly oft she depends, by corded roots:
So that sea-gods, beholding, bate their breaths.
The chilling wind, her golden hairs outbloweth.
She, bound about her, long fringed-mantle bears;
That sea-cast One, to cover from the cold.

Like as who finds some fallen fledgeling bird,
Out of the nest; or weanling of hedge-beast,
Uplifts, and home, in pious hands, it bears,
And cherisheth: and aye, twixt doubt he is
And hope, to nourish up; that such not miss,
Of kindly life, whereto born on the earth:
Much more, thou child, thing goodliest having found,
On sea's waste strand, tremblest and durst, uneath,
To him thou lovest, now call, for uncouth dread.

O joy, when dimly, at last, beholds each one,
The other's semblant, in this doubtful gloom.
Then whispered speech, sweet knitting of true palms,
Already knit their hearts. Her mantle, warm,
Of wadmel, then she splayed about them both.
They creep together, in that fear and cold,
In dim sea-cave. Smiles out, in firmament,
The hoary girdled, infinite, night of stars,
Above them: like as when, in sweet spring-time,
With wind-flowers white, some glade is storied seen;
Whereas, from part to part, like silver stream,
Shine hemlocks, stichworts, sign of former path.

To her innocent bosom, she him gathers, warm;
And girded, each, of other's arms, they sleep.
But Cloten, waking, spread, to heaven, his palms,
Calling high gods, to witness of his truth;
His being, knit to this nymph, for life and death.
O'ermuch she travailled hath, to-day, and run;
Nor, child, wist, risen, she hath known a man:
Yet feels that new in her, as were unmeet,
She as tofore, on Sena's sacred hearth,
Wait; wherefore gan she weep; but fears him wake.

    The moon's clear lamp shines, o'er wide silver deep;
When, kneeling, from first sleep, upon her knees,
On the pure sand, she purer Esla prays.
She morrow nigh sees, by these heavenly signs;
So, priestess, went, to bathe her gentle limbs.
Before her, fleeting, lo, in the dark tide,
Lies thing uncouth. She gathers then to her,
Her garments; and calls Cloten to the shore;
Upon whose eyelids sleep, sent from the gods,
Yet heavy lies. That timber fioat, it is,
Which waves uplift, the prince, at eve, gan knit,
On the shole strand: and now apparelled is,
With well-tressed bulwarks of those golden rods;
A work, the whilst they slept, for love of Esla,
Of the sea-nymphs; ready with helms and oars!

    Come, from sea-cave; and standing by loved Esla,
Feels Cloten whole his hurt. In all these things,
The heavens show favour to his enterprise.
Though Esla do these justling waves affray,
Her liever were die, with him, in the sea,
Than live from him apart; she wots not why.

    Then, embarked Cloten, in his manly arms,
His love, his spouse. Anon, the prince thrust out;
The whilst they pray, both, to the watery gods.
Quaked Sena's cliffs; for wakes the island-god.

Rose the weird sisters nine, in their 'lone bowers;
And to the everbrenning hearth, they run:
Where taking count, (low burns the sacred flame!)
There faileth none of them, but Esla, alone;
Whose name sounds, from the rumbling oracle.

    Then course they all, with fearful yelling cries,
To the cliff-brow; where, turned to barking hounds,
Those, frantic, leap, upon the utmost crags,
Making, as would they cast them down, from thence.
But ever as they fall, from steepling cliffs;
To lapwinged plovers changed, they, wailing, rise;
Which tossed and buffeted are, in madding blasts,
O'er sea and soil. Kindled the island-god,
Himself, a flaming beacon on his rocks,
Gives Cloten light to sea! and Sena's spouse,
Clear goddess of the moon, hath Esla blessed.
Though toucht the prince, to Sena's sacred coast;
He was, mongst fallen crags, the sea-god's guest.

    The same hour, spake the oracle, in isle Sena,
Weird nun interpreting; his priestess-choir
Be, henceforth, nine, should ten be told no more!
A king of Gaul offended hath, that gave
A changeling, to the god, for his own child.
Now lies, at point of death, that royal maid,
Guilt of her sire; but Esla did no wrong.

    Like little cowering bird, in fowler's snare,
In every dainty limb, yet trembles Esla,
Mongst tumbling billows. Come forth, from the rocks;
Cloten rows strongly, on the silver flood.
This jeopardy past, smooth lies large watery path,
Under sheen moon; which comforts their cold voyage.

    Their nimble withers undersetting, draw
Manloving dolphins, forth, their bark, in teams.
Whilst then, on the salt tide, twixt sleep, they swim,
And wake; a bridal lay, sing aery spirits,

Till morrow's break: then night-born dawning ray,
(Like to a bride, white-clad, glad eyed and mild,)
Mounts on sea-throne; and cometh forth soon the sun,
With rainbow, crowned; wherein, as would they grace,
From heaven, this marriage, set have holy gods,
The hew of every flower of the spring mead:
And rose the morning's wind, with a sweet breath,
On them that wake, of daisy-hills from land.

O, joy! before the opening eyes, appears,
Of Cloten, his own navy; (it late, dispersed;
Had gathered, under Gaul, a strong sea-god,)
Making their merry flight, with wingéd breasts!
Seven rushing prows, divide much sprinkling flood.
Is their approach like Cantion chariots.
Bowed down, they stride before a clear East wind.
In their firetops, flies dragon of his sire.

How vails her sails, the foremost keel, and luffs,
Now, among the billows wild, up, in the wind.
And surely, of those, is marked their little coque.
Her shipment let down barge; which to them rows!
And is it Cloten, those behold alive?
Sailing with one, that goddess seems; and drawn,
Upon great water's face, of finny teams;
Whose ship, men weened, was lost, not come to land!

Then immense joy; then shouting very great!
Almost was, in strong tumult, over-set
Their bark, wherein they now ben taken up!
Prince Cloten is indeed, none other is;
"Live Cantion's prince!" And, to the royal ship,
Those hastily row. Now mount they, on her board!

When was this seen, in their next consort ships,
Come sailing with square yards and wind apoop;
Which loosed, last flood, from Gaul, with blackened
     sails,
For the lost prince; that Cloten founden is!

The air, with trumps, they rend, and mighty shout.
Lie-to Kent's fleet; and who had, in cold billows,
Leapt down, in this first joy, to swim to Cloten,
Were taken then up, in their ships' skiffs, uneath.

Loost now broad sails, again, to merry wind;
Kent's keels, like coursers, spurn the clodded waves.
So run they all day on, towards Cantion cliffs.
Cloten, Kent's royal prince, which lately thrall,
Was bounden, naked, lost; now, in tall poop,
Sits, noblest, mongst them all, with godlike looks;
Girt in white-shining lawn, garded with gold.

By Cloten sits; wots no man what she is,
Some maid. Who look, fain, on her heavenly feature;
Deem they behold one of those blessèd ones!
For long gilt wounden locks, like sunny rays;
And purple-fringèd shining priestess-weed,
(White lawn, with ceint of gold,) Esla the bright,
Thing seemeth more fair than daughter of the earth,
Like goddess, clothed with grace. Who gaze, on her,
Think, that consent of music they do hear;
When sounds an harp, from heaven, of the sun-god!

Though she herself, be daughter to a king;
Her love, yet, none thought of his estate.
Amazed she is, so many living wights,
To see; well pleased, see Cloten, who hers is,
Be in this chief regard! For many lords,
In boats, with long row-banks, arrived aboard;
Sit bowed before him, reverent, with bared heads.

Blows aye the wind, in their full sails, forthright;
Under their feet, rush on the winged sea-steeds.
They nigh to haven and wide sea-strand, at length,
Of Dubris; neath white-shining Cantion cliffs.
Much people hie down, soon, to salt wave-brinks;
On Kent's returning fleet to gaze! Ere days,
Word come was to their ears; how Cloten's vessel,

From hence outsailed, in that swart tempest, perished!
   Run-in, with half-furled sails, they anchors shoot.
But when, who stand longs shore, see Cloten's barge,
(Wherein rowed forth, known by his shining weed,
The prince!) those cliffs wide-ring, with joyful shout.
Toucht to the chisel-banks, Cloten outleaps:
And bears his bride, to land, in his strong arms,
Esla, the bright; and gives his gods high thanks!

   Now Britons all, in their best garments, trim,
With guirlands on their heads, of the green oaks;
With songs, bring Cloten forth to Dover gates:
Where, eftsoon, ready-made the royal chariots;
Unto their journey, lo, the princes mount.

   Cloten, lest any messenger him outride,
Doth put on, till set of that happy sun;
And without pause, save often change of steeds.
The speedy wheels thus erst were to arrive,
In dim light of the moon, of happy Cloten,
Before Kent's royal dune, fair Durovernion.

   Loudly of the porter, Cloten gan enquire;
"What-ho! What means this wailing, that I hear,
From river meads?" Answers the drowsy ward,
(Who drunken seems of ale, that he discerns
Nor horse nor chariot, at his city walls;
Nor more knows Cloten's, his own king's son's, voice!)
"This town is all went forth to funerals,
Which makes the king, for the drowned prince, to-
     night."

   With Cloten, Esla alights; she weary is,
To chariot-riding all unwont. He bids
Who followed fast with him, here, silent, wait;
Whilst they twain, only, to the meadow, pass.
Eftsoon, they, from green hill, to Cloten known,
Look down; (and issues, clear, the labouring moon,)
Over much people's confused multitude.

Hark, how the king loud calls, on his son Cloten!
Thrice calls the sorrowing sire, with choking voice.

Cloten, an empty pyre, sees, in that place!
Druids blow embers, on an altar's hearth.
Sees Cloten young men, his familiars, stand,
Of even years; and each one armed, his hands,
With a sharp bronze, to smite himself to death.
(For such, mongst weeping kin, their custom is.)
Behold, some father kiss his loved son's knees;
Nor can his stubborn will he bend, from death!

One cries; he heard now noise of trampling steeds!
Shout other; they heard more than mortal voice,
Saying, "Cloten lives!" Then moved is all the press.
Leaps Cloten's heart, with bitter sweetness pierced.
Left Esla, a moment, sitting on dim grass;
Prince Cloten, cleaved thick back-turned multitude;
Comes, straightway, where the mourning old king is!
Murmurs the sire, who now, with dust, defiled
His royal hairs; how wot the only gods,
Where his son's life became, in vast salt deep!
"Tables were cast to strand, of his ship's wreck,"
The royal father sobs. Sudden, young Cloten,
Kisseth, closed in his arms, his wintered cheeks!
So turns, that light might shine on him, his face,
Light of bleak moon, that goeth down soon, to rest.

Quakes the hoar sire; and feels his knees to sink:
And feels his heart, was shut up in distress,
With fearful joy, oppressed. As saw he a spirit,
His voice sticks in his throat; and he lost breath.
Last his old tears, with hollow groans, break forth.

How stand astonished all! But him, prince Cloten
Had withdrawn privily. And, soon, ah, the glad prince
Returns, now leading, happy, by the hand,
On, weary, gentle Esla, in clear moonlight!
Then kneeled down both, at king Cocidius' feet;

They kiss his hands, and feeble knees embrace:
And quoth the prince; This lady saved his life!
Who wept, for sorrow, erst, weep now, for gladness:
And went up a great joyous people's shout!

All follow then, the princes from the field;
With mirth, returning, thence, in mourning weed.
Men enter carolling, in the city's gates;
And throng, together, to their market place:
Where sacrifice shall be made, they hear, and feast.
Are soon great bonfires kindled, in their streets.
Heralds cry up and down; "In the king's hall,
Is meat and mead, to-night, for all who will!"

But come, with immense joy, the princes home,
To the king's house: the sire Cocidius,
(Who chief of the four kings of noble Kent,)
His son and Esla, leading, by the hands;
To that derne bower, forlorn of hope, of late,
Declines, where Kerriduen, mother queen.

She, when went forth the king, with funeral train,
Was fallen, in a stupor on the floor.
Then seemed those like some revellers of the night,
Which, full of mead and impious, towards the gods,
With their untimely cries, and glare of lights,
Trouble this house of mourning; and whose noise
Wakens, for now she slept, the sorrowing queen.

How silent is this inner house, and dim!
Where dying embers glimmer, on the hearth,
The women's bower; that all this day resounded,
With woeful shrieks and baleful funeral wailing:
Where, with long loost locks, sate the sorrowing queen,
By empty bier, in mourning stole, among
Her women; which, displayed their fruitful paps,
Them cruelly did wrong! She bereaved queen,
Continually, did outrage her blubbered face;

And rent, with nails, her royal cheeks alas.

Her risen, behold, all trembling cold and wan,
At the king's voice. But, kindled, round the walls,
Soon, many torches; she Cocidius sees,
Turned, jocund: and smiles Cloten, like a dream!
Aye, and with them, one that nymph or goddess seems.
And her long shut-up and straightened heart,
Unfolds, uneath; and still is like to break;
Impatient, whilst tells of this happy case,
In few rapt words, the sire Cocidius.

She, to her mother's breast, her son embraced;
And, fixt, beholds! to her, returned alive!
Whom weened she, journeying now, in sunless paths,
In swart hell-wagon of the dread death-goddess.
Almost, stood still her heart, and swoons her sense.

But come queen Kerriduen to herself,
As one long lost, in sun-beat wilderness,
Slakes, at some well, his burning infinite thirst,
Long kisses drinks her mouth of her child's flesh.
And, dearly, hath Esla, sith, this queen embraced.
But, when they see her heaviness gin to pace;
From women's bower, as meet to their estate,
The kings wend forth, to sit in audience.

Hastes Kerriduen, washt her tear-worn face,
To put-on queen's apparel: and her women,
She bids make ready, that they sup, anon.
Sith, when they sit, at board; she, come her spirits,
Mother, o'er this new daughter, smiles and weeps.
Yet, hollow-eyed, she sighs, as wanting breath;
Like one whom hellish fiends effrayed, of late;
And scaped, (which certain seemed,) from some dread
        death!

Yet, whilst men tarry, in the king's hall, and sup;
Dights Kerriduen, now, thrice-happy queen,
Unto her bridal bower, Esla, the bright.

Combing her locks of gold; she, on her story,
Museth; which, shortly, had rehearsed Cocidius:
And Cloten said, This lady saved his life!
She marvels, and oft Esla all-new embraced;
And looketh, oft, in the maiden's heavenly face.

Great wonder is, in Esla's gentle breast,
Who priestess, from an isle, in Gaulish seas,
Is scaped, with Cloten, now, all evil hap!
The queen, (unclothed her bosom, ivory-white,)
Some birth-mark sees, neath this dear child's left pap
Much like to berry of holy misselden!
With trembling fingers, Kerriduen, queen,
Uprents her tunic of fine lawn. Ah, gods!
She another token finds, which, there, she sought;
Twixt Esla's gracious shoulders and white neck,
Much like to bee! For Gaulish Gwenneth, then,
She shrilly shright; was whilom her own nurse.
That old wife cometh, soon, hipping, on her staff;
And Gwenneth wox dismayed, at this sweet sight!
So quoth, when she, again, had caught her breath;
"Queen, and dear daughter, nursling of this breast,
Doubt not, thy sister's very child is this.
How is her image glassed, in this sweet face!
How yearns, beholding her, mine aged womb!

The tokens, thou seest, ben those, which I marked
     well,
What night, from twixt my lady's knees, in Gaul;
(My foster-child,) these hands, thy sister's babe,
Received." With amorous groans, then Esla embraced,
That ancient nurse, dear, to her withered paps,
With greedy great affect; and still she kissed.
"Dear queen," she cries, "our very child is this!"

Strain Esla, an hundred sithes, both, to their breasts,
Those weeping women. Gins then Esla weep,
For ruth: and as Spring-sun shines, after rain;

She smiles, for love, between. Like snowdrop, pale,
Heavy, with dew, at dawn, be her bright locks.
And, haply, these had wept forth, the long night,
Forgetful of the spouse; but that hoarse trump
Souneth the watch! from Durovern's ancient walls.

Behold! in royal ray, the mother queen,
Changed that late winter sadness of her face,
To summer's smiling pride, and springing gladness,
Forth issues, from her bower, leading bride Esla;
Where train of noble maidens of the town,
With joyous chant, receiving her, around
Her, cluster, bearing firebrands their white hands:
So pass before, to the bride-chamber door.
There stand, with mystic boughs of misselden,
The white-stoled druids; that sprinkle all the floor,
With holy water dew; the whiles they bless,
With many a murmured spell, this marriage.

Cocidius, king, there, his bride-daughter kissed.
The sire, that tiding, glad, tells forth, of her;
That, "this is the queen's sister's daughter dear,
Which Cloten saved, beyond the seas, from death!"

Lo, come is happy Cloten, mongst his peers;
Which (his *soldurii,*) would have died, to-night,
To be, in death, companions of his spirit.
With mirth and minstrelsy, those him, now, forsake,
At the bride-chamber door; where, enranged, wait,
The maidens, which, around bright Esla, sing!
For gladness, shedding piteous tears between.

(*Book IX, lines 269–786*)

A. E. Housman

(1859–1936)

On Wenlock Edge the wood's in trouble

On Wenlock Edge the wood's in trouble;
His forest fleece the Wrekin heaves;
The gale, it plies the saplings double,
And thick on Severn snow the leaves.

'Twould blow like this through holt and hanger
When Uricon the city stood;
'Tis the old wind in the old anger,
But then it threshed another wood.

Then, 'twas before my time, the Roman
At yonder heaving hill would stare;
The blood that warms an English yeoman,
The thoughts that hurt him, they were there.

There, like the wind through woods in riot,
Through him the gale of life blew high;
The tree of man was never quiet:
Then 'twas the Roman, now 'tis I.

The gale, it plies the saplings double,
It blows so hard, 'twill soon be gone:
Today the Roman and his trouble
Are ashes under Uricon.

From far, from eve and morning

From far, from eve and morning
　　And yon twelve-winded sky,
The stuff of life to knit me
　　Blew hither: here am I.

Now—for a breath I tarry
　　Nor yet disperse apart—
Take my hand quick and tell me,
　　What have you in your heart.

Speak now, and I will answer;
　　How shall I help you, say;
Ere to the wind's twelve quarters
　　I take my endless way.

Far in a western brookland

Far in a western brookland
　　That bred me long ago
The poplars stand and tremble
　　By pools I used to know.

There, in the windless night-time,
　　The wanderer, marvelling why,
Halts on the bridge to hearken
　　How soft the poplars sigh.

He hears: no more remembered
　　In fields where I was known,

Here I lie down in London
And turn to rest alone.

There, by the starlit fences,
The wanderer halts and hears
My soul that lingers sighing
About the glimmering weirs.

Look not in my eyes, for fear

Look not in my eyes, for fear
They mirror true the sight I see,
And there you find your face too clear
And love it and be lost like me.
One the long nights through must lie
Spent in star-defeated sighs,
But why should you as well as I
Perish? gaze not in my eyes.

A Grecian lad, as I hear tell,
One that many loved in vain,
Looked into a forest well
And never looked away again.
There, when the turf in springtime flowers,
With downward eye and gazes sad,
Stands amid the glancing showers
A jonquil, not a Grecian lad.

To an Athlete Dying Young

The time you won your town the race
We chaired you through the market-place;
Man and boy stood cheering by,
And home we brought you shoulder-high.

To-day, the road all runners come,
Shoulder-high we bring you home,
And set you at your threshold down,
Townsman of a stiller town.

Smart lad, to slip betimes away
From fields where glory does not stay
And early though the laurel grows
It withers quicker than the rose.

Eyes the shady night has shut
Cannot see the record cut,
And silence sounds no worse than cheers
After earth has stopped the ears:

Now you will not swell the rout
Of lads that wore their honours out,
Runners whom renown outran
And the name died before the man.

So set, before its echoes fade,
The fleet foot on the sill of shade,
And hold to the low lintel up
The still-defended challenge-cup.

And round that early-laurelled head
Will flock to gaze the strengthless dead,
And find unwithered on its curls
The garland briefer than a girl's.

Francis Thompson

(1859–1907)

The Hound of Heaven

I fled Him, down the nights and down the days;
  I fled Him, down the arches of the years;
I fled Him, down the labyrinthine ways
  Of my own mind; and in the mist of tears
I hid from Him, and under running laughter.
      Up vistaed hopes I sped;
      And shot, precipitated
Adown Titanic glooms of chasmèd fears,
  From those strong Feet that followed, followed after.
      But with unhurrying chase,
      And unperturbèd pace,
  Deliberate speed, majestic instancy,
      They beat—and a Voice beat
      More instant than the Feet—
"All things betray thee, who betrayest Me."

      I pleaded, outlaw-wise,
By many a hearted casement, curtained red,
  Trellised with intertwining charities;
(For, though I knew His love Who followèd,
      Yet was I sore adread
Lest, having Him, I must have naught beside)
But, if one little casement parted wide,
  The gust of His approach would clash it to.
  Fear wist not to evade, as Love wist to pursue.

Across the margent of the world I fled,
  And troubled the gold gateways of the stars,
  Smiting for shelter on their clangèd bars;
    Fretted to dulcet jars
And silvern chatter the pale ports o' the moon.
I said to dawn: Be sudden—to eve: Be soon;
  With thy young skiey blossoms heap me over
    From this tremendous Lover!
Float thy vague veil about me, lest He see!
  I tempted all His servitors, but to find
My own betrayal in their constancy,
In faith to Him their fickleness to me,
  Their traitorous trueness, and their loyal deceit.
To all swift things for swiftness did I sue;
  Clung to the whistling mane of every wind.
    But whether they swept, smoothly fleet,
    The long savannahs of the blue;
      Or whether, Thunder-driven,
    They clanged his chariot 'thwart a heaven
Plashy with flying lightnings round the spurn o' their
      feet:—
  Fear wist not to evade as Love wist to pursue.
    Still with unhurrying chase,
    And unperturbèd pace,
  Deliberate speed, majestic instancy,
    Come on the following Feet,
    And a Voice above their beat—
  "Naught shelters thee, who wilt not shelter Me

I sought no more that, after which I strayed,
    In face of man or maid;
But still within the little children's eyes
  Seems something, something that replies,
They at least are for me, surely for me!
I turned me to them very wistfully;

But just as their young eyes grew sudden fair
    With dawning answers there,
Their angel plucked them from me by the hair.
"Come then, ye other children, Nature's—share
With me" (said I) "your delicate fellowship;
    Let me greet you lip to lip,
    Let me twine with you caresses,
        Wantoning
    With our Lady-Mother's vagrant tresses,
        Banqueting
    With her in her wind-walled palace,
    Underneath her azured daïs,
    Quaffing, as your taintless way is,
        From a chalice
Lucent-weeping out of the dayspring."
        So it was done:
I in their delicate fellowship was one—
Drew the bolt of Nature's secrecies.
    I knew all the swift importings
    On the willful face of skies;
    I knew how the clouds arise
    Spumèd of the wild sea-snortings;
        All that's born or dies
    Rose and drooped with; made them shapers
Of mine own moods, or wailful or divine—
    With them joyed and was bereaven.
    I was heavy with the even,
    When she lit her glimmering tapers
    Round the day's dead sanctities.
    I laughed in the morning's eyes.
I triumphed and I saddened with all weather,
    Heaven and I wept together,
And its sweet tears were salt with mortal mine;
Against the red throb of its sunset-heart
    I laid my own to beat,

And share commingling heat;
But not by that, by that, was eased my human smart.
In vain my tears were wet on Heaven's gray cheek.
For ah! we know not what each other says,
    These things and I; in sound *I* speak—
Their sound is but their stir, they speak by silences.
Nature, poor stepdame, cannot slake my drouth;
    Let her, if she would owe me,
Drop yon blue bosom-veil of sky, and show me
    The breasts o' her tenderness:
Never did any milk of hers once bless
        My thirsting mouth.
        Nigh and nigh draws the chase,
        With unperturbèd pace,
    Deliberate speed, majestic instancy;
        And past those noisèd Feet
        A Voice comes yet more fleet—
    "Lo! naught contents thee, who content'st not Me."

Naked I wait Thy love's uplifted stroke!
My harness piece by piece Thou hast hewn from me,
        And smitten me to my knee;
    I am defenseless utterly.
    I slept, methinks, and woke,
And, slowly gazing, find me stripped in sleep.
In the rash lustihead of my young powers,
    I shook the pillaring hours
And pulled my life upon me; grimed with smears,
I stand amid the dust o' the mounded years—
My mangled youth lies dead beneath the heap.
My days have crackled and gone up in smoke,
Have puffed and burst as sun-starts on a stream.
        Yea, faileth now even dream
The dreamer, and the lute the lutanist;
Even the linked fantasies, in whose blossomy twist

I swung the earth a trinket at my wrist,
Are yielding; cords of all too weak account
For earth with heavy griefs so overplussed.
  Ah! is Thy love indeed
A weed, albeit an amaranthine weed,
Suffering no flowers except its own to mount?
  Ah! must—
  Designer infinite!—
Ah! must Thou char the wood ere Thou canst limn with
    it?
My freshness spent its wavering shower i' the dust;
And now my heart is as a broken fount,
Wherein tear-dripping stagnate, spilt down ever
  From the dank thoughts that shiver
Upon the sighful branches of my mind.
  Such is; what is to be?
The pulp so bitter, how shall taste the rind?
I dimly guess what Time in mists confounds;
Yet ever and anon a trumpet sounds
From the hid battlements of Eternity,
Those shaken mists a space unsettle, then
Round the half-glimpsèd turrets slowly wash again;
  But not ere him who summoneth
  I first have seen, enwound
With glooming robes purpureal, cypress-crowned;
His name I know, and what his trumpet saith.
Whether man's heart or life it be which yields
  Thee harvest, must Thy harvest-fields
  Be dunged with rotten death?
    Now of that long pursuit
    Comes on at hand the bruit;
  That Voice is round me like a bursting sea:
    "And is thy earth so marred,
    Shattered in shard on shard?
  Lo, all things fly thee, for thou fliest Me!

"Strange, piteous, futile thing!
Wherefore should any set thee love apart?
Seeing none but I makes much of naught" (He said),
"And human love needs human meriting:
    How hast thou merited—
Of all man's clotted clay the dingiest clot?
    Alack, thou knowest not
How little worthy of any love thou art!
Whom wilt thou find to love ignoble thee
    Save Me, save only Me?
All which I took from thee I did but take,
    Not for thy harms,
But just that thou might'st seek it in My arms.
    All which thy child's mistake
Fancies as lost, I have stored for thee at home:
    Rise, clasp My hand, and come."

        Halts by me that footfall:
        Is my gloom, after all,
    Shade of His hand, outstretched caressingly?
        "Ah, fondest, blindest, weakest,
        I am He Whom thou seekest!
    Thou dravest love from thee, who dravest Me."

Lionel Johnson
(1867–1902)

Dead

TO OLIVIER GEORGES DESTRÉE

In Merioneth, over the sad moor
  Drives the rain, the cold wind blows:
  Past the ruinous church door,
The poor procession without music goes.

Lonely she wandered out her hour, and died.
  Now the mournful curlew cries
  Over her, laid down beside
Death's lonely people: lightly down she lies.

In Merioneth, the wind lives and wails,
  On from hill to lonely hill:
  Down the loud triumphant gales,
A spirit cries *Be strong!* and cries *Be still!*

FROM *In Memory*

Ah! fair face gone from sight,
  With all its light
Of eyes, that pierced the deep
  Of human night!
Ah! fair face calm in sleep.

570

Ah! fair lips hushed in death!
  Now their glad breath
Breathes not upon our air
  Music, that saith
Love only, and things fair.

Ah! lost breath! Ah! sweet
  Still hands and feet!
May those feet haste to reach,
  Those hands to greet,
Us, where love needs no speech.

By the Statue of King Charles at Charing Cross

Sombre and rich, the skies;
Great glooms, and starry plains.
Gently the night wind sighs;
Else a vast silence reigns.

The splendour silence clings
Around me: and around
The saddest of all kings,
Crowned, and again discrowned.

Comely and calm, he rides
Hard by his own Whitehall:
Only the night wind glides:
No crowds, nor rebels, brawl.

Gone, too, his Court: and yet,
The stars his courtiers are:
Stars in their stations set;
And every wandering star.

Alone he rides, alone,
The fair and fatal king:

Dark night is all his own,
That strange and solemn thing.

Which are more full of fate:
The stars; or those sad eyes?
Which are more still and great:
Those brows; or the dark skies?

Although his whole heart yearn
In passionate tragedy:
Never was face so stern,
With sweet austerity.

Vanquished in life, his death
By beauty made amends:
The passing of his breath
Won his defeated ends.

Brief life, and hapless? Nay:
Through death, life grew sublime.
Speak after sentence? Yea:
And to the end of time.

Armoured he rides, his head
Bare to the stars of doom:
He triumphs now, the dead,
Beholding London's gloom.

Our wearier spirit faints,
Vex'd in the world's employ:
His soul was of the saints;
And art to him was joy.

King, tried in fires of woe!
Men hunger for thy grace:
And through the night I go,
Loving thy mournful face.

Yet, when the city sleeps;
When all the cries are still:
The stars and heavenly deeps
Work out a perfect will.

Rudyard Kipling

(1865–1936)

M'Andrew's Hymn

Lord, Thou hast made this world below the shadow of a
    dream,
An', taught by time, I tak' it so—exceptin' always Steam.
From coupler-flange to spindle-guide I see Thy Hand,
    O God—
Predestination in the stride o' yon connectin'-rod.
John Calvin might ha' forget the same—enorrmous, cer-
    tain, slow—
Ay, wrought it in the furnace-flame—*my* "Institutio."
I cannot get my sleep to-night; old bones are hard to
    please;
I'll stand the middle watch up here—alone wi' God an'
    these
My engines, after ninety days o' race an' rack an' strain
Through all the seas of all Thy world, slam-bangin'
    home again.
Slam-bang too much—they knock a wee—the cross-
    head-gibs are loose,
But thirty-thousand mile o' sea has gied them fair ex-
    cuse. . . .
Fine, clear an' dark—a full-draught breeze, wi' Ushant
    out o' sight,
An' Ferguson relievin' Hay. Old girl, ye'll walk to-night!
His wife's at Plymouth. . . . Seventy—One—Two—
    Three since he began—

574

Three turns for Mistress Ferguson . . . and who's to
    blame the man?
There's none at any port for me, by drivin' fast or slow,
Since Elsie Campbell went to Thee, Lord, thirty years
    ago.
(The year the *Sarah Sands* was burned. Oh, roads we
    used to tread,
Fra' Maryhill to Pollokshaws—fra' Govan to Parkhead!)
Not but they're ceevil on the Board. Ye'll hear Sir Ken-
    neth say:
"Good morrn, McAndrew! Back again? An' how's your
    bilge to-day?"
Miscallin' technicalities but handin' me my chair
To drink Madeira wi' three Earls—the auld Fleet Engi-
    neer
That started as a boiler-whelp—when steam and he
    were low.
I mind the time we used to serve a broken pipe wi' tow!
Ten pound was all the pressure then—Eh! Eh!—a man
    wad drive;
An' here, our workin' gauges give one hundred sixty-
    five!
We're creepin' on wi' each new rig—less weight an'
    larger power;
There'll be the loco-boiler next an' thirty mile an hour!
Thirty an' more. What I ha' seen since ocean-steam
    began
Leaves me na doot for the machine: but what about the
    man?
The man that counts, wi' all his runs, one million mile
    o' sea:
Four time the span from earth to moon. . . . How far,
    O Lord, from Thee
That wast beside him night an' day? Ye mind my first
    typhoon?

It scoughed the skipper on his way to jock wi' the sa-
    loon.

Three feet were on the stokehold-floor—just slappin' to
    an' fro—

An' cast me on a furnace-door. I have the marks to show.

Marks! I ha' marks o' more than burns—deep in my soul
    an' black,

An' times like this, when things go smooth, my wickud-
    ness comes back.

The sins o' four an' forty years, all up an' down the seas,

Clack an' repeat like valves half-fed. . . . Forgie's our
    trepasses!

Nights when I'd come on deck to mark, wi' envy in my
    gaze,

The couples kittlin' in the dark between the funnel-
    stays;

Years when I raked the Ports wi' pride to fill my cup o'
    wrong—

Judge not, O Lord, my steps aside at Gay Street in
    Hong-Kong!

Blot out the wastrel hours of mine in sin when I abode—

Jane Harrigan's an' Number Nine, The Reddick an'
    Grant Road!

An' waur than all—my crownin' sin—rank blasphemy
    an' wild.

I was not four and twenty then—Ye wadna judge a
    child?

I'd seen the Tropics first that run—new fruit, new
    smells, new air—

How could I tell—blind-fou wi' sun—the Deil was
    lurkin' there?

By day like playhouse-scenes the shore slid past our
    sleepy eyes;

By night those soft, lasceevious stars leered from those
    velvet skies,

In port (we used no cargo-steam) I'd daunder down the
    streets—
An ijjit grinnin' in a dream—for shells an' parrakeets,
An' walkin'-sticks o' carved bamboo an' blowfish stuffed
    an' dried—
Fillin' my bunk wi' rubbishry the Chief put overside.
Till, off Sambawa Head, Ye mind, I heard a land-breeze
    ca',
Milk-warm wi' breath o' spice an' bloom: "McAndrew,
    come awa'!"
Firm, clear an' low—no haste, no hate—the ghostly
    whisper went,
Just statin' eevidential facts beyon' all argument:
"Your mither's God's a graspin' deil, the shadow o'
    yoursel',
Got out o' books by meenisters clean daft on Heaven an'
    Hell.
They mak' him in the Broomielaw, o' Glasgie cold an'
    dirt,
A jealous, pridefu' fetich, lad, that's only strong to hurt.
Ye'll not go back to Him again an' kiss His red-hot rod,
But come wi' Us" (Now, who were *They?*) "an' know
    the Leevin' God,
That does not kipper souls for sport or break a life in
    jest,
But swells the ripenin' cocoanuts an' ripes the woman's
    breast."
An' there it stopped—cut off—no more—that quiet, cer-
    tain voice—
For me, six months o' twenty-four, to leave or take at
    choice.
'Twas on me like a thunderclap—it racked me through
    an' through—
Temptation past the show o' speech, unnameable an'
    new—

The Sin against the Holy Ghost? . . . . An' under all,
    our screw.

That storm blew by but left behind her anchor-shiftin'
    swell.
Thou knowest all my heart an' mind, Thou knowest,
    Lord, I fell—
Third on the *Mary Gloster* then, and first that night in
    Hell!
Yet was Thy Hand beneath my head, about my feet Thy
    Care—
Fra' Deli clear to Torres Strait, the trial o' despair,
But when we touched the Barrier Reef Thy answer to
    my prayer! . . . .
We dared na run that sea by night but lay an' held our
    fire,
An' I was drowsin' on the hatch—sick—sick wi' doubt
    an' tire:
"Better the sight of eyes that see than wanderin' o' de-
    sire!"
Ye mind that word? Clear as our gongs—again, an' once
    again,
When rippin' down through coral-trash ran out our
    moorin'-chain:
An', by Thy Grace, I had the Light to see my duty plain.
Light on the engine-room—no more—bright as our car-
    bons burn.
I've lost it since a thousand times, but never past return!

   .   .   .   .

Obsairve! Per annum we'll have here two thousand souls
    aboard—
Think not I dare to justify myself before the Lord,
But—average fifteen hunder souls safe-borne fra' port
    to port—

I *am* o' service to my kind. Ye wadna blame the
    thought?

Maybe they steam from Grace to Wrath—to sin by folly
    led—

It isna mine to judge their path—their lives are on my
    head.

Mine at the last—when all is done it all comes back to
    me,

The fault that leaves six thousand ton a log upon the
    sea.

We'll tak' one stretch—three weeks an' odd by ony road
    ye steer—

Fra' Cape Town east to Wellington—ye need an engi-
    neer.

Fail there—ye've time to weld your shaft—ay, eat it,
    ere ye're spoke;

Or make Kerguelen under sail—three jiggers burned wi'
    smoke!

An' home again—the Rio run: it's no child's play to go

Steamin' to bell for fourteen days o' snow an' floe an'
    blow.

The bergs like kelpies overside that girn an' turn an'
    shift

Whaur, grindin' like the Mills o' God, goes by the big
    South drift.

(Hail, Snow and Ice that praise the Lord. I've met them
    at their work,

An' wished we had anither route or they anither
    kirk.)

Yon's strain, hard strain, o' head an' hand, for though
    Thy Power brings

All skill to naught, Ye'll understand a man must think
    o' things.

Then, at the last, we'll get to port an' hoist their baggage
    ciear—

The passengers, wi' gloves an' canes—an' this is what I'll
 hear:

"Well, thank ye for a pleasant voyage. The tender's
 comin' now."

While I go testin' follower-bolts an' watch the skipper
 bow.

They've words for every one but me—shake hands wi'
 half the crew,

Except the dour Scots engineer, the man they never
 knew.

An' yet I like the wark for all we've dam'-few pickin's
 here—

No pension, an' the most we'll earn's four hunder pound
 a year.

Better myself abroad? Maybe, *I'd* sooner starve than sail

Wi' such as call a snifter-rod *ross* . . . French for
 nightingale.

Commeesion on my stores? Some do; but I cannot afford

To lie like stewards wi' patty-pans. I'm older than the
 Board.

A bonus on the coal I save? Ou ay, the Scots are close,

But when I grudge the strength Ye gave I'll grudge their
 food to *those*.

(There's bricks that I might recommend—an' clink the
 firebars cruel.

No! Welsh—Wangarti at the worst—an' damn all patent
 fuel!)

Inventions? Ye must stay in port to mak' a patent pay.

My Deeferential Valve-Gear taught me how that busi-
 ness lay.

I blame no chaps wi' clearer heads for aught they make
 or sell.

I found that I could not invent an' look to these as
 well.

So, wrestled wi' Apollyon—Nah!—fretted like a bairn—

But burned the workin'-plans last run, wi' all I hoped to
    earn.

Ye know how hard an Idol dies, an' what that meant to
    me—

E'en tak' it for a sacrifice acceptable to Thee. . . .

Below there! Oiler! What's your wark? Ye find it runnin'
    hard?

Ye needn't swill the cup wi' oil—this isn't the Cunard!

Ye thought? Ye are not paid to think. Go, sweat that off
    again!

Tck! Tck! It's deeficult to sweer nor tak' The Name in
    vain!

Men, ay, an' women, call me stern. Wi' these to oversee,

Ye'll note I've little time to burn on social repartee.

The bairns see what their elders miss; they'll hunt me
    to an' fro,

Till for the sake of—well, a kiss—I tak' 'em down below.

That minds me of our Viscount loon—Sir Kenneth's kin
    —the chap

Wi' Russia-leather tennis-shoon an' spar-decked yachtin'-
    cap.

I showed him round last week, o'er all—an' at the last
    says he:

"Mister McAndrew, don't you think steam spoils ro-
    mance at sea?"

Damned ijjit! I'd been doon that morn to see what ailed
    the throws,

Manholin', on my back—the cranks three inches off my
    nose.

Romance! Those first-class passengers they like it very
    well,

Printed an' bound in little books; but why don't poets
    tell?

I'm sick of all their quirks an' turns—the loves an' doves
    they dream—

Lord, send a man like Robbie Burns to sing the Song
   o' Steam!

To match wi' Scotia's noblest speech yon orchestra sub-
   lime

Whaurto—uplifted like the Just—the tail-rods mark the
   time.

The crank-throws give the double-bass, the feed-pump
   sobs an' heaves,

An' now the main eccentrics start their quarrel on the
   sheaves:

Her time, her own appointed time, the rocking link-head
   bides,

Till—hear that note?—the rod's return whings glim-
   merin' through the guides.

They're all awa'! True beat, full power, the clangin'
   chorus goes

Clear to the tunnel where they sit, my purrin' dynamoes.

Interdependence absolute, foreseen, ordained, decreed,

To work, Ye'll note, at ony tilt an' every rate o' speed.

Fra' skylight-lift to furnace-bars, backed, bolted, braced
   an' stayed,

An' singin' like the Mornin' Stars for joy that they are
   made;

While, out o' touch o' vanity, the sweatin' thrust-block
   says:

"Not unto us the praise, or man—not unto us the
   praise!"

Now, a' together, hear them lift their lesson—theirs an'
   mine:

"Law, Orrder, Duty an' Restraint, Obedience, Dis-
   cipline!"

Mill, forge an' try-pit taught them that when roarin' they
   arose,

An' whiles I wonder if a soul was gied them wi' the
   blows.

Oh for a man to weld it then, in one trip-hammer strain,
Till even first-class passengers could tell the meanin'
    plain!
But no one cares except mysel' that serve an' understand
My seven thousand horse-power here. Eh, Lord! They're
    grand—they're grand!
Uplift am I? When first in store the new-made beasties
    stood,
Were Ye cast down that breathed the Word declarin' all
    things good?
Not so! O' that warld-liftin' joy no after-fall could vex.
Ye've left a glimmer still to cheer the Man—the Arrtifex!
That holds, in spite o' knock and scale, o' friction, waste
    an' slip,
An' by that light—now, mark my word—we'll build the
    Perfect Ship.
I'll never last to judge her lines or take her curve—not I.
But I ha' lived an' I ha' worked. Be thanks to Thee,
    Most High!
An' I ha' done what I ha' done—judge Thou if ill or
    well—
Always Thy Grace preventin' me. . . .
                    Losh! Yon's the "Stand-by" bell.
Pilot so soon? His flare it is. The mornin'-watch is set.
Well, God be thanked, as I was sayin', I'm no Pelagian
    yet.
Now I'll tak' on. . . .
    'Morrn, Ferguson. Man, have ye ever thought
What your good leddy costs in coal? . . . I'll burn 'em
    down to port.

Cities and Thrones and Powers

Cities and Thrones and Powers
   Stand in Time's eye,
Almost as long as flowers,
   Which daily die:
But, as new buds put forth
   To glad new men,
Out of the spent and unconsidered Earth
   The Cities rise again.

This season's Daffodil,
   She never hears
What change, what chance, what chill,
   Cut down last year's;
But with bold countenance,
   And knowledge small,
Esteems her seven days' continuance
   To be perpetual.

So Time that is o'er-kind
   To all that be,
Ordains us e'en as blind,
   As bold as she:
That in our very death,
   And burial sure,
Shadow to shadow, well persuaded, saith,
   "See how our works endure!"

The Law of the Jungle

*Now this is the Law of the Jungle—as old and as true as
the sky;*
*And the Wolf that shall keep it may prosper, but the
Wolf that shall break it must die.*

*As the creeper that girdles the tree-trunk the Law
runneth forward and back—*
*For the strength of the Pack is the Wolf, and the
strength of the Wolf is the Pack.*

Wash daily from nose-tip to tail-tip; drink deeply, but
never too deep;
And remember the night is for hunting, and forget not
the day is for sleep.

The Jackal may follow the Tiger, but, Cub, when thy
whiskers are grown,
Remember the Wolf is a hunter—go forth and get food
of thine own.

Keep peace with the Lords of the Jungle—the Tiger, the
Panther, the Bear;
And trouble not Hathi the Silent, and mock not the Boar
in his lair.

When Pack meets with Pack in the Jungle, and neither
will go from the trail,
Lie down till the leaders have spoken—it may be fair
words shall prevail.

When ye fight with a Wolf of the Pack, ye must fight
him alone and afar,

Lest others take part in the quarrel, and the Pack be
   diminished by war.

The Lair of the Wolf is his refuge, and where he has
   made him his home,
Not even the Head Wolf may enter, not even the Coun-
   cil may come.

The Lair of the Wolf is his refuge, but where he has
   digged it too plain,
The Council shall send him a message, and so he shall
   change it again.

If ye kill before midnight, be silent, and wake not the
   woods with your bay,
Lest ye frighten the deer from the crops, and the
   brothers go empty away.

Ye may kill for yourselves, and your mates, and your
   cubs as they need, and ye can;
But kill not for pleasure of killing, and *seven times never
   kill Man!*

If ye plunder his Kill from a weaker, devour not all in
   thy pride;
Pack-Right is the right of the meanest; so leave him the
   head and the hide.

The Kill of the Pack is the meat of the Pack. Ye must eat
   where it lies;
And no one may carry away of that meat to his lair, or
   he dies.

The Kill of the Wolf is the meat of the Wolf. He may do
   what he will,
But, till he has given permission, the Pack may not eat
   of that Kill.

Cub-Right is the right of the Yearling. From all of his
    Pack he may claim
Full-gorge when the killer has eaten; and none may re-
    fuse him the same.

Lair-Right is the right of the Mother. From all of her
    year she may claim
One haunch of each kill for her litter; and none may
    deny her the same.

Cave-Right is the right of the Father—to hunt by him-
    self for his own:
He is freed of all calls to the Pack; he is judged by the
    Council alone.

Because of his age and his cunning, because of his gripe
    and his paw,
In all that the Law leaveth open, the word of the Head
    Wolf is Law.

Now these are the Laws of the Jungle, and many and
    mighty are they;
But the head and the hoof of the Law and the haunch
    and the hump is—Obey!

My new-cut ashlar

My new-cut ashlar takes the light
Where crimson-blank the windows flare.
By my own work before the night,
Great Overseer, I make my prayer.

If there be good in that I wrought
Thy Hand compelled it, Master, Thine—

Where I have failed to meet Thy Thought
I know, through Thee, the blame was mine.

One instant's toil to Thee denied
Stands all Eternity's offence.
Of that I did with Thee to guide,
To Thee, through Thee, be excellence.

The depth and dream of my desire,
The bitter paths wherein I stray—
Thou knowest Who has made the Fire,
Thou knowest Who has made the Clay.

Who, lest all thought of Eden fade,
Bring'st Eden to the craftsman's brain—
Godlike to muse o'er his own Trade
And manlike stand with God again!

One stone the more swings into place
In that dread Temple of Thy worth.
It is enough that, through Thy Grace,
I saw nought common on Thy Earth.

Take not that vision from my ken—
Oh, whatsoe'er may spoil or speed,
Help me to need no aid from men
That I may help such men as need!

A St. Helena Lullaby

"How far is St. Helena from a little child at play?"
What makes you want to wander there with all the
    world between?
Oh, Mother, call your son again or else he'll run away.
(No one thinks of winter when the grass is green!)

"How far is St. Helena from a fight in Paris street?"
I haven't time to answer now—the men are falling fast.
The guns begin to thunder, and the drums begin to beat.
(*If you take the first step, you will take the last!*)

"How far is St. Helena from the field of Austerlitz?"
You couldn't hear me if I told—so loud the cannon roar.
But not so far for people who are living by their wits.
(*"Gay go up" means "Gay go down" the wide world o'er!*)

"How far is St. Helena from an Emperor of France?"
I cannot see—I cannot tell—the Crowns they dazzle so.
The Kings sit down to dinner, and the Queens stand up to dance.
(*After open weather you may look for snow!*)

"How far is St. Helena from the Capes of Trafalgar?"
A longish way—a longish way—with ten year more to run.
It's South across the water underneath a falling star.
(*What you cannot finish you must leave undone!*)

"How far is St. Helena from the Beresina ice?"
An ill way—a chill way—the ice begins to crack.
But not so far for gentlemen who never took advice.
(*When you can't go forward you must e'en come back!*)

"How far is St. Helena from the field of Waterloo?"
A near way—a clear way—the ship will take you soon.
A pleasant place for gentlemen with little left to do.
(*Morning never tries you till the afternoon!*)

"How far from St. Helena to the Gate of Heaven's Grace?"
That no one knows—that no one knows—and no one ever will.

But fold your hands across your heart and cover up your
    face,
And after all your trapesings, child, lie still!

The Runes on Weland's Sword

A Smith makes me
To betray my Man
In my first fight.

To gather Gold
At the world's end
I am sent.

The Gold I gather
Comes into England
Out of deep Water.

Like a shining Fish
Then it descends
Into deep Water.

It is not given
For goods or gear,
But for The Thing.

The Gold I gather
A King covets
For an ill use.

The Gold I gather
Is drawn up
Out of deep Water.

Like a shining Fish
Then it descends
Into deep Water.

It is not given
For goods or gear,
But for The Thing.

Song of the Galley-Slaves

We pulled for you when the wind was against us and
the sails were low.
Will you never let us go?
We ate bread and onions when you took towns, or ran
aboard quickly when you were beaten back by the
foe.
The Captains walked up and down the deck in fair
weather singing songs, but we were below.
We fainted with our chins on the oars and you did not
see that we were idle, for we still swung to and fro.
Will you never let us go?
The salt made the oar-handles like shark-skin; our knees
were cut to the bone with salt-cracks; our hair was
stuck to our foreheads; and our lips were cut to the
gums, and you whipped us because we could not row.
Will you never let us go?
But, in a little time, we shall run out of the port-holes as
the water runs along the oar-blade, and though you
tell the others to row after us you will never catch us
till you catch the oar-thresh and tie up the winds in
the belly of the sail. Aho!
Will you never let us go?

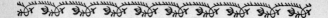

John Jay Chapman

(1862–1933)

Song

Old Farmer Oats and his son Ned
They quarreled about the old mare's bed,
And some hard words by each were said,
    Sing, sing, ye all!

CHORUS

Let every man stand for what is in his hand, say I,
Let every man give to keep a man alive, say I,
For it's all one when all's done,
Ye'll keep none when death's come, say I!

Then Oats he bade the boy be hanged;
So up he stormed and out he banged;
And away to the heath and the wars he's ganged.
    Sing, sing, ye all!—CHORUS.

Old Farmer Oats with his bent head
Is ever thinking of his son Ned,
And whether the lad be alive or dead,
    Sing, sing, ye all!—CHORUS.

And every beggar and every thief
May go to the old man for relief;
For love is love and grief is grief
    Sing, sing, ye all!

CHORUS

Let every man stand for what is in his hand, say I,
Let every man give to keep a man alive, say I,
For it's all one when all's done,
Ye'll keep none when death's come, say I!

Lines on the Death of Bismarck

At midnight Death dismissed the chancellor,
But left the soul of Bismarck on his face.
Titanic, in the peace and power of bronze,
With three red roses loosely in his grasp,
Lies the Constructor. His machinery
Revolving in the wheels of destiny
Rolls onward over him. Alive, inspired,
Vast, intricate, complete, unthinkable,
Nice as a watch and strong as dynamite,
An empire and a whirlwind, on it moves,
While he that set it rolling lies so still.

Unity! Out of chaos, petty courts,
Princelings and potentates—thrift, jealousy,
Weakness, distemper, cowardice, distrust,
To build a nation: the material—
The fibres to be twisted—human strands.
One race, one tongue, one instinct. Unify
By banking prejudice, and, gaining power,
Attract by vanity, compel by fear.
Arm to the teeth: your friends will love you more,
And we have much to do for Germany.
Organized hatred, *that* is unity.

Prussia's a unit; Denmark's enmity
Is so much gain, and gives us all the North.
Next, humble Austria: a rapid stroke
That leaves us laurels and a policy.
Now for some chance, some—any fluke or crime
By which a war with France can be brought on:
And, God be glorified, the thing is done.
Organized hatred. That foundation reaches
The very bottom rock of Germany
And out of it the structure rises up
Bristling with arms.

"But you forget the soul,
The universal shout, the Kaiser's name,
Fatherland, anthems, the heroic dead,
The discipline, the courage, the control,
The glory and the passion and the flame—"
Are calculated by the captain's eye
Are used, subdued, like electricity
Turned on or off, are set to making roads,
Or building monuments, or writing verse,
Twitched by the inspired whim of tyranny
To make that tyranny perpetual
And kill what intellect it cannot use.

The age is just beginning, yet we see
The fruits of hatred ripen hourly
And Germany's in bondage—muzzled press,
The private mind suppressed,—while shade on shade
Is darkened o'er the intellectual sky.
And world-forgotten, outworn crimes and cries
With dungeon tongue accost the citizen
And send him trembling to his family.

.   .   .   .

Thought cannot grasp the Cause: 'tis in the abyss
With Nature's secrets. But, gigantic wreck,
Thou wast the Instrument! And thy huge limbs
Cover nine kingdoms as thou lie'st asleep.

Edwin Arlington Robinson

(1869–1935)

Luke Havergal

Go to the western gate, Luke Havergal,
There where the vines cling crimson on the wall,
And in the twilight wait for what will come.
The leaves will whisper there of her, and some,
Like flying words, will strike you as they fall;
But go, and if you listen she will call.
Go to the western gate, Luke Havergal—
Luke Havergal.

No, there is not a dawn in eastern skies
To rift the fiery night that's in your eyes;
But there, where western glooms are gathering,
The dark will end the dark, if anything:
God slays Himself with every leaf that flies,
And hell is more than half of paradise.
No, there is not a dawn in eastern skies—
In eastern skies.

Out of a grave I come to tell you this,
Out of a grave I come to quench the kiss
That flames upon your forehead with a glow
That blinds you to the way that you must go.
Yes, there is yet one way to where she is,
Bitter, but one that faith may never miss.
Out of a grave I come to tell you this—
To tell you this.

There is the western gate, Luke Havergal,
There are the crimson leaves upon the wall.
Go, for the winds are tearing them away,—
Nor think to riddle the dead words they say,
Nor any more to feel them as they fall;
But go, and if you trust her she will call.
There is the western gate, Luke Havergal—
Luke Havergal.

George Crabbe

Give him the darkest inch your shelf allows,
Hide him in lonely garrets, if you will,—
But his hard, human pulse is throbbing still
With the sure strength that fearless truth endows.
In spite of all fine science disavows,
Of his plain excellence and stubborn skill
There yet remains what fashion cannot kill,
Though years have thinned the laurel from his brows,

Whether or not we read him, we can feel
From time to time the vigor of his name
Against us like a finger for the shame
And emptiness of what our souls reveal
In books that are as altars where we kneel
To consecrate the flicker, not the flame.

The Clerks

I did not think that I should find them there
When I came back again; but there they stood,
As in the days they dreamed of when young blood

Was in their cheeks and women called them fair.
Be sure, they met me with an ancient air,—
And yes, there was a shop-worn brotherhood
About them; but the men were just as good,
And just as human as they ever were.

And you that ache so much to be sublime,
And you that feed yourselves with your descent,
What comes of all your visions and your fears?
Poets and kings are but the clerks of Time,
Tiering the same dull webs of discontent,
Clipping the same sad alnage of the years.

FROM *Captain Craig*

I doubt if ten men in all Tilbury Town
Had ever shaken hands with Captain Craig,
Or called him by his name, or looked at him
So curiously, or so concernedly,
As they had looked at ashes; but a few—
Say five or six of us—had found somehow
The spark in him, and we had fanned it there,
Choked under, like a jest in Holy Writ,
By Tilbury prudence. He had lived his life
And in his way had shared, with all mankind,
Inveterate leave to fashion of himself,
By some resplendent metamorphosis,
Whatever he was not. And after time,
When it had come sufficiently to pass
That he was going patch-clad through the streets,
Weak, dizzy, chilled, and half starved, he had laid
Some nerveless fingers on a prudent sleeve,
And told the sleeve, in furtive confidence,

Just how it was: "My name is Captain Craig,"
He said, "and I must eat." The sleeve moved on,
And after it moved others—one or two;
For Captain Craig, before the day was done,
Got back to the scant refuge of his bed
And shivered into it without a curse—
Without a murmur even. He was cold,
And old, and hungry; but the worst of it
Was a forlorn familiar consciousness
That he had failed again. There was a time
When he had fancied, if worst came to worst,
And he could do no more, that he might ask
Of whom he would. But once had been enough,
And soon there would be nothing more to ask.
He was himself, and he had lost the speed
He started with, and he was left behind.
There was no mystery, no tragedy;
And if they found him lying on his back
Stone dead there some sharp morning, as they might,—
Well, once upon a time there was a man—
Es war einmal ein König, if it pleased him.
And he was right: there were no men to blame:
There was just a false note in the Tilbury tune—
A note that able-bodied men might sound
Hosannas on while Captain Craig lay quiet.
They might have made him sing by feeding him
Till he should march again, but probably
Such yielding would have jeopardized the rhythm;
They found it more melodious to shout
Right on, with unmolested adoration,
To keep the tune as it had always been,
To trust in God, and let the Captain starve.

He must have understood that afterwards—
When we had laid some fuel to the spark

Of him, and oxidized it—for he laughed
Out loud and long at us to feel it burn,
And then, for gratitude, made game of us:
"You are the resurrection and the life,"
He said, "and I the hymn the Brahmin sings;
O Fuscus! and we'll go no more a-roving."
We were not quite accoutred for a blast
Of any lettered nonchalance like that,
And some of us—the five or six of us
Who found him out—were singularly struck.
But soon there came assurance of his lips,
Like phrases out of some sweet instrument
Man's hand had never fitted, that he felt
"No penitential shame for what had come,
No virtuous regret for what had been,—
But rather a joy to find it in his life
To be an outcast usher of the soul
For such as had good courage of the Sun
To pattern Love." The Captain had one chair;
And on the bottom of it, like a king,
For longer time than I dare chronicle,
Sat with an ancient ease and eulogized
His opportunity. My friends got out,
Like brokers out of Arcady; but I—
May be for fascination of the thing,
Or may be for the larger humor of it—
Stayed listening, unwearied and unstung.
When they were gone the Captain's tuneful ooze
Of rhetoric took on a change; he smiled
At me and then continued, earnestly:
"Your friends have had enough of it; but you,
For a motive hardly vindicated yet
By prudence or by conscience, have remained;
And that is very good, for I have things
To tell you: things that are not words alone—

Which are the ghosts of things—but something firmer.
First, would I have you know, for every gift
Or sacrifice, there are—or there may be—
Two kinds of gratitude: the sudden kind
We feel for what we take, the larger kind
We feel for what we give. Once we have learned
As much as this, we know the truth has been
Told over to the world a thousand times;—
But we have had no ears to listen yet
For more than fragments of it: we have heard
A murmur now and then, an echo here
And there, and we have made great music of it;
And we have made innumerable books
To please the Unknown God. Time throws away
Dead thousands of them, but the God that knows
No death denies not one: the books all count,
The songs all count; and yet God's music has
No modes, his language has no adjectives."

"You may be right, you may be wrong," said I;
"But what has this that you are saying now—
This nineteenth-century Nirvana-talk—
To do with you and me?" The Captain raised
His hand and held it westward, where a patched
And unwashed attic-window filtered in
What barren light could reach us, and then said,
With a suave, complacent resonance: "There shines
The sun. Behold it. We go round and round,
And wisdom comes to us with every whirl
We count throughout the circuit. We may say
The child is born, the boy becomes a man,
The man does this and that, and the man goes,—
But having said it we have not said much,
Not very much. Do I fancy, or you think,
That it will be the end of anything

When I am gone? There was a soldier once
Who fought one fight and in that fight fell dead.
Sad friends went after, and they brought him home
And had a brass band at his funeral,
As you should have at mine; and after that
A few remembered him. But he was dead,
They said, and they should have their friend no more.—
However, there was once a starveling child—
A ragged-vested little incubus,
Born to be cuffed and frighted out of all
Capacity for childhood's happiness—
Who started out one day, quite suddenly,
To drown himself. He ran away from home,
Across the clover-fields and through the woods,
And waited on a rock above a stream,
Just like a kingfisher. He might have dived,
Or jumped, or he might not; but anyhow,
There came along a man who looked at him
With such an unexpected friendliness,
And talked with him in such a common way,
That life grew marvelously different:
What he had lately known for sullen trunks
And branches, and a world of tedious leaves,
Was all transmuted; a faint forest wind
That once had made the loneliest of all
Sad sounds on earth, made now the rarest music;
And water that had called him once to death
Now seemed a flowing glory. And that man,
Born to go down a soldier, did this thing.
Not much to do? Not very much, I grant you:
Good occupation for a sonneteer,
Or for a clown, or for a clergyman,
But small work for a soldier. By the way,
When you are weary sometimes of your own
Utility, I wonder if you find

Occasional great comfort pondering
What power a man has in him to put forth?
'Of all the many marvelous things that are,
Nothing is there more marvelous than man,'
Said Sophocles; and he lived long ago;
'And earth, unending ancient of the gods
He furrows; and the ploughs go back and forth,
Turning the broken mould, year after year.'. . . .

"I turned a little furrow of my own
Once on a time, and everybody laughed—
As I laughed afterwards; and I doubt not
The First Intelligence, which we have drawn
In our competitive humility
As if it went forever on two legs,
Had some diversion of it: I believe
God's humor is the music of the spheres—
But even as we draft omnipotence
Itself to our own image, we pervert
The courage of an infinite ideal
To finite resignation. You have made
The cement of your churches out of tears
And ashes, and the fabric will not stand:
The shifted walls that you have coaxed and shored
So long with unavailing compromise
Will crumble down to dust and blow away,
And younger dust will follow after them;
Though not the faintest or the farthest whirled
First atom of the least that ever flew
Shall be by man defrauded of the touch
God thrilled it with to make a dream for man
When Science was unborn. And after time,
When we have earned our spiritual ears,
And art's commiseration of the truth
No longer glorifies the singing beast,

Or venerates the clinquant charlatan,—
Then shall at last come ringing through the sun,
Through time, through flesh, a music that is true.
For wisdom is that music, and all joy
That wisdom:—you may counterfeit, you think,
The burden of it in a thousand ways;
But as the bitterness that loads your tears
Makes Dead Sea swimming easy, so the gloom,
The penance, and the woeful pride you keep,
Make bitterness your buoyance of the world.
And at the fairest and the frenziedest
Alike of your God-fearing festivals,
You so compound the truth to pamper fear
That in the doubtful surfeit of your faith
You clamor for the food that shadows eat.
You call it rapture or deliverance,—
Passion or exaltation, or what most
The moment needs, but your faint-heartedness
Lives in it yet: you quiver and you clutch
For something larger, something unfulfilled,
Some wiser kind of joy that you shall have
Never, until you learn to laugh with God."
And with a calm Socratic patronage,
At once half sombre and half humorous,
The Captain reverently twirled his thumbs
And fixed his eyes on something far away;
Then, with a gradual gaze, conclusive, shrewd,
And at the moment unendurable
For sheer beneficence, he looked at me.

"But the brass band?" I said, not quite at ease
With altruism yet.—He made a sort
Of reminiscent little inward noise,
Midway between a chuckle and a laugh,
And that was all his answer: not a word

Of explanation or suggestion came
From those tight-smiling lips. And when I left,
I wondered, as I trod the creaking snow
And had the world-wide air to breathe again,—
Though I had seen the tremor of his mouth
And honored the endurance of his hand—
Whether or not, securely closeted
Up there in the stived haven of his den,
The man sat laughing at me; and I felt
My teeth grind hard together with a quaint
Revulsion—as I recognize it now—
Not only for my Captain, but as well
For every smug-faced failure on God's earth;
Albeit I could swear, at the same time,
That there were tears in the old fellow's eyes.
I question if in tremors or in tears
There be more guidance to man's worthiness
Than—well, say in his prayers. But oftentimes
It humors us to think that we possess
By some divine adjustment of our own
Particular shrewd cells, or something else,
What others, for untutored sympathy,
Go spirit-fishing more than half their lives
To catch—like cheerful sinners to catch faith;
And I have not a doubt but I assumed
Some egotistic attribute like this
When, cautiously, next morning I reduced
The fretful qualms of my novitiate,
For most part, to an undigested pride.
Only, I live convinced that I regret
This enterprise no more than I regret
My life; and I am glad that I was born.

(Lines 1–256)

Miniver Cheevy

Miniver Cheevy, child of scorn,
　　Grew lean while he assailed the seasons;
He wept that he was ever born,
　　And he had reasons.

Miniver loved the days of old
　　When swords were bright and steeds were prancing;
The vision of a warrior bold
　　Would set him dancing.

Miniver sighed for what was not,
　　And dreamed, and rested from his labors;
He dreamed of Thebes and Camelot,
　　And Priam's neighbors.

Miniver mourned the ripe renown
　　That made so many a name so fragrant;
He mourned Romance, now on the town,
　　And Art, a vagrant.

Miniver loved the Medici,
　　Albeit he had never seen one;
He would have sinned incessantly
　　Could he have been one.

Miniver cursed the commonplace
　　And eyed a khaki suit with loathing;
He missed the mediaeval grace
　　Of iron clothing.

Miniver scorned the gold he sought,
　　But sore annoyed was he without it;
Miniver thought, and thought, and thought,
　　And thought about it.

Miniver Cheevy, born too late,
   Scratched his head and kept on thinking;
Miniver coughed and called it fate,
   And kept on drinking.

For a Dead Lady

No more with overflowing light
Shall fill the eyes that now are faded,
Nor shall another's fringe with night
Their woman-hidden world as they did.
No more shall quiver down the days
The flowing wonder of her ways,
Whereof no language may requite
The shifting and the many-shaded.

The grace, divine, definitive,
Clings only as a faint forestalling;
The laugh that love could not forgive
Is hushed, and answers to no calling;
The forehead and the little ears
Have gone where Saturn keeps the years;
The breast where roses could not live
Has done with rising and with falling.

The beauty, shattered by the laws
That have creation in their keeping,
No longer trembles at applause,
Or over children that are sleeping;
And we who delve in beauty's lore
Know all that we have known before
Of what inexorable cause
Makes Time so vicious in his reaping.

William Butler Yeats

(1865–1939)

Down by the salley gardens

Down by the salley gardens my love and I did meet,
She passed the salley gardens with little snow-white
feet.
She bid me take love easy, as the leaves grow on the
tree;
But I, being young and foolish, with her would not
agree.

In a field by the river my love and I did stand,
And on my leaning shoulder she laid her snow-white
hand.
She bid me take life easy, as the grass grows on the
weirs;
But I was young and foolish, and now am full of tears.

The Sorrow of Love

The quarrel of the sparrows in the eaves,
The full round moon and the star-laden sky,
And the loud song of the ever-singing leaves,
Had hid away earth's old and weary cry.

And then you came with those red mournful lips,
And with you came the whole of the world's tears,

And all the trouble of her labouring ships,
And all the trouble of her myriad years.

And now the sparrows warring in the eaves,
The curd-pale moon, the white stars in the sky,
And the loud chaunting of the unquiet leaves,
Are shaken with earth's old and weary cry.

The Song of Wandering Aengus

I went out to the hazel wood,
Because a fire was in my head,
And cut and peeled a hazel wand,
And hooked a berry to a thread;
And when white moths were on the wing,
And moth-like stars were flickering out,
I dropped the berry in a stream
And caught a little silver trout.

When I had laid it on the floor
I went to blow the fire a-flame,
But something rustled on the floor,
And someone called me by my name:
It had become a glimmering girl
With apple blossom in her hair
Who called me by my name and ran
And faded through the brightening air.

Though I am old with wandering
Through hollow lands and hilly lands,
I will find out where she has gone,
And kiss her lips and take her hands;
And walk among long dappled grass,

And pluck till time and times are done
The silver apples of the moon,
The golden apples of the sun.

He Thinks of His Past Greatness When a Part of the Constellations of Heaven

I have drunk ale from the Country of the Young
And weep because I know all things now:
I have been a hazel tree and they hung
The Pilot Star and the Crooked Plough
Among my leaves in times out of mind:
I became a rush that horses tread:
I became a man, a hater of the wind,
Knowing one, out of all things, alone, that his head
Would not lie on the breast or his lips on the hair
Of the woman that he loves, until he dies;
Although the rushes and the fowl of the air
Cry of his love with their pitiful cries.

No Second Troy

Why should I blame her that she filled my days
With misery, or that she would of late
Have taught to ignorant men most violent ways,
Or hurled the little streets upon the great,
Had they but courage equal to desire?
What could have made her peaceful with a mind
That nobleness made simple as a fire,
With beauty like a tightened bow, a kind

That is not natural in an age like this,
Being high and solitary and most stern?
Why, what could she have done being what she is?
Was there another Troy for her to burn?

The fascination of what's difficult

The fascination of what's difficult
Has dried the sap out of my veins, and rent
Spontaneous joy and natural content
Out of my heart. There's something ails our colt
That must, as if it had not holy blood,
Nor on an Olympus leaped from cloud to cloud,
Shiver under the lash, strain, sweat and jolt
As though it dragged road metal. My curse on plays
That have to be set up in fifty ways,
On the day's war with every knave and dolt,
Theatre business, management of men.
I swear before the dawn comes round again
I'll find the stable and pull out the bolt.

Paudeen

Indignant at the fumbling wits, the obscure spite
Of our old Paudeen in his shop, I stumbled blind
Among the stones and thorn trees, under morning light;
Until a curlew cried and in the luminous wind
A curlew answered; and suddenly thereupon I thought
That on the lonely height where all are in God's eye,
There cannot be, confusion of our sound forgot,
A single soul that lacks a sweet crystalline cry.

To a Shade

If you have revisited the town, thin Shade,
Whether to look upon your monument
(I wonder if the builder has been paid)
Or happier thoughted when the day is spent
To drink of that salt breath out of the sea
When grey gulls flit about instead of men,
And the gaunt houses put on majesty:
Let these content you and be gone again;
For they are at their old tricks yet.
                              A man
Of your own passionate serving kind who had brought
In his full hands what, had they only known,
Had given their children's children loftier thought,
Sweeter emotion, working in their veins
Like gentle blood, has been driven from the place,
And insult heaped upon him for his pains
And for his open-handedness, disgrace;
An old foul mouth that once cried out on you
Herding the pack.
                    Unquiet wanderer
Draw the Glasnevin coverlet anew
About your head till the dust stops your ear,
The time for you to taste of that salt breath
And listen at the corners has not come;
You had enough of sorrow before death—
Away, away! You are safer in the tomb.

That the Night Come

She lived in storm and strife,
Her soul had such desire
For what proud death may bring
That it could not endure
The common good of life,
But lived as 'twere a king
That packed his marriage day
With banneret and pennon,
Trumpet and kettledrum,
And the outrageous cannon,
To bundle time away
That the night come.

A Coat

I made my song a coat
Covered with embroideries
Out of old mythologies
From heel to throat;
But the fools caught it,
Wore it in the world's eye
As though they'd wrought it.
Song, let them take it
For there's more enterprise
In walking naked.

PROLOGUE TO *Responsibilities*

Pardon, old fathers, if you still remain
Somewhere in ear-shot for the story's end,
Old Dublin merchant "free of ten and four"
Or trading out of Galway into Spain;
And country scholar, Robert Emmet's friend,
A hundred-year-old memory to the poor;
Traders or soldiers who have left me blood
That has not passed through any huxter's loin,
Pardon, and you that did not weigh the cost,
Old Butlers when you took to horse and stood
Beside the brackish waters of the Boyne
Till your bad master blenched and all was lost;
You merchant skipper that leaped overboard
After a ragged hat in Biscayne Bay,
You most of all, silent and fierce old man
Because you were the spectacle that stirred
My fancy, and set my boyish lips to say
"Only the wasteful virtues earn the sun";
Pardon that for a barren passion's sake,
Although I have come close on forty-nine
I have no child, I have nothing but a book,
Nothing but that to prove your blood and mine.

Index of Titles and First Lines

615

Biographical Notes

ARNOLD, MATTHEW (1822–1888), born at Laleham, son of Thomas Arnold (later headmaster of Rugby), was educated at Rugby, Winchester, and Balliol College, Oxford (1844), and was a fellow of Oriel College. He was an inspector of schools 1851–86, from 1857–67 was Professor of Poetry at Oxford. *Essays in Criticism* (1865) and *Culture and Anarchy* (1869) gave him stature as a critic; *Empedocles on Etna* (1852), *Poems* (1853), and *New Poems* (1867) as a poet. C. B. Tinker and H. F. Lowry, eds., *Poems* (1950). H. Kingsmill, *Matthew Arnold* (1928); L. Trilling, *Matthew Arnold* (1939). L. Trilling, ed., *The Portable Matthew Arnold*.

BRIDGES, ROBERT (1844–1930), born at Walmer, was educated at Eton and Corpus Christi College, Oxford (1867), after which he studied medicine. After a period as surgeon at St. Bart's, London, he retired (1882) to a life as writer. His works were quietly received, though he was made Poet Laureate in 1913, but the philosophical *Testament of Beauty* (1929) had considerable popularity. *Collected Essays, etc.* (1927–36), 10 vols. *Poetical Works* (1914). A. Guerard, Jr., *Robert Bridges* (1941); E. Thomson, *Robert Bridges* (1944).

BRONTË, EMILY (1818–1848), born at Haworth, Yorkshire, was educated at a boarding school and later spasmodically taught by her father. As a novelist she is famous for *Wuthering*

Heights (1847); her poetry, except for *Poems* (1846) by Currer, Ellis, and Acton Bell (Charlotte, Emily, and Anne Brontë), was published posthumously. C. W. Hatfield, ed., *The Complete Poems* (1941). L. L. Hinckley, *Charlotte and Emily: The Brontës* (1945).

BROWNING, ROBERT (1812–1889), was born at Camberwell and privately educated. *Pauline* (1833), published anonymously, met with some critical success among poets. *Paracelsus* (1835) affirmed the literary course of his life, as *Sordello* (1840) did his attempts for an individual idiom. He eloped with Elizabeth Barrett (1846) and lived in Italy until her death. Sir. F. G. Kenyon, ed., *Works* (1912), 10 vols. H. W. Griffin and H. C. Minchin, *The Life of Robert Browning* (rev. ed., 1938).

CHAPMAN, JOHN JAY (1862–1933), born in New York City, was educated at St. Paul's School, Concord, N. H., and at Harvard (1885). He was active in reform politics in New York City, but *Emerson and Other Essays* (1898) began a noteworthy though not popular career as writer. He was the author of poetic dramas, *Songs and Poems* (1919), and many books of essays. M. A. De W. Howe, *John Jay Chapman and His Letters* (1937).

DICKINSON, EMILY (1830–1886), born in Amherst, Mass., was educated at Mount Holyoke Female Seminary. From 1854 she withdrew from town life until she

625

became a recluse. Her poems were her private life, only five being printed in her time. Published soon after her death, in *Poems* (1890, 1891, 1893), they met with instant success, and unpublished poems still continue to appear. M. D. Bianchi and A. L. Hampson, eds., *The Poems* (1937); M. L. Todd and M. T. Bingham, eds., *Bolts of Melody* (1945), a further collection. G. F. Whicher, *This Was a Poet: A Critical Biography* (1938).

DODGSON, CHARLES L. (1832–1898), born at Davisbury, was educated at Rugby and Christ Church, Oxford (1854), where he was mathematical lecturer from 1855–81. A distinguished mathematician and photographer, he is best known for *Alice's Adventures in Wonderland* (1865) and *Through the Looking Glass* (1872), published under the *nom de plume* of "Lewis Carroll." *Complete Works* (1937). S. D. Collingwood, *Life and Letters* (1898); F. B. Lennon, *Victoria through the Looking Glass* (1945).

DOUGHTY, CHARLES M. (1843–1926), born in Suffolk, was prepared for the navy, but shifted to Caius College, Cambridge (1865). He concentrated after college on linguistics and antiquarianism in preparation for such works as *The Dawn in Britain* (1906), 6 vols., but it is for his prose *Travels in Arabia Deserta* (1888), 2 vols., that he is best known. D. G. Hogarth, *The Life of Charles M. Doughty* (1928); A. Treneer, *Charles M. Doughty, a Study in His Prose and Poetry* (1935).

FITZGERALD,   EDWARD (1809–1883), born near Ipswich, was educated at Bury St. Edmunds and at Trinity College, Cambridge (1830). He

did some translations from the Greek dramatists, but is chiefly known for his letters and for his translation of Khayyám, a 12th-century Persian poet, said to have "helped to shape the melancholy hedonism and moral incertitude of late nineteenth-century England." G. Bentham, ed., *Poetical and Prose Writings* (1902), 7 vols.; W. A. Wright, ed., *Letters and Literary Remains* (1902–03), 7 vols. A. C. Benson, *Edward Fitz-Gerald* (1900); A. M. Terhune, *The Life of Edward FitzGerald* (1947).

HARDY, THOMAS (1840–1928), born near Dorchester, attended local schools and was articled to an architect (1855–61). *Under the Greenwood Tree* (1872) met with sufficient success to warrant his retirement from architecture. With *Wessex Poems* (1898), he quit the novel after the outcry against *Jude the Obscure* (1896), *The Dynasts* (1903–08) and volumes of lyrics bringing him a second reputation. *Works* (1914–31), 24 vols.; *Collected Poems* (1937). C. J. Weber, *Hardy of Wessex* (1940).

HOLMES, OLIVER WENDELL (1809–1894), born in Cambridge, Mass., was educated at Phillips Academy, Andover, and Harvard (1829), and studied medicine abroad (1833–35). He was Professor of Anatomy at Dartmouth 1838–40, and Dean of the Harvard Medical School 1847–53. His *Poems* (1836) distracted attention from his distinction in medicine, and with *The Autocrat at the Breakfast-Table* (1858) and succeeding volumes he became known as the wit of his age. *The Works* (1892), 13 vols.; H. E. Scudder, ed., *The Complete Poetical Works* (1895). M. A. De W. Howe, *Holmes of the Breakfast-Table* (1939).

HOPKINS, GERARD MANLEY (1844–1889), born at Stratford, Essex, was educated at Highgate Grammar School, and at Balliol College, Oxford (1867). He became a Roman Catholic (1866) and was ordained (1877). In 1882 he taught classes at a Jesuit foundation at Oxford, and 1884–89 was Professor of Greek at the Royal University, Dublin. He published almost no poems during his life, and had no reputation as a poet until Robert Bridges' edition of his work in 1918. R. Bridges and C. Williams, eds., *Poems* (1938). H. House, ed., *Notebooks and Papers* (1937). W. H. Gardner, *Gerard Manley Hopkins* (1944–49), 2 vols.

HOUSMAN, A. E. (1859–1936), born at Fockbury, Worcestershire, was educated at Bromsgrove School and St. John's College, Oxford (1882). He was in the Patents Office 1882–92, but was made Professor of Latin at University College, London, 1892, and in 1911 Professor of Latin Philology at Cambridge. To classical scholars he is known for his editions of Juvenal, etc., but to the public for *A Shropshire Lad* (1896). His later poetry is represented by *Last Poems* (1922) and *More Poems* (1936); his critical ideas by *The Name and Nature of Poetry* (1933). *Collected Poems* (1940). L. Housman, *My Brother, A. E. Housman* (1938).

JOHNSON, LIONEL (1867–1902), born at Broadstairs, Kent, was educated at Winchester and New College, Oxford (1890). A combination of the qualities of Roman Catholicism and the *fin de siècle* *Yellow Book* resulted in a late Pre-Raphaelite phenomenon. He wrote an excellent critical study on *The Art of Thomas Hardy* (1894), *Poems* (1895), and *Ireland and Other Poems* (1897). *Poetical Works* (1915).

KIPLING, RUDYARD (1865–1936), born in Bombay, was educated at the United Services College, in England, after which he returned to India and became a journalist (1882–89). From 1890 he lived chiefly in England, though for a while in the United States. *Departmental Ditties* (1886) and *Plain Tales from the Hills* (1888) launched him on his prolific and successful career as writer. *Writings in Prose and Verse* (1941), 28 vols.; *Rudyard Kipling's Verse* (1940), a collection. H. Brown, *Rudyard Kipling* (1945).

LANIER, SIDNEY (1842–1881), born in Macon, Ga., was educated at Oglethorpe University (1860), where he became a tutor. In 1861 he enlisted in the Confederate Army. A prisoner for four months, he was released at the end of the war suffering from tuberculosis. Later, he was flautist with the Baltimore symphony orchestra, and lecturer in English at Johns Hopkins University. *Poems* (1877) was followed by *The Science of English Verse* (1880). C. R. Anderson, ed., *The Centennial Edition* (1945), 10 vols. A. H. Starke, *Sidney Lanier* (1933).

LEAR, EDWARD (1812–1888), was born in London, son of a wealthy stockbroker of Danish origin, imprisoned for debt when his son was 13. At the age of 15 he began to earn his living as an artist. He was a member of the household of the Earl of Derby (1832–36) for whose grandchildren he composed his *Book of Nonsense* (1846). From 1836 his chief interest was landscape painting. H. Jackson, ed., *The Complete Nonsense* (1947). A. Davidson, *Edward Lear* (1939).

LONGFELLOW, HENRY WADSWORTH (1807–1892) born in Portland, Maine, was educated at Bowdoin College (1825). From 1826–29 he studied abroad. He was Professor of Modern Languages at Bowdoin 1829–35, and at Harvard 1835–54. His public career as a poet began with *Voices of the Night* (1839). *Evangeline* (1847) and *The Song of Hiawatha* (1855) had enormous success. H. E. Scudder, ed., *Complete Poetical Works* (1893). S. Longfellow, *The Life of Henry Wadsworth Longfellow* (1891), 3 vols. L. Thompson, *Young Longfellow, 1807–1843* (1938).

LOWELL, JAMES RUSSELL (1819–1891), born in Cambridge, Mass., was educated at Harvard (1838), and graduated from Harvard Law School (1840). *A Year's Life* (1841) and *Poems* (1844) began his career as a poet, and *Conversations on Some of the Old Poets* (1845) as a critic. In 1855 he became Professor of Modern Languages at Harvard, 1863–72 was joint editor of the *Atlantic Monthly*, and 1880–85 Minister to England. C. E. Norton, ed., *The Complete Writings* (1904), 16 vols.; H. E. Scudder, ed., *The Complete Poetical Works* (1917). H. E. Scudder, *James Russell Lowell* (1901), 2 vols.

MELVILLE, HERMAN (1819–1891), born in New York City, attended the Albany Academy, but received no formal schooling after 15. He went to sea in 1837, and shipped (1841–44) on the whaling voyage which was the basis of *Moby-Dick* (1851). *Typee* (1846) began a period as prose writer which ended with *The Confidence-Man* (1857). Discouraged, he took a position in the New York Customs (1866–85). Turning to poetry, he wrote *Battle-Pieces* (1866), *Clarel* (1876), *John Marr and Other Sailors* (1888), and *Timoleon* (1891). R. Weaver, ed., *The Works* (1922–24), 16 vols.; H. P. Vincent, ed., *Collected Poems* (1945). N. Arvin, *Herman Melville* (1950); Jay Leyda, ed., *The Portable Melville*.

MEREDITH, GEORGE (1826–1909), born at Portsmouth, England, was educated locally and at a Moravian school in Germany. He studied law but turned to journalism and literature. *Poems* (1851) contained an early version of *Modern Love*, which appeared in its final form in 1862. He is known also for his essay *On the Idea of Comedy . . .* (1877), and for his novels. *The Works* (1909–11), 27 vols.; G. M. Trevelyan, ed., *Poetical Works* (1912). R. E. Sencourt, *The Life of George Meredith* (1929); G. M. Trevelyan, *The Poetry and Philosophy of George Meredith* (1907).

MORRIS, WILLIAM (1834–1896), born at Clay Hill, Walthamstow, was educated at Marlborough College, and at Exeter College, Oxford (1855). Independently wealthy, he studied architecture and painting, and wrote poems and prose romances. *Sigurd the Volsung* appeared in 1876. His private press and his activities in the decorative arts were also influential. May Morris, ed., *Works* (1910–15), 24 vols. J. W. Mackail, *The Life of William Morris* (1899), 2 vols.

NEWMAN, JOHN HENRY, CARDINAL (1801–1890), born in London, was educated at Trinity College, Oxford, becoming a fellow of Oriel. Here he came under the influence of Keble. In 1828 he was made vicar of St. Mary's in Oxford, from which his famous sermons were made. He became a Roman Catholic in 1845 and a priest in 1846. *Apologia pro Vita Sua* (1864) was written to explain his position. He was made cardinal in 1879. *The Dream of Gerontius* (1866) was the result of warnings of possible death. C. F. Harrold, ed., *Works* (1947——). C. F. Harrold, *John Henry Newman* (1945).

PATMORE, COVENTRY (1823–1896), was born at Woodford, Essex. He was educated privately, and began to write verse in 1840, but in 1845 his father's financial reverses caused him to take a position in the British Museum. *The Angel in the House* (1854), a dramatic sonnet sequence of domestic life, was very popular, but *The Unknown Eros* (1877) and *Odes* (1886) are most highly regarded today. F. Page, ed., *The Poems* (1949). B. Champney, *Memoir and Correspondence* (1900), 2 vols.; F. Page, *Patmore, a Study in Poetry* (1933).

ROBINSON, EDWIN ARLINGTON (1869–1935), was born in Maine, and educated in the local high school and as a special student at Harvard (1891–93). A business life proved impossible for him, and he devoted himself to a literary career, publishing at his own expense *The Torrent and The Night Before* (1896). In 1897 he moved to New York City, where he met the original of *Captain Craig* (1902); and published *The Children of the Night* (1897) and *The Town Down the River* (1910). He held a minor position at the Treasury. His later work was chiefly long narrative poems, such as *Tristram* (1927). *Collected Poems* (1937). H. Hagedorn, *Edwin Arlington Robinson* (1938); Yvor Winters, *Edwin Arlington Robinson* (1946).

ROSSETTI, CHRISTINA (1830–1894), born in London, the sister of Dante Gabriel (q.v.), was educated at home. A small collection of her verse was privately printed in Italy at her grandfather's press in 1847. *Goblin Market* (1862) was followed by volumes of verse and religious prose. W. M. Rossetti, ed., *Poetical Works* (1904). Marya Zaturenska, *Christina Rossetti* (1949).

ROSSETTI, DANTE GABRIEL (1828–1882), born in London, the son of a Neapolitan political exile, was educated at King's College School and studied art. In 1848 the Pre-Raphaelite Brotherhood was founded, including Rossetti, Millais, and Hunt. In 1850 *The Germ* and *Art and Poetry* were issued as bulletins, containing among other writings "The Blessed Damozel," which was closely related to his painting. *The Early Italian Poets* (1861), a series of translations, was followed by *Poems* (1870) and *Ballads and Sonnets* (1881). W. M. Rossetti, ed., *Works* (1911). O. Doughty, *Dante Gabriel Rossetti* (1949).

SWINBURNE, ALGERNON CHARLES (1837–1909), born in London, was educated at Eton and Balliol College, Oxford (1859), but left without a degree. In 1857 he came under the influence of Rossetti and Morris. *Atalanta in Calydon* (1865), *Songs Before Sunrise* (1871) and *Poems and Ballads* (1866, 1878, 1889) were among his many volumes. E. Gosse and T. J. Wise, eds., *Complete Works* (1925–27), 20 vols. (including Gosse's *Life*). S. C. Chew, *Swinburne* (1929).

TENNYSON, ALFRED, LORD (1809–1892), born at Somersby, where his father was rector, was educated by his father and at

Trinity College, Cambridge (1831). The death of his friend Hallam (1830) occasioned the beginning of *In Memoriam* (published 1850), but he had already published *Poems by Two Brothers* (1827), *Poems, Chiefly Lyrical* (1830), and *Poems* (1833). He was made Poet Laureate in 1850. *The Princess* (1847), *Maud* (1855), and *Idylls of the King* (1859 ff.) were highly successful. He was made a baron in 1884. H. Tennyson, ed., *Works* (1907–1908), 9 vols. Sir C. Tennyson, *Alfred Tennyson* (1949).

THOMPSON, FRANCIS (1859–1907), born at Ashton, Lancashire, the son of a doctor, studied medicine, but spent a chaotic life in London, where his intense Catholic faith was insufficient to steady him. The *Poems* (1893), including "The Hound of Heaven," and *New Poems* (1897) were his chief works. T. L. Connolly, ed., *Poems* (1941). E. Meynell, *The Life of Francis Thompson* (1931).

THOMSON, JAMES (1834–1882), born at Port-Glasgow, Renfrewshire, the son of a drunken sailor, spent his boyhood in orphan and military asylums and his youth as an army schoolmaster. Discharged (1862), he later wrote for the *National Reformer*, and spent a life of illness and drink. *The City of Dreadful Night* (1874) is his best-known poetry. B. Dobell, *The Poetical Works* (1895), 2 vols. J. E. Meeker, *The Life and Poetry of James Thomson* (1917).

WHITMAN, WALT (1819–1892), born at Huntington, N. Y., attended the public schools of Brooklyn. At 13, as printer's devil, he began a long connection with newspapers, which culminated in his editorship of the Brooklyn *Daily Eagle* (1846–1848). *Leaves of Grass* (1855) was the initial collection of verse, expanded in many editions throughout his life and incorporating other books of poems later. During the Civil War he acted as a volunteer nurse. H. S. Canby, *Walt Whitman* (1943). G. W. Allen, *Walt Whitman Handbook* (1946). M. Van Doren, ed., *The Portable Walt Whitman*.

YEATS, WILLIAM BUTLER (1865–1939), born at Sandymount, Ireland, the son of a Protestant Irish painter, was educated at Godolphin School, Hammersmith, and Erasmus School, Dublin, after which he studied art. At 21 he became a professional writer. His interest in Irish mythology is represented in *Fairy and Folk Tales* (1890) and *The Celtic Twilight* (1893); in the theater by *The Land of Heart's Desire* (1894) and *Cathleen ni Houlihan* (1902); in poetry by *The Wanderings of Oisin* (1889), *The Wind Among the Reeds* (1899), and *Responsibilities* (1914), with which he began a new manner. *The Collected Poems* (1950). W. B. Yeats, *Autobiographies* (1926); R. Ellmann, *Yeats* (1948); A. N. Jeffares, *W. B. Yeats* (1949).